COYOTE

*A novel of love, honor
and personal sacrifice*

by
Della Van Hise

Coyote (by Della Van Hise)

Publisher: Eye Scry Publications
All rights reserved, Copyright © 2013

ISBN 13: 978-0-9766897-8-2
ISBN 10: 0976689782

WHOLESALE INFORMATION

For information about wholesale rates,
or to order additional copies, please email us at...
contact@eyescry.com

For Wendy...
the poet and the muse

~

For Diane...
and a friendship spanning centuries

~

For He Who Shall Remain Nameless...
who inspired this trickster tale

~

...and for all my imaginary
friends and lovers

~

May you all live happily ever after.

PROLOGUE
The Traveler

1988

Psychiatrists who have examined my case have speculated that
River Willows is either a pathological liar or a deluded neurotic, yet
I state for the record that I am neither. I am simply a traveler - at
least that's the best explanation anyone has been able to give me.

And yet, the roads on which I travel do not appear on any
maps. They do not exist in Newtonian time and space. Some would
say they do not exist at all.

It was in Land o'Lakes, Florida that my first awareness of
Synjin and Ch'en Po came, though even that is not altogether
correct. It was there that my first *contact* with them came. I had held
the *awareness* of them since before the day I was born, twin echoes
playing on the surface of my mind, the tranquil voices of insight
and guidance at times when no mere human mentor would suffice.

I should mention that I was isolated from an early age, running
as a wild child through orange groves and swamplands, better
friends with the redwing blackbirds and fireflies than with the
human children from school. Mom worked. Dad was never around,
and when he was they fought as if spawned from two incompatible
species, the end result being that I slipped through the cracks of any
so-called ordinary upbringing.

That was perhaps the greatest blessing I could have received,
for it meant an escape from most of the typical indoctrination into
society, leaving me free to be me instead of whoever or whatever
the world at large wanted me to be.

As a child, I considered myself relatively normal. I dreamed of
starships and sunk my toes in the alien sands of far-flung worlds in

my imagination; the ascended spirits of my ancestors danced on the surface of lake on the eve of my thirteenth birthday to celebrate my coming of age; I interacted with The People of the Dream each night for as far back as I can remember, traveling between the quantum molecules of here and there to a space/time that existed non-locally between tick and tock, at right angles to reason, but was no less real than the world we thought of as our own. It was in that world that I first saw the temple - a vision of a great fortress which housed the Masters and their many secrets.

Whether it was the result of watching too many old reruns of *Kung Fu* and longing to *be* Kwai Chang Cain in a world otherwise inhabited by mall-crawling zombies, or whether it came after reading the collected works of Carlos Castaneda, who's to say? All I know is that I had never felt at home on Planet Earth, drawn instead to that otherworld where words like honor and respect and nobility still held some meaning, a world where there was life beyond the comforting blue glow of the television, a world where one might *be* the character in the book on her grand adventure, instead of just another lonely black-clad girl *reading* the book in the back of the bus on her way from home to school to work, just one meaningless day following every other.

I could not be that girl. I *would* not.

Perhaps I should have given some thought to the old cliché, *'Be careful what you wish for. You just might get it!'*

And yet, what real dreamer is ever cautious about her dreams? Dreams are made of untamed things and woven with filaments of risk and mystery. Otherwise they are only idle thoughts caught in the droning churn of mediocrity.

And so, perhaps it stands to reason that I embraced the world of the Dream with an unrelenting intensity that would be off-putting to some, or labeled as madness by others. I cared little for labels, and understood at a very young age that 'madness' was a word attached to anything not immediately understood by the consensual agreement of humans at large.

Put simply: despite my mother's best intentions and the very best efforts of the public school system, I was a stranger in a strange land and a social oddity long before it was popular.

When I was seventeen, I selected my own mate from among The People, birthing his image from some ancient future memory.

Six foot four, with shiny black hair that fell to his shoulders and moved like a restless shadow. His eyes were obsidian magnets, piercing yet tender, his yin/yang soul made of wild ivy - strong enough to hold my rebel heart, not so strong it would strangle me. He was, in essence, the male mirror of me, for it's no secret to anyone who *sees* that we are all in love with our opposite, who is simultaneously the highest potential of our Self.

When I spoke to the Old Woman who was the match-maker of The People, I requested that he should be of a type - an enigma even among his own people, a rebel, a teacher, a Master of the temple. He was to be a mystery, a book with a black cover and blank pages - ink visible only to those who knew how to read it.

The Old Woman went on her way with a knowing smile and vowed to find this man before the midnight of my thirtieth year. Until then, she told me, I would walk my world alone. Until then, my spirit must grow, turning from a girl into a woman as the lines in my palm deepened into meaning. She told me quite simply that I must become whole within Myself before I could avow myself to one of The People.

Perhaps she believed that I would no longer visit the Dream once I left childhood behind. The veil between our worlds is thin for children, but solidifies into an almost impenetrable wall as adulthood intrudes - that terrible day when imagination must be traded for responsibility and obligations, when the world we are taught to think of as fantasy is exchanged for what we are programmed to believe is Reality... and somewhere in that twisted equation, truth gets sold off as a lie, and the lie becomes the deceitful truth, and most humans live out their lives never suspecting that they have sold their souls for thirty pieces of silverware somewhere around the onset of puberty.

My soul was not for sale.

Driven by the vision of the temple, haunted by the voices of the Masters in the winds that blew through the orange groves and over the surface of the black lake where I grew up, I took up martial arts at seventeen, going to the only school in town and slowly gaining a mild respect for being the only female in the class. Most afternoons for the five years following high school were spent with Master Barrows - learning, absorbing, hungry for this new knowledge. It was the first step on the road to the temple – the road *home* - that much I knew.

At night, when I once again traveled the quantum astral realms with The People, I taught the children of the other world the kata I had learned, the philosophies and the fighting techniques. The Old Woman attended my classes once or twice - watching discreetly from a thicket of live oaks as she sat in her wheelchair with a golden shawl thrown across her useless legs. Perhaps she wanted to see if I could be worthy of the mate she would find for me. Or perhaps she simply wanted to walk again, or run, or dance.

All these normal childhood things I did and saw.

What I did not understand was that few of them could be considered normal. I learned a difficult lesson that summer when I told my mother of the journeys I went on each night, when I related to her that a mate was to be found for me, and that I would one day find this temple I had been seeking since childhood.

I was in the shrink's office before the echo of my last words died. Invisible friends, the doctor said. Flights of fancy. Schizophrenia. Childhood fantasies which should be put to sleep like a sick animal.

They tried to do just that - to strangle the Dream, to make me blind to that other world. I fought it for the first three months and probably ended up validating their whisperings about that word of theirs. Madness. But one afternoon a deep sense of serenity settled within me as the answer came, whispered in my ear by some passing spirit at the edge of the Dream. So simple it broke my heart and mended it in the same perfect moment.

Truth means nothing to those who hunger for a lie. Tell them what they want to hear, for that is all they <u>can</u> hear.

"It doesn't happen anymore," I told them - my properly worried mother and the doctor and his anorexic nurse. "I don't travel in my dreams any longer. I don't think I ever did."

And so I was cured. I even thanked them for saving my soul.

But I traveled nonetheless, - right up until the day I died.

CHAPTER ONE
The Little Old Man At the Bottom of the Lake

"Come *on*, River!" Dara shouted, her voice seeming a hundred miles away.

We were horseback riding near the lake as we did every morning. It was sometime in the summer of 1988, nearly five years after graduation, and not much had changed for either of us. Thoughts of college had died with the economic recession, and my life was put on hold when my parents finally separated. My father had always been my anchor, and without him in my life I felt adrift, maybe even abandoned. It wasn't his fault, of course. No sane being could have lived with my mother, who had been possessed by the demons of her menopause and the fanaticism of her religion.

I found myself out of a job by the time I was twenty one. Now, at twenty two, I had little to do with my time other than tend to the horses and practice the Art. I taught at the studio every afternoon, and studied with Master Barrows in the evenings. I'd earned my second degree black belt a few months earlier, and teaching had settled into my blood. It wasn't a bad existence, even if socially unproductive and financially unrewarding.

"River, come *on*!" Dara shouted again.

I looked up to see Dara's back disappearing into a row of orange trees. Her little stud pony, Firefly, was tossing his head and hopping from one foot to the other. I noticed that even Widow, who was usually content to drop her head and pick up fallen oranges, was dancing slightly more than usual, her ears pinned back flat against her head, nostrils flaring as if sensing something in the thick, unmoving air.

Still, nothing struck me as unusual until I glanced down a long, dark row of trees and saw someone standing there. It was just a glimpse of black and red, and at first I wondered if it were one of the migrant workers seeking shelter from the blazing afternoon sun. I kept on thinking that until we came out of the grove and stood looking over the lake, our horses prancing and shying.

"You see that guy?" Dara asked, running her wrist across her face until it came away wet with sweat.

"What guy?" I asked, pretending ignorance.

"The one back there - in the grove," Dara said.

"I didn't see anybody," I lied. No point ending up in the shrink's office again.

Dara practically snarled, her lip curling upward into a grimace of disgust as she looked me up and down. "Forget it!" she snapped, her eyes hardening. "I've probably just been around you too long! You didn't see him because you didn't *want* to see him! I *saw* you look at him!"

She'd been a schizo bitch since her boyfriend dumped her a month before, but I'd learned the discipline of the Art enough to let it pass. Dara needed her anger.

She looked over her shoulder, face red with the heat. "Sorry," she muttered as she started toward the lake again. "I didn't mean to take it out on you, River."

"I know. Forget it, okay?"

Dara nodded wordlessly, then urged her mount deeper into the cool lake. There was no sensation closer to flying than riding bareback through deep water. We leaned forward and grabbed around their necks as they waded into the lake and eventually started to swim,

It was just natural to let my eyes close and pretend I was somewhere else. I wanted to be looking for the temple. I wanted to be with The People.

To this day, I'm not sure what happened.

The only thing I remember is hearing Dara's scream, and then something hit me in the middle of the back. Jarred from my fantasy world, I gasped in a lungful of water as Firefly's weight came down on top of Widow - *and* on top of me. Crushed between the two of them, I was already under water, disoriented and in agony from the impact of hooves against my back when the stud mounted my mare. Stallions were a lot like their human counterparts – when it came to breeding, they would mount anything, anywhere, anytime.

I was vaguely aware of sliding out from between the two animals. My left arm wasn't working, and the water was so black with mud that I couldn't see which way the bubbles were traveling.

It was then that I felt myself being kicked. Hooves flailing to find purchase impacted with my skull, water filled my lungs and I let go of consciousness and sank to the murky bottom of the lake.

My last thought was something about the black-clad hallucination in the grove, and a deep sense of regret that I was going to die a virgin. I almost laughed.

I drowned instead.

~

I'm not religious despite the best wishes of the local church ladies, so I knew that the little old man sitting in front of me was neither god nor devil. He looked to be a hundred-and-ten-going-on-death, of Asian descent, and oddly at peace with himself regardless of the fact that he was sitting on the bottom of the lake breathing water instead of air. He smiled as I floated awkwardly down next to him, then reached out one weathered hand to steady me when I drifted with the current.

"Ta ta ta!" he scolded. "You not supposed to be here, little ram. Go now!" He tried to push me away, looking anxiously up to where the sky would have been had we not been fifteen feet under water.

I hadn't been dead a minute, and already someone was trying to chase me out of Valhalla. Not knowing what else to do, I tried to swim away, but stopped when I realized that my body was lying flat on the bottom and that *"I"* was sitting cross-legged several feet away from it. A moment of panic began, then abruptly subsided. That twenty-two-year-old body seemed strangely unimportant. Fragile and yet cumbersome, it drifted obscenely with the eddies from an underground spring with no more significance than a discarded beer bottle.

"You go," I grumbled. My heavenly head was throbbing.

The little old man stared at me, eyes widening. "Not time for you to be here, River Willows," he said, speaking in a rushed voice. "I send Synjin to keep you out of trouble, and you already dead! Ta!"

"Who?" I asked, taken off guard by the word 'dead'. I *was* dead. I must have seemed perplexed as I looked from him to my own body, which had already floated several yards away. "Who's Synjin?" Under the circumstances, it was as good a question as any.

He shook his head, long gray hair and beard floating in the current. "Your mate. Now go! If you die, Synjin die! If Synjin die, many people die! Go now, little ram! Back into body like hermit crab!" he said in badly broken English which seemed to come and go.

Without waiting for my response, he pushed off from the bottom of the lake and drifted over to my now-face-down body. Then, grabbing the water-logged shell, he began to push it upward, toward the surface.

"Need help!" he insisted, motioning me toward him with one crooked finger. "Quick!"

His words carried power, and I found myself at his side, under my own body, pushing with all my might before I fully realized what I was doing. I think I finally understood then that I *would* die if I didn't listen to him. The will to survive kicked in with a vengeance, and I didn't question how this watery little mentor came to be conveniently sitting on the bottom of the lake. I assumed he was simply a traveler like myself or just another hallucination, but intuition told me that his desire to help was genuine.

It seemed like minutes but couldn't have been more than a few seconds when sunlight started breaking through the water. I glanced at the old man only to see him grunting and straining as he continued to struggle with the physical husk where my Self had once resided.

I stopped, then looked at him more closely. "Synjin is my mate?" I whispered. It was in that unlikely moment his previous statement penetrated my mind.

His ancient blue eyes met my green ones and he smiled once more. "The Old Woman said he's very special - like you. But the time isn't ripe for you to be with Synjin. Eight more years, then you'll both be ready."

The fact that he sounded like a cross between Yoda and some 1950s cartoon was irrelevant. He was *my* hallucination, so he could be whatever I needed him to be.

I stared at him through cloudy water. "Ready? For what?"

He shrugged enigmatically. "You're impatient, little ram. Come looking for Synjin at bottom of lake. Make old man tired on nice sunny day." He jerked his head toward the lifeless cargo we held above us. "Go live now," he urged again, not answering my question.

It explained nothing. "Who *are* you?"

"My name is Ch'en Po, and I am Synjin's master," he said, as if that should explain everything in all the universes. Had I been thinking clearly, perhaps it would have. It didn't occur to me just then that his English was perfect again.

Then, before I realized what was happening, he shoved my body upward once more until it broke the surface of the lake and began to float, face up and eerily silent. At least, it would have appeared to be floating to anyone looking on. In reality, we were both treading water underneath it and probably sweating - if dreaming bodies could sweat.

Trying to ignore the implications. I looked once more toward the little old man.

"Do I know you?" He seemed terribly familiar.

He only smiled, this time more wistfully. "Lesson number one in life: there are no answers. Lesson number two? There are no accidents."

"No accidents?" I muttered, wondering what I was doing on the bottom of the lake.

Gray brows lifted with admonishment. "Little ram does not yet know the extent of her own powers, or her purpose. Would do well to start at the beginning."

I frowned. "The beginning?"

He seemed about to shrug and probably would have had he not been occupied holding my mortal remains above the surface of the lake. "The start," he said with a little grin.

I intuitively trusted the crazy old man, though I couldn't have said why. "I'm not sure there is a beginning. Consciousness is existence. Maybe that's all there is."

He grimaced with a weary sigh. "Ta! Words they teach you in school are just words. Must learn to *feel* the thoughts, *hear* the color of blood, *taste* the wind's music. Then maybe you start to understand something. Until then, you just take up space and eat innocent cow for dinner when not even hungry."

My jaw dropped. The little delusion had a lot of nerve. "Who the hell *are* you?" I asked again. Far away, voices that had once been familiar were shouting; a woman screamed; a boat's motor whined; eerie tremors made the water tremble.

Not surprisingly, Ch'en Po didn't answer. Instead, he reached out with one hand, running the backs of his fingers down my cheeks. "You want to live, or you want to die?" His voice was voice soft and melancholy. "Make choice."

"*Will* I live?" I asked, afraid of the answer. The boat was coming closer. Further away, a siren wailed. An abject terror brushed me with cold black wings at the thought of what was happening - what was *going* to happen. Strangers were going to find me, handle me like so much dead meat, perhaps even bury me in some lonely cemetery beneath a conglomeration of chrysanthemums and wilted gladiolas. Dead was an ugly word with no future.

Finally, drawing his hand away, the little old man gave me what passed for an answer. "A long time ago, men with strength and hope were taught how to live by men who had *lived*," he said with great emphasis, his accent disappearing and giving way to perfect English. "The gifted were taught to sow the seeds that make the tree, learned to water the seed to make the tree grow. Now men just cut trees down... no understanding of the path of the warrior or the heart of the tree."

I didn't have time to understand what Ch'en Po was talking about – he seemed most adept at babbling - so I did as all self-centered humans have done since the dawn of time: I brought it down to a more personal level. "So what does that have to do with *me*?"

"You the seed," he said mysteriously, looking at me as if I were some curious and fragile object. The accent was back. "Puny little seed now, but might grow with proper nourishment. Go live now. Tell no one about me. Tell no one about Synjin. Silence is strength."

It was then that the old man released his hold on my floundering physical body and began sinking back toward the murky bottom of the lake.

"Wait!" I called after him.

I started to follow him, yet the will to survive refused to allow me to go. I held fast to that water-logged husk which had once housed my spiritual essence, lost in a drowning nightmare as a life I'd never lived flashed before my eyes. A mother's love. A father's absence. Dinners with grandma. Lies. Someone else's life, not mine. I started to tremble, afraid I would die, afraid I wouldn't.

From deep below me, I heard the old man laugh. "Remember lesson number one, little ram!"

There were no answers.

It was then that I began to choke. The sun was burning my dead-open eyes, and someone was pushing on my chest. Three ribs cracked. I felt my Self fall back into myself - an odd sensation, since I'd been below my actual body instead of above it.

I didn't try to sort it out.

I was too busy coming back from the dead while the little old man sat on the bottom of the lake, playing a flute filled with water and cold black silt.

~

Within four days of meeting the mystical Ch'en Po, my life turned to chaos. The first three days were spent in a comatose state in the local hospital. On the fourth day, I killed a man.

On the fifth day, I ran, and it was there that life as I had known it ended.

CHAPTER TWO
Renegade

Nothing made sense. Time seemed to be running backward or sideways, skipping like a rock over water in such a way that my life became non-linear, some quantum-crazy nightmare that played out in fits and starts, beginning where it should have ended, ending where it all began.

The trip across country took two weeks and three days - mainly because I had no idea where I was going. The late summer days were hot and sticky until I got through Texas and after that, the desert lay before me, hotter still, yet somehow sentient.

The camping gear in the back of the car made it easy to stay out of sight. I drove during the night and slept during the day. Sometimes I'd stay for a day or two and check out the area, though nothing I could find on a map or in reality seemed right, yet I wondered if I'd know 'right' when I tripped over it.

At the very least, the car's radio kept me well-informed of my whereabouts. I'd been spotted in Miami Beach, boarding a small commuter plane that was hijacked to Cuba. A few days later I was seen again, this time in Jacksonville, selling hamburgers at the Dog 'n Suds. Some old lady in Maine swore to reporters that she'd seen me at a drive-in with James Dean riding shotgun in the passenger seat of a '59 Chevy.

I was starting to feel like Elvis.

But eventually, the reports became less frequent, and by the time I reached Houston, I was lucky to hear anything at all about the armed-and-dangerous River Willows. The public was losing interest and the Air Force was taking a lot of media heat for being unable to locate and capture one allegedly deranged young woman.

The disconcerting thing was looking in the mirror. The face that looked back at me was still my own, though the hair belonged to Miss Clairol. I made a point of staying in the sun as much as possible, allowing it to darken my skin until I began to look more like my ancestors than myself. It was reaching the point that I could barely remember what "I" looked like anymore.

Once along the road to wherever I was going, I ran into the police. It was in El Paso, where I'd pulled into a truck stop for gas. The cops pulled up next to me in their squad car and politely told me that a nice young lady like myself had no business in such a rowdy joint. Concerned for my safety, they offered to lead me to a nearby restaurant where I could freshen up. They even bought me breakfast.

What I learned from the experience was that being a fugitive was not a fine art. As long as I played the game, as long as I pretended to be nothing more than a young woman on a vision quest to California, no one cared who I was or what I'd done in the past.

The hunt for River Willows was all but over.

~

The man at the agricultural check point border took away my Granny Smith Apples. He apologized profusely, mumbled something about the Med fly, then welcomed me to California - "the state of utter confusion," he called it with a grin.

I took advantage of his easy attitude to ask him what he recommended as far as places to see, deliberately flirting to keep him off guard. "I hear the desert's nice this time of year," I commented.

"If you're a tarantula or a side-winder. Of course, if you don't mind driving, the high desert's slightly cooler, up around Joshua Tree. Still, in the middle of summer, you're likely to run into trouble out there if you're not careful."

"What kind of trouble?" I asked.

"Well, for one thing, there's not many people around out there. If you had a flat on one of those back roads, you could roast to death before the ranger even came around to check. But the camping's free - and in this day and age, anything you get for free's a good deal."

I'd fixed more than one flat in my time, and living in Florida all my life had prepared me for whatever heat heaven wanted to send down. I smiled again. "Thanks for the advice."

Pulling away from the checkpoint, I glanced into the rear view mirror only once. He was talking to the driver of the next vehicle in line and eating one of my apples. I saw him score a bunch of bananas and a huge watermelon.

I liked California already.

~

The fruit-filching guard had been right about two things: the desert was hot, and Joshua Tree National Monument was about as deserted as any place I'd ever been.

For the first hour or so, I wasn't impressed with the scenery. The lower Colorado Desert with its white sands and jumping cholla cactus wasn't the most spectacular thing in the world. But as I started gaining altitude, proceeding through the transition zone and into the high Mojave, I realized I had found the right place. It was a deep-rooted knowledge which defied explanation, and I gave into the feeling without question. It smelled like home.

The oddly-shaped rock formations were alien and alluring, and I could almost believe I was on the surface of some distant planet. Joshua Trees which had been alive since before the white man came stood like sentinels over the desert, unmoving in the brisk wind, unconcerned for the fate of humanity. And there was a silence in the high desert that I'd never heard before - the silence of the temple, the silence of a dead man's heart, the silence of the soul. Joshua Tree was the soul of the Earth. I knew it then. Or perhaps I was only delirious from the heat.

The sun was at its zenith when I came to a campground, appropriately named Jumbo Rocks for the massive boulders that seemed to have been piled into haphazard mounds by some insane god. A drive through the entire camp revealed only one other visitor - a twenty foot Winnebago with its air conditioner blasting, its generator groaning.

My life was to consist of moving from one camp to another until some additional insight revealed itself to me. For a short time, the adventure of it all might be sufficient, yet I couldn't fathom continuing that type of existence for eight years.

Eight years, Ch'en Po had said. Eight years before I would be with Synjin. Why?

CHAPTER THREE
The Time In Between

Summer thinned into autumn sometime during the last days of October. Winter came, and with it the storms and the snow. It was hard to believe that a place which saw temperatures in excess of 120 degrees in the summer could get snow, even hold it on the ground for weeks at a time. With the arrival of spring, the desert bloomed, casting alien blossoms into the air and bringing a scent of life to the otherwise barren stillness. And then the summer was back again - the destroyer, the game master, the ruling force. It sent the spring campers back to the safety of the city; it took the rock climbers and hikers behind a boulder, threatening that they would not survive should they remain too long in the heat. Summer spoke of mirages and death, and drowning in a dry river bed.

I was alone again.

Each morning, I rose with the first light of dawn and practiced the kata and the fighting techniques I had learned over the years. The Joshua Trees kept me company, the coyotes sang to me at night, the wind whispered Synjin's name when I stopped to listen. Occasionally, I would travel with The People while I slept, teaching the children, learning of their world and bringing a part of it back with me in the form of hope when I awakened the next morning. From time to time, new children would join my classes and older ones would simply disappear.

In that way our two worlds were very much alike. The children there could travel as I did so long as they remained children. The moment they gave up that mystical childhood, they became grounded in their own world and the astral door closed to them forever.

It saddened me, yet I had come to realize that not everyone was meant to exist in the same limbo I did. Some people wanted their families and their friends and their quiet little homes and their mortgages and their jobs. Some people wanted to be normal.

I envied them.

~

One evening as I taught the kata in a plane that existed between two realities, a young boy by the name of Jaden came to tell me of a message from Ch'en Po and a gift from Synjin. He wore the white gi of an initiate, and explained that he had studied with Master Synjin since he was three. The message was a simple one even if typically cryptic, and it was delivered when Jaden slid his small hand into mine. I heard Ch'en Po's voice in my mind then.

Oak tree cannot grow without water. And even when water plentiful, still need company of other tree if branches to develop strength enough to hold nest of bird. Take care to send roots deep.

I wasn't especially psychic, but I understood what Ch'en Po was saying – as much as anyone *could* understand what Ch'en Po was saying. If I weren't careful, existence in the desert would become easy - maybe *too* easy. Already, after barely a year, my body had adapted to the extremes in temperature. As long as the sun rose around me, I was a part of its heat. When the wind blew, I followed its direction instead of moving against it.

As for the company of this other tree, however, I hadn't a clue as to what Ch'en Po really meant. Most likely it was a euphemism for some other person I was to meet, or some new change in consciousness. It might have helped had he simply said what he meant, though I had learned that riddles were his stock in trade and figuring them out was part of the lesson.

I stood on the astral plane for several moments after the young messenger drew his hand away. Then, as I looked at him, he held out his hand with a tender, boyish smile. In it was a book, bound in silver. There was no title, but when I opened it at random, I saw that it contained the total accumulated knowledge of all systems of martial arts ever taught. Inside the pages were the ancient wisdoms of Hung Gar kung fu, shotokan, kenpo, tae kwon do, chin na, jeet koon do, jujitsu, aikido, kendo, and all the rest. The text was written in manuscript, intricate and beautiful, with drawings and diagrams to illustrate the Art and how to use it. It didn't matter that the inside of the book was larger than the outside – the sum of the knowledge held in a space that was insufficient to contain it. Such was the magic of the temple, the mystery of the Art. I didn't question it.

What I felt wasn't unlike what a priest might feel if he were suddenly to be handed a book containing the entire religious knowledge of the world, complete with a map leading to heaven.

"Master Synjin asked that I should deliver this book to his beloved," Jaden said, his voice clear and beautiful. "He asks that you read it whenever you visit this place, and he tells me that you are now ready for this knowledge."

I smiled at the boy. "Do you know where this place is?"

He nodded. "Of course, Master Willows. It is the universe which exists between space and time. It is the soul's bedroom."

My brows lifted. "I'm not a Master, Jaden. Only a student like yourself." I wanted to straighten that out before I tackled something as intriguing as the soul's bedroom.

"My teacher has also asked me to tell you that Mastery lies not within the pages of this book, but in how the knowledge is used by each individual. He said that you will know what to do with the book, how to read it." He paused, then tilted his dark head to one side. "Do you think Master Synjin will one day allow me to study this book?"

I smiled and touched him fondly on the shoulder. "If you stay on your path, Jaden, I'm sure he will."

He seemed satisfied with that, for his smile widened.

"Jaden, would you do something for me?" I asked.

He nodded. "It would be an honor to be of service, Master Willows."

"Good," I said, smiling. I held the book out to him. "I want you to keep this for me. Bring it to me when I come here next, and keep it safe while I'm away."

He smiled warmly. "And don't read what's inside because I'm not ready?"

I chuckled. "Is that what Master Synjin said?"

"He promised to make me sweep every corner of the Temple of Kalpa if I read so much as one word before permission is given." Still, Jaden seemed amused.

"Well, if I were you, I'd listen to what Master Synjin says unless you like to sweep," I suggested.

He took the book and tucked it under his arm. "I hate to sweep," he said with a grin.

Then he was gone, back into his own world, back to his morning, back to his body.

~

I watched the seasons change three more times in my world. What lay behind me now were four years of almost complete isolation. What lay ahead, I couldn't be certain. I only knew it would come soon or not so soon, in its own time and not a moment before. Twenty six years of living had taught me to accept it, though it was seldom easy.

The book Synjin had given to me kept my nights occupied, and my knowledge of the Art increased exponentially. Through the mental and physical disciplines in the book, I learned to control my time in the astral plane, and to enter it at will through alpha meditation. I studied the art of acupuncture and herbal medicine, how to heal as well as how to kill. I saw the world differently by the end of that fourth year, yet I was no more than a hundred pages or so into the thick volume of knowledge.

When supplies ran low, I would travel into the town of Joshua Tree to buy groceries at the market. The man behind the counter never questioned me, never seemed to care that my order always consisted of precisely the same thing: beans, rice, tortillas, vitamin supplements, propane canisters, and Miss Clairol.

I hadn't grown careless. I'd be a blonde for two months, then a brunette, then a redhead. My skin stayed dark from the desert sun, and I bore little resemblance to the person I'd been when I left Land o'Lakes for the last time.

That River Willows was lost forever when Avery Madison's life ended.

I'd gone through each of the campgrounds within Joshua Tree National Monument several times, and it had become easier to tear down the tent and move my life two miles to the left or right, ten miles to the north or south. Even the rangers had come to accept me as a semi-permanent fixture, and looked the other way even though my extended stay violated park policy.

From time to time, a sheriff's deputy would come through the park, patrolling the grounds as if searching for someone or something. But the only trouble I ever ran into was one day in November of '92.

Deputy Ernie Drake pulled me over as I was leaving the monument on a wood-gathering expedition one evening. He told me politely that my tags had expired and that I needed to have them renewed within thirty days to avoid a stiff penalty. He commented briefly about the fact that they had been expired for over three years, asking me why. I made some excuse about being a starving college student, and threw myself at his mercy.

When he asked to see my driver's license, I began to wonder if something more than expired plates had caused him to stop me. I handed it over nonetheless, then waited with controlled terror while he went back to his cruiser and called it in.

After an eternity, he came back to my car and handed the license through the window, along with a warning citation about my out-of-date Florida plates.

"I'm not gonna fine you this time, Ms. Raynor, because I was in college once, too," he said with typical police courtesy. "But I do want you to get this taken care of as soon as possible."

I nodded politely. "Where's the nearest DMV?"

He inclined his head toward the east. "There's an office in 29 Palms. You might as well renew your license, too. It doesn't expire for a few more months, but if you're like me, you won't want to stand in line more than once."

I smiled at him, trying to keep it light. "I'll take care of it first thing in the morning."

"You going to be staying in California for awhile?"

"Yeah," I replied, making it all up as I went along. "I go to school part-time at UCLA. When I'm not there, I come out here to work on my writing."

"Got any books published?" he asked, surprising me with the abrupt change of subject. He wasn't suspicious, just bored.

"Not yet. This'll be my first."

He loosened up after that. "I wrote a book once," he said, resting his hands on the door frame of the car as he laughed. "Never could find a publisher for the damn thing - probably because it was a piece of shit. Oh, pardon my language. It was, though, a piece of..." His face darkened and he tapped the roof of the car, then backed away. "Well, you stay out of trouble, Ms. Raynor. And have a nice stay in the desert."

I thanked him for his leniency, then started the engine and pulled back onto the road. I was shaking like hell; it had been a long time since I'd had to worry about the police, and even though the search for River Willows had long since been ignored by the media, I suspected that some bureaucrat somewhere was still interested in tracking me down.

For the rest of the night, I prowled the back roads, gathering scrap wood and loading it into the car – mainly to keep myself occupied and work off the anxiety. When the back was full, I parked near a church to wait for dawn. For several hours, there was only silence and darkness and then the church bells pealed, startling me from my semi-meditative state as they announced the coming of another day.

I wondered fleetingly where time went when it was gone. Four years in the desert, each day blending seamlessly into the next, time accumulating itself for a purpose that remained entirely obscure. Life was a strange collection of daydreams and nightmares, memories and hopes, whispered in the voice of those bells that were lonesome and somehow terribly sad, like castrati sirens weaving their melody around crumbling tombstones in the church cemetery at the edge of a dilapidated town.

An unwelcome melancholy filled me, and for the briefest of moments I came close to feeling sorry for myself. What might my life had been had things gone a different way? Who might I have become had I not become a fugitive?

Pointless speculations, the little voice of wisdom whispered from the back of my mind. *Might as well ask the moon what she dreams when the Earth is full.*

Starting the engine, I pulled back onto the main road and headed in the direction of town. When I arrived at the center where the Denny's was located, I cruised by the DMV to check their hours.

Having two hours to kill, I parked in with the herd of pick-ups and mini-vans near the restaurant, then got out and started to walk. I was filled with a restlessness I hadn't experienced in years, and a very real frustration. The money was running dangerously low. Registration on the car was bound to be expensive, and I'd be needing food and supplies again within the week.

Walking for several blocks in the early November morning, I was grateful for the coolness of the late autumn. Now the desert was coming alive again; campers planning a Thanksgiving away from the hassles of the city were starting to flood the desert towns.

I was drawn from my reverie when I came upon a small newsstand tucked into the corner of a shopping plaza. The store itself was nothing special - a less-than-glorious imitation of a 7/11, with several racks of magazines, paperback books, newspapers and the traditional touristy necessities.

I thumbed through a couple of magazines, found nothing of interest, then replaced them on the shelf. But when I saw the December '92 issue of *Martial Artistry*, something caused my hand to tremble as I reached for it.

Fighting the peculiar reaction, I picked it up and began glancing through the table of contents. Various articles featured different fighting styles; an essay on the importance of chi manipulation; the usual fare. But as I came to the bottom of the page, something caught my eye that caused me to gasp aloud.

The article was entitled *The Execution of a Master*. I quickly began to read.

> *He was a master in every sense of the word, yet his life ended along a lonesome road on the outskirts of Yuma, Arizona on October 20 of this year. Evidence found near the scene indicated that a struggle of incredible proportions had taken place, and it is rumored that the FBI removed two bodies in addition to Master Mark Barrows' bullet-ridden corpse prior to the arrival of local officials.*
> *There were also several other pieces of this complex puzzle which suggest that...*

I couldn't make sense of something that made no sense. Master Barrows' photograph stared up at me from the page, his eyes shining bright, his smile crooked, his hands pressed together in the traditional salute. In the background, several students whom I recognized stood at attention, myself among them. I even remembered that the photo had been taken by the local paper to honor Master Barrows for community service.

My body trembling, I stared down at the photograph for several minutes, until I heard the store clerk cough politely. Drawing a deep breath which did nothing to calm my nerves, I turned to the register and slapped the magazine down on the counter. The young woman looked at me rather oddly, and I wondered if the whole thing had flared up again, if I were about to be surrounded by the police after she'd sounded some silent alarm. My Master was dead; I was bound to be paranoid.

"Do you study?" the woman behind the counter asked.

She might as well have been speaking Portuguese. "What?"

She tapped on the magazine. "Do you study?" she repeated.

My fortitude was weak, faltering. "I used to," I managed. "A long time ago."

She made a grunting sound. "Just curious. A lot of the students from that dojo around the corner come in here," she added. "I've read a lot about it - Zen books, mostly, and some stuff on Buddhist philosophy. I've thought about getting into it, but I don't have the time."

I remembered something Master Barrows had always emphasized. "You make time for the Art," I said, dazed.

She reached for a candy bar, then stuffed half of it into her mouth. "You look like you just lost your best friend," she commented, holding out the package and offering me a piece. "Chocolate usually helps, honey."

For nearly five years when I was his student, Mark Barrows *had* been my best friend. If it weren't for him, I wouldn't be alive.

I turned toward the door, my eyes bleeding tears until I was blind.

~

Somewhen in The Past

I'd done well. More than six hours after the death of Avery Madison and I was still alive. But if I wanted it to stay that way, I was going to need help.

On the entire planet, there were no more than four people I could trust - Master Barrows, Dara, my father, and one half-crazy ex-schoolmate by the name of Martin Quaid. Going to my father's house or to Dara's would sign my death warrant; and the feds certainly would have figured out that I spent more time at Master Barrows' studio than at home. That left Martin, a boy I'd known since we were children. He'd had a crush on me years before, and we'd become friends of a sort.

The exodus away from the combined forces of the police and the Air Force MP's took an hour longer than I'd estimated. By the time I reached the outskirts of Land o'Lakes, the first silver sliver of dawn was beginning to pierce the eastern horizon. Crickets and bull frogs read Shakespeare to one another with myriad voices. Whip-o-wills spoke of their latest journey among the stars, and alligators from the swamp croaked a warning that not even the other night creatures could comprehend.

It took another half hour before I arrived at Martin's place. If he were still the same person he'd always been, he'd still be working at the same job - which meant he'd come out of his house at around 6:30, climb into his hot-rod Mustang, and drive into Lutz to the tiny mom-&-pop supermarket.

As usual, Martin was ten minutes late, but he finally came ambling out of the house and started toward the car, fumbling with the keys in his hand, dropping them once, then trying again.

Moving quickly, I ducked low under the trees and emerged into the back yard, concealing myself behind the wall of the garage and inching along until I came to the front. Martin was still fidgeting with the door lock when I stuck my head around the corner. I hadn't seen him in almost a year, but he still looked the same. Tall, pale, gangly, awkward.

"Martin!" I whispered loudly.

He looked over his shoulder in the wrong direction, then back toward the house, seemingly perplexed.

"Martin!" I tried again.

He finally saw me, but the surprise caused him to drop his keys again. "River?" he said in a voice that was too loud.

I motioned for him to keep his voice down, then jerked my head toward the safer sanctuary of the orange grove. "I have to talk to you."

His expression was one of suspicion and trust, paradoxically intertwined.

"Mom and dad don't live here anymore. They moved back to Virginia last year," he said unexpectedly. He inclined his head toward the house. "Come inside."

I hoped I could trust him. "Go around and unlock the back door."

He did as he was told, though it seemed to take forever until I heard the sliding glass door open. Staying low, I ran across the back yard and through the door, emerging into the kitchen.

He stared at me a moment longer, shaking his head with a sigh. "Damn, River, I don't know what you really did, but it must've been good. You made CNN this morning." He said it as if I were a celebrity and he was impressed.

I groaned inwardly, then reached out to touch him on the arm. "Look, Marty, I don't have much time. I need you to do something for me."

He stared at me again. Finally, he nodded. "You know I'd do anything for you, River," he said, his voice sad and elated at the same time. Marty was a living contradiction – probably one of the few natural goths, just a gentle poet who saw the world too clearly.

I glanced around the room. "Pen and paper?"

He went into another room and came back with a small note pad and a pencil. I took it and hastily began to write.

Dear Master Barrows:

I'm sure you've heard what's become of me by now. I want you to know, as my Master and my friend, that I have acted in self defense. Through circumstances, however, my own honor is not enough to clear me of the charges which will result should I be captured. Indeed, I have reason to believe I would be killed before any legal action ever reached the courts.

If you feel that I have acted dishonorably, you may bring the police with you to the meeting place I will propose and I will turn myself in. If you can still believe me though, after all that's certainly been said in the media, I would like to speak privately with you this evening. You taught me the first moves of the Tiger and the Crane in a location of significance. I hope to see you there again tonight.

I deeply regret any dishonor I have brought to you, to the studio or its other students.

With respect, RW

I folded the note and handed it to Martin, knowing that no man or woman alive would be able to follow Mark Barrows if he decided to accept my proposal. If we met, we'd be alone.

"I want you to take this to my Master," I said, careful to make my instructions clear. "The studio is on School Road, about half a mile from the junction. Master Barrows lives in the cottage behind the building."

Martin stared at me curiously. "You don't think the cops'll have the place under surveillance?"

"Absolutely," I agreed, "which is why this is so important. Just walk up to the door of the cottage and knock. Act like you belong there. Don't be looking over your shoulder." It was impossible to impart my instincts to him in the short time I had. "When Master Barrows answers the door, ask him if you can come in. Whatever you do, don't hand him the note until you're inside."

Martin nodded, then smiled. "No problem." His brows lifted, concern grew on his face. "What really happened, River?"

I drew a deep breath and looked away from him, out the back door and toward the grove. "I'm not sure myself. What are they saying on the tube?"

He shrugged. "That you're an escaped mental patient," he revealed. "And that you killed three Air Force guys."

I jolted. "*Three?*"

"Did you?" he asked innocently.

"No!" I wasn't sure how much I should tell him - maybe everything, maybe nothing. Truth usually worked the best. "I killed one man, Martin," I said at last. "In self defense."

He seemed to relax a little, gave a curt nod, then we stood there looking awkwardly at one another.

I forced a smile. "You'd better get going. Just drop off the note, then go on to work. You have to act as if nothing's out of the ordinary." I touched him again, both hands on his arms. "I owe you one."

He shook his head shyly, then studied my face once more. "You could stay here, River," he said. "Nobody ever comes around. You'd be safe if you wanted to sleep for awhile. There's food in the fridge."

"Thanks," I said, weary and exhausted. "It's only a matter of time before someone thinks to look through the records back at school. Eventually, somebody will come around asking questions about me."

He was still looking at me. "I won't see you again after this, will I?"

My lips pressed together. "I don't think so, Martin."

He gave me a sad little smile. Then, before I knew what he was doing, he leaned down and kissed me shyly on the cheek. "I hope you know what you're doing."

So did I.

He went to the front door, but turned toward me with a quizzical look.

"You always did seem to know something the rest of us didn't," he commented, surprising me with his perceptions. "Is that what it is? Is that why all of this is happening to you?"

I smiled, somewhat wistfully, I suppose. "I really don't know. Someone I admire once said something that makes a lot of sense."

"Which is?"

"There are no answers."

He looked perplexed, then nodded as if he understood. Maybe he did. "Take care of yourself, River."

I never saw Martin Quaid again after that.

~

The stuff on the tube was worse than I'd imagined. From the local network stations to CNN, I was the big news, it seemed. I damned my timing, wishing the death of Dr. Avery Madison had happened on the day of some great natural disaster or some sleazy political scandal.

I sat in front of Martin's nine inch television for about an hour, getting the various versions of what I'd supposedly done. The news anchor on Channel 13 had me flying over the hood of a military ambulance like a ninja madwoman and twisting Madison's head around backward on his shoulders. Channel 8 reported that a mental patient suffering from acute schizophrenia had attacked the driver of the ambulance, and had subsequently gunned down one of the kindly doctors with his own weapon, broken another's neck, and killed the third man by running over him with the ambulance itself. CNN kept it brief, but said that I had indeed killed three high-ranking Air Force officers, and had fled into Tampa, taking a hostage from a nearby bus stop.

Misinformation. None of the reporters were that incompetent. They were simply repeating what some spokesman for the Air Force had told them. And undoubtedly each one was given a slightly different version of the truth. In such a manner, eyewitnesses could easily be discredited, and the general public would be so terrified that my own mother might have considered turning me in.

After checking to make sure all the doors and windows were locked, I went down the long hallway and into what appeared to be a guest bedroom. The covers were dusty; Martin had been telling the truth when he said no one would come around.

I had planned to sleep only an hour before returning to the orange grove to wait until dark. When I woke up, the sun was low on the western horizon.

It was ten hours later and time to start moving again.

~

The sun had been down for more than two hours when the crickets went suddenly still. I listened intently, the silence so deep that my ears hurt from it after a few minutes. From my vantage point among a thicket of oaks, I could see the entire clearing easily, even without the moon.

The only time I'd been to the location had been with my Master. It was near a road that had once been used by the early Florida settlers - a logging trail used to haul downed trees from the forest. Over the years, the road had been abandoned, and immature saplings grew in a clearing where proud oaks had once stood. Master Barrows had impressed that symbolism onto me one afternoon, saying that the clearing was one of his favorite locations.

I waited.

The crickets sang again, stopped, sang. Nothing.

Sighing with frustration and weariness, I leaned against the trunk of an oak, tilting my head back until I could see the stars. It was in that moment that something fell at my feet. Startled, I jumped back, snapping my head in either direction until I could discern the familiar silhouette of a man about three feet behind me.

"Master Barrows," I said instinctively.

He took a step closer, breathed a heavy sigh and indicated the bundle he'd dropped at my feet. "Your gi and your belt. I found them in your locker and thought you might want them." Then, squatting, he rested his back against a tree, motioning for me to sit with him. "We'll be safe here for awhile. Tell me what happened."

I started at the beginning. The drowning, the hospital, the coma, Dr. Madison, the Air Force. I gave serious thought to telling him about Ch'en Po and the rest of it, but didn't. *Tell no one about me. Tell no one about Synjin'.*

When I was finished, he sat there for a long time, studying the ground at his feet. "Damn," was all he said.

It was the most uncharacteristic thing I'd ever heard come from his lips.

"I knew it had to be something like that," he continued. "The feds were on my doorstep an hour after it happened, asking all sorts of questions. They've had the studio under surveillance since yesterday afternoon." He laughed lightly. "Of course, they think I don't know about it, but I've never had much trouble spotting trouble, especially when it parks half a block up the street in an unmarked van."

"I'm sorry, Master Barrows. I didn't intend to dishonor you." It was important to me that he know that.

"There's no dishonor in protecting yourself, River. From what you've told me, your life was in danger." He paused, studying me intently. "Want to tell me the rest? As far as I know, the government isn't in the habit of grabbing people out of the hospital just because they were in a coma for three days."

I looked away. Then, drawing a deep breath for composure, I met his eyes. "I would if I could, Master," I said. "There are other lives at stake. And I will dishonor a friend if I say too much."

He didn't push it, but reached out to take my hand. "For what it's worth, I'll do anything in my power to help you." He paused, choosing his words carefully. "When you first came to me, I have to admit that I didn't think you'd stick with it - largely because you seemed so completely unconcerned with the world in general." He chuckled again, softly. "But when I saw the amount of devotion you gave to the Art, I started to realize that you were probably more like the old Masters than any of my other students."

I frowned. "I don't understand."

"In each soul, there's a blueprint if you will, an inner knowledge of what's right and what's wrong. The old Masters lived in their own world - not unlike you do."

"Sometimes I think it's a better world," I said, surprised that I had an answer for him, surprised at the depth of his perception, though I shouldn't have been.

Looking at me closely, he smiled just a little. "Have you ever wondered why I teach at the studio?"

"Because it's in your blood," I replied.

He shook his head. "That's part of it, sure. The Art either gets into your blood or it doesn't; but that's not why I teach." He paused, looking around at the silence and the darkness and the night and me. "I remember that other world, River, and I know that through the Art, enough discipline can be developed to understand it better." He laughed, surprising me. "Did you know that I have a master's degree in engineering? But I gave it all up. I went back to Okinawa and Beijing and spent another five years with the Masters, trying to get back what I lost somewhere along the way."

My heart pounded. "Have you - have you been there - to that other world, I mean?"

He looked at me curiously, then shrugged. "When I was younger," he said. "When I was a *lot* younger..."

"What do you remember about it?"

"I'm not sure it's a physical place, River," he said then. "But it's a world nonetheless - a place in the soul. It's what teaches us, helps us grow. It's like an allegory, or a fairy tale."

It was much more than that, though I began to realize that each individual saw it differently. "What if you found you could get there?" I asked. "Physically, I mean. Would you go?"

"Probably not."

That took me off guard. "Why?"

Holding my hand so tight that it turned numb, he looked far away, perhaps into that other world itself. "Because it's not where I belong. You've studied for five years, almost six. You know what techniques work for you and which ones don't. In the same way, I know that I belong here." He studied me again. "Do you understand?"

"Yes," I said, trying to smile. "For what it's worth, I think I might even understand why."

"Oh?"

"If you hadn't been here, there would have been no studio in this little town. There would have been no Art for me, or for your other students."

He nodded understanding. "River," he said fervently, "I've given you all the knowledge I can. Now you're going to have to take that knowledge and use it as best you can."

"You remind me very much of someone I met recently. Another Master," I said, thinking of Ch'en Po.

He frowned thoughtfully, then chuckled. "After awhile, maybe we all start to sound alike. There are a lot of different roads to the same knowledge. Four is still four, whether you got there by adding three and one, or two and two. That's what my first Master was fond of saying."

I considered that. "Who was he?

He smiled in fond remembrance. "He was an old man I met in Beijing on my first trip to China. Older than the hills and still quicker than a fox. You see, my first love was White Crane Kung Fu, but I didn't have the build for it - too thick in the shoulders and legs. Ch'en Po spent two years trying to convince me of that, but I was a stubborn young man who wanted what I wanted. I have him to thank, though, for pointing me toward kenpo and shotokan."

I wasn't hearing a word he was saying. There couldn't be two of Ch'en Po, not in this world or any other. I felt my mouth open to say something, to proclaim that I had also met the elusive and masterful Ch'en Po, but the words wouldn't come.

'Tell no one about me. Tell no one about Synjin'.

"You okay?" I heard Master Barrows ask.

"Yeah... sure." I shook my head to clear the cobwebs of clashing realities. "Just trying to make some sense of everything." I knew now precisely why Master Barrows and I had met. Intersecting paths. Converging lines. Crossroads. Maybe Ch'en Po engineered the whole thing from the abacus that kept track of time and lives and destiny.

"Where will you go, River?" he asked very quietly.

"I don't know yet, but it has to be far away from here," I said, knowing that at least one part of my life was over.

He was silent for a moment. "I thought so. I've taken care of a few things for you."

I looked up from where I'd been staring at the ground.

"It isn't much," he began, "but if you're going to get out of this mess alive, you're going to need transportation." He inclined his head toward the far side of the sapling-oak clearing. "There's a dirt road that dead ends about half a mile from here. At the end of it you'll find a car with some clothes and food. If you're smart, you'll move with the herd until you're out of Florida, then head west somewhere and travel at night."

I blinked, protesting. "I can't take your car, Master Barrows. You can't—."

"It's not my car, River," he interrupted. "My brother fixes junkers for a living; he owed me a favor." He shrugged nonchalantly. Then, reaching around to his back, he withdrew a small pouch from somewhere in the folds of his clothes.

"In here, you'll find a driver's license and enough cash to keep you out of harm's way for awhile. Take it."

I didn't reach for it, so he took my hand, turned it upward, and placed the pouch in my palm, closing my fingers around it.

"I can't-."

"Don't say it," he interrupted again. "Besides, you've been with the studio nearly six years; you've helped me teach; and you can't afford to say no." He paused, then chuckled. "Besides, how do you think it would look if one of my top students couldn't evade something as minor a nationwide search? Hell, if you get caught now, it's going to wreak havoc with business!"

I felt his sincerity and appreciated his humor, but that didn't make it any easier. "If I ever get out of this mess..." My voice trailed off; the possibility seemed unlikely.

He stood up, pulling me to my feet until we faced one another in the wooded glen. "If you ever get out of this mess, River, come back and teach with me."

I smiled, though my heart was heavy.

He stepped away from me then and placed his right fist into the palm of his left hand - the gesture of respect from one martial artist to another. I repeated the formality, then bowed from the waist to honor my Master, my eyes closing as part of the ritual.

When I opened them, he was gone.

Parting from my Master was the hardest thing I'd ever had to do. He had offered me security and knowledge, a safe haven when my spirit was weak or my flesh was tired. Now I would never enter the sacred doors of his studio again. It made no difference that the hinges squeaked or that the building itself was only a store front in a tiny town. It had been a sanctuary to me, and now it was lost in the maze of anarchy that had become my life.

The things my Master had said had astounded me, yet how could I really be surprised by any of them? Four was still four. We both loved the Art and, in the end, it was probably for the same reason: Ch'en Po, and the mystical temple that lived like Oz in the hearts of martial artists.

For more than an hour, I remained there, coming to terms with myself and what I had become. Ch'en Po was right about one thing - there were no answers.

I picked up my gi, the belt, and the pouch my Master had given me. I started walking then, and didn't stop until I found the car he had hidden at the end of the long dirt road. I found great symbolism in that, but attributed it to the fact that my mind was imploding in on itself, looking for meaning in the sand, omens in the wind.

The car itself wasn't what I'd expected. Master Barrows had said that his brother fixed junkers for a living. This could hardly be labeled a junker. It was sleek, white, and low to the ground. I recognized it as an older Camaro from the late 70s, but the fact that it had obviously been rebuilt left it looking shiny and new.

Feeling guilty and humbled at the same time, I rifled through the pouch Master Barrows had given me until I found the keys. After opening the door, I slid into the driver's seat and turned on the dome light.

Taped to the steering wheel was a note.

> *My beloved student:*
> *I'm an only child. Sorry for lying to you about my nonexistent brother, but I know how martial artists are. We're a humble yet proud breed who don't readily accept charity. Anyway, the car goes fast and should keep you two steps ahead. It belonged to a friend of the family who recently died of cancer, and is still registered in her name. So's the driver's license, insurance, etc.*

You're a new person, so you can stop feeling guilty right about now.

I've tried to give you some of the same knowledge my Masters over the years have given me. I hope it will be enough to keep you safe and help you find the wisdom and the courage that seem so elusive in this world.

I almost envy you your quest.

Love and honor – Mark

I was suddenly alone in the world, and as I took my first breath as my new self, the air was cold and terribly empty.

Some time later, I opened the pouch and looked inside until I found the driver's license. The photo didn't look much like me, but it was a legal license, and at least the woman in the picture was about the same age. Looking further, I found a wad of cash - more than forty five hundred dollars. My Master wasn't a wealthy man; he must have drained the studio's account to get the money, and I struggled with the emotions that overcame me.

A quick glance at the back of the car also revealed camping gear - a sleeping bag, tent, propane stove, and several grocery sacks filled with food. A Hershey Bar was sticking out the top of one of them - Master Barrows' final tribute. He'd been trying to get me to give up chocolate for years.

~

And now, four years and a lot of miles later, the grocery clerk at a tiny convenience store on the other side of the country was tempting me with it all over again, conjuring up ghosts I'd thought well insulated with time and distance.

I thanked the woman for her concern, then quickly left the store, my mind too numb to think, my heart shattered, my hope lost.

My Master was dead, and with him a part of the temple had been lost.

CHAPTER FOUR
Discovery

I found myself a block away with the magazine clutched in numb fingers. The plaza was called 'Desert Plaza' for originality, and in the far end I could see the painted red letters over the door to one of the store fronts. 'KARATE', was all it said.

It wasn't any later than 7:30, and I needed time to think. There was a row of benches in front of the studio and I flopped onto one, forcing back the tears that wanted to come.

I opened the magazine again and picked up where I'd left off.

...were also several other pieces of this complex puzzle which suggest that Master Barrows might have been attempting to contact a former student, the now infamous River Willows, black belt kenpo instructor turned fugitive in a bizarre incident which began in 1988.

In an interview with Barrows in 1989, he maintained that Ms. Willows was innocent, and that he was attempting to intercede with the FBI in an attempt to have her name cleared and a formal acquittal declared.

It was shortly after that when Master Barrows was accused of cocaine possession, and charged with soliciting minors from his studio for sexual acts. No formal charges were brought, but the damage to his reputation from these allegations resulted in ruination of his career and the closure of his business.

Whatever really happened to Mark Barrows that night near Yuma will probably always remain a mystery, as will the whereabouts of River Willows.

The martial arts community is deeply saddened by the loss of Master Barrows. He was 53, and is survived by his parents, Mr. & Mrs. Andrew Barrows; and one twin brother, Kevin Barrows - a martial artist with a degree in engineering. Mr. & Mrs. Barrows declined to be interviewed, but, Kevin told me that while he's saddened by his brother's death, "I can almost envy him his quest into that other world."

I couldn't help it; I started to smile as I finished the article. Kevin Barrows, with a degree in engineering. My Master was an only child. I didn't need to know the hows and whens and the whys. Somehow, perhaps in the same way he'd arranged for my new identity, Master Barrows had arranged for his own.

Obviously, something had happened back there in Land o'Lakes, and I didn't doubt that he'd been set up as a result of trying to have me acquitted. But survival was his stock in trade, even if he had to die to make it happen.

~

"I see you're reading *Martial Artistry*," a voice said, breaking into my thoughts. "Are you interested in lessons?"

I lifted my head to see a man standing over me. He wore a black gi with the traditional belt tied around his waist. Five red strips on the ends of the belt denoted his rank, and he smiled openly as I met his blue eyes. Sandy blond hair was cut just below his ears, and grew longer in the back, where the fringe had been tied into a four-inch tail. He seemed enthusiastic and energetic even if somewhat young to hold a fifth degree black belt.

"What system do you teach?" I asked out of curiosity, momentarily startled.

He grinned broadly, then asked with a gesture if he could share the bench. I nodded and he sat down.

"I've never been much on labels. The system I teach is a combination of a lot of different things - aikido, tae kwon do and kenpo, mostly," he added. "With a little kung fu thrown in to hold everything together."

I liked him instinctively and told him so with a smile. "I haven't studied actively for a long time," I replied. And I also couldn't afford the lessons even if I'd been interested, but I did enjoy the company of another student of the Art.

He looked me over. "It's never too late to get back into it," he reminded me, genuine warmth in his tone. "Mind if I ask what you studied?"

"Kenpo, mainly... with a little kung fu thrown in for glue," I said, mirroring his words back at him.

He laughed easily. "The studio doesn't open for another hour yet, but if you want, come on inside and let me show you around."

I saw no harm in it and got to my feet. "Sure," I said, following as he led the way. When we reached the door, I automatically kicked off my tennis shoes and left them just outside the training area.

Once inside, I was impressed with the set-up. A yin/yang symbol was drawn on the floor, its black and white paint worn thin from the footprints of many years of students. There were several mats toward the back of the room, and traditional weapons were hung along the walls. Running along the other side were full-length mirrors, above which appeared a hand-painted mural. It depicted the ancient warriors of China conferring with Samurai and ninja. The characters in the painting sat at a central round table which was also painted with the age-old yin/yang.

He noticed my interest. "Something one of my students did," he said with obvious pride. "He wanted to show that all martial arts stem from the same source - the balance of dark and light, if you will."

I smiled, turning to face him. "It was obviously very inspired."

He held out his hand in a gesture of friendship. "Jerry Davin," he offered.

"Lynne Raynor," I replied, impressed with the firm warmth of his handshake.

He released my hand and took a step backward. For a moment, we were awkward with one another, but the feeling passed when he strode purposefully toward the back of the studio.

"The stretching machines and weights are back here," he said, urging me to follow as he disappeared behind a wall. When I emerged into an impressive exercise area, he added, "I try to have enough equipment to keep the kids interested in coming. Sometimes, the littler ones just come and watch." He shrugged. "Some of them join the school when they get older."

I admired him. "How long have you been teaching here?"

"About two years now," he responded. "The studio used to belong to Master Chang, but he went on an indefinite sabbatical to China. I'm certainly not his equal, but the kids seem to like me."

The studio felt good. I didn't doubt his word. "How many students do you have?"

At that, he gave a disbelieving chuckle. "Last time I actually counted, there were two hundred and fourteen kids and sixty five adults on record," he said. "Of course, they don't all come regularly, but each belt-rank has about thirty five people in the class."

I was surprised. "I didn't think this area was that big."

"Neither did I. All I know is that they just seem to keep coming. I used to open up at noon and close at seven. Now the doors open at nine a.m., and I'm lucky to close before ten at night. As you might have guessed, there's not much to do out here, and a lot of the parents send the kids here just to get them out of their hair at home." He sounded almost apologetic.

"It was the same way where I used to study," I said, finding him easy to talk to. "But the ones who are serious will stick it out; the ones who aren't will find something else to do."

He eyed me curiously. "Were you serious?"

He was straightforward and I liked that. "Yes."

Inclining his head toward the training arena, he spoke with a smile. "Ever do any sparring?"

I knew what he was getting at, and for a reason I couldn't define, I wasn't adverse to the idea.

"Some," I replied with an evasive grin. "Is that a challenge?"

"Consider it an invitation," he laughed, moving past me and back into the main part of the studio.

I followed him to the mats and waited for a moment before stepping into the designated sparring area. "You've either got one hell of a sale's pitch or else you're completely out of your mind," I commented, amused.

He stretched, loosening his muscles as I took his lead and did the same. "Guilty on both charges," he replied.

Placing his right fist into his left open palm, he bowed. I repeated the gesture of mutual respect, then stepped onto the mat, dropping into a low fighting stance as I anticipated his first move.

He was quick and agile, and I appreciated the fact that he didn't treat me like an inferior. He didn't underestimate me once. When either of us connected with a target, it was with enough pressure to make the blow felt, yet not enough force to injure.

We sparred for several minutes, testing one another's strength and skills. There was one moment when he could have taken me if he'd moved in, and another when I could have defeated him had I seized the opportunity. It seemed that neither of us was in the mood to end the game; the competition itself was enjoyable, and we were well matched.

In the mock battle which continued for nearly twenty minutes, I learned a few tricks I hadn't known before, and I think Jerry picked up a few of my unusual techniques. By the time it became obvious that there wasn't going to be an actual winner, we were both dripping with perspiration.

The competition ended when Jerry finally dropped his guard and took a step back, bringing his empty hand and closed fist together once more.

"Whew!" he commented in an exaggerated sigh. "If you're telling the truth when you say you haven't practiced in a few years, I wouldn't have wanted to spar with you when you were at the peak of your training. Where'd you learn that stuff anyway?"

Catching my breath, I shook my head. "I didn't say I didn't practice. I just haven't studied formally for awhile." I evaded his direct question altogether, something I'd learned from Ch'en Po.

Stepping off the mat, he returned to the back room. I followed as he opened a locker and tossed me a clean white towel. After wiping his face and neck, he looked at me again, the amusement leaving his eyes as he studied me.

"What's the matter?" I asked, still slightly out of breath. I felt good about myself and about him.

His leaned up against the back wall. "You're River Willows, aren't you?" he asked then, his voice very still.

I didn't have the controls to avoid breaking eye contact with him for just a moment. I considered running; he was out of breath. But so was I.

"I told you who I am," I said without indignation. "Why would you say something like that?"

He didn't buy it. Instead, he only shrugged, his posture relaxed. "Don't panic," he said quietly. "I knew who you were the minute I saw you sitting outside the studio."

My body tensed and I gave up the pretenses. "Can I expect the entire police force to pull up at any moment?"

He admonished me with a frown. "Not unless you want to call them." He continued lounging against the back wall, his demeanor natural, casual. "You may not believe me, but if there have to be sides in this thing, I'm on yours."

I wasn't sure I *could* believe him. He might just be stalling long enough for the cops to arrive.

I couldn't risk it and turned to walk away. Somewhat surprised that he didn't follow, I moved through the studio and toward the front door, listening for footsteps that didn't come. When I reached the exit, however, heart slamming wildly in my chest, I found it locked. With a sinking feeling in the pit of my gut, I glanced over my shoulder to see Jerry standing just inside the training arena, the towel still draped around his neck.

"I wouldn't advise trying to kick it down," he said matter-of-factly.

His tone said he was amused at me, and that awakened my anger. My body jerked toward him, eyes narrowing. "Yeah? Well you'll forgive me if I don't take that advice!" I replied. Then, spinning toward the door and summoning my chi like an ally, I connected with a front thrust kick to an area about three inches below the knob. It should have resulted in a shower of splinters, but the door didn't budge, and the reverberation sent pain shooting through my right leg, causing me to stumble back. Out the corner of my eye, I could see Jerry moving toward me at an unconcerned pace, but I estimated that I had time for another try at the door.

"Take it easy, River," his voice said, coming closer. "I didn't lock the door to lock you *in*, but to keep everyone else *out*." He was closer now, and the world was spinning.

Pivoting into position, I drew my left leg back to try the door again, mentally sealing off the throbbing ache that had already begun in my knee.

I'm not sure what happened after that. I remember my foot impacting with the door, and the door mocking me as it continued to stand, undamaged. Jerry was on me by then, and I turned to fight as if my life depended on it. I believed it did. I felt an elbow connect with flesh, but it wasn't the target I'd thought would be there. Nothing vulnerable. I think I caught him on an arm. Somehow, he'd circled around behind me and my right wrist was suddenly seized in a well-practiced grip until my entire shoulder went numb and limp.

"Would you relax?" he asked from behind me, holding me immobile. "Just let me talk to you!"

I used my other elbow in an attempt to knock the wind out of him. But as a martial artist, he was prepared for the attack which would have taken a normal street thug off guard. He blocked the blow with his forearm, cushioning the impact entirely.

I heard him sigh, struggling to hold me. "You going to stop it?"

It infuriated me that I'd been so easily subdued, and I lashed out again, bringing my head back hard against his chest until I heard him grunt.

And then I felt his hand move. Strong fingers tightened at the apex of shoulder and neck; there was a pressure in my head; and the world was going away. The bastard actually neck-pinched me, never mentioning his expertise in *chin na*.

I heard his voice, distant. "Take it easy. I'm not your enemy, River."

Then there was nothing.

~

"Young ram butt head against the wrong wall this time!"

It was Ch'en Po's voice again, and I opened my eyes to find myself sitting next to him in the center of Jerry's studio. I found it both symbolic and ironic that I was seated on the black half of the yin/yang, while Ch'en Po sat, wise and aloof, in the light area.

Whatever the deep inner meaning, I was happy to see the old man again.

Shaking his head, he scoffed. "Ta! Look at fine cucumber get self into this time!" he chastised, jerking his head toward the front door of the studio.

"Fine *pickle*," I corrected automatically, following his gaze.

While I looked toward the front door of the studio, Jerry picked up my unconscious body and lifted it easily into his arms. Carrying it across the room, he took it to the mat and gently laid it down. He even sat down next to it, then lifted my head into his lap, mumbling some soothing mumbo-jumbo.

I started trusting him then. He had no reason to cater to an asparagus. I turned back toward Ch'en Po. "I didn't know."

"If you learn to think with chi, might stop ending up at outer limits of astral bus stop so often!"

I lowered my head in respect. "I understand," I said, humbled.

Reaching out, the old man smacked one of my hands with his bony fingers, causing me to yelp with the unexpected sting.

"Old man didn't waste time just to come here and say what you're already supposed to know."

I wasn't angry, just puzzled. "Then why *did* you come?" I asked, rubbing my hand.

His gray brows lifted in what might have been disbelief. "Came here to slap young ram on hand!" he said as if I should have known that, too. The look he was giving me spoke volumes, but I couldn't read a single word of it.

"What?" I asked, starting to feel self-conscious.

He never answered and I never fully understood *why* he came to me that day. Maybe it was just curiosity. Maybe it was protectiveness. Maybe he didn't need a reason.

He started to hover above the ground while still sitting cross-legged. I didn't even question it as he went floating upward, his body thinning until it was only the molecules of the air.

~

I awoke with my head in Jerry's lap and a strange lethargy permeating my entire body. Instinctively, I tried to sit up, but his large hands pressed against my shoulders, holding me still against the mat.

Unable to move, I looked up to find him gazing down at me, an out-of- place smile playing across his lips.

"The door's reinforced with steel. You never had a chance." He eyed me curiously. "I'm sorry – I tried to tell you."

My head hurt like hell and I groaned when I tried to move my neck. In response, he slid his forearms under my arms and hoisted me up until my back was leaning against his chest. He began massaging my neck and shoulders until the cobwebs started to clear from my mind.

"What...?" I started to say. *'What do you want from me?'* That's not how it came out.

He chuckled softly. "Ten Jao chin na," he said in way of explanation. "There's a nerve junction running along the pericardium meridian. Apply enough pressure and you can stop a bull moose."

It wasn't the answer I was looking for. "I'm not a bull moose," I managed, my voice hoarse. My thoughts were fuzzy, indistinct. I still couldn't move easily, and had no choice but to continue leaning against him.

He pushed my body slightly forward and continued the massage lower on my back. "You'll feel better in a few minutes."

I doubted it as I lifted my head just enough to see the clock. 8:48. No sirens. No cops.

"What do you want from me?" I asked at last, grateful that I could breathe somewhat easier. Sensation was returning to my legs and arms, though I still felt drained. My right knee throbbed and I could see the swelling through the faded sweats.

His hands slowed their work for a moment. "I'd like to help you," he said.

"Bullshit," I snapped, surprising myself. "Nobody wants to help anyone other than themselves." I hated myself the minute the words were out of my mouth.

Jerry's fingers dug a little deeper into sore muscles, maybe to teach me a lesson. "You can't be as good as you are with your karate and still believe that, can you? Or did you just learn to fight and ignore everything else?"

My face darkened. I didn't answer for a long time. "Sorry," was all I mumbled when I did reply.

A soft sigh pressed through his lips and he ran his hands down my back. "How's that? Any better?"

I rotated my head experimentally and found that the pain and numbness all but gone. "Yeah."

He slid out from behind me and got up. Standing in front of me, he offered a hand to help me to my feet. I only looked at him and stood up without accepting his assistance. But the moment my weight came down on the right knee, my leg buckled under me, almost toppling me back to the mat. He caught me easily by an elbow, steadying me as he inclined his head toward a bench against the far wall.

"Here - sit down," he instructed. "Let me take a look."

I didn't have much choice. It didn't take a rocket scientist to know that the knee cap had been dislocated in my first savage kick to the door. Red knives shot through my entire body, exploding in my leg.

"I'll get some ice from the back," he said once I was seated on the bench, my back pressed to the wall. "In the meantime, get out of those sweats."

I looked up at him, my brows lifting and speaking more than any words I could have come up with. He only sighed, shaking his head as he unfastened the black belt and laid it reverently on the bench next to me. Then, untying the gi top, he stripped it off and tossed it onto my lap with a grin.

"I'm sure your body's nothing to be embarrassed about, but if you're shy, throw this over you," he suggested.

He had me again and I knew it. The body was a temple, nothing to be ashamed of. As far as his belt rank went, he was only threes steps past where I'd been when I'd left Master Barrows' studio. Yet in wisdom, he seemed years beyond me. I'd learned much from the silver-bound book Synjin had given me on the astral plane, yet without human contact there was seldom an opportunity to apply my new knowledge. I wondered fleetingly if Synjin had been correct, if I were ready to receive such knowledge, or if I should now be required to sweep every corner of the temple.

I forced myself to relax. If Jerry had wanted to hurt me, he'd had his chance; I'd been unconscious for nearly twenty minutes, watching from another world as he displayed nothing but tenderness and concern.

I shucked off the sweats without too much trouble, but almost wished I hadn't when I looked down at the injured knee. Angry and red, it stared up at me in silent accusation, the knee cap several centimeters to the left of where it should have been. I didn't look forward to having it manipulated back in place, and had it not been for the fact that my identity wasn't as secure as I'd believed, I might have considered going to the local hospital.

After another minute, Jerry returned through the open door. He hadn't bothered to put on another gi jacket, so I ignored the urge to cover my legs with the one he'd given me earlier.

In one hand he carried a towel filled with ice, in the other was a tray of acupuncture needles. Coming up next to me, he set the tray on the bench, then knelt at my feet and placed the ice on the injury. The numbness spread almost immediately.

Taking one of the needles, he traced his fingertip in a line up my leg, stopping at a point just above where the knee cap should have been. Then, placing the needle at the point where his finger stopped, he turned it until it penetrated the skin. I wasn't surprised to feel the pain disappear instantly; I'd studied acupuncture in Synjin's book, and Master Barrows had used it from time to time to treat injuries.

Jerry worked in silence for several minutes, applying eight more needles to various locations of my body. By the time he was finished, the pain had stopped altogether and a pleasant laziness had settled in my body. He continued turning the needles from time to time, stimulating the nerve endings at the various contacts, looking up to judge my reaction occasionally. I barely felt the pressure when he slid the knee cap back into position.

"You're pretty good at that," I said, breathing easier.

"Something I learned from Master Chang," he explained. "He believed that a martial artist should be able to repair whatever damage he did to another person or to himself."

I nodded, then brought myself back to reality. "You still haven't answered my question, you know," I reminded him.

He frowned. "What question?"

"What you want with me," I clarified. "I don't mean to appear ungrateful. I'm just curious as to why you didn't turn me in to the police."

He laughed, surprising me. "Why should I?"

"Don't you believe what the media was saying a few years back?" I asked. "I'm supposed to have killed three Air Force officers while in the throes of a schizophrenic episode."

He looked up at me, his face showing no emotion. "Yeah, I read the papers. I even watch the news sometimes. That doesn't mean that I believe everything I see."

I didn't understand his nonchalance. "As far as you know, I'm still a dangerous criminal."

He stood up and went to a locker against a back wall. Taking out a stretch bandage, he knelt in front of me again as he began to wrap the knee.

"Dangerous criminals make dangerous mistakes," he replied. "If you were really the lunatic the media made you out to be, you never would have gotten out of the city, and you certainly wouldn't have made it all the way to California."

"You seem to know a lot about me."

He finished wrapping the injury and fastened the bandage. Then he began removing the needles, leaving the one nearest the damage for last.

"One of the martial arts magazines did an article on you a couple years back," he replied. "They said you were probably one of the best, if not *the* best female martial artist alive today."

I drew back and laughed. "Not in this world or any other, Jerry. I just got lucky, and I had a lot of help. Besides," I pointed out, "I just got my ass kicked by a door!"

After a quick chuckle, he sat on the bench next to me, becoming serious. "There's no such thing as luck, River. Don't sell yourself short."

"Don't oversell me," I countered.

"I'm not," he replied. "You're a little rough around the edges still, but that'll work itself out in time."

I wasn't insulted. He was right.

"What've you been doing for the last few years?" he asked when an awkward silence fell between us. "I assume you've been hiding out in the desert somewhere."

I grunted an acknowledgement. "And?"

"How's the leg?"

I allowed him to change the subject. "Better," I said truthfully. "Did you learn the fine art of evasion from Master Chang, too?"

His laughter came again. "Maybe."

Despite everything that had happened, I couldn't dislike him. "I'll accept that you haven't turned me in. *Yet*," I stressed. "There must be a reason."

He took my hand and held it between both of his own. Under other circumstances, the gesture may have been intimidating, but instead it grounded me at a time when I *needed* grounding.

"Granted, you have no reason to trust me. But I hope I haven't given you too many reasons *not* to trust me," he added. "It's just that something came clear to me when I saw you sitting outside the studio. I need you, and you probably need me, too."

My body tensing, I looked away.

He squeezed my hand tighter. "That's not what I meant." He inclined his head toward the training arena. "I can't give enough individual attention to all the students. I need someone who's qualified to teach."

I held my breath, warring between whether to believe him or not. "You must have a few advanced adult students. They could handle the lower belt ranks, couldn't they?"

"They already do. I have qualified green and brown belts to teach the white and orange, but I need another black belt instructor who's qualified to teach green, brown and even first degree black." He paused as if to let that sink in. "You interested?"

Taking a deep breath, I looked into his eyes, trying to discern the truth. "This all seems rather coincidental," I commented, that old paranoia coming back to haunt me. "The only reason I came into town at all was because I have to go to the DMV. If you'll pardon my saying so, you're a little too good to be true."

He shot me a meaningful smile.

"What's so funny?"

"You," he said, but then turned solemn. "Everything happens for a reason, River," he added, sounding a lot like Master Barrows. "From my point of view, I'm looking at what the old Masters would have considered a gift of good fortune."

"I'm not sure I understand."

"Normally, I don't come into the studio until 8:45, yet for a reason I can't explain, I came down here an hour earlier this morning – fate put us in the same place at the same time. When I went to the front door to open up, I saw you sitting there and, yes, I did recognize you. Maybe I shouldn't have led you on under false pretenses, but I had to know for myself that you weren't everything the media had hyped you up to be."

I considered his words and found them surprisingly rational. "Why the sparring match?"

"Mostly for enjoyment," he admitted. "And I also wanted to see if you were as good as you were touted. You know, you became something of an anti-hero in the martial arts community after you disappeared. There were all sorts of speculations - everything from rumors that you'd been taken under the wing of a Shaolin Master and smuggled out of the country, to the possibility that you'd simply taken on a new identity, gotten married and settled down with a husband and kids somewhere in the midwest."

"Neither," I commented, embarrassed at so much attention.

He squeezed my hand again with genuine affection. "For what it's worth, a lot of martial artists covet your experiences - myself

50

included. You've evaded the cops under the worst of circumstances, used the Art to help you get away from the government - not an easy task. And," he added after a momentary hesitation, "I have to admit that I have selfish reasons for wanting you to stick around. I could certainly use another instructor, and if my guess is correct, you could probably use the money."

He was right about that, though I'd never considered taking money for teaching. He must have read that in my eyes.

"I know," he said. "It was hard for me at first, too. But you have to realize that very few people respect what they get for free. Am I right?"

He was. Still, the logistics escaped me. "And how do you propose to explain me to your students?"

His answer was simple and immediate. "I don't have to. What I'm proposing is that you open another studio - over near Joshua Tree, if you like." He shrugged. "At least a third of the students who study with me live over there anyway."

I gestured for a halt. "Wait a minute," I said, shaking my head, confused. "Run this by me again?"

He spoke more slowly, taking the time to explain his vision to me. "We'll open a second studio in Joshua Tree. I'll come up with whatever up-front cash you need to get started, and you can enroll as many new students as you want. The money's yours, and it should be enough to start supporting the studio within a couple of months. Just kick back a percentage once in awhile to pay off the loan, if you want to think of it that way."

Finances had never been my strong point. Neither had manna from heaven.

"What?" he asked when I didn't respond.

"Why would you do this for me?"

"I'm not doing it for you," he said at last. "I'm doing it for my students, and for myself - hopefully in that order. Like I said, I have more than I can effectively handle. If they're going to get anything out of the Art at all, they need more personal attention than I can give them right now. I don't want to cheat them out of learning, and I don't want to kill myself keeping the doors open until midnight, either."

I wondered about him for a moment. "Question?"

He nodded.

"Why did you accept more students than you could train properly?"

"Because you never know who's serious and who isn't," he said quietly. "I can't make arbitrary decisions about who to let into the school and who to turn away - not before I see what each student wants from the Art and what they're willing to give back to it. What if your Master had turned you away without even giving you a chance, all because he had too many students at the time?"

It wasn't a pleasant prospect. "Another question. Not that I'm complaining, but why not just let me teach here? Wouldn't that be easier than trying to start another studio from scratch?"

"Sure it would," he agreed. "But it's been my experience that two instructors seldom have the same approach. I don't want to step on your toes - and I don't want you stepping on mine."

He didn't pull his punches, for which I was grateful. "What about my little popularity problem with the law? How's that going to affect you if I get caught."

He laughed warmly. "I knew who you were because I've followed the news since all those things happened back in Florida. Master Chang was fond of saying that a person's life story was written in their eyes. I was just able to read yours, that's all."

"The police are trained observers, too, Jerry," I reminded him. "I wouldn't want to find my eyes being read by some cop who decided to take a few karate lessons to impress his buddies."

"The cops aren't interested in you anymore, River," he insisted.

I weighed my options carefully. I had a lot to lose if I blew my cover now. On the other hand, Jerry was right about one thing: I desperately needed the money. I could either accept his proposal to do something I'd always loved, or try to find some meaningless job which might expose me far more than teaching karate to kids.

"Look," he said, reading my uncertainty, "take some time to think it over if you want. If you decide not to, no hard feelings. You can walk out of here right now and we can pretend we never met." He paused, putting a pressure on my hand. "But if you decide to go with it, come back and we'll get started."

His willingness to let me go made me want to stay. I didn't think about my answer any longer. Looking up, I met his eyes and held his steady gaze. *'Still need company of other tree.'* Ch'en Po's voice made my decision, for I began to understand why I'd been led to Jerry Davin's studio.

"Let's get started, then," I said, letting go of my hesitations.

He grinned broadly, reminding me of a kid. He volunteered to cancel his classes for the rest of the day, and I didn't argue. Once that was done, he drove me over to the DMV and waited around while I took the exams and filled out the forms for new registration. Deputy Ernie had been right; the penalties for having the car unregistered for three years were stiff. When I was done paying for everything, I had less than a hundred dollars in my pocket, but I'd stood for more than an hour in the cop-shop without repercussions. State troopers came and went. No one gave me more than a cursory glance.

When the lady behind the counter asked for my mailing address so that new plates could be sent, I found Jerry by my side, giving the studio's street number.

By the time I followed Jerry back to his pick-up, I was California legal.

The path had just widened, showing me what lay around the curve where I'd been stalled for nearly four years.

CHAPTER FIVE
Birth Day

The new studio was actually an old house situated along Highway 62, which ran through the town of Joshua Tree in between 29 Palms and Yucca Valley.

When Jerry and I first found the place with the For Rent sign tacked crookedly to the door, I think we both knew it was right. Personally, I wasn't about to be picky. I was still inundated with the feeling that he was something akin to a gift from the gods. I liked him – maybe more than I was comfortable with, and I know he had feelings for me that went beyond whatever we had spoken.

Now, nearly a month after Jerry and I first met, I stood in the new studio and surveyed our handiwork. We'd removed several walls in the antiquated three bedroom house, opening the structure up until what remained vaguely resembled a karate studio. Unlike most of the houses in southern California, this one wasn't built on a cement slab. Instead, the wooden floors creaked, and occasionally a cold winter draft would sneak in through the ill-fitted windows.

It was a palace as far as I was concerned. With Jerry's help, we'd managed to find enough mirrors to completely cover two walls, and a fresh coat of paint gave the place a scent of cleanness. One of his students had even come over to help out with the more intricate decorations, and by the time I was ready to open for business, the interior looked more like a temple than any American studio I'd ever seen. Chinese and Japanese writing appeared above the mirrors and along the back walls, telling the history and origins of various systems of martial artists. And, taking heed from Jerry's studio, I'd painted the yin/yang symbol over the entire exposed surface of the wooden floor.

The back of the studio housed a bathroom and dressing room area; and there was even a place where I could throw down my sleeping bag if the necessity ever arose. In a small refrigerator, I kept the perishable herbs Jerry had bought.

Regardless of my love for the new studio, I found myself returning to the desert in the evenings. After four years of living in a tent, the thickness of walls seemed too confining, and I suppose there was still a reasonable degree of suspicion residing in my chi. I didn't want to wake up in the middle of the night to find the studio surrounded by the police.

I found my old gi and belt among the stuff I'd hidden in the storage well of the car, and put it on for the first time in early December of '92. When I tied the well-worn black belt around my waist again before teaching my first class, I had to struggle to contain the emotions that came over me.

By the first of the new year, with the studio open for barely a month, I'd taken over fifty three of Jerry's former students and signed on thirty seven new ones. I found myself working semi-regular hours for the first time in my life, and by the end of March, I was able to start paying the studio's rent out of my own funds. I could afford to buy gasoline for the car again and even invested in some new sparring and exercise equipment for the studio's tiny gym.

I devoted my life fully to the Art for the next year and a half.

By the time I'd been a fugitive for five years and ten months, I began to believe that I might indeed make it the full eight years Ch'en Po and I had discussed. A glance at the calendar told me I'd be twenty eight in another week.

~

Jerry arrived at the studio unexpectedly on my birthday, carrying a massive sheet cake decorated with miniature Oriental lanterns and bearing the inscription 'For chi and harmony - we love you, Lynne'.

He'd also arranged a surprise party, and by the time the afternoon was over, the studio was filled with our combined students. Jerry kept shoving cake in my hand, telling me when I protested that even the old Masters celebrated life once in awhile.

Finally, the crowd began to thin out until eventually only Jerry and I were left behind. We glanced silently over the studio, then began picking up the trash and putting things back in order. When we were finished, we went back into the small office in the front of the studio and flopped onto opposite ends of the sofa. Looking over at him, I smiled, feeling warm and happy and filled with a sense of belonging I hadn't experienced in a very long time.

"Have a good time?" he asked with a grin.

I nodded. "Thanks. You didn't have to do that, you know."

"I wanted to. I'm really glad this is working out for you - for both of us."

"I'm glad, too," I replied. Yet I began to understand in that moment that it couldn't last forever. Eventually, if I stayed on my mystical, unmapped path, I would be leaving this world, going with Synjin on whatever quest life had laid out for the two of us together. Almost six years had passed since Avery Madison died, since the day I first met Synjin, since my life turned to anarchy incarnate.

Jerry must have read something in my aura, for he leaned closer, his brows tightening. "You all right?"

I tried to find the right words. "Jerry," I began slowly, "there's something you should know about me."

He grinned. "You think I'm the greatest thing since sliced bread and can't live without me one more day?"

"You already know that," I said, returning his good-natured teasing. But my smile slowly faded. "It's just that... I may not be around much longer." It didn't come out right, and I shook my head to chase the words away. "What I mean is..."

Sliding closer to me on the couch, he placed one hand on my arm. "I know," he said as if he meant it.

"You do?"

He smiled again, more wistfully. "A person like you doesn't stay in the same place for too long. You've been at the studio for nearly two years now - more than that if you want to count the time it took to get this place ready." He paused, squeezing my arm with tender reassurance. "I never expected you to stay here forever, River, because I know you *can't*."

It was the first time he'd called me by my real name in a long time, and though the word sounded almost alien, it made his sincerity all the more genuine.

"I just don't want to leave you in a bind," I said. "You've been good to me - good *for* me. I've learned things from you about the Art that I might never have known otherwise." He'd taught me *chin na*, some aikido, and other unusual techniques.

"You would have learned those things anyway," he said without hesitation. "So let's not get maudlin about something that hasn't happened yet."

I suppressed a yawn, surprised at how tired I was. It wasn't often that I could sit around the studio and relax in the company of a good friend. Finally the yawn came. "Sorry," I mumbled.

A comfortable silence dropped between us. He pulled me closer until his arm slid around my back. I didn't protest; the warmth and the closeness felt good. I had the strangest feeling that he was about to kiss me, and though I wouldn't have minded, he never did.

I leaned back against him, exhausted from the party and the months of teaching without much time off, then slipped into a deep and restful sleep.

The People were there again in the void, smiling as they brought me flowers and wished me well in the beginning of my twenty-eighth year. Some of the children who were my students on the astral plane celebrated by performing the intricate moves of the Leopard Set without flaw, their bodies moving as one, silhouetted against a red and purple sunset. It was a perfect gift.

Further away, perhaps in another world still, I saw Synjin once more. His back was to me, yet I recognized his aura immediately - power and grace and deep green serenity. He seemed to be talking to someone, a man in a business suit with cold blue eyes. It was incongruous. The fact that it was other-worldly was irrelevant. It still made no sense. Synjin in his gi, the man in his suit. The buildings around them looked like slum tenements in any major city.

I could not hear their words, yet I knew they were arguing.

The man drew a gun.

And then Synjin moved against him. Placing one hand on the man's chest, Synjin pushed him hard against a wall as the gun fell away and disappeared into the fog at their feet. The man in the suit lost his life when Synjin broke his neck with cool, lethal efficiency.

Something had changed him, just as time and experience had changed me. Perhaps neither of us were the people we had been when we first met - on the day I had also learned to kill.

CHAPTER SIX
Synjin

Avery Madison was dead, and though I would have preferred it another way, there was no going back.

The military ambulance was half-on, half-off the curb, its lights still flashing, siren still blaring. Motorists had stopped to watch whatever it was that had just happened. I heard Colonel Segar moaning softly to himself, nursing a dislocated shoulder and trying to breathe again. The soldier on the ground was still unconscious. Neither was badly hurt, though that was more than offset by the dead man lying in the street with his cold gray eyes staring up toward heaven.

Luckily, the human mind doesn't react fast when presented with a series of seemingly inexplicable events. Not one of the motorists made a move to come toward me, nor even to help Madison. Maybe they knew he was already beyond help. Maybe, like most humans who lock their doors at night and hide from shadows, they simply didn't want to get involved.

Whatever the reason, I met with no resistance as I abruptly started to run, needing to put as much distance as possible between that ambulance and myself. I was surprised to discover that I *could* run, though my legs trembled and I stumbled twice.

Through the distant streets, growing closer, sirens began calling to one another, miscreant demons wailing. Segar had probably regained his ability to speak, and it wouldn't be long before a full-scale search was implemented.

It didn't take more than five minutes for exhaustion to overtake me. After the absurd drowning incident, a few days in the hospital had been enough to drain my strength, and the energy I'd expended in the fight had taken the rest.

After nightfall, if I could get back to Land o'Lakes, I knew the terrain better than anyone alive. Between the horseback riding in the summer and the childhood exploring, there wasn't a bush or back-road I hadn't met.

'*Always set a goal that gives you the advantage. Never fight the lion in her own den*'. Master Barrows' voice. All those words of wisdom I'd thought I'd never need. All that training I'd hoped I would never have to use.

I discovered a large shopping plaza less than half a block away. I hoped I could rely on the fact that the majority of people didn't pay much attention to anyone other than themselves. If anyone did notice a half-crazy woman in a flimsy hospital dress, they'd probably pass her off as a bag lady and politely look the other way.

Fighting the urge to run, I cut across the parking lot until I reached the back of the buildings. I passed only one other person along the way - an old man who smiled sweetly and commented about the heat of the day. I hadn't noticed it, though my eyes were occasionally blinded by perspiration.

I spoke to him courteously and continued on my way, slipping around the back of the complex where a narrow alley allowed delivery trucks access. The entire maze of shops was the length of a city block and, across the alley, a row of office buildings from the next street over was butted up against a six foot tall cinder block wall.

A stray cat skittered from a dumpster, drawing my eye to a pile of clothing obviously tossed out from one of the many stores – damaged goods, last week's style now out of fashion, who's to say? A quick rifling of the discards turned up a pair of 501s in something close to my size, and a black tank top emblazoned with a glittery peace symbol.

The fact that the pants were missing a button and the top was sun-damaged from too long in the front window was entirely irrelevant. It was a godsend as far as I was concerned, and I took advantage of the deserted alley to yank the jeans on, burying the hospital gown in the bottom of the dumpster and shrugging into the tank top. My feet were still bare, and whatever guardian angel had provided the clothes had left no shoes, but it was a hardship I was willing to accept, all things considered.

Not too far away, another flock of sirens was assembling. They were closer than before, crawling like ants over a mound of sugar. There had been more than ample time for Colonel Segar to tell the authorities what had happened. And the Hillsborough County Coroner had undoubtedly pronounced Dr. Avery Madison dead at the scene.

I was officially a murderer and a fugitive.

~

The two-story office complex across the alley was smaller and more compact than the shopping plaza, and as such the police would consider it a less-likely hiding place. If I wanted to survive, I had to out-think them, stay not one step ahead, but two.

I walked across the alley and ducked behind the wall, then looked up and down until I spotted a metal service door fifty feet away. The plastic sign read: MAINTENANCE PERSONNEL ONLY. It was locked with only a small pad lock, one which yielded easily when smashed with a rock.

I found what I needed in the form of a janitorial closet. Opening it, I slipped inside and then let the door close behind me. The interior space was no more than five feet by six feet - room to sit, stand or even lie down if need be.

And it was private. The only disconcerting factor was that the light bulb was burned out - not that I would have dared turn it on anyway.

There I stayed in total darkness until nightfall. I tried to sleep and couldn't. Dr. Madison's ghost made sure I stayed awake.

~

At some point in the dark isolation of the janitor's closet, it occurred to me that the mess I now found myself in was due largely to something I could neither explain nor even see at will. I wondered fleetingly if perhaps Dr. Madison had been right in his insinuations; maybe I *was* insane and just didn't have the good manners to know it.

I thought again of Ch'en Po, and finally of Synjin, and an hour passed in silence. Synjin... man of my dreams, all right. Yet if I understood the situation at all, *he* was the one who had broken the windows and shut down the power at the hospital. He was the one who had shoved an orderly through some dimensional hidey-hole. And I was the one who was facing the consequences.

I felt angry and betrayed - not only by Synjin, but by Ch'en Po as well. Yes, I knew the code The People lived by. When I turned from a child to an adult, I would have been perfectly free to leave behind that other world, to abandon it back to the Dream where I first found it. No ill will would have been generated had I simply drifted away as most children did. I didn't have to seek out the Old Woman, and I didn't have to avow myself, body and soul, to a man from a world existing at right angles and quantum loopdiloops to our own.

I'd never even seen Synjin - at least not as anything more than a glimpse among the orange trees - yet I couldn't help loving him. He was, after all, my perfect match, the culmination of all the Old Woman's magic and power. No, she didn't sit before a cauldron boiling bat wings and frog spleens. She merely studied life in all its components - herbs and healing, air and water, fire and earth. And she understood people - their dreams, their motivations, their needs. Most of all, she understood loneliness.

As I sat there listening to the drum beat of my own heart, I began to fully comprehend how different I was. It was a scary realization, for it meant I wasn't normal, could never *be* normal. Now more than ever, for an Air Force officer lay dead - killed by my hands.

Maybe it was nothing more than the pressures of the past few hours venting themselves, but my fingers clenched into fists. I had taken a life. Avery Madison must have had a family. I had brought grief to them, shame to myself.

"Damn you!" I whispered. "*Damn you!*" I didn't know if I were cursing myself or Synjin or Avery Madison himself.

I sat there for a long time feeling sorry for myself and estimated that about two hours had passed. One more hour to wait before it would be safe to travel. Occasionally, there was a sound of tires crunching through the gravel alley, and my imagination did the rest. The cops were right outside. Someone had seen me. Someone had turned me in.

For a few insane moments, I gave serious thought to simply turning *myself* in. At the very least, the police would have to take into account some awfully peculiar happenings. For one, Madison had told my mother that I'd died in the hospital. Certainly the cops would find that of interest. Or would they? The fact remained that I had killed someone - in the presence of witnesses - and as far as the police were concerned, that was usually the bottom line. I'd be tried and found guilty in the media before The Late Show. Or more likely, I'd be shot on sight. The military couldn't afford to have me taken alive.

"Ta!" someone said right in front of me, startling me so much that I jolted, gasped. "Feel sorry for self when out of danger!" It was Ch'en Po's voice, though I didn't know if he were actually there or if I'd imagined him.

"Go away," I muttered miserably. Whether I was speaking to a mental apparition or a physical manifestation didn't seem to matter. Delusions, Madison had said. Maybe he was right.

"Ta ta ta!" the old man scolded in total blackness. His voice softened then. "Self punishment won't bring back the dead."

My jaw tightened. "*I - killed - a - man,*" I said, stressing each syllable.

"Death is tragic, yes. Avoidable, no. Self defense."

"Blame doesn't matter, Ch'en Po. A man is dead," I reminded him. "This isn't how I envisioned my life."

There was a surprised silence. "Universe is not interested in your preference. In another eight years, you'll be with Synjin—."

"Eight years?" I interrupted. "Eight *years*? I'll be lucky to be alive eight *hours* from now!" I shook my head, frustrated and scared. "And for that matter, how do I even know Synjin really exists? You keep talking about him, but I've never seen him! It's been five years since we were matched! How am I supposed to believe in something I can't even see?"

"Cannot see a mortal breath yet you witness its effects on dandelions scattered on the wind of a wish," the old man replied, though I could hear the disappointment in his voice. "Synjin not seen, yet your paths already tangled together like vines of jasmine."

"Yeah? Well I'm starting to think maybe I should untangle them," I countered, despondent.

For a few long seconds, there was no response. Then, in the darkness, I heard Ch'en Po sigh heavily. "You worse than Synjin! Stubborn!"

I didn't answer. No point talking to a hallucination.

"If I let you be with Synjin for five minutes, then will you trust old man?"

My heart pounded so hard that it gave me a headache. It got my attention. "Wh-what?" I stammered.

"Gone deaf from banging head against wall?"

I had to admit that I *didn't* completely trust him - not after what had happened. I wasn't even sure I still believed in him. After seeing Madison's dead eyes staring up at me, I couldn't help thinking that Ch'en Po could have prevented it. That's what imaginary friends were for.

Too many thoughts were crowding my mind. "But what about the path? You said I couldn't be with Synjin because we'd both ignore the path." I figured he'd bring up that argument next, so I saved him the trouble.

"Never broken the rules before," Ch'en Po admitted softly. "Maybe time to start. You and Synjin two yins in search of yang," he added matter-of-factly. "But maybe it won't crack universal egg if you meet. Dark enough that neither of you get too caught up in romantic interlude. Not enough room in puny closet for love."

I felt my face flush in the darkness. "I - uh - I'd just like to *meet* him," I stammered, embarrassed.

"Hmmph!" the old man commented, then laughed. "Can't lie to me, River Willows!"

Still, it unnerved me to think of what might happen if we somehow *did* stray off this mystical path the old man was always talking about. In my dreams, I'd traveled with The People since I was very young. I knew them as well as I knew myself. Their philosophies taught that each soul had a purpose, a reason for being on the Earth. I didn't want to overlook my own, didn't want to believe it was just another delusion, another lie I'd told myself in my sleep. As it stood, society was doing its job: it was taking the child in me away, forcing me into emotional adulthood and thrashing everything I'd ever believed.

I made myself trust Ch'en Po again. "I need to know, Master" I said haltingly. It was the first time I'd called him that, yet stress made the word come easily. I needed a Master right about then.

A gentle hand reached out to touch my arm. "Things happen when things happen. Not too soon, never too late."

I wanted him to understand me. "Dreams and feelings aren't always enough. My world isn't kind to dreams."

The old man squeezed my arm with understanding. Then, as abruptly as he'd appeared, he was gone.

At first, I thought I'd been abandoned again after a few words of wisdom from the ether. But as I drew in a sharp breath, I sensed another presence in the tiny room with me. He was standing against the door, and though I couldn't see anything with my physical eyes, I detected an aura of heat surrounding him.

I couldn't breathe. His presence was overwhelming, his scent intoxicating, somewhere between sandalwood and myrrh. Intuitively, I understood who and what I was encountering. Emotionally, reality overloaded and shut down.

For several seconds, neither of us moved. Then, very slowly, I felt him come toward me.

When the silence was finally broken, it was by him. "River?"

A word I vaguely recognized as my own name. His voice was quicksilver, settling in my blood like a pleasant yet fatal poison. It made him real.

I nodded, then realized we were in total darkness. "Synjin?"

For a few moments more, neither of us spoke. After that, he came forward, and I felt warmer-than-human hands on my arms, just below my shoulders. I trembled, embarrassing myself in the process, for I'd never given any man that type of power over me.

"Please believe me when I tell you I've wanted this moment as much as you," he said. "I did not think Ch'en Po would bend on such a matter, though I'm grateful he's given us this time together." He paused, touching me softly. "It will be brief, though."

"I know," I said, my heart breaking and soaring at the same time. "Better brief then not at all."

Not knowing what else to do, I followed instinct, allowing my own hands to come unfrozen and touch him. His arms were muscular yet not incredibly thick. The fabric of his shirt was a familiar canvas - the soft cotton of a well-worn gi. It felt black, like the one I wore at the studio. It created a common ground, and I relaxed very slightly.

"I had to know you were real," I said, confessing the truth as I looked up toward where his face would have been had there been any light in the room.

Surprisingly, I felt his arms slide around my back, pulling me against his chest. I tensed at first, unaccustomed to such an intimate embrace, but as I felt his warmth, inhaled his alien scent, I closed my eyes and allowed myself to be held. A moment later, my arms were around his back, though I couldn't recall placing them there. The ends of his hair caressed my wrists.

He held me tighter, as if to confirm my reality. Sanity did a cartwheel and finally stabilized somewhere between us.

"So what now?" I asked. We didn't have long to be together, and I began to realize how very right Ch'en Po had been. If I stayed with Synjin now, neither of us would ever let go.

A soft fingertip traced the outline of my cheekbone. "Now," he said, his words almost a whisper, "you must take everything you have learned and go away from this place. It doesn't matter what part of the world you travel to, for I will always be able to find you, just as you'll always be able to find me. We *will* be together, River."

That was the confirmation I'd been seeking since I was a child. It was the proof of subjective reality. That was what mattered, and I'd do anything to keep it, to make it happen even if it had to be eight years in some unimaginable future.

"Tell me about yourself," I said, holding tight to him. "Please?"

One hand was drawing circles on my back. "What would you like to know?"

I was suddenly elated as years of doubts fled. "Oh, nothing much... just where you were born, what you've done for as far back as you can remember, what you do now, what you know about Ch'en Po, what your world is like - *everything*."

He laughed softly against my chest , a deep, masculine vibration. "That might take a little longer than we have right now."

He had a point. Drawing my head back, I looked up at him again. It didn't matter that I couldn't see anything. "Then tell me what's important to you." I wanted to know all of him in a single instant, yet I wanted to take forever to learn about him.

He laughed again - an infections rumble. "All right," he agreed. "I would guess that the things which are most important to you are also the things most precious to me: equality, justice, harmony, balance." He paused for a moment, his hands creating a hypnotic trance around me as they stroked across my back. "The Art itself has become much of my life. I teach at the Temple of Kalpa, under the guidance of Ch'en Po, who is also my Master."

"Kalpa?" I repeated.

He held me closer. "An ancient word known to your world and mine as well. Its meaning, in essence, is a long period of time. If there were a rock of the hardest granite and 50 miles square, and if a sparrow were to come once every four years and brush the rock with her wing, kalpa is the length of time it would take for the stone to be worn to the size of a grain of sand." He paused, his chin brushing the top of my head. "It is also how long it would take to fully understand all aspects of life, or to truly master the Art."

I found myself falling deeper under his spell; for once in my life, I didn't fight the emotion of love, even though I recognized it as a drug more addictive than cocaine. "You think you might get tired of me in a couple of kalpa?"

He shook his head. "No. You?"

"Never." Never before had I experienced what I was feeling in that moment. It made me dizzy, light-headed. "It's almost like you're inside my thoughts," I said, trying to explain the sensation.

He smiled; I felt it. "I am."

I knew it was true. He was inside my mind, a part of me now, a mental communion that followed the lines of physical contact. Touch telepathy. That was his gift, as mine was the ability to open doorways between his world and mine. Most children could see into his world. One in a hundred thousand could open the vortex and travel physically between the two diverse dimensional planes. I didn't know where the knowledge came from, only that Synjin transmitted it to me.

For the first time in my life, I started to understand who - *what* - I was. "Do you mean that I could go into your world?" I asked. "Right now?"

Bringing one hand to my face, he caressed my cheek once again. "You could. Yet you would soon discover that what Ch'en Po says is true. If you and I come together before the day time has chosen for us, many lives will be lost."

I grew suddenly cold inside. "Why?" I whispered. "Why must it be that way?"

"Even I am not privileged to such information," he said, his words filled with regret. "I only know that there are things you must do - things *we* must do together here in *this* world before we live together in mine."

"How do you know this?" I asked, holding him against me, warming my soul in his heat. "Can you actually see the future?"

He smiled again, his lips brushing my hair with soft breath. "*That*," he said, "is one of my Master's many gifts."

My head lifted. "Then Ch'en Po has future sight?"

The deep, gentle laughter came again. "Some of the Masters say he travels through time the way you and I travel through air."

I tensed, considering the enormity of such a speculation. There was so much I wanted to ask him, so much I wanted to tell him, yet I fully understood that we were cheating the universe by being together at all. His knowledge became mine - part of it anyway - and I began to fathom some of the things Ch'en Po had said. If we stayed together, the future would somehow be changed.

"I think I understand," I told him.

His smile radiated into me; our thoughts touched again. "I know you do."

An incredible surge of pride filled me. "It's so natural for me to be with you like this."

He nodded. "We were carefully matched."

Still, I couldn't help wondering what he thought about it. "Would you... I mean... would you have chosen someone like me?" I was almost afraid of the answer. I didn't want to go on thinking that the Old Woman had yanked him out of his life and thrown him into mine just for my own personal desires.

"I might ask the same of you."

I frowned thoughtfully, and then the understanding came. "You mean... the Old Woman... you went to her, too?"

He was tracing my spine with his fingertips until my entire body tingled. "I consulted her when I was very young, and then didn't hear from her for many years. I told her of my vision - a mate who could fight by my side in battle, a woman who would understand the ancient Art and pursue its knowledge with me." He paused, pulling me tighter against him as his voice dropped to a whisper. "You are all those things, River. You have the beauty, the strength and the power."

My mouth opened to speak, but nothing came out. I *wanted* to be all those things. I hoped I could. "You have a lot of faith in me," I said, humbled by his words.

"Not faith. *Certainty*. It took the Old Woman many years to find you for me - many years and two different worlds. How could there be any doubt?"

I struggled to encapsulate a lifetime of dreams and imaginations and astral travels into a few words. "I've always known your world is out there, Synjin," I began haltingly. "But now, with everything that's happened, it seems so far away. I never thought it would be like this. If someone had told me a week ago that I was going to kill a man..."

He held me close, his aura warm and soothing against the coldness and fear I felt inside. "Did you kill a man, or did you stop him from killing you?"

I tried to make myself believe that. "I've known how to kill since I first started studying the Art, Synjin," I murmured. "But I've never *wanted* to kill. I never knew it would hurt so much."

"If it didn't hurt," Synjin said gently, "you wouldn't be human anymore."

I considered that in thoughtful silence, trying to come to terms with the fact that my life had changed so abruptly.

"I love you, River," Synjin whispered, deep and soft against my forehead. "And I *will* love you."

I closed my eyes, felt wetness on my cheek.

It was then that he kissed me for the first time, our lips brushing together in the darkness until my body slumped against him. I felt his affection, his power and his magic through the telepathic touch, and wondered at the miracle of how two souls from such divergent worlds had ever been allowed to meet. I wanted to love him, to make love to him, to hold him that way forever.

But it was an instant later that Ch'en Po had the bad manners to return, popping back into the room like some unruly jumping bean.

"Ta ta ta!" he scolded, his words clipped. "Two young love birds get stuck together in lip-lock now, won't even hear when police break door down!"

Synjin released me and I felt him tremble. Yet when he spoke to Ch'en Po, his voice was level, controlled. "Master," he sighed, "have you never been in love with a woman?"

"Been in love many times, youthful Master Synjin. Still know the difference between bedroom and broom closet, right time and wrong time!" Ch'en Po paused for only an instant. "River must go now - find path back home, then take path out of town."

It didn't matter. Shock made a lot of things more acceptable, and at least I knew where the path led now. It led back to Synjin. Still in his embrace, I hugged him once more, then took a step backward until we were two separate entities once again, only our hands still touching. It hurt, but I knew I'd break altogether if I didn't let him go.

"I know," I said softly. "I know." I told Synjin with a pressure on his hand that it was all right, though we both knew it wasn't.

His hands were powerful and reassuring. So much meaning in his touch. So much love. "Eight years isn't such a long time," he promised. "After that, there will be no more separation."

I didn't try to speak. I couldn't. He held on an instant longer, and something was slipped into my hand. Synjin closed my fingers around it just before he let me go. I didn't know at first what it was, only that it was made of metal.

And, he told me with a telepathic rush of feeling to hold my silence. It was a gift - a shared secret to confirm his reality for the eight years that lay ahead.

After another moment, before I could respond, I felt him blend back into the shadows, and I knew it the moment he left my world. There was a hollow space where he had been, a Synjin-shaped hole that could be filled by nothing and no one else.

Ch'en Po remained for a few seconds longer. The old man placed one weathered hand on my shoulder, communicating his own affection with touch. "Love more painful than death. The deeper the love-wound, the worse the pain."

He was right about that.

"*Can* I live like a fugitive for eight years?"

"If you keep inner vision sharp, if you keep body and mind attuned to chi, live happy long life with Synjin at Temple," he promised. "If not, if ignore voice inside Self and walk along easy paved road, might end up in cold silver box with soul trapped in between time."

'*Eighteen Tourists already in cold sleep*'. Avery Madison's meaningless words, spoken in the back of a military ambulance just before I sent him to Hell. I started to say something about that, but Ch'en Po was already gone.

I might have thought him an illusion again had it not been for what I held in my hand.

~

A short while later, I slid back into the corridor, though the sudden light in the hall caused me to wince. But as I looked down to see what was nestled in my palm, a deep chill passed through my soul.

The metal was like nothing I had ever seen – a darkly burnished green with irregular striations of silver, formed into a ring that was clearly made by a wizard in some alien forge – at least that's what I chose to believe. And though I didn't know *how* I knew, I understood that this was the ring given to Synjin when he had attained Mastery of the art – something that had been worn until the metal was thin and formed to his hand. Inside the band was an inscription, written in a language I could not read, scripted in characters as mysterious as the being who had placed it in my palm. I could only imagine what it said, or who had written it, and when.

Trembling, my eyes wet, I slipped it on my middle finger, though it was large enough that I could have put it over two of my fingers with room to spare. But to my surprise and, as soon as the ring was on my hand, it seemed to morph as if made of living tissue, forming itself perfectly to my finger as if custom made to fit.

I gasped with surprise, with wonder.

The ancient magic. The ancient Art. The mystery that was Synjin's world, the world of The People.

For several minutes, I stood there looking at this object which transcended words, this mystical symbol which was born of another world and bound me utterly to this man whom I barely knew, yet whom I knew better than I had ever known even myself.

Then, feeling the living warmth of the ring as it permeated me, knowing time would not stand still even for this, I slipped into the black embrace of the night.

CHAPTER SEVEN
Steale

I awoke back in my own world again, back in the linear flow of time, to discover Jerry gone. The sun was almost gone, too, and long shadows from a grove of Joshua Trees reached into the office from the open window. For a moment, it was almost as if I could step backward through time itself, though I wondered what I would have found had I pursued that dangerous thought.

Perhaps I would have found Synjin - though I understood intuitively that neither of us were the same people we had been then. Time had intervened. And distance. And the meddlesome hand of fate had destroyed some shred of the idealism we had shared in that long-ago broom closet on the other side of reality.

Still, he was my match, his aura brushing against me like a ghostly presence, his ring still clinging to my finger where it had been since the day he slipped it into my hand. In that moment, I wanted nothing more than to tempt destiny and go bounding off through the ether to find him. Yet Ch'en Po's words haunted me like a minor-keyed melody from the past. *'Eight years must wait'.* Change that and many lives would be lost. I no longer needed to understand it in order to accept it.

I found myself on the sofa, my head cushioned on a pillow. When I sat up, the note Jerry had left on my chest fell into my lap.

> *Hope you had a nice nap. I didn't want to wake you, but I had to get back for tonight's classes. Besides, I didn't trust myself to sit there holding you while you slept any longer.*
> *Happy birthday.*
> *Love and honor -*
> *Jerry*

I smiled wistfully as I got up, taking the note and placing it in the drawer. The mischievous smiley-face drawn at the bottom grinned up at me. There was a definite attraction between us, yet it was a completely safe relationship. Neither one of us would ever make the first move.

But as I closed the drawer, my thoughts returned abruptly to Synjin. For several minutes, I sat in the chair, rubbing my eyes with the palms of my hands.

It occurred to me that I had always thought of Synjin as some benevolent, kindly figure. I fully understood that he was capable of killing, yet I could imagine no circumstance in his world which would *require* that he kill. It was a gentler place, even if not perfect.

Trembling as the image of the man with the gun replayed in my mind, I didn't immediately notice when the front door of the studio opened and someone stepped inside. I became aware of him only when footsteps came into the office and the springs in the old sofa groaned under a man's weight.

Looking up sharply, I found myself face to face with someone who caused the color to drain from my face. For a split second, I thought Synjin had broken down the door between time and sanity, and that he had come to rest in my humble studio with the dead man's soul still lingering like blood on his hands.

I blinked, my mouth opening to speak. But as I looked at the man more closely, I realized that the body was not quite right. The shiny black hair was not long enough, though it covered his collar in back; the aura was different. He wasn't Synjin, though I knew instinctively that he was of the same ilk, the same dark breed.

His eyes said he was too cold to be one of The People; the air that surrounded his aura said he was too gentle to live in my world. He was, if possible, cruel and delicate at the same time. He looked clean, yet hadn't shaved in a couple of days. A faint growth of stubble that some women found attractive gave him an air of mystery and foreboding.

Still, he was impressive, sitting there in tight-fitting jeans and a low-slung tank top which showed off his excellent physique to a fault. I could be impressed with his beauty. And I could also be unnerved by it. It wasn't often I found myself physically attracted to anyone - certainly not after I'd met Synjin, and never so abruptly.

I was also uncomfortable with the slight bulge which extended from his right hip. He was carrying a gun, yet I knew he wasn't a fed. He was the type of man who stood out in a crowd, not someone who could disappear under cover or blend in.

Pretending not to notice his attractiveness *or* his weapon, I opened the conversation with a smile. "What can I do for you?" I asked, standing up and coming around to the front of the desk.

He looked me up and down - somewhat openly - then met my eyes. "I'd like to talk to the Master here," he said, his voice deep and cool.

I admit I probably didn't look much like a Master. I was wearing jeans, a t-shirt, and no shoes. "I'm the head instructor," I told him. "Lynne Raynor," I added, offering my hand.

He took it with some reluctance, then leaned back against the couch without ever standing up. "You're a woman," he said without inflection, without judgment – just an observation.

It wasn't the first time I'd encountered that reaction. I nodded with a slight chuckle. Just as my first Master wasn't what I'd expected, I wasn't what most people envisioned when they enrolled in a karate school. "Does that make a difference?" I asked.

"No," he said, then smiled for the first time as if coming to the decision that it didn't. He hesitated, looking at me with intense eyes which were somewhere between deep green and pale brown. "I want to learn to fight."

He was telling the truth, but only part of it. "Why?"

"Why not?" he replied, trying to appear relaxed. I knew he wasn't. His body language spoke volumes despite his teasing grin.

I gave the answer that Master Barrows gave to a new student who said only that they wanted to fight. "Karate can teach you to fight, but that's only a small part of the Art," I told him gently. "If you want to fight, there's a gym in Yucca Valley. They teach boxing every Thursday and Saturday."

His reaction took awhile to come. When it did, he smiled again, more openly this time. "I went there a couple of times," he confessed, amused with himself or with me or with something. "It wasn't what I wanted."

I considered his answer, leaning against the desk as I spoke. "If you decide to join the studio, the first year or so of the training concentrates on the basics," I warned. "You won't even come near the sparring arena until you've earned an orange belt - and then only if I think you're ready."

He seemed about to protest, then nodded, that little smile still playing in his eyes, that lethal quality still lingering in his aura. "I'll be ready," he promised.

His voice more than his words gave me chills. "We'll see," I commented. "You have a name?"

He never broke eye contact. "Steale," was all he said.

"Just Steale?"

He shrugged, mischievousness in his eyes. "Just Steale."

I didn't press. I didn't need to. He could call himself whatever he liked, and living in the desert for six years had taught me that it was a place filled with eccentrics and loners and maybe even a fugitive or two.

"All right," I said at last. "If you're interested, I can show you around the studio."

He nodded graciously, then stood up. I wasn't surprised to notice that he was quite tall, at least six foot three. I felt small next to him as I gestured through the open door of the office and toward the training area.

He started to walk past me when an odd feeling came over me. "By the way," I said lightly, "you can leave your gun on the desk." I wasn't afraid of him, but I'd learned not to underestimate an opponent. Arrogant over-confidence could kill as quickly as fear.

His black brows lifted as he stopped just inside the office, looking down into my eyes and standing a fraction of an inch too close. "You got something against guns?"

"No," I replied, knowing he was teasing me. "I've just never had any use for one."

He shrugged, then reached inside the waistband of his jeans and withdrew the weapon. It wasn't like any hand-gun I'd ever seen, but such things weren't my specialty. I waited until he placed the long-barreled, brushed metal weapon on the desk.

"Feel better?" he asked.

I didn't let him unnerve me. Instead, I politely gestured toward the training area once again. "Thank you," I said, not answering his question.

As we walked through the studio, I explained the various symbols on the wall, gave the abbreviated version of the meaning of the yin/yang symbol on the floor, then led him into the back where the gym was located. After showing him the miscellaneous exercise equipment and weights, we returned to the training area once again, on the way to the office.

About half-way there, however, Steale put one hand on my arm to stop me. "Show me something," he said with a disarming grin.

It was a common request - and one that I seldom honored. But I suspected I was about to make an exception.

"What would you like to see?" I asked, holding his gaze as I planned my move.

He shrugged. "Anything. Impress me."

I smiled deceptively. "All right," I agreed. "Throw a punch."

He seemed to like the idea, and chuckled softly. Then, drawing his arm back, he came toward me with a right step-through punch.

Using one of the simpler techniques against his attack, I dropped back into a fighting stance, blocking his blow with my left arm. A well-controlled kick to his leg informed him that I could just as easily have deflated the family jewels. Finally, finishing my defensive move, I followed him as he staggered back, delivering a right heel-palm strike just under his chin - not sufficient to injure him, just enough to get his attention. When my foot snaked behind his ankle and swept forward, he lost his balance and fell on his butt with a stunned, "Oof!"

He sat there on the mats looking shocked as I stepped back out of range. Then he met my eyes and started to grin.

"Impressive enough?" I asked.

"I guess so," he replied noncommittally. He got back on his feet, staying respectfully out of range. "Well?"

"Well?" I repeated, confused.

He inclined his head toward the office. "I'm in if you'll have me."

There was something about him that I couldn't quite place. It wasn't that I didn't like him. It could have been that I liked him too much. At the very least, he had awakened my curiosity.

I nodded, feeling an unusual flutter in the pit of my stomach. "You're in then," I said with a smile, offering my hand in friendship.

When we talked about costs, he said only that money was no object. He paid for a full year's lessons in cash. I tried not to act surprised, though I was. Maybe that explained why he carried a gun, for I noticed several other large bills in his wallet.

"Adult classes are held Monday through Thursday from six until eight in the evening," I explained. "Also, there's an open-belt class that anybody can come to on Saturday morning. It usually has a lot of the kids in it, and I'll warn you that they can be a handful."

"When can I start?" His tone said he wasn't in a hurry despite his words.

"Any time you want," I replied. "For starters, I recommend being here as much as you can. I'll be covering the basics every night, with an emphasis on self-defense techniques on Tuesdays and Thursdays." I paused, hoping I wasn't moving too fast. "It takes about six months for most people to feel comfortable with the material. There's a lot to learn, especially at first."

He nodded nonchalantly. "What about tonight? No classes?"

I laughed softly. "Today was my birthday. Things got a little off schedule. Is tomorrow soon enough?"

His brows lifted with amusement. "Happy birthday," he said, ignoring my question for a moment. Then he added, "Sure, tomorrow's fine. Anything else I need to know?"

"You'll also be receiving an hour-long private lesson once a week if you're interested," I told him. "That way, if you're having trouble with anything, we can talk about it and work it out."

He stood up casually. "Anything special I should wear?"

He'd rattled me more than I thought. "I'll get you a gi from the back. When you come in for your first class tomorrow night, I'll show you how to tie the belt."

He followed me when I went through the studio and to the locker in the back. Picking out a size four man's gi, I handed him the black bundle with the white belt folded neatly on top.

He just kept smiling that indefinable smile. "What should I call you?" he asked. "Master... or mistress?"

I didn't let him get the better of me. "When we're not actually in training, you can call me whatever you like," I said, enjoying his mischievousness. "But once you step through the doors of the studio for a lesson, you'll refer to me as Ms. Raynor."

He inclined his head in agreement, then turned and headed toward the door with the gi tucked under his arm. "I always wanted to have a mistress," he commented, deliberately low so that I barely heard him.

I didn't follow after him. "Let me know if you ever find one," I called after his retreating back.

He disappeared into the dusky afternoon and drove away in a shiny red sports car the likes of which I'd never seen before. The customized California plate read 'COYOTE 1'.

CHAPTER EIGHT
The New Student

Steale No-Last-Name came to class the following evening, waving a mock salute from the doorway as he started through the studio and toward the back room. I made my way through the assembling class and met him at the door.

"Glad you could make it," I said, feeling a sudden warmth and even a protectiveness toward him.

He nodded an acknowledgement.

"Now that you're a student, you should always remove your shoes before entering the training area."

"Sure," he said. He wasn't smiling now and I wondered why.

Determined not to make him uncomfortable before his first lesson, I gestured toward the dressing room. "Go ahead and get into your gi, then I'll show you how to tie the belt."

He nodded, then bent over and began removing his Nike's. I fought back a shiver as I caught the scent of his body. Clean. Like sandalwood.

Turning back to the training area, I began a series of stretches to loosen up my muscles, and to gather my own controls. He was an unnerving presence despite my years of training.

Several of the students were talking among themselves, others practicing recently-learned moves in the mirrors. A few of the lazier ones stood quietly to the back, waiting.

I saw Steale out the corner of my eye when he came out of the dressing area. Dressed all in black, he looked even taller and more ominous, but I tried not to let that observation intimidate me. Instead, I pulled myself out of a split and went to him.

He handed me the white belt without comment, lifting his arms so I could slide it around his waist. I demonstrated the proper way to tie the flat reef knot, then watched while he did it for himself. I could tell a lot about a student by how well they could learn to put their belt on correctly. Steale would do all right.

When I was finished, I looked up at him. "Ready to get started?"

He still did not smile. "I'm ready."

Turning back to the arena, I taught him the bow of respect, then gestured him in amongst the others. He stood several inches above my tallest student, and I found myself looking at him intermittently as I led the class through the warm-up exercises.

Two of the recently acquired teenage girls whispered to themselves and nudged one another while Steale pretended not to notice. Not wanting to make a scene and risk spooking the new student, I shot a stern look toward the girls and made a mental note to deal with them later.

Secretly, I couldn't really blame them. Steale was an enigma – raven wing and desert heat and black magic. Even I was not immune.

~

It continued that way for several weeks. He came to the studio nearly every night, and I could tell he was one of the serious ones. What surprised me was that, for the first two months, he didn't stop by to schedule a private lesson. The one time I mentioned it to him, he said his business was often uncertain, and that he didn't want to stand me up if he couldn't make it.

I let it go at that. He had a problem, though I didn't know what. Whatever it was, it made his eyes sad and difficult to read. His aura was dark, concealing things I intuitively knew I did not care to imagine. On rare evenings, he would tease me. Other nights, I don't think he noticed I was in the room.

Maybe I should have pressed him a little harder in the beginning, encouraged him to open up. I had a growing and uneasy feeling that he was somehow a part of my path, though whether an obstacle or an ally, I didn't know.

~

"What'd you have to do to convince *him* to study?" Jerry asked one night after my adult white belt class had emptied out.

I looked up to see what he was talking about and found him staring at Steale's back as my progressing student disappeared out the front door.

"What do you mean?" I asked, bowing out of the training area and going to the back of the studio to sit down.

Jerry sat next to me with a perplexed look. "That guy used to hang around my studio," he commented. "He even paid for a whole year, then never came back after the fourth or fifth lesson."

I looked automatically toward the door, though Steale was long gone.

"He showed up after that birthday party you threw for me," I said, remembering it well. "I showed him around, knocked him on his butt, then signed him up for lessons. He's been coming regularly ever since."

"Watch yourself around him, River," Jerry was never one to over-react to any given situation. If anything, he'd always been understated and mild. A warning like that was incongruous.

"Why?" I asked, chills raising on my arms.

"One of my students said he'd seen the guy around town a couple of times - once at a fancy restaurant with some shady-looking characters, then again at that biker hang-out near Morongo Valley."

I thought it over and came back to lesson number one. Where Steale was concerned, there were no answers.

"You worked with him for awhile," I said. "What did you think?"

Jerry shrugged. "He's intense. And don't ask me to explain it, but there's something behind those eyes."

Taking a deep breath, I considered Jerry's statement. "He's a good student," I commented, feeling a strange protectiveness toward Steale.

Jerry looked at me for a long moment. "You're not falling for him, are you?"

I laughed. "No," I said, hoping I was telling the truth.

"He might have underworld connections," Jerry warned.

I thought about that, remembering the gun Steale had brought into the studio with him on my birthday. "Then maybe the Art will do him some good. I think he's probably just confused about a lot of things - like most people in this crazy world."

"Well," Jerry sighed, "maybe you can make a difference with him. I always had the feeling that he was looking for something. If you can set him on the right path, maybe he'll find it."

Jerry often spoke of paths. It was no longer odd to discuss it with him. "Maybe. I'm still trying to get him in here for his private lessons."

Jerry frowned, but it turned to a grin as he reached out to tousle my hair. "Maybe he's just afraid you'll knock him on his butt again. Now *that's* an unorthodox sales pitch!"

I laughed a little, enjoying the easy rapport between us. "I seem to recall a time not too long ago when someone who shall remain nameless locked me inside his studio."

Jerry sighed fondly. "Guilty. And glad of it."

I was glad, too, but I turned the conversation back to Steale. "Did you ever learn anything else about him?"

"Not much," Jerry replied. "The only other thing I know about him, aside from the fact that he seems to have money to burn, is that his nickname is Coyote."

"You think he could be from one of the reservations around here? Maybe it's a tribal name."

Jerry shook his head. "I checked. The address he put down on the contract turned out to be bogus, as did his phone number."

It didn't make sense, but it definitely aroused my curiosity. We didn't have the opportunity to talk further, for it was then that the orange and blue belts began drifting into the studio.

When the classes were finally over at ten o'clock, Jerry suggested driving into town for pizza and a movie.

We climbed into his pick-up, not saying much as the desert night blew its balmy July warmth through the open windows. But we found the city dark, the restaurant eerily silent, the theatre deserted. Power failure - a big one by the looks of it. There was no light on the horizon in any direction.

After the customary groans of disappointment, Jerry turned the pick-up around and started back toward Joshua Tree. By the time we got there, we were lucky to find an all-night liquor store doing a booming business with a generator hooked up out back. We bought some cheese and crackers and a bottle of wine, then returned to the studio and lit candles for what had turned into a midnight snack.

When the wine was gone, it was almost two in the morning. Neither of us went home that night. Instead, Jerry fell asleep on the office sofa and I found a comfortable spot on the mat inside the sparring arena.

When I drifted into sleep, I found my students among The People once more. We discussed the flow of the chi with the seasons, and practiced kata for a long time. I never tired of it, and found myself more awake and alive on mornings after I had visited the astral realms.

Then Jaden came to me again, solemn as he gave me the silver-bound book once more.

"Master Synjin wishes me to express his sorrow to his beloved," the crystal-clear voice stated. The familiar smile had gone from his eyes.

My heart wrenched. "Why, Jaden?"

Jaden's dark head bowed. "Some time ago, my Master took a life," he began haltingly. "It is only now that he has returned from a period of spiritual cleansing in the mountains. His first wish upon returning to the temple was that I should bring this news to you. He said you would understand."

I wasn't sure I did. "Why did Master Synjin kill this man?"

"I do not know, Master Willows," the boy replied. "I believe this man was an assis – an assass-."

"An assassin?" I supplied when Jaden struggled with a word he should never have had to learn at his age.

He nodded with a stoic grace. "I believe the man was an assassin," he said, pronouncing the word perfectly. "Master Synjin said he was a traveler who had brought harm to some of our people and who would have harmed many more if not stopped." He spoke clearly, succinctly, a deep regret in his tone.

I drew a shaky breath, not fully understanding what had happened, wondering if I needed to. The vision I'd seen had shown me that Synjin had killed to save his own life – and apparently the lives of others, if what Jaden had said were true. A very long time ago, I'd found myself in a similar situation.

Reaching out, I raised Jaden's chin until our eyes met. "Tell Master Synjin that he's allowed to be human," I said, trying to smile for the boy's sake. "Whether in my world or yours, no one can achieve perfection, Jaden. You understand that, don't you?"

"My Master is a great man," he said. "It troubles me to see him so sad. What can I do?"

I had no immediate answer and considered my words carefully. "Sometimes we have to heal our injuries with time,

Jaden," I said. "Stay close to him when he wishes it and leave him when he needs to be alone."

The boy seemed dubious. "Nothing more?"

I smiled softly, my own heart breaking. "Do you remember lesson one and two?"

"There are no answers, and there are no accidents," he recited. I wished I'd been his age when I learned that. It would have made life a lot simpler.

Kneeling in front of him, I pulled him close. "Perhaps Master Synjin needs to be reminded of that, too."

I felt a tear slip down Jaden's cheek and light on his shoulder. It was golden in color. The soul's blood. The heart's rain.

I held the boy until he fell asleep in my arms. Then, like a shadow melting in the sunlight, he slipped back into his own world, his own body, his own life. My arms were empty.

~

I spent a few days alone in the desert after that. Luckily, one of the adults I'd inherited from Jerry was able to take on the class-load. Part of the requirements for graduating from first degree black to second degree were one hundred hours of teaching. Jeff Morrison was happy to oblige, and I was glad to let him.

For the first day, I just drove through the monument from 29 Palms all the way south to Cottonwood Springs. From there, I took the 1-10 west and into the outskirts of Los Angeles.

It was the first time in over six years that I'd been in a city any larger than Yucca Valley, and though it was something of a culture shock, it was also fascinating. If I'd disliked cities before, that dislike had evolved into an odd combination of dismay and despair. The air smelled thick and sour, a grimy yellow layer hanging in the sky the nearer I got to town. Smog turned the sunset a shade of molten amber that might have been beautiful had it not been poison.

I also noticed that the freeways were crowded long past when rush-hour should have ended, and the expressions on the faces of passing motorists could only be described as grim. People no older than myself drove BMWs and Mercedes, sitting in the grid lock with their windows rolled up and their eyes cast straight ahead.

The world was afraid. The zombies had come, and they were us.

I took an off-ramp which led down into the city, parked the car, and walked the streets for awhile, looking into shop windows and marveling at the things for which people would spend good money. The latest fad in food seemed to be oat-bran-burgers and tuna burritos.

It also seemed that the 60's were alive and well again. Tie-dye t-shirts and long flowing skirts filled the shop windows, and I noticed young people wearing cheap love beads and flowers in their hair. The fact that it was just another uniform probably never occurred to them. It was popular, and that was all that mattered. Trends. Fashion. Fitting in. Even if my life hadn't taken a sharp turn into the bizarre, I could not have lived in that world.

When I stopped in a book store out of curiosity, I found that the peace movement could have used a boost. The war in Iraq had claimed the lives of thirty five thousand American soldiers; Moscow was in the throes of political rebellion; Israel was defending its borders against invading Iranian terrorists; Mexico had closed her doors to the majority of foreign visitors; two species of whales had been officially declared extinct; AIDS was alive and well, mutating each time a cure seemed imminent; the Star Wars Defense Initiative had indeed been put in orbit, but had seriously malfunctioned during the first week, killing eight thousand people in the Hunan Province of China when the newly perfected (or *not* so perfected) lasers burned a hole the size of Manhattan into the Earth's crust. The ozone problem had worsened; the rain forests of South America were still being hacked down at a phenomenal rate; NASA had been disbanded after the sabotage and destruction of the Space Shuttle *Copernicus*; and children were still starving in Mississippi.

Yes, the zombies were alive and well, though I wondered if it had ever been any different, or if it ever *could* be.

I left the book store with a feeling of futility and continued on down the gray concrete sidewalk. At one point, I was approached by three young hooligans who offered to show me the time of my life in the back seat of a Mustang. They didn't want to accept my negative answer, but came to the conclusion I was right after I dropped one of the more physically aggressive to the pavement.

Chin na was an impressive art. It looked as if the user had only to touch his victim to induce unconsciousness.

After that, the other two picked up their buddy and didn't look back as they dumped him into the car and sped away. They certainly wouldn't call the cops; they were probably wanted for at least as many crimes as I was.

By the time I'd walked the streets for a couple of hours, I was more than ready to return to the sanctuary of the desert. At that moment, the studio seemed as much a haven as the Shaolin Temple in China must have seemed to the weary priests of long ago.

The whole damned planet had gone mad and there was nothing I could do about it.

~

I reached the entrance to the monument around ten in the evening, and continued on toward my campsite. I found two jack rabbits hanging around the tent, waiting for their evening hand-out. I could have sworn I heard one of them complain that I was late.

The following morning I loaded the backpack with enough food and water for two days, folded the sleeping bag down to a reasonable size, and took off into the desert. The heat was oppressive by ten, so I stopped in the shade of a boulder to meditate, marveling at the silent strength of a pinyon pine which grew through solid rock and offered bird-song from its branches.

I spent the rest of the day there, and the night, too. It wasn't that I was looking for something or even running away from something else. I simply needed to find a place where I could see nothing man-made for the entire 360 degrees of the horizon, where I could try to make some sense of the world, my life, my path, all of it.

It truly seemed that people had lost all sense of direction. For one thing, there were no more role models, not even the fictional likes of Captain Kirk or Mr. Spock, not even the heroes who lived in the pages of beloved books. I thought of Ray Bradbury and *Dandelion Wine* – life as it must have been in those simpler times written of with such poetry and grace that it caused one's heart to expand, one's mind to swell with possibility. I thought of Heinlein and Michael Valentine and *Stranger In A Strange Land*. All the old sci-fi classics that gave Man some small sense of hope, some idea that maybe – *just maybe* – we could go to the stars one day, if we could only get past our own global madness and social dis-ease.

And yet...

The world had changed. In the aftermath of so much mass insanity, people had lost their faith not only in their government and their society and their religion, but in themselves. They had gone from believing in *something* to believing in the cold and abject certainty of *Nothing*, with the end result being a slow but inevitable fall from hope to despair, a shift from peace to violence, a deterioration from the idea that one might achieve their highest potential, to the dark acceptance of the lowest common denominator of mere survival of the organic body and the certain death of the inorganic spirit.

The world was at war with itself on levels it could not even begin to comprehend, and the undead were winning.

I wanted to feel great sadness for that, and yet I could only conclude that every living being has choices to make – and it is only when we make the impeccable choice that we *might* have the opportunity to make the *next* choice. Put simply: we can actively evolve or passively de-evolve. We can choose our own path or wait for governments and societies and religions to choose it for us. We can have blind faith in our keepers, or we can throw off the chains and think and live as individuals instead of being another mindless sheeple worshipping the dictates of the program – one meaningless step following the next from cradle to grave.

For several hours, my mind was flooded with thoughts like this – a dark but undeniable revelation that exposed with painful clarity what was wrong with the world, but gave absolutely no hint of how to fix it.

Perhaps there were no answers and no accidents, but must it also be that there are no solutions? Was *that* the third lesson?

In the past, that might have been Ch'en Po's cue to pop out of the nowhere and into my head, but there was no fanfare to announce his arrival, not even a stirring of the wind or the howl of a coyote. I was alone.

It's just your own self-importance that makes you think you should be able to save the world, you know.

Not Ch'en Po's voice. Not Synjin. Just myself, telling me what I already knew but didn't want to accept. I *did* want to save the world. I *did* want to be the hero – but now I had to ask myself if I wanted those things for any noble purpose, or only – as the little voices suggested – to feed my own self-importance.

You can't change the world, River. You can only change yourself.

It wasn't what I wanted to hear. I started to stand up and head back toward camp, but the little voice took me firmly by the shoulders and shook me until I was sure my teeth rattled... though in reality I never moved at all.

If you want to make a difference, save yourself first and help those who cross your path. You don't need to go looking for causes. Trust me – the cause will find <u>you</u>. Isn't that how all of this started in the first place?

It sounded so... *selfish*. I wanted to argue and protest, but what purpose would it serve to have a battle with myself in the middle of nowhere while the stars were shining down and the crickets were singing in the cool of the evening and when I knew intuitively that the little voices were right.

You don't need to go looking for causes, they repeated for emphasis.

As that realization assimilated, I began to understand that I was exactly where I needed to be, exactly where I *had* to be on my path.

A comforting sense of serenity slowly replaced the turmoil and frustration. I didn't need to fully understand *where* the path was leading – I simply had to trust *myself* to walk it as it opened before me, and to be the director of my own destiny rather than an actor in my own drama. Simple enough – I'd always known it – but coming face to face with it in my own mirror had an impact that seemed to shift my view of the world, but more importantly, my view of myself and my role.

I sat in silence with these revelations for a long time that night, hoping they would still exist in the cold, harsh light of day. But when I started back toward camp in the cooler evening, I was suddenly overwhelmed with a sense of foreboding. An instant later, as if manifesting from my thoughts, the ground rumbled beneath my feet, causing the desert to groan as gigantic granite boulders rubbed and bumped together like insignificant pieces of flint. At first I thought it was an earthquake, but then there was a sound of air being forced through a garden hose until a piercing whistle filled the desert.

It was so intense that I had to cover my ears, and still it surrounded me, almost deafening. Then, as abruptly as it had come, it was gone again. I had the horrifying thought that the bombs had fallen and the world really was dying, yet there was no fire-flash or nuclear mushroom for as far as I could see.

The desert grew eerily silent until the coyotes began to howl their inexplicable commentary. Then the ground rumbled once more, a shorter length of time, and not with the previous intensity. It had no specific source that I could discern, everywhere and nowhere.

After the second rumble, I stood without moving for several long seconds, my heart hammering loudly in my chest. Finally, forcing myself to stir, I scrambled up one of the rock formations. When I made it to the top, I stood looking out over the desert as the last silver light bled away from the horizon, clouded over by night's ebony ink.

Looking toward where Yucca Valley should have been, there was only darkness against the sky. No tell-tale light contamination blotted out the evening stars, and even the microwave tower with its glowing red beacon on a high mountain to the east was gone.

Power failure. The second one within three days. It seemed too coincidental to be a coincidence. The only light came from what few cars were moving like ants on a snake's back. Highway 62, almost ten miles away.

The night winds had started almost immediately after the sun went down, and though the breeze was warm, I shivered against it. I sat down on top of the boulder and waited for several more minutes, my eyes continuing to scan the horizon and the desert below, looking for *something*.

When I finally saw it, my breath caught in my throat. About five miles to the northwest, in an area where I estimated the Wonderland of Rocks to be, a bright light had appeared close to the ground. A brilliant blue in color, it appeared to oscillate, not unlike a star might twinkle on a particularly clear night.

I stared at it for several minutes, noting that it neither brightened nor dimmed. It also didn't vanish under scrutiny as I'd thought it might. It simply waited there, like a beacon or a warning or an alien mirage.

I considered scrambling down the boulder and setting off across the desert to locate it, but common sense stopped me. Between the cholla cactus, the nocturnal sidewinders and the rough terrain, I'd never make it on foot.

Shortly after that, the moon crept cautiously over the eastern horizon. It took another hour before her light began to outline the terrain, but by midnight, I had a fairly good idea of where to look in the morning.

I pinpointed its location as being somewhere in the vicinity of Barker Dam - an old cattleman's watering hole left over from the early part of the century. Deep washes cut through the area, and massive rock formations towered as high as five hundred feet.

I dozed once or twice during the night, but for the most part, I didn't sleep at all.

At first light I scrambled down off the rock shortly before the full strength of the sun came over the horizon, and began making my way back to camp. It took another hour to reach it, and by the time I saw my diminutive tent in the valley below, exhaustion was taking its toll. I wouldn't be able to travel to the Barker Dam area during the full heat of a July day.

I climbed wearily into the car, then headed back to the studio. When I turned on the radio to keep me awake for the drive, *Blue Moon* was playing on the local station. *Nights In White Satin* followed it up. Nothing unusual about that, until the announcer reminded me that the old love song was performed by The Moody Blues.

Blue... blue... blue.

I took it as an omen.

What I couldn't precisely determine was whether I was going looking for a cause, or if the cause had indeed found me.

CHAPTER NINE
The Fortune Cookie

I caught myself napping in the cool sanctuary of the studio until noon, when the first private lesson showed up. I taught four students that day, then put in a call to Jeff Morrison again for the evening classes.

After hanging up, I went to shower and change out of my gi. When I was finished, I rounded the corner from the back room, a towel still wrapped around my head, then looked up to find Steale standing in the outer foyer. He was dressed in jeans and a skimpy, tight-fitting spandex top. I wondered if he knew what his attractiveness did to people; I wondered if he used it as a weapon. He was extraordinary, though I realized I'd gotten no closer to him than when we'd first met.

Composing myself, I tossed the towel through the bathroom door, grabbed a comb, and headed out to meet him. Looking up, I smiled, dragging the comb through wet hair.

"What brings you here an hour before class-time?" I asked, hoping to lead him down my path for a change.

He shrugged nonchalantly, amusement in his eyes. "I thought I should come down and sign up for one of those private sessions," he said, following me into the office.

I sat in the chair behind the desk while he took a seat on the couch, leaning forward to rest his elbows on his knees.

I watched him as I worked the last tangle out of my hair. Then, opening the top drawer, I pulled out the schedule. "When's good for you?"

He hesitated for a moment, and I hoped he was trying to figure out my seeming lack of interest. I'd tried the sugar; now it was time for the stick.

"When's good for *you*?" he countered, a question for a question.

"I can take you tomorrow at nine in the morning or four in the afternoon." I didn't look up.

His hesitation turned to silence. Finally he spoke. "Afternoon."

I penciled him in on the schedule, otherwise ignoring him. Timing my actions, I glanced up a few seconds later. "Anything else?"

He looked at me very oddly, then started to stand. "No... I guess not."

I inclined my head in acknowledgement. "Then I'll see you tomorrow at four."

He stood there for a beat longer than necessary, then started for the door. I thought I'd blown it, but he stopped just inside the room, turning toward me once again.

"Was there something else?" I asked.

His brows narrowed as he studied me. "Not really. Just trying to figure you out."

It was a start. "Oh? How so?"

He leaned against the door frame, crossing his arms. "For one, how come you're here," he said, surprising me with his straightforward approach. It was better than a continued stand-off, so I allowed him to take the lead.

"You mean why do I teach here instead of some place else?" I couldn't help the reaction he produced in me. It wasn't love. It might have been lust, but I didn't have the experience to know.

"For starters, yeah," he said casually.

"One of my Masters was fond of saying that the road seldom leads where you want it to go," I said. "It just sort of happened."

He seemed to consider that, and I noticed that he had taken another step back inside the room. He tilted his head to one side. "What about Jerry Davin?"

That surprised me. "What about him?" I asked with a smile. "He helped me start the studio; we're old friends."

The amusement came back to his eyes. "Just friends?"

"Just friends," I confirmed. "Why?" I observed that my heart had quickened a bit. It felt too hot in the room. Was he really interested in my relationship status?

He shook his head as if to dismiss the topic, casually walked back over to the couch and sat down. "Just curious."

My brows lifted. "You don't lie very well."

He looked up sharply and for a moment, I thought he might bolt. Instead, after a few tense seconds, he started to smile. The mask again. The one he wore so well.

"All right," he said, "the truth is that you remind me of someone I used to know and I wondered if you might want to go out for something to eat."

"Who?" I'd tackle that first. It would give me time to get over the shock of being asked out to dinner.

He shrugged with a seeming indifference, but I saw the facade slip for just an instant. Behind it, the pain was there again, and the secrets. "Her name was Kirin." He quickly changed the subject. "So how am I doing so far - with the karate, I mean."

I allowed him to alter the conversation. "Well enough," I replied truthfully.

His long brows rose. "Just well enough?"

I smiled again. "Maybe a little better than that," I said, then took another chance. "Care to tell me why you studied with Jerry awhile back and then dropped out of sight?"

He seemed about to protest, then nodded with a well-practiced nonchalance. "I had other things to do at the time," he evaded. "I wasn't ready."

I held his wavering gaze. One thing I *had* mastered was the art of reading people. "No matter how terrible you may think the truth is, if someone's your friend, it won't make them like you any less."

He held my gaze, his eyes hardening. "Wouldn't it?"

I didn't back down. "No. It wouldn't."

"Are you telling me you're my friend?"

"I am if you want me to be," I said honestly. As I looked at him, some of his animalistic magnetism was losing its control over me. He was becoming more of a person and less an icon. I liked him better that way, although I couldn't quite drown out those little voices that had found me the night before. This one *had* crossed my path. Now what?

He took awhile to think about it. Leaning back on the couch, he clasped his hands behind his head, his olive-colored skin stretched taut over lean biceps. So I noticed. A coma patient would have noticed.

Finally, with a heavy sigh, he shook his head as if in embarrassment. "You know, I can't help wondering if you'd be this virtuous if I hadn't paid you eight hundred dollars. Would you be as willing to befriend a drunk sleeping it off in a ditch?"

Without breaking eye contact, I opened the top drawer of the desk, pulled out the studio's check book, and picked up a pen to write. "Eight hundred and *fifty* dollars, Steale," I corrected. "How do you want the check made out?"

I wasn't angry, but I was dead serious.

He got up off the couch, came over to the desk, and grabbed the pen out of my hand. He stuffed it into his jeans' pocket, then stood there looking down at me, hands on his hips as our eyes locked. As close as he was standing, I could feel the heat of him, the scent of his cologne that was exhilarating and intimidating and altogether male.

"I don't give a damn about the money," he said, almost a whisper.

I didn't let him rattle me. "Then why'd you bring it up?" I didn't need to raise my voice to make the point.

And I knew I'd struck a raw nerve. He turned all the way around, presenting his back to me. In the training arena, it was a gesture of disrespect. But we weren't in the studio. This was one on one - infinitely more dangerous than a room full of black belts.

For nearly a full minute, he just stood there with his head lowered and his hands crammed down into his pockets. When he turned to face me, the mask was carefully in place once more. "Look, I'm sorry," he said. "It's been a rough week."

I gestured toward the couch. "Apology accepted," I said, waiting until he sat down. "You want to talk about it?"

He looked up at me with that unconvincing smile. "Not really," he said. "You hungry?"

I was constantly amazed by his rapid shifts. Making my decision, I looked up into Steale's unreadable eyes. "Maybe," I replied, using his own evasive tactics as a tool. "What'd you have in mind?"

"Chinese?"

"You going to tell me what's going on in that head of yours over dinner?" I asked with a leading smile. "Or is this just a way to take the heat off for awhile?"

He seemed surprised by the question. "If I wanted to take the heat off, I could just walk out that door."

"You could," I agreed. "Is that what happened when you were studying with Jerry? Did he get too close to something you didn't want to talk about?"

"Nope," Steale replied. "You're way off. Dinner?"

I gave in, recognizing the stone wall I'd butted my head against. "All right," I agreed, my tone becoming casual again. "Dinner."

Finally I stood, then looked down and realized what I was wearing. Faded black stone-washed jeans and a ratty t-shirt. I'd been planning on scouting out that mysterious light in the desert, not going to dinner with an enigma.

"Let me change into something a little less homeless," I offered.

"Don't bother," he grinned. "Wu keeps a table waiting for me, and he doesn't ask questions."

I considered that, looking at him. His clothes were more expensive than mine, but appeared well-worn. He probably paid extra for that.

"Okay," I said, then started for the door, wondering what the hell I was doing. "My car's out back."

"We'll take mine." He gestured toward the low-slung red sports car parked outside the building.

I didn't argue despite the fact the car was almost as intimidating as its driver could be. The silver plate on the bumper said 'Lamborghini', with the numbers '5000S' appearing just below. And that license plate was staring up at me again. 'COYOTE 1'.

When I got inside and the door closed, I inhaled the aroma of Italian leather and Steale's unique scent. It was a mixture which produced a reaction in me that I did *not* want to acknowledge and therefore chose to ignore.

I waited until he got in, then turned sideways in my seat, curling one leg underneath me. "Nice car," I commented, hoping to draw him out.

He shrugged as the engine purred to life. "I like nice things," he said, a teasing smile on his lips. "Is that a sign of weakness, Master?"

I let him get away with calling me that. It seemed to make him feel better. "Not unless the nice things start to own *you*."

He grunted an answer, then swung the car onto the open road. It went from zero to dizzying in about half a second. Sitting back, I pretended not to notice, despite the fact that Joshua Trees were flying past the window faster than the wicked witch in a Kansas twister.

"So who's Coyote?" I asked casually. "You?"

He glanced at me out the corner of one eye, trying to judge my reaction. "Coyote's a scavenger. Jack of all trades. The Native Americans call him the trickster - the one who brought chaos down

94

on the once-peaceful world." He shrugged indifferently. "Original sin, I guess."

"Is that what you are?" I asked to give the pretense of keeping it light despite the growing flutter in my stomach.

He kept his profile to me, eyes straight ahead as he drove. "Sure you want to know?"

Much as I wanted to, I didn't take the bait. "Coyote's also the code name applied to someone who runs illegal aliens across the border," I recalled. "It can also be a name given to someone who's split from the mob and starts working alone. They don't usually live long when they start cutting into the godfather's business."

"Now where did a nice young lady like you learn something like *that*?' he asked with a chuckle.

I shrugged. "I also read in addition to teaching karate to up and coming smart-asses like yourself. And besides," I added, "I'm not that young."

Shaking his head, he turned his eyes back on the road. "Well don't trouble your head with it," he told me. "I don't work for the mob. And if I *did*, I wouldn't advertise it on my license plate."

I wasn't sure I believed him, but I let it pass.

Neither of us spoke again until we pulled up in front of what looked to be a very expensive Chinese restaurant. Steale came around and opened my door before I could figure out how to unfasten the seat belt.

"I'm not that much of a lady either, you know," I told him, slightly embarrassed at the treatment.

His brows lifted as he gestured me through the front door of the restaurant. "And I'm not much of a gentleman," he whispered, so close to my ear I could feel the warm breath of him.

That I could believe.

~

We talked very little during dinner. The head waiter, an elderly Chinese fellow by the name of Wu, kept coming around to fill our water glasses, and I noticed that other patrons were staring at us occasionally. It was the first time I'd been into a restaurant in over six years, and I wasn't entirely comfortable with it. It felt decadent compared to how I'd learned to live. It also felt nice.

When we did talk, it was about nothing in particular. Steale was fascinated with the history of martial arts, and I was happy to tell him as much as I could. I wished I'd gotten further in Synjin's book, yet I discovered as I studied that the writing, even the text itself, was deceptive. I'd read for hours, only to discover that I hadn't covered more than two pages. Still, I knew far more now than I had when I'd left Master Barrows, and I did my best to impart some of that knowledge to my curious pupil.

By the time we finished eating, I realized I'd been doing most of the talking.

"You haven't said much," I told him, finishing off the last of my jasmine tea. "Did you plan it that way?"

He smiled a little, more relaxed. "I'm interested in what you have to say."

I started to pursue that, but Wu came back then, presenting us with a tray which held the bill and two plastic-wrapped fortune cookies. Without even looking at it, Steale pulled out a hundred dollar bill and set it back on the edge of the table.

Turning back to me, he held out the two fortune cookies in the palm of his hand. Feeling a strange tightness in my stomach, I accepted, peeling off the outer wrapping. Then, breaking the cookie in half, I looked down to read the tiny slip of paper.

It was hand-written in red ink. *'By the time the sun rises again, a truth will be revealed to you'.*

I stared at it for a moment, feeling goosebumps raise up on my arms. Omens from the beyond had a tendency to produce that reaction in me.

"What's it say?" Steale asked.

I held it out by the corner and let him take it. Reading it, he raised his brows, then handed me the one he'd received.

'The time to act will soon be upon you'.

I chilled again, looking up as I handed him the slip of paper. Finally, forcing a false lightness onto myself, I met his eyes. Some unspoken message passed between us, but it was as cryptic as any fortune cookie, indecipherable. The moment passed.

Setting his tea cup back onto the table, he gestured toward the door. "Ready to go?"

I hadn't seen Wu come back, but the bill had been settled and a generous tip was left on the table. I stood and followed my elusive pupil out the door, climbed into the car, and sat making awkward small-talk as he drove back toward the studio.

He was getting to me, whether I liked it or not. What scared me most *was* that I was starting to like it.

~

I experienced an uncharacteristic rush of panic when Steale failed to turn into the driveway at the studio.

"My car's back there," I said, a bit sharper than I'd intended.

He seemed altogether unconcerned. "I was hoping we could talk for awhile longer."

I considered that. "Do you mean *we*, or do you mean me? And while we're at it, where are we going?"

He shrugged, continuing into the tiny town of Joshua Tree. "I thought we could take a drive through the monument. Wu liked you," he added, completely out of sequence. "That's why he was hanging around so much. We didn't really have much of a chance to talk."

I liked him a lot better when he took the time to explain himself. "Oh." Nothing else came to mind.

He turned off the main road about a mile later, onto Park Boulevard. When we passed the ranger's station it was empty, and darkness had already fallen. It occurred to me that I could invite Steale to my humble campsite for stale crackers and cheese, but I wasn't sure I wanted him to know where I spent my nights. I also wasn't sure I *didn't*.

It surprised me more than a little that I could be so affected by him, and hardly at all by Jerry Davin, even though Jerry had always been open and forthcoming, while Steale was a mystery wrapped in ambiguity with a thick coating of secrecy. From time to time, perhaps I had felt a curiosity about Jerry, even wondered what might have happened if he *had* kissed me on my birthday. But the feelings Steale was beginning to awaken in me were far darker and more dangerous, and all but impossible to ignore. Whether he knew it or not, he was a walking pheromone, a lethal dose of temptation.

With the exception of Synjin, I had never felt so drawn to another human being, and certainly not with the intensity that gripped my stomach somewhere in between excitement and nausea.

And while I *wanted* to believe he was aware of it, I came to the conclusion that he was entirely oblivious to the effect he was having on me.

I was annoyed with myself most of all – I was supposed to be his teacher, neutral in all matters, an icon of virtue and self-control.

The little voices laughed out loud. *Get over yourself,* they advised. *If you __didn't__ notice, you'd be dead. Nothing wrong with admiring the scenery.*

Steale kept his eyes straight ahead, unaware of my atypical line of thought. I was simply grateful that the darkness concealed the flush that had almost certainly risen in my cheeks.

Determined not to make an issue of it, I sat back and listened to the car's engine as we continued along for several minutes longer. Slowing, he pulled into the circular parking area at Keys View – an isolated overlook which provided an unparalleled view of the valley below. Palm Springs lay spread out like a blanket of stars, with other communities nestled in nearby valleys. Further to the south, the Salton Sea appeared as a black hole in a galaxy otherwise comprised of pixels of light and shadow.

A deep and somehow profound eeriness filled the desert, the winds more pronounced at the higher elevation, drafting up from the valley and whistling ominously around the curves of the car. While the landscape below was a study in chaotic illumination, the world at the elevation of 5500 feet was so dark that I could barely make out Steale's silhouette against the driver's window.

It startled me when he spoke.

"I like to come here at night sometimes," he said, his voice deep and low, penetrating. "The desert's eternal. It never changes - not in our lifetime, anyway."

There was a sense of comfort in what he said. Though he was still only an outline of black against black, I sensed him looking at me.

"That's one thing that's kept me here for so long," I said, only then realizing it to be true. "I went into LA a few days ago, and it just reinforced my belief that man was never meant to live like that."

"Ummm. And how *is* man meant to live?" he asked philosophically.

I laughed just a little. "I'm not really sure. Just not like that." I heard the shallowness in my voice. Steale deserved better than some hollow platitude. Digging deeper, past the nervous hesitation to which I was unaccustomed, I looked at the shadow in the driver's seat and said what I was really thinking.

"The world has become a caricature of itself," I began, recalling how I had felt on the heartless streets of Los Angeles. Lifeless expressions. Doll's eyes staring equally at car wrecks and kittens – seeing no difference in anything anymore. Automatons going through the motions of a reality that was entirely unreal to them.

"Why do you think that is?" Steale asked. "Do you think it's always been that way?"

I wondered. I suspect everybody wonders at some point. "People are so busy trying to be who they *think* they are – who they've been programmed to *believe* they are – that they have no idea of who they *really* are, or who they *could* be beyond the roles they're playing." The phenomenon itself perplexed and simultaneously fascinated me. "Everybody's wearing a uniform and carrying a flag – whether they ever realize it or not."

"Yeah," he sighed. "Every time I go into the city, I can't believe how people live in their little houses and shut out the rest of the world."

His words were an echo of my thoughts. "Most of them don't know any other way. And the ones who do are afraid to let go, to try something different. It's easier to stay in a bad situation than to walk off into the complete unknown."

For a moment, he didn't reply. When he did, I knew the mask was lowering. "I walked away from it." A pause, then: "You obviously walked away from it." I felt him looking at me. "Or ran."

His observation raised the hair on the back of my neck.

"What happened?" I asked, hoping he was ready to open up, and eager to take the attention away from myself.

His knuckles tightened on the steering wheel. "It isn't important." There was a long silence before he added, "Let's just say there came a time when it finally dawned on me that heroes are best left in books and monsters are more often men in suits than anything else."

It wasn't difficult to sense the rage hiding close to the surface of what might otherwise have been dismissed as a nonchalant comment on the state of the world. But this wasn't casual.

Whatever had happened to him was personal, and in some dark corner of his spirit, he was poised for revenge.

This knowledge came to me as if downloaded directly from the universe itself. A simple knowing. *"Gnosis with the Infinite, knowing without knowing how you know,"* Ch'en Po had once said to me in a dream when I'd asked how the old Masters always seemed to have the right answer even before the student had asked a question.

Whatever the mystical process might have been, I simply knew in that moment that Steale's past was every bit as twisted as my own. What I *didn't* know was if he were running from the authorities, or from himself, or both.

"You okay?" he asked, and only then did I realize I had been wrapped in the silence for more than a full minute.

"Sorry," I muttered with a little chuckle. "I was just thinking about what you said." I gathered my thoughts, proceeding with caution. "In my experience, heroes are just people who find themselves in extraordinary circumstances, and villains are usually the ones who *created* those circumstances – whether intentionally or not."

I felt him smile through the same strange gnosis. "So there are no real heroes and no real villains?"

"Yin and yang," I replied automatically. "We may be predisposed to one or the other, but there's a little of both in everybody."

Turning in his seat until his back pressed against the door, he stared at me for a long time. "You're not who you seem to be, are you?" he said, his words more a statement than a question.

I felt a twinge of panic, but wrestled it under control. "What do you mean?"

"Just an observation. Don't let it worry you."

It did worry me, but I quickly put it back in his lap. "It works both ways, you know. You're not what you seem to be either."

He laughed easily. "And what do I seem to be?"

I considered it, more grateful than he would ever know to change the subject. "You seen to be a chameleon as much as a coyote – the camouflaged trickster. But I don't think you're a drug dealer or some mob assassin, if that's what you want to know."

"Is that how people see me?"

I didn't want to hurt his feelings, but I didn't have the luxury of lying to him. "Sometimes," I said. "You drive around in this car, you carry a gun, you flash a lot of money, you wear expensive clothes..."

"Like I said, I enjoy nice things. And I've never particularly cared what other people think of me."

Considering his seemingly contradictory words, I tried another angle. "Why did you really come into the studio this afternoon? You could have called to schedule a private lesson."

I heard the hesitation that was only silence. "Maybe I just wanted to talk. Even a camouflaged coyote needs company once in awhile. You want me to drive you back to your car?"

I couldn't ignore the slight tone of bitterness in his voice. It hurt. "No. But I do wish you'd be more honest with me, Steale."

He hesitated again, though not as long. "All right," he said with an uneasy laugh. "What would you like to know? I'll answer any questions you can come up with."

It seemed too easy. "Why?"

His silhouette shrugged. "Why not? When you get to know me, you'll probably decide I'm not nearly as interesting as the images you've conjured up in your mind."

Taking a deep breath, I struggled to stay on equal footing.

"I want you to know that I can accept you for whatever you are. It doesn't matter to me if you're some eccentric millionaire, or if you're running illegal aliens across the Mexican border." I thought about what I'd said, then amended it slightly. "As long as what you do isn't harmful to anyone, it's not my place to judge you."

He didn't hesitate this time. "And what if it *is* harmful?"

I didn't like the sound of it, but I gave him the truth. "I wouldn't like it, but I wouldn't turn you over to the authorities, if that's what you're asking – not my job."

He chuckled softly. "And what *is* your job?"

I shared in his momentary amusement. "My job is to try to teach you how to avoid trouble. By studying the Art, you learn that there are better ways than fighting. There's personal integrity, diplomacy, honor."

"Tell me about honor."

I smiled in the darkness. "That's sort of like the student who asked the old sage to give him all the knowledge of the universe while standing on one foot. Honor is something every living soul is born with. It's also something that a lot of people lose the older they get. Sometimes, though, if they're lucky and if they have someone to guide them, they can regain their honor through the practice of living."

He was silent for a moment, as if contemplating my answer. When he spoke again, the mask lowered a little more. "And what if another person dishonors you? What if someone takes something that belongs to you? Do you lose your honor if you try to get it back?"

I thought long and hard before I spoke. "If someone takes a physical object from you, it becomes important to define how important that object really is."

He leaned closer. "What do you mean?"

"Well, if someone steals money from you to buy food, it would dishonor you if you took that money back and spent it on gambling while the beggar starved."

He was silent for a moment. Then: "And what if the object wasn't money? What if someone took away a husband, or a wife?"

I wasn't sure what he was getting at. "Since a husband or a wife can't be owned, they can't really be stolen," I said. "Each person makes up their own mind as to what they want to do, who they want to be with."

He shook his dark head. "No, no. That's not what I mean. What if someone came and physically took that husband or wife away against their will?"

I grew abruptly cold, the hair raising on my neck as I realized he was close to revealing some dark and dangerous truth. I didn't want to scare away it away by asking too many questions. I tried to project myself into the nebulous situation he was discussing. "If someone kidnapped one of my students, I would be honor-bound to do everything within my power to get that student back."

The silence between us was eerie for a moment. "But if you tried everything and failed? Would your own honor be lost? Could you live knowing that someone who had depended on you was lost because you couldn't help them?"

Chills raked along my arms, running hot and cold down my spine. I squinted through the darkness, wishing I could see his face.

Reaching out, I found one of his hands resting on his leg. I took it and held it tight. "What are you trying to tell me, Steale?"

102

He tensed, trying to draw his hand back. The mask came up. "It was just a question."

Listening to my own instincts, I backed off, though his abrupt retreat hurt. "Okay." I loosened my grip on his hand until it dropped back into his lap. "We don't have to talk about it."

To my surprise, he didn't launch into a long list of denials. Instead, he said only one word. "Thanks."

For several minutes, neither of us spoke. The wind had picked up considerably, whistling around the contours of the Lamborghini, a chorus of disturbing voices. I wondered if the conversation were at an end, though I wasn't content to let it go. Being with him in the desert, in the silence, in the weird sorcery of the night, made me understand that our roads were somehow interconnected. I wanted to be there with Steale, and had the impression he was trying to decide if he wanted to be with me. He was testing me. That much I knew.

Taking a gamble, I opened the car door and walked over to the cement retaining wall ten feet in front of the car. No more than thirty inches high, it made a good place to sit. Straddling it, I looked out into the distant valley, down into the mouth of the canyon, until I heard the car door open again. A moment later, Steale straddled the wall facing me, following my gaze as the wind lifted his shaggy hair.

"I'm sorry," he said, reaching out to take my hand.

I could see him fairly well now. Without the roof of the car to block the starlight, my eyes had started to adjust. I could even see his expression, which was one of genuine despair. It made my chi ache, especially when he held my hand tighter than necessary.

"Tell me how to help, and I will," I said, meaning it.

"I want to, Lynne," he whispered. "Just... not now."

I forced myself to accept that answer. It still hurt and I think he knew that.

He smiled wistfully. "For now, I'd like you to be my friend - if the invitation's still open, that is."

I nodded, giving him the space he seemed to need. "It is." I deliberately chose what I thought to be a less sensitive topic of conversation. "You still haven't told me why you want to study the Art so much, why it's so important to you?"

I felt an indefinable tension in him, but he didn't pull away. Instead, he laughed almost inaudibly. "My brother got me interested in it, I suppose," he said at last. "That was also a long time ago. We haven't seen one another in years."

I wondered if there were anything about his past that *wasn't* painful for him.

"Time can mend a lot of things, Steale," I told him, hoping it would be enough.

"Not this," he said.

He was hurting - soul deep. "Mind if I ask what caused the rift between you?"

He shrugged with seeming indifference and didn't answer for a long time. "A woman," he said at last. "Kirin."

The name he'd mentioned before. The woman he'd said I reminded him of. "Your brother fell in love with her?"

At that, surprising me once again, Steale laughed aloud. "No, nothing like that," he replied. "Our falling out came a long time after Kirin and I were already apart."

It was clear that he didn't want to say any more. I gazed at the distant line of mountains on the horizon, leaving him in silence for a few moments.

"What about you? What's the tragic story of your past?"

My body tensed despite my resolve to be open with him. He felt it, too.

"What?" he asked with a grin. "I hit a nerve?"

I shook my head, forcing calmness onto myself. "I got into some trouble awhile back." Then, mirroring his own words, I added, "It was a long time ago."

He didn't let me get away with it. "So you want me to strip my soul naked, but you're going to clam up?" He wasn't angry, just persistent. I liked that.

"I had some trouble with the police," I said, then tried to shrug it off. "You were right when you said I'm not the person I seem to be." It was more than I'd ever confessed to anyone, and that scared me when I realized how little I knew about this man.

He was silent while the wind ran summer fingers through his hair. "Do I want to know who you really are?"

I laughed softly. "Probably not."

He laughed, too. It broke the tension between us.

Regardless of Steale's questionable past, I found myself trusting him, or at least wanting to trust him.

For a few minutes, neither of us spoke. Then, sighing softly, Steale revealed a secret to me - perhaps the one the fortune cookie had spoken of.

"Look, Lynne," he said gently, "I don't want you to get the wrong idea. It's important to me. *You're* important to me," he stated fervently, taking me off guard again. "When I studied with Jerry Davin, it wasn't right for me. But with you, I feel I can finally start to learn what I need to know."

That tender confession touched me deeper than anything any student had ever said to me. I looked at him for a long time. I felt it, too. That mystical connection, that inexplicable link between us. If I believed in reincarnation, I might have thought he was a brother from some long-ago past life.

Or a lover.

The thought disturbed me. It also excited me in a way I found dangerously erotic. And just plain dangerous.

"I'll teach you everything I can, Steale," I promised. "But there will come a day when you're going to have to trust me."

He nodded silently, then inclined his head upward, back to the stars. When he spoke again, his voice took on an ethereal quality, surreal. "Did you ever wonder what's out there?" he asked unexpectedly, ignoring my comment altogether.

I followed his gaze to Polaris, Arcturus, Mizar and Alcor. "People, I suppose. Maybe like us, maybe not." I wondered fleetingly in that moment if Synjin's world were closer or much further away. It existed within my own, overlapping it and permeating it, yet I could see the stars much clearer than the place where my mate was born.

Steale seemed to draw himself out of his reverie then, squeezing my hand as he stood up. "It's late," he said. "If you plan on giving me that private lesson tomorrow afternoon, you'd better get some sleep."

I was tired, yet I didn't want it to end. I felt I had just run my toes through the first layer of some incredibly deep ocean. Still, I hadn't learned what I knew of the Art overnight. I wouldn't find Steale's tragic secret in the first attempt.

"You're probably right," I agreed, getting up and walking with him back to the car. Once inside, I relaxed in the seat and watched him drive. Without trying, he was impressive. Cool, controlled, tightly-wound.

Coyote.

We arrived at the studio about twenty minutes later, where he dropped me at my car with a promise to see me the next afternoon. We didn't linger and there was no awkwardness between us when he drove away.

I climbed inside the Camaro after watching his tail lights disappear over the hill, started the engine, and drove back to my campsite. The jack rabbits did not come that night, nor did deafening thunder nor a brilliant blue light. The desert was at rest.

I thought of Synjin again.

But now I thought of Steale, too.

CHAPTER TEN
One Foot In Another World

I was awake before the sun rose the following morning, refreshed and restless at the same time. I dressed quickly, pulling on a pair of light-weight jeans, a white shirt to reflect the heat, and a hat to protect my head.

It seemed my body knew where I was going long before the thought entered my mind, for I climbed into the car and began driving toward the Wonderland of Rocks just as the first streak of silver light shone over the horizon. With any luck, I should have about two hours of relative safety before the sun parched the land dry of the cooler night air.

I took the dirt road which led away from the Hidden Valley campground and into the Barker Dam area, followed it to its end, and parked the car off to the side. Then, taking two canteens, I started the mile-long hike toward the dry river bed at the mouth of the dam.

I deliberately thought of anything *but* Steale – which meant I was thinking of him by trying *not* to think of him.

It took less than half an hour to hike from the parking area to the actual dam, which wasn't terribly impressive at close range. Made of cement block and rough grout, it stretched about sixty feet across, joining a massive granite rock formation to the north, and a much lower outcropping of boulders to the south.

It took another few minutes to scramble down from the trail and into the wash itself, and by the time I was standing in the middle of it, the sun was peering over the mountains, taking the shadows and the coolness of the morning away.

Closing my eyes for a moment, I mentally summoned the image which had burned itself to my inner eyelid two nights before - specifically a saddle in the mountain where two tall peaks were surrounded by dozens of alien-looking spires.

Once that image was clear, I began walking toward the northeast, following the bend of the dry river toward the base of the mountain.

What surprised me most was the suddenly cool breeze which began snaking its way through the river bed, lifting my hair and drying the beads of perspiration that had risen on my face. It was alien, out of place, and though I was grateful for the reprieve from the heat, it caused a chill to pass through me from head to toe.

I drew a sharp breath, then pivoted in place to look over my shoulder. I thought I'd sensed something - a shadow, perhaps, or the sound of footsteps.

There was nothing.

Opening the mouth of the canteen, I drank several swallows. Old legend had it that the desert was sometimes a merciful killer. If he liked you, he'd let you think you'd found a cool place to sleep, that you'd stepped into a gentler world.

I didn't want to become part of that legend, and though I didn't feel dehydrated or delirious, I moved to the side of the wash and into the shade of the jagged mountain. Sitting down, I put my head between my knees, breathing slowly in through my nose, then out through my mouth.

I didn't feel any different. The coolness hadn't given way to desert heat; delirium hadn't given way to clarity of thought; reality hadn't altered.

It wasn't *me* who was delirious; it was the desert.

I sat there for another minute, losing precious time as I tried to rationalize what I was experiencing. The air that caressed my face was cool - like a spring wind blowing down from the mountains, brushing snow on the way to the valley.

The dry river bed snaked around toward the dam, which was now out of sight around a bend. The terrain was identical to how it had been when I'd walked through it five minutes before, and the indentations of my footprints lead through the loose sand to find me where I sat.

Finally I rose and stood looking to the left and the right. I began walking back the way I'd come, carefully retracing my exact footprints in the sand. For nearly thirty seconds, the cool wind stayed on my back, but as I went from one step into the next, I was inundated with a blast of heat as if from a furnace. The wind stopped; the silence grew thick. Above my head, high atop the mountain, a raven cried out.

I stood for just a moment inside the hot desert, then walked two steps backward until I felt the cool wind against my shoulders and back. One step into the heat. A half-step back into the cool.

For several minutes, I stood half-way between the two realities, searching my mind for any rational explanation. Even though the desert was filled with tricks, there could be no scientific reason for what I was experiencing: a temperature variance of at least thirty five degrees from one footstep to the next.

Deciding to experiment further, I walked about twenty feet to the left of my former footprints, then paralleled them back toward the heat. My footprints now made a cross in the sand, with one arm extending some twenty feet to the west, back toward the dam to the south, and about fifteen feet in either direction to the east and north.

It occurred to me then that it was some sort of doorway rather than an anomaly of nature - like stepping from the desert into an air-conditioned room. Approximately thirty five feet wide at the arms of my footprint cross, it seemed to begin and end at the cross's apex.

Taking a deep breath to steady my nerves, I fought to remember something I had learned from Synjin's thoughts, a long time ago, in a part of my life that seemed distant and indistinct now.

One in a hundred thousand could open the vortex.

Was that it?

But I hadn't done anything to open some mystical, invisible vortex. My thoughts hadn't even touched on Synjin or his world when I'd started the walk from the dam to where I now stood, one foot in my world, one foot in another.

For a long time, I simply remained there. It occurred to me to keep going and never look back - to keep walking until, eventually, I found Synjin. But I was also impressed with the thought of what might happen if I *couldn't* get back. And what if this wasn't Synjin's world at all? If one parallel place could exist, why not several?

An image of Steale flashed through my mind, and I began to fully realize that my work in my own world wasn't yet finished. I still had no genuine idea what that work was to be, yet I knew I couldn't abandon a man who thought of himself as original sin any more than I could have walked away from my own Self.

I stood for a moment longer in what I had defined as a doorway, looking toward the mountains where it led. If my estimations were correct, the blue light I'd seen in the desert two nights before had been at the base of the foothills - almost exactly where I now stood.

For a brief time, I found my mind playing back memories of things I'd learned in school a long time ago, things I'd read in books more recently. Admiral Byrd and his rich, green landscape which suddenly appeared at the North Pole. Two teenagers in Galveston, Texas who had gone for a summer evening drive but had returned home with the bed of their pick-up filled with snow. Legends of fairy circles where the unwary traveler might simply fall through a hole in the ground and awaken in a land where elegant elves served lavender wine in green crystal goblets. The remote jungles of South America, the mystical fields of Ireland, the lochs of Scotland, the deserts - all places where humans had reported strange encounters with things they could not explain.

Many legends were based in fact.

And the fact was that I had one foot in the place where many of those legends were born.

~

"Doesn't young ram have classes to teach?" a voice said from a few feet behind.

Drawing a sharp breath, I spun around to find myself face to face with the last person I'd expected to see.

"Ch'en Po!" I gasped. It was the first time I'd actually seen the old man in the flesh. There had been the incident in the janitor's closet in Tampa, but the darkness had been so thick that physical eyes were useless. I knew he wasn't astral this time because I wasn't asleep; I wasn't dreaming; I wasn't delirious.

He stood slightly taller than he'd seemed in our previous meetings, and very real. His astral Self was a combination of how he saw himself and how I saw him - a combination of our images. Physically, he was different, yet still the same.

Walking toward me, he inclined his head, his long gray beard touching the middle of his chest and lifting in the cool breeze.

"Is this your world?" I asked.

He frowned admonishment. "Why you come here? Can't stay. Go back to your studio. Water young trees. Those that don't wither might grow strong."

"You know," I said with a grin, "you're always trying to chase me out of some place. First, you made me go back to my body when we were under that lake in Florida. Then you basically told me to get out of the ambulance and fight for my life. Then there was the time Jerry used that chin na technique and knocked me out. Now you're trying to chase me out of here, too." I paused to let that sink in, then added with a chuckle, "Don't you have anything better to do, Master?"

He smiled then, surprising me just a little. "Old man have many things to do. Sweeping travelers out of vestibule only one of many chores."

"So this *is* an entrance into your world? A doorway?"

He nodded. "Place where fabric of space between here and there is weak. Many such places in desert, since no man-made boundaries to distinguish what rock belong where, no building or highway to tell Joshua Tree to grow in your sand, or grow in mine."

I frowned, trying to fully internalize that. "Did I open it with my mind or something - the doorway, I mean?"

The old man laughed, tossing his head back and howling into the wind. "Unless scared for own life, young ram not have enough power to open can of Pepsi with mind!" he giggled. "But sometimes have enough vision to see vestibule and wander inside like mouse wander into temple basement."

It was frustrating when he spoke in analogies. "My path *led* me here," I told him firmly. It was the first time I'd come close to arguing with him.

He looked at me for a long moment. "Path lead in many directions. Young ram must retrace steps sometimes - like cross of footprints in desert sand."

That made only a little more sense than what he'd said before. "In other words, I'm not supposed to be here."

His gray brows lifted. "If not supposed to be here, wouldn't be here," he said wisely. "Just not supposed to *stay*."

"I'd already decided that on my own," I told him with a smile.

He inclined his head curtly. "Good thing," he commented. "Otherwise, frail old man have to toss strong young ram through door of vestibule. Might strain muscle or bruise foot in process."

I chuckled lightly. "You don't look frail to me, Master. And I certainly don't want to be on the receiving end of getting tossed out of here by you. Can we talk for awhile?" There was so much I wanted to ask him, so much I needed to know.

He inclined his head back toward the dam, answering me with a smile. "Students waiting. Go water forest now."

I remembered then that Steale was one of those students. "Master, there's a man who studies with me."

"Only one?" Ch'en Po asked, seemingly shocked.

I shook my head, then said what I really meant. "There's one who stands out. And..." I wasn't sure what I was going to say, how to say it, if it needed to be said at all.

"And young ram fears her own feelings?" he asked.

"That's part of it," I confessed. "He's a mystery to me. I can't always read him, and I'm afraid of making a mistake. He needs a Master, and I don't feel qualified to fill that need."

"Being Master doesn't mean one is suddenly given all knowledge," he pointed out. "Must always follow your instinct, look for answer within Self. Never be afraid to say you don't know when you don't know. Find guidance in natural kingdom, strength in hearts of men. The snake is honest for he doesn't know how to lie. White crane is free because he doesn't know laws of gravity. Monkey sleeps well at night because he's not eaten up by guilt for stealing banana from hungry rat. Understand those things first; the rest will follow."

On one level, I already did. On another, I wasn't sure I was qualified to pass that knowledge along. "He needs a Master," I repeated, almost to myself.

The old man's smile was back again, though wistful and perhaps sad. "That why he come to *you*."

I started to protest, but Ch'en Po reached out to place his full hand over my mouth, silencing me.

"I was still a student long after young rams start calling me 'Master'. Someday you realize that everything in life is learned from living – not from book, not from old man." He paused, still keeping his hand over my mouth. "You're already Master, River Willows - because it pleases *me* to say so. Still have much to learn - refine techniques, stop butting head, learn healing, study chi."

Aside from his fingers clamped over my mouth, I could think of no response. If Ch'en Po wanted to think of me as a Master, I could only try to live up to that expectation.

"You honor me, Ch'en Po," I told him as I bowed my head in respect.

112

He gestured elaborately toward the dam again. "Then go honor old man. Soon you'll be with Synjin, then we all sit down with bottle of saki and play checkers. But for now, much work still to be done, many curves still left on path before road winds home."

Home. I rolled the word over in my thoughts. I'd been without one for a very long time, though it hadn't really occurred to me until that moment.

"As for young ram's feelings," he added, "you must act on instinct and honor. Cannot live in spiritual harmony if out of physical balance. Body and mind must work together. Cannot shut down feelings any more than you can make heart stop beating." He gestured toward the mountains in the distance. "Cannot climb pinnacle without first falling down, bruise body, skin knee, maybe even break heart."

I started to ask him to clarify what he meant, but he was already walking away - to the north, into the cool wind, away from my world. He said only one more thing to me that day, and that he called over his shoulder as if in retrospect.

"Go butt head against stubborn student," he suggested, his words carried on the wind. "If young ram *be* Master, then student learn respect. If young Master falter, fear feelings, student never reveal Self. Water tree. Tend garden. Sleep well. Drive safe. Bye bye..."

I stared after him for several minutes. "And don't forget to brush your teeth before you go to bed," I muttered to myself long after he was gone.

As much as I wanted to, I did not try to follow him.

CHAPTER ELEVEN
Matters of Honor

Steale came in the front door of the studio at 3:59:30, hurried into the dressing room, and reappeared a minute later, gi in place, belt tied properly.

I suppressed a smile as I stood in front of him. "Lose track of time?"

He seemed flustered, uncentered. "Business. Sorry, it couldn't be helped."

Once the formalities were completed, I stood there looking at him for a moment. Then, gesturing toward the painted yin/yang, I motioned him into position.

"You can start by stretching out," I told him.

I noticed a mild amusement in his eyes. It was the kind of humor which spoke of the conversation we'd had the night before - and it was precisely the reason I'd never allowed myself to become involved with students. Now I'd simply have to deal with it. I *was* involved.

When he finished his warm-ups, he rose gracefully to his feet. "Good enough?"

Standing there with the late afternoon sun streaming in through the window, he was a flawless silhouette cut into the fabric of space and time, a riddle written in the ashes of some unimaginable past that haunted him and made him seem both fragile and impenetrable at once.

I didn't want to want him. At least that's what I tried to make myself believe.

In answer to his question, I smiled and gave a quick nod. "What would you like to work on today?"

He shrugged, unconsciously crossing his arms in front of him. "You're the Master, Master. You tell me."

I allowed myself to be casual with him. "Well, you can start by unfolding your arms. In here, it's disrespectful. Out there," I added, inclining my head toward the outside world, "it's body language for the fact that you're trying to initiate a challenge."

He didn't argue. Instead, his arms dropped to his side with a grin. "Sorry."

I was determined to take Ch'en Po's words to heart. If I wanted this man to open up with me, he first had to respect me. If I wanted to be a Master, I had to start acting like one.

"Show me Blocking Set One," I requested, standing to one side so he could use the mirrors behind me. He performed it easily, faltering in only one place, which he corrected when reminded.

"Not bad," I commented. "Work on the focus." I stepped in front of him and threw a well-controlled punch which he blocked expertly, though not with much strength. "Your arm should become a deflecting wall to stop my blow," I added, using a different punch which required the second move of the blocking set. "Watch the movement of my shoulder to anticipate what kind of punch I'm going to throw, and meet my fist with your arm before it impacts."

He did it very well, better than he should have been able to manage at his rank.

Finally, satisfied that he was competent in the blocks, I motioned him back into the center of the yin/yang. "Let's see how you're doing with your basics."

We progressed through the blocking and stance sets twice more, and I had him demonstrate Short Form One three times. It was a combination of foot maneuvers, stances and blocks - the basic defense techniques of the white belt's material combined into a moving kata. It was the first step along a much longer road, but if he continued with the same degree of devotion he was demonstrating, I had no doubt he'd succeed.

He performed the movements with grace and efficiency, the lean contours of his body moving with a fluidity that was unexpected for a new student.

The Art was in his blood.

When he finished the kata, he stood waiting.

"Not bad," I said again. "Let's go through some of the self defense techniques. I'll attack; you defend."

He nodded, dropping into a ready stance as I called off the techniques by name. We got through the entire list of material twice, and I could find no serious flaw in any of his moves. As we finished the last of the techniques, I stepped back and looked at him for a moment. He wasn't even breathing hard.

"You're better than you should be at this point," I said, not realizing I'd spoken aloud.

A little chuckle was his response. "Don't look so surprised. I have a lot of free time to practice."

"It shows." I smiled, realizing I seldom offered compliments.

We finished the private lesson with the traditional salute and bow, then stepped back from one another. Regardless of the fact that I was impressed with his progress, there was a certain distraction in his demeanor throughout the time I spent with him, as if his body had been trained to perform the moves required of him by rote, yet his mind was elsewhere.

He disappeared into the dressing room for a few minutes, then returned to find me still in the studio. I'd been taking advantage of the empty floor to practice my own material - the new things Jerry Davin had been teaching me whenever we found time to study together. I felt my student's eyes on me but continued with what I was doing. When I finished the difficult maneuvers of the Dragon kata, I'd worked up a slight sweat.

"Nice," Steale commented from the doorway that led into the back of the studio.

"Thanks," I said. "I don't have it fluid yet, but I'm working on it."

He gave me a very peculiar look that was almost scary in its intensity. "What?"

"I said I don't have it fluid yet," I repeated, perplexed by his question when I knew he'd heard me. "It's not just a matter of memorizing the moves. In order for the kata to have meaning, it should flow together. Like a ballet - fluidity is the key to strength and speed."

The immediate confusion left his eyes, but he was still staring at me, his expression unreadable. It went right through me.

Finally he smiled. "Looks good to a lowly white belt," he commented.

I laughed softly, then became more serious. "So where you off to tonight?" I asked, trying to give the appearance of not caring.

He continued leaning against the door frame. "I've got some business to take care of between eight and ten, but I'm free after that. Why? You asking me for a date?" Amusement was in his eyes again, flickering in the late afternoon sunlight.

I didn't let him rattle me. "I enjoyed talking with you last night and thought we could do it again."

"I'd like that. You teaching tonight?"

I nodded, catching my breath. "I've got the white belts until eight. Jeff's taking over the blues and oranges for the next couple of weeks - teaching requirements."

"Want to meet somewhere?" he asked.

I wasn't sure why, but I knew that the moment had come to earn his respect. Going to the back of the studio, I motioned him into the gym area. After he sat down, I stood in front of him, looking into his expectant gaze.

"What's going on with you?" I asked softly. "I have the feeling that you're in some kind of trouble."

His brows lifted but he didn't reply at first. When he did, it was another of his no-answer answers. "Feminine intuition?"

"Teacher's observation," I countered, deciding not to take the intentional bait that was intended to distract and maybe even to offend. "You were preoccupied during your entire lesson."

When he spoke again, his words were measured, carefully chosen. "How do I know I can trust you if I tell you this deep dark truth you seem to think I'm hiding?" No anger. Just curiosity.

"If you can trust me enough to tell me the truth, you can trust me to guard that truth as well, Steale."

For a moment, I thought he would simply get up and walk out the front door forever. But he looked up at me for a very long time, studying me with unwavering eyes. "Why is it so important to you?" he asked at last. "I don't see you trying to dig some deep inner meaning out of all your other students. Why me?" It was a sincere question.

"Let's just say you're hardly my average student, Steale."

"Not good enough."

I could respect that. It was honest. "All right. The truth is that I don't know why it's important to me," I said, recalling Ch'en Po's advice. It was all right not to know. "All I'm sure of is that it *is*. And, for what it's worth, you're just going to have to trust me when I tell you that I'm not here to hurt you."

"I know that," he replied fervently. "If I didn't, I wouldn't be here. I have a certain amount of intuition, too."

"And what is that intuition telling you now?" I asked, hoping to make him listen to his own inner voices.

He glanced away for just a moment, then sighed heavily. "It's telling me that I need more time."

I'd foolishly believed I could push him, force the issue.

"All right." I turned away from him, unaccustomed to running up a brick wall so many times within a twenty four hour period. "I just hope you won't wait too long."

Releasing a breath he'd been holding, he came to where I was standing. He started to reach out as if to place a hand on my shoulder, but stopped half-way, his arm dropping back to his side.

"It'll happen when it happens, Lynne," he said, taking me off guard with his soft-spoken gentleness. "Please try to understand that."

His voice was deep and pleasant - and sincere for a change. "I do understand it," I told him. Reaching out, I did what he was afraid to do. Placing one hand on his arm, I squeezed reassuringly., attempting to impart through human contact what I had clearly failed to communicate with words alone.

Before I could say anything more, however, I looked up to see the six o'clock white belts arriving sporadically. I let my hand drop back to my side just before one of the new students came ambling through the gym on the way to the dressing room.

For a moment, Steale's gaze remained locked with mine, and then he smiled a message that I couldn't quite read. "Don't give up on me," he said with that easy grin. "I'll swing by after I'm done with my business tonight. If you're still speaking to me by then, I'll try to explain a few things."

"Answer one question for me."

"I'll try."

I phrased my inquiry carefully. "Why do you suddenly want to study the Art when we both know you carry a gun?"

A faint smile came to his lips. "A gun can't answer my questions, and it's a lousy dinner partner."

I shook my head, mildly irritated by the flippant reply. "That's good, but not good enough. Why now? Is it just a novelty to you?"

He seemed genuinely hurt by the question, for which I was sorry. I hadn't intended to be unfeeling.

"It's not a novelty, Lynne," he said. "It's something I'm going to need - maybe very soon." He paused, the mask lowering just

118

enough for me to read the despair in his eyes. "And... it's a matter of honor."

His answer chilled me to the bone. I wanted to question him further, but two more students wandered through the gym. He was right about one thing: now wasn't the time.

Again, he tried to tell me something with his eyes, but I couldn't hear them speak. They were too filled with pain, regret, secrets.

"Be here at ten thirty," I told him.

He nodded, then turned and disappeared around the wall. I heard his footsteps moving across the wooden floor of the studio and out into the afternoon twilight.

I was trembling. His scent hung in the room like a restive spirit.

~

Teaching was an excellent diversion, especially when the students were white belts with minds like a blank slate. They absorbed the new knowledge easily is most cases, and they asked enough questions to keep my mind away from Steale for the next two hours. When I did dismiss the class, however, I was irritated by the fact that he was the first thing that came back to my thoughts.

Jeff Morrison showed up a few minutes later and, after a brief discussion with him, I went into the back to change, pulling on a pair of dark jeans, a long- sleeve black t-shirt, and tennis shoes. I glanced at the clock in the dressing room, then grabbed the hunting knife from my travel bag and ran the sheath through the belt of the jeans. It was barely eight o'clock, and Steale wouldn't be around until ten thirty – *if* he showed up at all.

I had two and a half hours - and some inner voice was tempting me with secrets I didn't want to hear. *'Barker Dam'*, it whispered. *'Barker Dam'*.

Leaving the studio, I got into my car and drove until I reached Hidden Valley Campground, then turned onto the dirt path which would lead to the area where the natural doorway was located. I wasn't sure what I expected to find, yet the compulsion to go was overwhelming.

I turned off the car lights as soon as I started down the dirt road. The path itself was composed of pale sandy-colored clay, and there was enough light from the stars to see where I was going.

Several small signs along the way read DAY USE ONLY - AREA CLOSED FROM 6 P.M. - 6 A.M. Still, I'd lived around the monument long enough to know that the rangers seldom drove into those areas at night to check.

I would have preferred to simply walk, but it was at least two miles from the campground to the parking area near the dam, and another mile over rough terrain to get to the dry wash.

Still, not knowing what I was likely to find, I parked about three-fourths of the way there, just off the side of the road behind a pinyon pine. The car wouldn't be readily visible from the main path.

From there, I jogged through the loose desert sand at the road side until I came to the Barker Dam parking area. As I rounded the final curve, however, my heart pounded into my throat. Instinctively ducking down and almost impaling myself on a yucca in the process, I muttered an inaudible curse, struggling to hold the panic in check.

Parked near the entrance to the trail and almost hidden behind an outcropping of rock was a low-slung red sports car. I didn't need to see the license plate to know what it said, and I'd stopped believing in coincidences a long time ago.

My body pressed to the ground, I scanned the area, unconsciously holding my breath. The Lamborghini was empty and the only sound was a burrowing owl talking to herself nearby. The stars and the distant glow from the city of Yucca Valley to the west provided the only illumination, yet I felt utterly exposed, as if I were being watched.

The fact that I had good reason to be paranoid didn't occur to me. I only thought of what would happen if Steale thought I'd followed him, if he caught me prowling around in black garb while he conducted his mysterious business.

On some level, I had already known. On another level, I had chosen to engage in the fine art of denial. Now the two worlds collided, smashing my idealism in the maelstrom.

Trying *not* to speculate, and relying on my years of training, I drew a few deep breaths, stayed low to the ground and moved away from the dirt road. Moving as quickly as possible, I made my way through the open desert toward the mouth of the trail that would lead toward Barker Dam. It took longer than it should have, and I was inundated with the fact that Steale had said he'd return to the studio at ten thirty. If he went there to find me gone, it could jeopardize everything I'd accomplished. Then again, his being *here* could easily have the same results.

But now more than ever, I had to know how he was involved - whether he was some lost soul from that other world, or a traveler like myself.

Eventually, after only one minor entanglement with a cholla, I reached the trail. Staying to one side, I sat down on a rock, drew the hunting knife from my belt, and cut away the cactus spines which had chewed their way into my shoe.

Sheathing the knife, I started to move again, then stopped abruptly when I heard approaching footsteps. Coming from the direction of the parking area, I determined there were two people walking a few feet apart.

Crouching low behind the rocks and peering over the top, I hoped the sound of my thundering heart wouldn't be audible. It took another minute before the two figures appeared at the mouth of the trail, and I was surprised to observe that Steale was not one of them. Both of the intruders were male, each of average height and build, dressed in casual clothing. Each carried a small duffel bag, and I could discern that the taller of the two wore glasses.

"...lot of money, Brannigan... son-of-a-bitch had better be telling the truth..."

I could make out only about half of what they were saying. The rest was swallowed by the peculiar acoustics of the desert.

"...you rather wait around here for the feds to show? ...starting over is the only chance I got left..."

It made no sense, though I began to discern more of their conversation as they made their way along the trail, passing no less than fifteen feet from my hiding place.

"Shit, Jackson, all I know is that it's the craziest thing I ever heard of," the one with the glasses said. "How was I supposed to know that the guy I hit was a DEA man?"

"We don't get paid to ask questions," Brannigan replied. "You take the money and you take your chance. I didn't know it either, or I never would have taken the job. Ain't hindsight grand?"

They laughed nervously.

"So how'd you meet this guy?" Jackson asked.

They were further away now, their words starting to fade.

"...found me... said he'd read about it in the paper... for a fee he could arrange passage out of the country..."

More laughter. "...the country? ...out of this goddamn world..."

"...just better be telling the truth... that's all I've got to say... didn't even *make* twenty five grand on the hit... lucky I had some stashed away...."

And that's all I heard, though it was more than I'd bargained for. From what I could make out, it was obvious they were assassins - whether from the mob or the CIA made no difference. And they were going somewhere. That, too, was obvious.

I didn't have to guess *where* they were going. They certainly weren't midnight hikers on their way to Barker Dam for the view.

I waited until they were out of sight, then started on my way again. It took forty five minutes to make the same hike I'd made that morning in less than half an hour. Prowling had its disadvantages. It slowed me down.

Eventually, however, still paralleling the trail some thirty feet to the east, I saw the dam and the rock face to the north. It occurred to me that I'd have to cross over the lower outcropping to the south, crawl along the top of the dam, and then start the climb up to a reasonable height for a vantage point. The journey wouldn't be difficult, but it would mean being out in the open for at least a full minute - the time it would take to cross the rocks and the top of the dam. And while black was normally the prescribed night color, the pale whiteness of the southern rock formation meant I'd stand out like a bug on a platter until I was across the dam.

It couldn't be helped and, knowing I had no alternatives, I scurried out from my hiding place and crawled along the top of the rocks on my stomach. Once I reached the southern tip of the dam, I squatted low and crawled on all fours to the other side, forcing myself not to look down. The drop wasn't severe, but it would terminate on jagged boulders if I made a wrong move.

Reaching the other side a few seconds later and taking care with the natural hand holds and crannies in the rocks, I skirted along a ledge of the huge granite formation until it started bending around to the northeast. It took another several minutes of careful climbing and one near-fall before I reached my destination.

The ledge widened with the curve of the rock and several smaller boulders formed a natural ladder to another ridge some twenty feet higher. Once I reached the top of the crest, my legs were trembling, my breath coming in irregular spurts. The climb was more difficult that I'd thought, yet it wasn't the reason for my exhaustion. For the first time since I'd killed Avery Madison, I was terrified.

Wedging myself between two stable boulders, I sat looking out over the desert below, my eyes gradually adjusting until I could make out the silhouette of the mountains, the long white snake which was the dry river bed, and the sound of voices coming from far away.

Squinting, I finally found the source. Walking in the middle of the wash I'd explored that morning were the two men I'd seen at the mouth of the trail. I couldn't understand what they were saying, only that they were talking in nervous tones.

I could detect no one else in the desert. But almost as that thought manifested, I suddenly saw another solitary figure walking toward the two men from further to the north. It occurred to me that the latest silhouette was already *beyond* where I had encountered the door to Synjin's world.

I shivered slightly at the implications. The silhouette of a man was in another world.

It took another minute before the solitary figure met up with the two assassins, and then there was a tense stillness as they spoke among themselves. Again, I couldn't discern their conversation, just a low rumble of male voices.

After that, the third man walked back in the direction he'd come while the two assassins stood utterly still in the middle of a mud wash in the middle of the desert. The man then disappeared out of sight behind a formation of rocks. I didn't want to believe it was Steale, yet my doubts were quickly disappearing. The lean body. The measured steps. The haunted aura of secrets and pain.

The night grew thicker and more eerie, the wind whipping through the crevices of the boulders where I was hidden, creating a night song that was somehow lonely and sad. I had started to wonder if the two assassins would simply stand there forever, perhaps the victims of some incredible scam, when I first sensed it.

That low rumbling again, almost inaudible at first, felt more than heard. After a few seconds, it became louder, like a clap of thunder from a clear sky. Almost immediately, the high-pitched whistle came again, deafening in its intensity. I wondered as I instinctively covered my ears how the two assassins could stand so near the source and still tolerate the sound at all. But as I looked at them, they seemed oblivious.

As the sound increased in pitch and volume, the low rumbling came once more, not as loud this time, like a purr in the chest of the Earth itself. Then the blue light was suddenly there, blinding, illuminating the entire valley and casting an eerie glow over the landscape which suddenly seemed alien, like some *Voyager* picture of Saturn.

While I looked on, the screaming whistle died down; the rumbling stopped; only the blue light remained. It was actually rectangular in shape, extending some twenty feet high and thirty feet across, pulsing like an irregular heartbeat. It was also three dimensional despite the fact that it looked to be the shape of a door laid on its side.

It was, I surmised as I stared at it, the same corridor I'd entered that morning - only somehow enhanced so as to be visible to the naked eye. It extended to the north for as far as I could see - beyond the bend of the dry river bed and through the jagged mountain itself. Where it terminated, I had no way of knowing.

My breath was coming in sporadic spurts, my eyes blinking against the powerful winds as I tried to make sense out of what I was seeing. I noticed that the two assassins, now easily visible in the brilliant blue light, had taken several steps back. One of them had even turned his back to the thing and covered his eyes with his arm.

And then I saw Steale. The way the lone man had walked, the cat-like silhouette dressed in black. Now, cast in pale blue light, there could be no mistake.

I stopped breathing.

He came through the corridor and into the desert, stopping as he drew up alongside the two terrified assassins. I couldn't hear what he said, but he gestured toward the blue light, his deep voice a murmur through the stillness.

The taller of the two hit men shook his head violently, arguing. The shorter one had taken another step back, and I wondered if they would both bolt, run back to sanity, and take their chances with the law. Indeed, that might well have happened had it not been for whatever it was that Steale did next.

I saw him reach around behind himself and retrieve something from the back of his pants. Then, pointing it toward the near-hysterical man, he pulled the trigger. There was no sound of a gunshot, not even the lethal pop of a silencer. But as I looked on, the horrified assassin slumped to the ground.

Steale kept the weapon aimed at the second man, and I heard what was said next quite well.

"You never said nothing about this!" the one I pegged as Jackson shouted, backing away. "Screw you, you crazy bastard! Just screw you!"

"You don't have much time!" Steale replied, also shouting as he gestured with the weapon toward the corridor. "Now pick up your buddy and get moving! You've got six minutes to get to the other side! If the door closes while you're in the passageway, you'll never get out! Now *go*!"

But Jackson continued backing away, shaking his head frantically. "Yeah? Well how do I know where that damn thing goes?" he shouted, almost shrill.

Steale was on him then, catching him by one arm and shoving him toward the entrance to the corridor. "We've been through this! Now get through there, or I'll shoot you, too, and leave you *both* to rot in the sun!"

"We had a deal!" Jackson protested, though I noticed that he wasn't offering much of a physical resistance as Steale forced him toward the corridor.

"That's right - and part of it includes that you get through there and don't come back!" Steale replied. "Now *move*!"

With that, he released the man's arm and shoved him toward Brannigan - who lay unmoving on the blue-lit desert sand. Jackson kept his head up as he watched Steale warily, but he managed to pick up his companion into a fireman's carry hold.

"You're crazy!" Jackson shouted. "He's dead!"

Whatever Steale replied to that, I'll never know, for he was back to speaking in a lower tone of voice. He jerked one finger toward the corridor, and as I looked on in shock, Jackson stepped into the light with his buddy thrown over his shoulder. He started walking, looking back only once, and then he was gone, running.

I couldn't tell whether he vanished into thin blue air, or if he merely moved out of my range of vision. I'd thought the corridor was transparent, but now I began to wonder. It had physical properties of some description, though I couldn't discern whether it was a solid anomaly or some ethereal tunnel of light leading between one world and another, maybe even between life and death.

For nearly a full minute, I continued looking down into the desert, my eyes riveted on Steale as he replaced the weapon into the back of his jeans, then stood there as if nothing at all were out of the ordinary, his body relaxed, his demeanor casual. He glanced down at his arm once, checking a watch, then went to lean on a rock, as cool and imperturbable as I'd always known him. This was not new to him.

After another few minutes, he checked the watch again. Then, miraculously, the blue light simply turned itself off the same way it had done when I'd observed from a much greater distance several nights before.

It took awhile for my eyes to adjust to the loss of the light, and when I was able to see again, I noticed Steale walking casually back toward the south - toward the trail and, eventually, his car.

It occurred to me to simply remain where I was and wait for him to drive away. Even from where I was sitting, I'd be able to hear the Lamborghini's engine when it fired to life. But as that thought struck me, it was interrupted by another. I'd parked my own car on the way to the Barker Dam area, and while I didn't think it would be noticed by casual late-evening hikers or even rangers on the night shift, Steale was a more trained observer.

If he found it where I'd left it, he'd guess where I'd gone, and if that happened, I'd probably end up like Brannigan.

Forcing myself to act, I looked down to see that he was walking at a leisurely pace, and I estimated that I had just enough time to get in front of him and stay two steps ahead.

I moved on instinct, scrambling back down the face of the rock, across the top of the dam and over the white-wash granite boulders until I crossed the trail. Distantly, I could hear Steale's footsteps coming up from the wash, crunching over the loose pebbles, climbing.

Taking care to make no sound, I made it to the far side of the trail and began retracing my previous path. I couldn't hope to stay ahead if I faltered at all, so I relied on blind luck to keep the sidewinders occupied somewhere else. I scrambled as quickly as stealthing would permit, realizing only when I reached the parking area that I'd lost track of Steale altogether. The last I'd heard was a soft crunching of booted feet about a quarter of a mile back.

Not taking any chances, I made a wide arc around his parked car. I'd have just enough time to get back to the Camaro and lay down a thick layer of dust before he reached the Lamborghini.

I heard nothing of him even as I came onto the dusty path that would emerge at Hidden Valley campground. It occurred to me that he might have stopped for some reason, or that he was in no hurry to get back to his car. He had no reason to think he wasn't alone.

But that thought didn't slow me down. I continued as quickly as possible until I was well away from the Barker Dam parking area. Then, knowing he would have no reason to walk any further than the Lamborghini, I stood up and began to jog, eventually breaking into more of a terrified sprint.

It took another couple of minutes to reach the car, and I still hadn't heard Steale's engine start. Jamming my hand into my jeans pocket, I grabbed the keys and fumbled to unlock the door.

"Please don't move, Lynne."

My eyes closed in automatic response to the dread that rattled through my stomach. My hand froze as my chi surged.

It was Steale's voice, less than fifteen feet away. Not close enough for a spinning roundhouse kick. Not far enough away to think I could outrun a bullet.

Swallowing the dryness in my throat, I turned very slowly toward him, not surprised to find him holding the same weapon on me that he'd used on Brannigan. I'd seen it before - in my studio the day we'd met. A sleek thing with a long silver barrel.

"You going to kill me, Steale?" I asked. At that moment, I could think of no logical reason why he shouldn't.

He shook his head, but didn't come closer. Instead, he adjusted something on the barrel of the gun. "No, I'm not going to kill you," he said, his voice level, controlled, cold. "But the effects of the drug aren't pleasant - especially if you try to struggle. It's best if you don't," he added with an out-of-place smile.

I drew a breath, hoping it wouldn't be my last. "For what it's worth, I already knew about the corridor." My voice wasn't working properly; the words came out as little more than a whisper as I gauged the distance between us, my hand poised over the knife.

He glanced down at his weapon again, making another adjustment. "I know," he said. Then, looking at me, he added, "You'll only be out for about twenty minutes. Long enough for me to figure out what to do with you. Sorry, Lynne. You didn't leave me much choice." He had the audacity to sound as if he meant it.

My muscles strained for action, yet I was too far away. "Why not just talk to me?" I asked, but even I could hear the fear in my voice. "Why not trust me, Steale? I'm on your side, remember?"

He shook his dark head, then aimed the weapon at my chest. "You'd probably kick my face in the first opportunity you got," he said, a wistful smile on his face.

He was probably right. I drew a deep breath and came to a decision. It was the only one possible, since it was obvious he had no intention of talking. Better to die in a blaze of fury than live in fear.

I launched myself toward him, both feet off the ground as I tried for a flying thrust kick. The ridiculous thought entered my mind that I didn't want to hurt him. If I could get him on the ground, disarm him, maybe reason could reach him.

But almost before I could take the first step, he pulled the trigger on the strange weapon, his hand not even trembling. Something impacted on my left shoulder and a moment of stunned disbelief flashed through me. Then I felt the sting, warmth spreading through my chest, reaching soft fingers into my mind. The bastard actually shot me.

"You son of a bitch!" I managed, hoping those indelicate words wouldn't be my last.

But it was already too late. My muscles turned to glue as I fell.

I was vaguely aware of fighting to hold my eyes open, looking up into the night to see Steale bending over me. He picked up my fallen car keys, then lifted me into his arms. I tried to struggle, but my head was growing heavier against his shoulder, my breathing becoming deeper.

"The more you fight it, the longer you'll be out," he warned with contradictory gentleness, perhaps in response to the disbelieving look in my eyes. "You can't win this one, so close your eyes and go to sleep."

Ridiculously, it sounded like a good idea.

An instant later, I was flying.

~

"Good," a soft-spoken voice stated. "It's about time you woke up."

Something cool was pressed against my lips and I drank instinctively. It made focusing slightly easier, and I realized I'd been staring at the overhead dome of the Lamborghini. I was in the passenger's seat, which had been fully reclined, and a hand was pressed against my shoulder.

Memory slowly seeped through the pores of returning consciousness and I recalled falling. Someone had picked me up. Steale. I groaned, my head moving from side to side as if of its own volition.

"Better?"

Than what? I wondered. I struggled, but he held me back against the seat.

"Trust me," Steale's voice said, slightly amused. "You don't want to sit up just yet. Give it a minute."

The world was still spinning in at least three different directions and my head throbbed. But as some semblance of rational thought returned, the pounding behind my eyes lessened and I was able to focus. I found myself looking up into his face to find a grim expression residing behind the mask of a smile.

"You bastard," I commented without raising my voice.

His brows lifted and, reaching over me, he did something which caused the seat to raise to a more comfortable angle.

I noticed then that my wrists were hand-cuffed together, and that a second set of cuffs, attached to the first, extended over to the door. I was secured to a steel bar just below the arm rest by both hands and ankles.

"So what now?" I asked sarcastically. "A tomb of rocks in the Mojave or a shallow grave in the low desert?"

Steale laughed, shaking his head. "What I had in mind was more along the lines of driving you out to my place, pouring some coffee into you, and trying to figure out what you were doing out there tonight."

I couldn't help but laugh at that. When you really believed you were about to die, it wasn't scary any more. It was just a matter of when. And how.

"I might ask the same thing," I commented.

A deep sigh pressed through Steale's lips. "Look, Lynne, you can stay pissed off if it'll make you feel better, but if I'd wanted you dead, we wouldn't be having this conversation. I could just as easily have killed you with an overdose."

He had a point, but I was too angry to care. "Uncuff me, Steale," I snapped, yanking the bonds tight until my wrists ached.

He leaned over me until we were alarmingly close. "And if I do, you'll either jump out of the car and I'll have to shoot you again, or else you'll start a fight that I can't win." He paused, eyes sparking danger and devilment all at the same time. "Personally, I like the odds better the way they are."

Infuriated, I yanked on the cuffs again.

"You want to tear up your wrists, be my guest," Steale invited. "But it won't change anything."

I subsided back against the seat and turned to look at him. It took every ounce of control I could muster to center my chi, and even then the balance was precarious at best.

"All right," I said, taking a breath. "It's your move." I wanted to know more, yet I was also afraid to know more. For the first time, I was afraid of *him*.

He studied me as if not quite trusting me. I wouldn't have trusted me either. "I'll uncuff you, but only if you swear on your honor that you won't try anything."

I thought about that, then nodded.

But he didn't move to fulfill his end of the bargain. "That includes not opening the car door, not taking a swing or a kick at me, and not trying to get away once we get to my house." He paused to let that sink in. "Deal?"

"Yes!" I snapped.

"On your honor," he demanded.

I didn't like being pushed, but my alternatives were severely limited. "On my honor, Steale," I agreed miserably. Now I was bound by those words.

He studied me for a moment longer, then reached into a pocket of his jeans to retrieve a key. Leaning over me, he uncuffed my ankles first, then my wrists. I didn't make a move. Instead, looking over at him when he settled back in his seat, I noticed we were parked just inside the entrance to the Hidden Valley campground.

For nearly a full minute, we simply stared at one another. Then, sighing, Steale shook his head. "You know, I was going to tell you tonight anyway. I'm sorry if I hurt you."

My lips pressed together. "I'm all right." But every muscle in my body was trembling.

"You sure?"

"Yes, already!" I said begrudgingly.

A few moments later, he started the engine and pulled the car back onto the road, glancing at me occasionally as he drove. He didn't speak, and I was surprised when he reached over the console between us to touch my arm.

Not wanting his touch, I pulled away. Or maybe I wanted it too much.

My reaction seemed to hurt him, though it didn't stop him. He slid his fingers down my arm until he took my hand. "Just relax," he told me in a voice which was a gentle contradiction to his nature.

To my surprise and a moment of horror, I felt my body doing just that as dizziness overtook me. A strange lethargy came over me when he squeezed my hand and the tension and fear left my body. My head relaxed against the soft leather seat, my eyes wanting to close. For a split second, I thought he'd drugged me again, but that fear dissipated an instant later.

I understood it then, without the complications of emotions.

Steale was from that other world. Now there could be no doubt. And he possessed the same gift as Synjin. Telepathy. A suggestion could become reality, as his suggestion for me to relax resulted in my body obeying him. In that way, I was powerless against him.

"Damn you," I heard my voice saying, as if from a great distance.

He laughed softly, keeping the pressure on my hand as he drove on into the night. I felt my breathing even out. Against his telepathic magic, I had no chance - or desire - to fight or run.

"In answer to your question: no, I'm not from around here," he said with amusement.

No shit. It was easier now - easier to accept it all. Another effect of the telepathy. I was drifting, almost pleasantly. I couldn't even be pissed at him anymore.

In what I estimated to be another ten minutes, the engine slowed as the car pulled into a long driveway. A moment later, he released my hand, turned off the ignition, and got out.

My head was starting to clear when he opened my door and offered a hand to steady me as I slid my legs out and stood up. I felt like hell, and had he not caught me, I would have fallen. My head spun. Even the dim light of the stars burned my eyes.

I noticed that the house was one I'd seen before. Located about half-way between Highway 62 and the entrance to the monument, it was an oversized dark-wood-shingle creation of unusual design. Against the backdrop of the sky were odd angles and dark windows, an intriguing structure I'd admired on my hikes into town for supplies years before.

Once inside, he guided me toward a sofa, gestured for me to sit down, then stood looking at me for a moment.

"Want something to drink?" he asked, hardly seeming like the ogre I'd made him out to be earlier.

"No." I didn't want anything from him right then, but my throat felt like fluffy cotton.

He left me alone, disappearing around a wall and into what I assumed was the kitchen. I heard him scrambling around in a cupboard, water running, the sound of a microwave door opening, cups rattling. He obviously hadn't taken no for an answer, and if I'd looked at myself in a mirror, I wouldn't have blamed him.

His absence gave me time to look around the room, and I was grudgingly impressed with what I saw. The place looked like a magazine spread on eccentric millionaires. A black leather sofa and matching love seat formed an L-shaped area toward the middle of the room, with a free-form wooden coffee table in the center. The table itself was actually a hollowed-out tree trunk, and in its center, under glass, several lush plants grew green and healthy. The shades on the lamps were obviously hand-made, stained glass depicting intricate dragonflies skirting over a still lake. A gas fireplace sat in the corner.

Along the wall which butted up against the foyer where we'd entered, Steale had a magnificent collection of martial arts weapons. An intricately carved *bo* hung on the wall, the faces of dragons peering out from a forest of leaves. There were shurikens, nunchaku, two steel sai, a three-sectional staff, Samurai swords, and an assortment of other weapons I'd only seen in books.

He was an enigma in more ways than one. He probably stayed up late working on it.

A few seconds later, he came back carrying two steaming cups. I recognized the scent of the tea as chamomile - an herb which produced calming effects.

I took the cup without comment, not flinching when he sat down next to me on the sofa. He set his cup on the glass table top, looking over at me as he leaned back against the arm of the couch.

"Better?" he asked, a faint smile curving his lips upward.

I hadn't decided how to feel about it yet. "Care to tell me what that was all about tonight?"

He fiddled with his tea cup. "I seem to recall your saying you knew about the corridor just before I shot you."

Whatever I'd said at the time was gone. "Speaking of which, that was a shitty thing to do."

He laughed aloud, surprising me as he did so often. "Probably. But I wasn't going to stand around and wait for you to rearrange my face." He paused, then took the gun out of its shoulder holster and placed it on the coffee table. "I keep it around for people like Brannigan. Some folks have a tendency to panic, and for obvious reasons, I couldn't let him change his mind about leaving."

"How *did* you get in front of me?" It wasn't an important question, but I didn't like mysteries.

He shrugged, then extended his wrist. On it was what appeared to be a common watch. "It takes a licking and keeps on ticking," he commented with a grin.

"You watch too much TV," I muttered.

He shrugged. "Probably. Anyway, I knew where you were from the minute you crossed the dam and climbed up on that ledge."

A strange sense of destiny had settled in my blood. "Then why didn't you do something sooner? You obviously didn't intend for me to find out about your little operation."

"You would have found out eventually anyway," he conceded. "There wasn't much point in me climbing all the way up there to get you down when I could just take a couple of short cuts and meet you back at your car."

He had a point. He was a wild card in a deck of jokers. If he were one of The People - and I knew he could be nothing else - he was like none I had ever met or imagined. They were a gentler breed. They had reason. They had honor.

He caught me studying him.

"You're thinking that I don't fit in with your image," he said, startling me with the eerie accuracy of his perceptions.

I looked away but didn't deny it. "What else *can* I think?"

"You could stop judging me and just listen to what I have to say," he suggested.

I started to protest, then made a concentrated effort to hold my silence. Looking up at him, I tried not to fear him.

He sensed my wariness, leaning closer. Then, taking me by both shoulders, he turned me until my back was to him. He began a skilled, deep massage, not stopping even when I tried to pull away. I think he knew I didn't really want to.

"I'm willing to be totally honest with you, Lynne," he said. "But it has to work both ways. If I tell you who I am and what I do, I have to know you meant what you said yesterday."

I frowned. His hands had a way of making memories vague. "What did I say?"

"That you'll still be here," he reminded.

"You mean I have a choice?" I asked, my voice sharper than I'd intended.

"If you want to leave, I'll take you back to your car," he offered with obvious disappointment. "But I hope you'll stay. There's a lot at stake."

"Such as?" I asked. I couldn't help it; my words were clipped, cold. I didn't like that in myself. Regardless of what he'd done, I didn't sense malevolence in him - just frustration, chaos, and a very genuine human fear. He was the trickster.

It softened me a little, forcing me to remember that I was still his teacher. I'd said a lot of words with high ideals - words about friendship. If I didn't live by them, I couldn't very well expect him to either.

He didn't reply for a long time. Instead, he continued rubbing my back and shoulders, letting his sorcery work on me. When he did speak, he was more in character: he avoided my question.

"Come in the kitchen with me and I'll fix us some dinner," he offered.

I almost laughed when I realized that I was hungry. Cataclysmic events normally dulled the appetite, but I was starved.

Making an effort not to judge him, I followed him through the living room and around the wall which led into the kitchen. The room was compact and efficient. Decorated in dark wood and virgin-white tile, it was a striking contradiction - much like its owner.

He gestured toward a small dinette which was located in one of the peculiar cut-aways of the house. From the outside, it would have looked something like a bay-window with a view to the east. Now, gazing out the tinted glass, I could see only my own reflection and one distant light from another house.

Steale went to the refrigerator, rummaged around, then stood looking at me over the counter. "I can either do some stir-fry vegetables, or I've got some of those frozen lasagna things that I could throw in the microwave," he offered.

He seemed out of place in a kitchen, but who didn't? "Throw the lasagna in the microwave," I suggested.

After unwrapping the two pre-packaged items, he put them into the microwave and turned it on. Then, pouring us each another cup of tea, he came over to the table and sat down.

There was an awkward moment as we looked at one another, glanced away, tried again, failed, and finally sat staring out the window. It occurred to me that we were both behaving like clumsy teenagers, and I made the move to bring an end to it.

Forcing myself to look into his eyes, I refused to look away even when I wanted to. "Let's just agree that this isn't going to be easy for either one of us. Maybe then we can both get through the night."

He nodded, mirroring my nervous smile. Then, taking a sip of his tea, he sat looking out over the desert for a moment. "I do what I do because it's the only thing I know *how* to do," he said quietly, warming his hands on the sides of the tea cup. He wasn't looking at me when he spoke. "I'll tell you why some day, but for now, I just want you to understand what."

"That's fair," I agreed. "Tell me about those two men tonight."

He looked out over the desert again. "Michael Brannigan and Richard Jackson. To make a long story short, they're a couple of cheap thugs who make their living doing clean-up work for anyone with enough money to hire them."

I came to the conclusion I'd already made at the dam. "You mean they were assassins."

"Among other things," he agreed, then gestured his words aside with one hand. "I don't know a lot about them; it's not my job."

I took my cue. "And what *is* your job?"

He went back to staring at his own reflection in the window. "I guess you could say I'm a travel agent," he said without humor.

"For a fee, you help criminals make the perfect get-away," I translated.

He looked at me as incredulity came to his eyes. "Not just criminals," he said without inflection. "I've arranged transportation for people who just want to disappear, too. A few days ago, I did some charity work - three women whose husbands were abusers. Earlier this month, a woman came to me with a four-month-old baby. I helped her get away, too."

I thought about myself, my past, Dr. Madison. "There was a time a few years ago when I could have used your services myself."

"Yeah," he said. "I know."

My stomach knotted. "You do?"

"I know who you are," he said with an easy chuckle.

I didn't want to be bluffed into saying something I might regret later. "And who am I?"

He held my eyes without flinching. "You're River Willows." Then, before I could speak again, he gestured me to silence. "For what it's worth, I didn't know at first - not when I first came to the studio."

I waited.

He sighed with seeming unconcern. "Don't worry - nothing I found would mean anything to anybody else."

I considered that, hoping he was right. "Go on."

Tilting his head back, he stared up at the ceiling for a moment. He was a study in contrasts and angles, yin and yang.

"As you know, I studied with Jerry Davin a couple years back. I hung around the studio a lot, got to know most of the other students. I would remember you if you'd been there. You weren't."

I frowned. "I never said I was."

"No, but I've seen how you and Jerry are with one another. He thinks you walk on water."

My puzzlement grew. "I don't follow."

He held my gaze as he spoke, his eyes mischievous. "When I was studying with him, he always had current issues of all the martial arts magazines in the studio. A lot of them went back a few years, and since I had about three thousand years worth of catching up to do on martial arts history, I borrowed them one night." He chuckled. "After awhile, I started noticing that several of them always fell open to articles about you."

"And from that you made the connection?"

"I didn't make the connection until this afternoon," he said. "Oh, I'd suspected, but I wasn't sure until I came out of the dressing room and saw you practicing the Dragon by yourself."

"What do you mean?"

"Student's observation."

I laughed, remembering the words that had passed between us earlier. "Oh?"

"One of those old articles was an interview with your former teacher... I don't remember his name... sorry."

"Master Barrows?"

Steale nodded. "When the interviewer asked Barrows how you approached the Art, he said that one of the most important things in your kata was the fluidity of movement - and that that's why you could move like the wind... something like that."

I was embarrassed at the praise. "And from that one comment I made in the studio this afternoon, you put all the pieces together." It explained why he'd looked at me so strangely when I'd said it.

Smiling, he sipped his tea. "I knew Jerry had always been fascinated with River Willows. Hell, he used to have this female black belt in one of his classes, and he was always riding her to study your methods. It's obvious that he's in love with you, River."

Now I *was* embarrassed. Apparently, a lot more mystique had been built around my past than I had ever realized. "That still isn't much to go on, Steale," I said, uncomfortable talking about Jerry.

Steale just laughed. "Actually, I wasn't one hundred percent sure until an hour ago."

"An hour ago?" I repeated.

Reaching out, he placed one hand over mine and I felt the distant brush of his mind.

"Telepathy usually cuts through the pretenses," he said with a devilish wink.

He had a point. "Oh."

I started to say something, but the microwave chirped.

Steale remained seated for a moment longer, our eyes locked together. "Don't go away," he said with an easy smile. "I nuke a mean lasagna."

He still thought I was going to bolt. I had to admit the thought had crossed my mind.

~

"So," he said after we'd finished the meal and pushed our plates aside, "tell me how this all started for you."

He already knew most of it, and if he hadn't turned me in, it stood to reason that he had other plans. And for a strictly irrational reason, I was starting to trust him.

I told him about the drowning, the strange events at the hospital, the fact that I'd killed a man, and concluded with how I'd met Jerry Davin and opened the studio. I left out the parts with Ch'en Po and Synjin, however, not seeing a need to bring it up. *'Tell no one about me. Tell no one about Synjin'*. It was a secret which was becoming harder - and perhaps even more important - to keep.

When I'd finished, he poured another cup of tea and we sat looking at one another with the safe buffer zone of the table between us.

"You've done well," he commented.

"I've had a lot of good fortune on my side. That helped." I looked at him once again. Throughout dinner, he'd relaxed a little, and though the dark aura of pain was still in his eyes - would probably always be there - the set of his shoulders had loosened, the tension in his hands was diminishing. "Your turn now. Tell me about how you came to be here."

He smiled wistfully. "You might not like it."

He had the uncanny ability to give me chills with the most unexpected statements. "I like *you*," I reminded him. "I'd just like to hear what made you who you are."

He leaned back until the dining chair tilted up on two legs. Then, rocking forward, he began toying with his half-full tea cup, running one long finger around the rim as he spoke.

"Where I'm from," he said slowly, almost as if discussing it for the first time, "I used to be an Argus - what someone in this world might think of as a police officer." He shrugged, looking at himself in the window again, looking at the darkness beyond. In that moment, I was surprised he had a reflection at all, for he was more like some haunted and tragic immortal than any human I had ever met.

"Remember when I said I knew about the corridor?"

He nodded.

I chose my words carefully. "I've been into your world, Steale," I told him at last. "One of my Masters is from there - at least I think that's where he's from."

"You're a traveler." He didn't seem surprised.

I took a sip of my tea. "That's what I've been told. Anyway, I travel into your world in my sleep - in dreams," I clarified. He was a telepath. Maybe my yammerings about astral travel wouldn't seem so strange to him. "That's where I met the Old Woman."

"The Old Woman?"

"Yeah. She's the one who matched me with one of The People," I tried to explain.

"Is that what you call us?" he asked with a smile.

It was infectious. "That's what I called you when I was seventeen," I confessed. "Anyway, this Old Woman - or my image of her, I guess - was some sort of a matchmaker... or something like that."

Steale nodded knowingly. "You're talking about Chalyn Thorn. I met her once... a long time ago."

I waited.

"She'd been confined to a wheelchair for over half her life," he explained then. "She became a gifted psychic after some sort of fire in her house half killed her. She started this match-making thing. People would come to her for a consultation and she'd go into her meditation chamber for days at a time. When she came out, she usually had some sort of insight into the future."

I studied Steale for a long time, thinking about what he'd said. "Did she find Kirin for you?"

Nodding, he bent his head down and rested it on his arms, his face turned toward the window. "Kirin had gone to her for a reading, I guess. My first awareness of her was when I got this call from Chalyn telling me that she had to see me." He laughed to himself. "It would be the same thing as if you got a call from the president telling you your presence was needed as a matter of national security. Whether you agreed with his politics or not, you'd probably go, just to hear what he had to say. Chalyn was a bit of a legend in my world – probably still is."

I smiled, watching the top of his head. Other than his reflection in the window, it was all I could see of him. "You didn't believe in her abilities?"

"I'd just never given it much thought. Where psychic things were concerned, I always figured they were better left to psychics." When he spoke again, his voice grew softer, more distant. "But Chalyn made a believer out of me. She told me about Kirin, and said that we'd meet when we were twenty-five." There was a far-away sadness in his eyes. Then, lifting his head, he looked at me with a curious openness that I hadn't seen in him before. "What did she tell you?"

"She said that I'd be with my mate before the midnight of my thirtieth birthday," I said at last.

Steale nodded thoughtfully. "Mind if I ask how old you are now?"

"I'm twenty-eight. I'll be twenty-nine in May - nine more months, I guess."

"Have you met him yet?" he asked.

"Once - in a dark room for five minutes."

"Sounds interesting."

"It was," I agreed. "But there was a strong warning in what the Old Woman said, too. She made it clear that we couldn't be together until I turned thirty."

Steale frowned. "Any idea why?"

"Not really. My Master's fond of telling me my path is here until then."

"And after that?"

"I don't know. I wish I did."

Steale perused me for several long moments. "Do you love him?" he asked, his voice soft and tender.

It was the most personal question I'd ever been asked, but I answered without hesitation. "Yes."

"I don't doubt it," he said, surprising me slightly. "I mean, I've never known Chalyn to make a mistake."

I was relieved to hear it. "Want to tell me about Kirin?"

It took him a long time to begin, but when he did, I knew his words were sincere.

"She was a lot like you," he began. "Not so much in physical appearance, but in the way she looked at things." He started running his finger around the rim of his tea cup again. "She was a research scientist at a prominent university. She was working on a variety of projects, and was asked by our government to go on the first probe we launched into your world. We were both just about to turn twenty-six when she found out there was a position on the probe for a security person. That's how I got involved."

"Probe?" I repeated, curious. "What kind of probe?"

"Our scientists first discovered how to penetrate the barrier into your world in what would have been the mid-Forties, your time," he explained. "Not being a physicist myself, I can't tell you exactly how it's done, but it has something to do with rearranging the quantum super-structure of space so that it's an exact match between here and there."

I considered that, thinking back on all the science fiction movies I'd watched as a kid. "You mean something like an interdimensional door?"

"Similar," he confirmed. "There have always been legends in my world about places were people can interact with different races. Fairy legends; stories about people who would disappear into some enchanted world. Sometimes they came back; sometimes they didn't. They exist here, too, right? The legends?"

"Sure."

"Anyway, there were certain places in my world where these so-called encounters and disappearances were more common," he continued. "So some of our best scientists began investigating the phenomena - which led to the development of certain types of sensor equipment. From that, they were able to discover that there are places and conditions in nature which cause a weakness in the structure between this world and mine."

"In other words, the fabric of space is weaker in some spots than in others," I offered, recalling Ch'en Po's explanation.

"Exactly." He poured himself another cup of tea. "It's more common for these doorways to appear in remote locations. Places that are eternal - like the desert or the mountains, remote regions of the jungles. Those places don't change much. And as a result, certain areas co-exist in both places at the same time. At least that's how I understand it. But when cities start springing up, it's just natural for the human mind - in your world *or* mine - to build walls against what it can't explain. Sooner or later, the doorways close, or people stop seeing them anyway."

I tried to follow him and wasn't sure I could. Certainly not after all that had already happened that night.

He looked up at me, then continued slowly. "The physicists and the engineers figured out how to actually *create* these doorways. That first probe was launched through one of those corridors."

"And it's also how you send people from my world into yours?"

He was looking out the window again and didn't answer my direct question. "It was called Project Gateway, one of the missions Kirin worked on. I just appropriated some of the equipment after..." His voice trailed off and he shook his head to dismiss the topic. "They left a lot of their equipment behind," he rephrased.

I wasn't sure what had happened to Kirin, yet it was obvious that what*ever* it was had torn a hole through his heart, maybe even through his soul. I ached for him, for the loss that had destroyed so much of his life.

"Care to tell me *why* you do it?" I asked.

He seemed about to speak, then glanced at the clock on the kitchen wall. "You tired?"

"Not terribly. You?"

He fidgeted and I knew he was uncomfortable with the conversation.

"Yeah," he said, not looking at me. "I could use some sleep."

I didn't let his sudden silence disturb me. After what we'd already shared, we were committed. At least that's what I wanted to believe.

Reaching across the table, I rested one hand on top of his. "I should go," I offered. "Take me back to my car. We'll talk more tomorrow."

He didn't look up, just kept staring out the window. "Stay here tonight." It wasn't a request.

I didn't argue, not keen on the idea of letting him out of my sight. Even though he'd told me a lot, I wouldn't have put it past him to simply vanish into his own version of thin blue air.

"All right," I said with a soft smile. "I'll take the couch."

At that, he *did* look up, his eyes sparkling a sudden mischief. "Like hell," he said.

For once, I had no answer. I sat there, speechless, then looked away. My stomach fluttered.

He stood and came around the table, placing both hands on my shoulders, pushing me down into my chair and causing me to shiver beneath his touch. Then, leaning over me, he murmured something close to my ear. "If you don't trust yourself, then trust me," he suggested, devilment in his voice. "I promise not to start anything if you do."

That could be taken either one of two ways. It also scared the hell out of me. Not because I *didn't* trust him, but because I *did*. He had a distinct advantage that I didn't have; I felt that pleasant laziness seeping into my blood again as he used his telepathic ability once more. It left me lethargic, comfortable, almost entranced.

"Damn you, Steale," I whispered, the tension leaving my body as he forced it away.

He laughed deep in his chest, then gave me back control of my body. "Old habits die a slow death. Sorry."

I breathed deeply, entranced by the warmth of his hands, the strength of his aura, the darkness of his power. "Don't apologize."

He continued touching me, but only with his hands, no longer with his aura, his mind. "Look, River," he said gently, "I just don't want to be alone right now. Humor me?"

I understood that very well, and realized I didn't want to be alone either. I acquiesced without speaking, and allowed him to guide me down the hall and into the bedroom before I could change my mind.

Like the rest of the house, it was decorated in a deep forest green, the walls felt close and comforting. The over-sized bed had four huge posts and was covered with a white goose-down comforter. It looked more like a nest than any bed I'd ever seen, and I had the amusing but disturbing thought that the trickster had lured me to his lair.

I stood in the middle of the floor, unconsciously folding my arms across my chest. The large window which faced the southwest was open, allowing the warm night air to waft in on little gusts that lifted the black drapes and caused them to dance like restless spirits.

Turning toward me, he looked me up and down with a smile. "You can start by unfolding your arms," he said, mirroring words back at me that I'd used on him in the studio.

My face darkened, but I let my arms fall back to my sides. Not knowing what to do with them, I stuffed my hands into the pockets of my jeans. I admit it, I was nervous, scared and downright inexperienced with men on a personal level.

I'd certainly never slept with one.

Steale moved easily around the room, going to a large walk-in closet and coming back with a soft white cotton shirt with long sleeves. He handed it to me - tossed it in my direction, actually. It was followed by a pair of black sweat pants.

"You can sleep in those," he said, gesturing to the north side of the room. "The bathroom's down the hall and to the right."

I took the clothes and after a muttered, "Thanks," disappeared into the sanctuary of the hall. I found the guest bath and closed the door behind me, leaning against the wall.

I didn't like that my legs were trembling or that my heartbeat sounded ominously loud. I also didn't like the fact that Steale could have so much power over me. The fact remained that I *allowed* him that power, that control. I'd given him my word, made promises on my honor. Knowing he could snatch my reason right out of my head left me more vulnerable than I'd ever felt – yet it was a vulnerability that held no fear, no hesitation.

Taking a moment to compose myself, I turned on the faucet and splashed cool water on my face. It didn't help much. It certainly didn't make the world any clearer. I took a towel from the rack, dried myself, then started to undress. But as I peeled off my t-shirt, I wasn't surprised to find desert sand in unexpected places. The climb up the side of the mountain hadn't helped, nor had falling face-first into the dirt after I'd been shot with the tranq bullet.

After removing my shoes and finding more sand, I made the only choice I could. Turning on the water in the shower, I wrapped a towel around myself, opened the bathroom door and stuck my head out.

"I'm borrowing some of your water," I called down the hall.

There was no response at first, then he came to the bedroom door. Sticking his head around the corner, he smiled. "Just put it back when you're done. Otherwise I'll have to charge you for it."

His casual attitude allowed me to relax. "How much?" I asked, enjoying the rapport between us.

His eyes sparkled playfulness as he disappeared back around the corner without answering.

Grimacing, I closed the door again, found the stash of clean towels, then finished undressing and stepped under the warm spray of water. By the time I'd rinsed my hair of the conditioner I found under the sink, I felt somewhat better physically even if not altogether settled mentally. I stepped out of the tub and wrapped one towel around my body, another around my head, then slipped into the shirt Steale had given me, fastening all but the top two buttons. It hung almost to mid-thigh, causing me to realize how tall he was. It also smelled like him - an alien sandalwood scent that clung like some exotic oil. Under other circumstances, it would have intoxicated me. As it was, it made me uncomfortable with my own thoughts. Again.

For a moment, I allowed myself to simply enjoy it, burying my face in the collar and inhaling the essence of him which defied all explanation. Finally, I climbed into the too-long sweat pants, drew a deep breath, and rubbed the towel over my head again for good measure. My hair hung almost to the middle of my back now, still a sandy blonde mane that had its own agenda. Wet, it was going to be a problem.

Running my fingers through it to remove the tangles, I opened the medicine cabinet and looked around until I found a pack of unopened combs. There was also an unopened package with a toothbrush, and a tube of toothpaste.

It occurred to me when I was finished that I had nothing left to do but return to the bedroom. It took another minute of talking to myself to actually do it, but I eventually padded back down the hall, leaving my clothes folded on the vanity.

When I came to the bedroom door, I heard the sound of running water and smiled to myself. It was another few minutes before the bathroom door opened and Steale came out, preceded by a rush of steam.

I'd sat in one of the chairs along the wall and was pretending to read a magazine I found on the dresser, but I glanced up automatically when he came back into the room. Instinct caused me to look away the moment I noticed that he was wearing only a pair of ragged cut-off shorts. His chest and legs were bare, his hair still moist from the shower. My face heated - something to which I was unaccustomed.

Admonishing myself for the childish reaction, I drew a deep breath and looked up into his eyes. He was standing at the foot of the bed, his weight tilted onto his right leg, gazing down at me with that unreadable smile. I had the unnerving thought that he was an animal spirit in a man's body – all angles and bone and raw male power, alien and human at the same time.

It didn't matter that I was the teacher and he the student. It didn't matter that the temple was in my blood, my strength and my protection. Steale could tear through those defenses and roles as if they were a spider's fragile web. He could rip my heart from my chest and devour it without effort.

And I would have let him – for somewhere along the way I had surrendered to my fate, to my destiny, to the dark and winding road that was my path.

Without any preamble, I knew then what was going to happen, and that knowledge left me light-headed, as if I'd suddenly stepped into a daydream that had never been even a possibility until that moment. What surprised me most of all was that I *wanted* it to happen.

His smile broadened and he turned down the comforter down to reveal cobalt blue sheets and king-sized pillows with black cases. Then, sitting on the edge, he slid his long legs under the covers, lacing his fingers behind his neck and lifting his head to look at me with the sheets pulled up to his waist.

It was a bed, I told myself. A place to sleep. No different than the air mattress in my tent or the cot I'd finally put in the back of the studio. No different.

A *lot* different. *He* was in it.

I concealed my apprehension behind a smile, got up, and went to his side.

The corners of his lips were dancing with amusement.

Reaching out, he took me by the hand and pulled me to him until I was sitting on the edge of the bed. The scent of him, fresh from the shower, was crisp and clean and cool. The heat of him was a contradictory fire – musk and spice and all things masculine.

The feel of my hand in his steadied my nerves only a little. He must have seen the apprehension in my eyes, for he tightened his grip, though whether to impart reassurance or prevent me from bolting, I was never certain.

Our eyes met, and I understood on some deeply intuitive level that he was just as scared as I was – even if for different reasons. Something had hurt him. Badly. If he could trust me enough to share this kind of intimacy, I knew I had to trust him enough to do the same.

"I – just so you know... I've never been with a man, Steale."

His eyes glistened with mischief. "That's okay. Neither have I."

I couldn't believe he said that – but it was the right thing at the right moment, breaking the tension and causing me to laugh at myself and my uncharacteristically girlish nervousness.

The next thing I knew, he had activated some sensor on the head of the bed and the lights dimmed until it was almost dark. As my eyes adjusted, there was just enough light to mimic the glow of a crescent moon. Though I hadn't seen him turn on the stereo, soft chords of music filled the room – a piece I occasionally played in the studio to facilitate meditation.

We were suspended in some perfect moment outside of time and far to the left of normal space. The desert night winds blew through the open window and as I gazed out into the stillness, a feeling of calm came over me while I looked at the stars setting behind a range of mountains.

Steale made no attempt to rush. Instead, he lay there looking up at me, letting time and space find their natural balance.

I closed my eyes, pleasantly surrounded by the music and the feeling that I had accomplished a great task by remaining alive until that late hour of the day. There had been more than one moment when it had seemed unlikely. I had cornered the coyote, though now it appeared the coyote had cornered me, living up to his reputation as the trickster by letting me believe I had ever been in control of my own fate.

He was a mystery painted in shadows and silhouettes. The beauty of him was so intense it had taken my reason away, causing the world to stop.

With an ease of movement that was astonishing, he slid one arm behind my shoulders and pulled me down next to him, so close I could feel the slow, measured beat of his heart. Giving myself over to his power, I lay in his arms, basking in the alien heat and strength of him. His cheek brushed my neck, nuzzling with a playful insistence that was rendered dangerously masculine by the roughness of his ever-present 5 o'clock shadow. He was the incarnation of everything erotic, everything carnal. He was temptation and the promise of salvation all at once.

Or maybe I was simply a delirious virgin in the unrelenting arms of the devil.

He toyed with me that way for a long time – his hands running up and down my back, cupping my face as he tormented me with seductive nibbles and nips that soon had me on the edge of a different kind of abyss.

When he finally pushed me down into the thick mattress and straddled my hips while holding my wrists gently pinned, I looked up into his face in the dim glow and understood for the first time how two mortal beings could complete one another, how the merging of two into one made both greater than the sum of their individual parts.

Leaning over me, he traced the outline of my ear with the tip of his tongue, the heat of his breath causing my body to surge with wanting him, craving the completion we both needed so desperately.

"Say my name," he whispered – not a request but a command.

I could deny him nothing. "Steale," I murmured. It was the one word that had been on my mind since he first wandered into my studio. "*Steale...*"

His name was the essence of him, and with the echo of that single syllable still on my mouth, he kissed me for the first time. A cautious brush of lips to lips at first, giving way to a darker demand when his tongue slipped inside my mouth and caused my body to arch up off the bed as if possessed by the spirit of some tantric sprite.

Our worlds collided then – and there was no discerning where one ended and the other began. Unfastening the buttons on my shirt – *his* shirt – he slid it from my shoulders, gazing down at me in the quasi-darkness with the eyes of a perfect predator, the essence of something not quite wild, yet never-to-be-tamed.

The warm desert air blew over my body, caressing my breasts. He touched me there, too – with reverence, with tenderness, but also with a raw passion that left me breathless. It occurred to some distant corner of my mind that I *wanted* him to take command – for clearly he was confident and experienced in areas where my own knowledge was sorely lacking.

"Touch me," he said, so soft it might have been my imagination whispering against my ear. But I touched him anyway, running my palms over the flat musculature of his chest. His body was smooth, and remarkably devoid of hair – a trait common among The People – and when I traced one fingertip over the erect nipple, his dark head arched backward and a low murmur of arousal purred softly in his chest.

"*Yes*... touch me."

His voice created a raging turmoil in my body, something I hadn't felt since the day I'd met Synjin. And since that day, I'd grieved for my mate, longing for a missed touch, a shy kiss that had ended too quickly, an embrace that couldn't be simulated by clutching a pillow to my chest each night as I slept.

Steale was *there*. He was *real*. His touch could heal the damage time had done to me, as I hoped I could heal a small fragment of the loneliness he had suffered.

At his command, I touched him. The contours of his back, still damp from the shower. The planes of his olive-skinned shoulders. And when I touched him, the sensations echoed in my own body as he mirrored my explorations until we were both beyond words. Mouths colliding. Clothing shed until we lay naked together with only the stars and the wind to witness our madness.

"I'm afraid." The words fell unbidden from my lips in between our kisses. Afraid it would end. Afraid I was dreaming. Afraid I wasn't.

Seeming to know what I meant, he held me tighter. "So am I," he confessed, and bit at the tender flesh of my neck until I was delirious, my hands tightening on his back to pull him to me.

His heat grew more intense as he pressed the full length of his body against mine, drawing me into a tight embrace. In the semi-darkness of his lair, he knelt before me, a sorcerer conjuring the wind to cease, time to stop, the world to end.

Then, settling his weight down over me, he brought us together in a union that took my breath away and caused me to cry out with the unparalleled joy and simultaneous anguish of being filled so completely with the divine presence of another living being.

We fit together like moon and penumbra, pain and pleasure, yin and yang. My body welcomed him as if it had always known him, and he took sanctuary within me as if coming in out of a storm.

We lay together without moving, just the synchronized rocking of our hearts to remind us we were still human at all. The breath of him against my neck was like a drug. Lifting my face to his kiss, I caught his lower lip between my teeth, intoxicated by the power each of us held over the other.

"Say my name," I whispered, tightening mind, body and spirit around him.

He was melting into me, dissolving my sovereign identity until my name was all that remained.

"River," he murmured, injecting the word into my mouth as if breathing me back to life after a long and terrible sleep. "*River...*"

Then he plunged us both into the abyss, where I was falling with him through the cracks of eternity until we landed, gasping and exhausted, on the far shore of indescribable fulfillment.

I didn't fall asleep. I think I fainted.

CHAPTER TWELVE
Roswell, New Mexico

The fields behind the campus were lush and green, still damp with morning dew. Tall evergreens reached skyward, glistening moist against the dawn, and a serenity permeated the windless sky. A distant bird whistled a complex aria, a flock of white herons alighting nearby.

Further away, near a clear blue lake, the silver craft waited, somehow out of place in the otherwise idyllic setting. Approximately thirty feet in diameter and fifteen feet tall, it was shaped like two inverted salad bowls pressed together. A row of oblong ports lined the craft half-way up, with a ramp extending some twenty feet into the field.

All was still.

The crew of was awakened at dawn by a group of white-coated lab scientists, given their breakfast, and put through the final pre-flight briefing. In a blur of movement and distorted sound, an elderly but enthusiastic Dr. Callahan McFee informed the four crewmen of the importance of the mission, its historic value, its scientific significance, and anything else he could think of. He also mentioned briefly that the project was funded by the government now, and that security was of the utmost importance.

Steale took it all in silently, a mischievous half-smile playing over his lips as he winked at Kirin from across the table. She smiled, blushed, and looked down at the papers in front of her, clearly trying not to lose control and break into a nervous laugh. Her pale lavender eyes sparkled in the fluorescent lighting, sandy-brown hair resting on her shoulders.

Teasing her again, Steale lifted both brows, his expression speaking more than words ever could as he inclined his head toward a door at the back of the room. Crew's pre-flight quarters. Where they'd slept the night before. Where he and Kirin had made love for the thousandth time since their marriage. What had it been? Two years? It seemed more like two weeks.

Eyes widening with disbelief and amusement, Kirin mouthed 'Stop it!' But she had to look away again to keep from laughing.

Steale only shrugged, then leaned back in his chair, his eyes fixed on his mate as the briefing continued.

"Make no mistake," McFee was saying, "we cannot risk any type of contamination in the parallel society. This includes social, cultural and biological contamination. We estimate that the chances of biological contamination are minimal, since we've already confirmed that people from their world and ours have been interacting since time began. Whatever germs exist here exist there, too. But their society is in a state of technological and cultural development which seems to be about fifty years behind ours, therefore - Steale, are you listening to me?"

Caught in the act of attempting to seduce his wife, Steale looked up into McFee's long-suffering eyes. "Yes, Callahan, I heard you," he said with an easy grin. "I especially liked the part about the religious implications of inter-dimensional travel. Did you stay up all night thinking that one up?"

Across the table, Kirin groaned, putting her head down on her arms when the other crewmembers laughed.

Shaking his head with dismay but also with obvious affection, McFee sighed audibly. "You know, Steale, I never wanted an Argus on this mission in the first place," he said, shaking a bony finger at the mischievous crewman. "But Kirin probably won't go without you - for which I question her taste sometimes - and the government wants you here for reasons I'll never understand. So I'm stuck with you. You're the only non-science personnel on this mission, taking up space which could have been used by a talented geophysicist. Do you have to be a wise-ass, too?"

Steale shrugged elaborately. "I'm also a Gemini."

The group laughed again, and the crewman sitting next to Kirin spoke up.

"There's your answer, Doc."

McFee rolled his eyes, chuckled warmly, then continued with whatever he'd been saying before.

Finally, seeming to realize he'd said everything more than a dozen times, the older man brought his speech to a conclusion. "In short, this is the first mission of its type, and we hope it won't be the last. For the time you're in our sister world, you're our ambassadors there. Try to avoid any direct contact with the inhabitants, but if you do run into unexpected situations – *Steale*," he stressed, "for Lethe's sake, don't hurt anyone."

Steale's dark brows lifted as he reached inside the white uniform jacket bearing the Project Gateway emblem. Holding McFee's gaze with a grin, he pulled out a long-barreled gun and laid it on the table in front of him. "Want me to leave it behind?"

McFee grimaced with a laugh. "I should have known you'd bring that thing along."

"If I'm being given the dubious honor of protecting this group of helpless book-worms, foul language doesn't always do the job."

McFee seemed to consider that as he eyed the gun. "What are you packing?"

Steale shrugged, looking at a port on the side of the barrel, close to the handle. "A little of this, a little of that," he said. "Tranq bullets, mainly."

The crewman sitting next to Kirin laughed again. "You should have been here for the simulation last week, Doc," he said, elbowing Kirin affectionately. "Big Bad Steale here shot himself in the foot with one of those damn things and we had to carry him back through the field and let him sleep it off in his room."

"Yeah, well, Fegan, that might not have happened if you hadn't tripped over your own big feet and bumped into my arm."

Fegan shrugged. "I'm a helpless book-worm. We're clumsy as a breed. But if you're the only protection we've got, I think I'm going to hand in my resignation. Dr. McFee, could you draw up the paperwork?"

McFee stood at the head of the table, shaking his head. Then, gesturing toward the door, he released a weary sigh. "Just go get on board, children," he instructed. "And may Lethe have mercy on the souls of anyone you run into on your journey."

Steale stood, replaced the gun in its shoulder holster, then walked around the table to meet Kirin. He slid one arm around her waist, walking with her as they left the building and began the short trek across the field.

Once they were outdoors, he deliberately slowed his pace, taking a moment before they reached the craft to turn his mate toward him. "You sure you want to do this?"

Kirin slid her arms around his waist until their bodies were pressed together. "There's another whole world out there, Steale," she said, standing on her toes to kiss him. "Aren't you curious?"

He shrugged, devilment in his eyes. "I'm more curious about you."

Kirin smiled softly, holding him close. "We've got at least a lifetime together, maybe more. You'll know more about me than you ever wanted to know by the time we're thirty."

Steale seemed unconvinced, his eyes sparkling "Want to get a head start?"

She studied his face for a prolonged moment, her expression darkening. "Are you apprehensive about this mission, Steale?" she asked softly. "Do you want to change your mind?"

Steale pulled her face against his shoulder, his hand in her hair. "I'm not letting you go off alone. Besides, it's a little late to back out now."

Kirin slid her fingers down his arm and took his hand as they continued on toward the waiting craft.

When they reached the ladder, they could hear Fegan's voice speaking to the on-board computer. He seemed to be having a prolonged conversation with it, giving instructions which only another scientist would have understood. The crew knew it was his baby; he'd programmed the beast with every scrap of scientific information available to him, arguing with the project administrators that one never knew when one might need the accumulated knowledge of humankind at their fingertips.

Catching Kirin's eye as they cleared the last step and the automatic door sealed shut behind them, Steale mimicked drawing the gun and pointing it toward Fegan's back. Pulling an imaginary trigger, he winked.

Kirin shook a finger at him, then slid into one of the chairs and went to work. The on-board instrument check took another two hours, during which time Steale lounged and fidgeted in his own chair - a lone seat away from the rest of the crew toward the back of the craft. McFee had said it would give him a better vantage point; Steale suspected it was meant to keep him out of the bookworms' hair.

He took the time alone to look around the craft once more, marveling at the elaborate equipment, much of it still in the experimental stages. Along one side of the vessel were banks of computers which fed information to the minuscule engine. The ship wasn't built for speed, only for durability. It was an exploration vessel, not a war bird.

Further away from the command area were stacks of equipment and specimen containers. Five stasis chambers had been prepared, each large enough to hold a man. While this mission wasn't authorized for human contact, they had been carefully instructed to bring back animals - cats, dogs, whatever they could find. The stasis chambers were to insure against contamination as well as to lessen the shock of the animal's first inter-dimensional travel. The life-force could be stopped for an hour, a year, or perhaps even indefinitely.

By the time the craft was ready to launch, it was mid-afternoon. A weather front in the sister world delayed the launch for another three hours, and when things were finally ready, the sun was low on the horizon.

"Well, kids," McFee's voice said over the base to ship transmitter, "you're on your way. We'll monitor and control the dimensional overlap frequency from here. Once the corridor opens, you'll have six minutes to get through to the other side. You're going to be coming through in an area of southern Arizona. When you're ready to come back, just give us the signal and we'll send the corridor."

At her station, Kirin laughed pleasantly. "We *know*, Callahan," she told him, casting a knowing look over her shoulder to her husband.

The craft moved. The blue light came.

The world ended.

~

"Kirin!" Steale shouted, picking himself up off the floor of the mangled craft and crawling through the rubble toward where his wife had been at the controls. He found her wedged half-way underneath the console, still breathing, unconscious.

Heart hammering wildly, he hurled the debris aside, carefully untangling her limp form from the wreckage. Then, lifting her into his arms, he took her to the far side of the craft, placing her on the floor away from the shower of sparks that flew from the control panel. Frantic, he determined that she was injured, though not badly. With some sense of relief he took her cool hand, pressing it between both his own until the Way opened between their thoughts.

Her mind was undamaged. Her left arm was badly sprained, maybe broken. Her leg was bleeding from a gash torn through the white uniform by the now-jagged console, requiring stitches, but not life-threatening. Her head hurt from the impact.

Steale's telepathy told him those things, gave him a course of action. Moving on instinct, shock-numbed into motion, he scrambled through the maze of scattered equipment until he found the first aid kit. A pressure bandage. Cold compress. Injection of Morphinol for the pain. His hands trembled, then he went to the others. It wasn't good.

When he returned to her side, Kirin's eyes fluttered, opened, closed again. Her head moved; a soft moan pressed through her lips. "Fegan and Lissi?" she murmured, trying to sit up.

Steale slipped one hand behind her neck, the other pressing her shoulder to keep her still. "I've given you a shot for the pain. Just stay quiet."

She grimaced; coughing. "Fegan and Lissi?" she said again, her voice filled with desperation.

Steale's dark eyes closed, grief masking his features. "Lissi's dead. Fegan's lost a lot of blood; he might not make it. I did what I could for him."

But the drug was taking effect. Kirin didn't reply. She slumped back against the floor.

He gripped her hand, held it tight, using his telepathy to open the Way between them once more, willing his beloved to live.

~

The automatic beacon was destroyed in the crash. Eight hours later, and still the corridor hadn't come. After the first five hours, it should have arrived automatically if there had been no contact between the probe and the base. But the corridor didn't come.

Through the fore port, Steale watched while a violent thunderstorm raged on. Either the corridor itself or the vessel had been struck by lightning; the navigational equipment malfunctioned; the ship was buffeted back and forth against the electromagnetic walls of the corridor and finally slammed down into the Earth. But *where*?

The few instruments that still worked told Steale nothing. Fegan's computer told him less. New Mexico was all the computer's voice kept repeating sporadically, its memory tapes damaged in the crash. Somewhere in New Mexico.

As the night grew darker, Fegan started to breathe a little easier. Kirin's strength pulled her through the worst of it, but she needed another shot to numb the pain in her arm. Fegan needed two more, and by the time the first light of dawn cast a silver haze over the downed vessel, the last of the pain-killer was gone.

Steale discovered that the ramp still functioned, though barely. He opened up the craft after several attempts, having to use physical strength to force the opening wide enough to let his body pass through. When he stepped outside, he found himself in an alien world.

The desert. It didn't look that different from the deserts in his own world, and he wondered for a moment if the corridor had been destroyed while they were still on their own side, in their own universe. If so, they might be lucky enough to be stranded a couple hundred miles from the university instead of in another world.

But the rescue party never came.

~

Kirin was stronger and Fegan was starting to stabilize by the time the sun reached a forty five degree angle on the eastern horizon. It was summer; the heat was oppressive, stifling.

The area around the crash site was littered with debris and the silver shielding material from the exterior of the craft. Peeled back when it had slid along the ground and up against a pike of boulders, the vessel's exoskeleton glistened, blinding in the sun.

At one point, some distance away, Steale thought he heard footsteps, voices, a horse whinnying. But by the time he came out of the craft where he'd been tending to Kirin and Fegan, the horizon was empty. Only the desert stared back at him, whispering of hallucinations and mirages.

The sun set again, and Kirin was stronger still. Fegan's condition remained the same, but at least he hadn't slipped further into death. After the shock of the crash had worn off, Steale took Lissi s still body and laid her down in the back of the craft, covering her lifeless form with one of the silver tarps they'd brought along. He was almost glad Fegan remained unconscious. His mate was dead. His beloved Lissi was gone.

Throughout the long night, Steale held Kirin in his arms, and though she passed out from the shock, he managed to set the broken arm, immobilizing the fracture with a piece of cloth torn from his own jacket. He slipped into her unconscious mind then, and gave her the suggestion to sleep through the night.

It was the following dawn that the military came with their Jeeps and their trucks and their generals.

Among them was an ambitious young punk by the name of Avery Madison, a second lieutenant with delusions of godhood. Steale went out to meet them, hoping. Even praying. Certainly they would have doctors. They could help Kirin. Maybe they could even help Fegan.

After that, the real nightmare began.

~

I awoke abruptly to find myself still in Steale's arms. His body was relaxed, his breathing coming in the steady rhythms of a natural sleep, his head resting on my shoulder where he'd fallen asleep the night before. The dream had stopped.

Taking care not to awaken him, I saw that the clock on the dresser read 3:38. We'd only been asleep for a few hours and our bodies were still joined together, his weight still heavy on top of me.

I realized abstractly that a peculiar wetness was clinging to my face. It was also on my shoulder. He'd been crying in his sleep, and as a result, I'd cried, too. For Lissi. For Fegan. For Kirin.

Most of all, for Steale.

Drawing a ragged breath, I slipped my arms around him under the covers, holding him against my chest, stroking his hair, soothing him. I hadn't realized it when we went to sleep, but the physical contact between us created a natural pathway for his telepathy to use. His dreams had become mine.

Not moving, I remained awake for several hours, my mind spinning as I tried to fit the pieces together. I'd heard something long ago about an incident in the New Mexico desert. A so-called flying saucer had crashed near Roswell in the late Forties - 1947, if I could rely on my own rattled memory. There had even been a newspaper article wherein the United States military had admitted to having an alien spacecraft and four alien bodies, but it had later been retracted to state that the first press release was an error. The "crashed saucer", they said, was only a weather balloon.

Nothing had been said about the fact that three of those bodies were alive. Indeed, when I tried to remember the article I'd read in the paper several years before - to commemorate the fortieth anniversary of the crash - it seemed that the majority of information anyone could uncover was sketchy at best. There were reports from the friend of the brother of the guy who had supposedly loaded the bodies into the military truck for transport to Wright-Patterson Air Force Base in Ohio, usually stating that the four occupants of the craft were three-feet tall, grayish-green in appearance, hairless, and with oversized eyes that resembled an insect.

Certainly no report I'd ever heard, nothing I'd ever read had insinuated that the occupants of the craft were very much human. There were the typical rumors of the crashed saucer, the legend of Hangar 19, and the occasional flare-up of interest in the Roswell crash whenever a flap of UFO sightings occurred.

Granted, I was no expert on the matter, but it was the one case anyone who'd ever heard of unidentified flying objects had encountered. In the late 1980's, it had even developed something of a cult following, with hordes of amateur UFOlogists traipsing through the deserts of New Mexico in search of what had once crashed on Mac Brazel's ranch.

My head started to ache with the bits of previously-useless information that tried to claw their way to the surface. There had been rumors in the late 60's of another crash - a much larger one this time, in Montana - rumors that several of the bodies were still intact. One supposition stated that one of the bodies had been turned over to MacDill Air Force Base in Florida for study for several years, and had subsequently been transported to a top-secret para-military organization near San Diego.

My heart slammed hard against my ribs as it started to come clear.

Something Madison had said, nearly seven years ago now. A drug-haze conversation in the back of a moving ambulance. Something about Tourists. *'Eighteen Tourists already in cold sleep'*. That's what Madison had said.

My mind wasn't working properly. I suspected that part of it had to do with the fact that Steale was still sleeping on my chest. As long as we were in physical contact, his natural telepathic abilities were wide open. I had no doubt that a part of my Self was still sleeping, too - somewhere inside him, perhaps.

My own body was trembling again. His closeness was overwhelming; our passion had left me drained. His dream had finished the job. I closed my eyes for just a moment, then fell into a restless sleep.

~

When I woke for the second time, it was to discover Steale's eyes gazing down into mine. His hands were on either side of my shoulders, and a mischievous smile was playing with the edges of his lips. Out the corner of my eye, I could see that the clock now read 5:33.

He didn't speak at all, just made love to me again with the same intensity of the night before. I had neither the strength nor the desire to resist him. Instead, looking up at him as he brought us together again, I started to understand the pain behind his eyes a little more.

When it was over, he rested against my chest again, his breathing slowing to normal as the first light of morning filtered through the open window. For several minutes, neither of us spoke, and I knew he didn't remember dreaming.

Not wanting to spoil the aftermath, I held my silence. There would be time to speak of dreams and losses later. For that one hour, I wanted to hold him against me and pretend we belonged together despite the fact that I knew we didn't.

It was another few minutes before Steale moved, lifting himself up on his arms until he was above me again. He traced his fingertips over my cheekbones, down my neck.

"Damn," he whispered.

It was the last thing I'd expected him to say. I laughed, running my fingers through his silky hair.

Reaching out, he ran his hand down my arm, his expression turning sober. "You know, there's still a lot I haven't told you," he said, his words not what I'd expected.

"I know. We have time," I said.

He studied me. "Don't you have to be at the studio in a few hours?"

I mentally ran time backwards. The studio seemed a million miles away. Something inside me had changed, and though that thought scared me more than a little, I recognized the truth for what it was.

"Look, I don't want to be so forward as to scare you away for good, but I've been thinking about what you said when you first came to the studio."

"Whoa. Slow down," he suggested, pulling me into his arms. When we settled again, my head was resting on his shoulder and I was looking up at him. "Now, let's try that again. Whatever you say isn't going to scare me away, so don't be afraid of that."

His voice rumbled against my ear, soothing, calming. I took a deep breath and settled my own thoughts, centering my chi.

Placing my arm over his smooth chest, I tried to impart my intentions through touch as much as through words. "You dreamed last night," I told him, then waited for his reaction.

When it came, he tensed very slightly and held his breath. "Oh."

I held him close. "If I'm going to help you - and I think I can -I have to know everything." I stopped, and when he didn't answer, I added, "What happened to Kirin and Fegan after the Air Force came?"

His heartbeat came faster against my cheek, but he didn't retreat behind his usual mask. "I guess I did dream last night," he said, almost as if to himself, then lifted his head to look at me. "Do you understand about the Way?"

"I think so. It's the path your thoughts travel when you communicate telepathically with someone."

He petted my back. "You must have followed the Way into my mind while I was sleeping. That's how it is between mates," he said, causing me to tense. "No, don't get the wrong idea. It's just that it doesn't work unless two people are extremely compatible." He paused and seemed to be searching for the right words. "Last night in the car?"

I remembered. "You took my hand and gave me a suggestion to relax. That was different?"

"That was different," he confirmed. "Most of my people have telepathic abilities to one degree or another. What I did last night was something that almost anyone in my world could have done - a simple transfer of thought, the suggestion for you to relax. But when you were inside my dream, you saw the images as if they were your own memories, right?"

Those images still terrified me. "Yes."

He sighed softly. "That's how it was with Kirin, too. It was as if we were the same person."

"What happened to her, Steale?" I pressed, almost afraid of the answer.

"How much do you remember from my dream?" he asked.

I told him what I'd seen, what I'd felt.

Again there was a long hesitation. "After the Air Force came, the three of us were taken to a base somewhere in New Mexico," he said at last. "The bastard who was in charge told Kirin they had facilities there that could help Fegan. I didn't trust him from the beginning, but we didn't have much choice. Fegan was hurt pretty bad. We thought he was dying."

He trembled slightly as the memory solidified in his mind. "When we got to the base, they took Fegan into another area - away from Kirin and me," he explained, speaking slowly. "They said he needed surgery, and that we could wait with this man called Colonel Schaeffer. There was another guy there, too."

"Avery Madison," I supplied, even his name bitter on my tongue.

Steale nodded, not questioning how I knew. "Kirin and I were interrogated for hours - without any offers of medical assistance. Her right arm was broken just below the elbow, and she'd lost a lot of blood.

"She was also an eternal optimist. Whenever Madison and Schaeffer went out of the room - supposedly to check on Fegan's progress - she kept telling me that it was going to be all right. She honestly believed they intended to just let us walk out of there."

I felt a sadness for her. "Because that's what would have happened in your world."

He nodded. "If the Argus had wandered up on what looked to be an alien ship, the first thing we would have is get medical attention for anyone who was injured. But your world was still new to us; we were naíve and ignorant in a lot of ways."

"I know it's hard for you, Steale," I whispered when his voice drifted away. "I'm sorry."

His gaze fixed on the ceiling. "I guess I've tried to forget. At first, I swore I never would - that I'd get her back if it took the rest of my life. But later..." His words trailed off into the silence of the morning. "That's not how it worked out."

Not wanting to push him, I curled against his side. "We don't have to talk about it right now. We have time," I repeated, though I wondered if my words were for him or for myself.

A weary breath pressed through his lips as he shook his head. "For a long time, I told myself none of it ever really happened - and I think I even started to believe that after awhile. But now--." He turned his head toward me, brows narrowing as he studied me.

"What?" I asked, taking the hand that lay over his chest and twining my fingers through his.

"You scare me," he confessed.

"Why?" I whispered, chills raking through me.

He didn't break eye contact, but squeezed my hands more tightly. "Because being with you brings it all back again. It's as if I've always known you - but it's more than that, River. Sort of like *deja vu*."

I tried not to tremble at the honesty in his words. "You scare me, too. For what it's worth, I know we were meant to meet, Steale. And your dreams last night - they're somehow connected."

"What do you mean?"

My head rested on his shoulder, my hand gripping his until my knuckles turned pale. "It's not over, is it?" I asked, not fully understand what I meant myself.

His body tensed beneath me. "It ended a long time ago. For Fegan and Kirin, it's over."

"Is it?" I persisted gently. "How much haven't you told me, Steale?"

For a very long time, he didn't answer. Finally, releasing my hand, he slipped his fingers under my chin and forced me to look at him, to meet the ghosts who lived behind his eyes.

"There are some things I can't talk about, River," he stressed. "Not for lack of wanting to, but because I don't know the right words to make you understand everything that happened."

Forcing myself not to look away, I drew a ragged breath. "Then show me. Telepathically," I offered, not fully believing what I'd just said. "Is that possible?"

He remained tense, saying nothing.

"Steale?" I murmured gently. "Is it possible?"

"Yes."

"But?"

He hesitated. "I don't want to lose you."

His words touched something deep inside me. "You won't," I promised. "If you have any doubts, look inside my mind for your answers."

He smiled just a little, his body gradually relaxing. "It doesn't work that way. I can't read direct thoughts any more than you could. But with the Way, I can look at the memories again, and you could see them, too."

He tried to shrug it off. "It's been a long time since I've wanted to share myself with anyone," he explained. "Opening the Way is just about as personal as sex."

I smiled, reassuring him with touch. "As I recall, we did all right with that last night."

The amusement came back into his eyes. He lifted his head off the pillow and kissed me affectionately on the lips, pulling me into a tight embrace. "Sure you want to do this?"

I nodded, feeling my Self merging with him just from the intimacy of our touching. "Yes. No. Yes."

I didn't know what to expect, but it certainly wasn't the firestorm of images and emotions which suddenly burst onto my mind. My individuality was gone before I understood what was happening.

I became the color of night, the scent of despair, the sound of death.

I became Steale.

~

"Roswell Army Air Field," the grunt who drove the ambulance said, answering Steale's inquiry as to their destination before being ordered to silence by Colonel Schaeffer.

The following morning, the young soldier was transferred to Guam and never heard from again.

~

Steale sat on the edge of a green naugehyde sofa in a locked room, looking at Kirin through red-rimmed eyes. He hadn't slept, hadn't eaten, hadn't been able to think rationally for forty eight hours. Now, in the dusty waiting area, exhaustion took its toll.

"It's been hours since they brought us here, Steale," Kirin murmured, careful to keep the arm still. Her face was pale and drawn, her aura spiking pain. "I'm worried about Fegan."

Steale experienced her agony within himself. "I know," he whispered. "I know."

Several hours later still, the door opened, admitting Colonel Schaeffer and Second Lieutenant Avery Madison. Both appeared grim, wary.

"A doctor's been summoned," Schaeffer revealed, his eyes wavering.

Steale didn't buy it. "That's what you said five hours ago," he snapped.

"These things take time." Madison's voice. Madison's lies.

"How *much* time?" Steale countered, standing, his eyes narrowing dangerously.

They ignored his questions. "Let's talk about your ship while we wait," Madison suggested callously.

"We've been through this a dozen times!" Steale shouted. "I've already told you everything! Now get a doctor!"

The doctor never came.

~

A nurse eventually tended to Kirin's arm, though it was a sloppy job, done with trembling hands. She did at least administer

166

some sort of powerful sedative and local anesthesia, and though Kirin remained semi-conscious, her body was lax, unresponsive.

Steale knew intuitively that this young woman wanted to help them, yet despite the fact that they were left alone in the room with her, she motioned him to silence.

"They've taken the body of the young woman who was killed in the crash to Wright-Patterson Air Base for an autopsy," the nurse whispered, glancing nervously over her shoulder toward the door.

Two MP's were stationed outside, peering in through the glass window. The nurse took care to keep her back to them at all times as she worked on applying the cast.

Kirin cried softly to herself in her drug-induced haze. For Lissi, Steale understood. And for Fegan.

"What about us?" he whispered to the nurse. "What do they intend to do?"

The young woman's pale green eyes studied him with compassion. "I don't know. They're having a plane brought in from Houston. I overheard one of Schaeffer's assistants saying something about a facility in San Diego. I think you'll be taken there. It's a top security installation."

Steale frowned, glancing toward the MP's. They seemed unconcerned. "Why?"

The nurse shook her head. "I'm not sure. They're dismantling your ship right now and flying it to Wright-Patt in pieces. They'll probably interrogate you. Be prepared."

Steale considered her words cautiously. "They've already interrogated us. About the ship, its technology, who flew it, where we came from. All of it. We have nothing to hide; we've already told them everything we can." He studied her more closely, cautious. "Why do you want to help us? Why do you believe me when no one else has?"

A wistful smile pressed through the woman's lips. "Because you look like you could use some help. And because I know there are four qualified doctors on this base who could have helped - and didn't." Her eyes were wide and wet.

"Why?" Steale asked, horrified at the cruelty of which this world was capable.

"They're afraid."

Brows lifting, Steale considered that. "Of what?"

167

After a jittery glance toward the door, the nurse sighed softly. "They probably think you're here to invade the planet."

Steale frowned. "Invade the planet?" he repeated. "We're *from* the planet."

The woman nodded. "I know."

"You do?"

A tender smile pressed through the nurse's lips. "A long time ago, there was a little girl who could walk through a hole in her bedroom closet and disappear into another world. I've never forgotten that. Your world gave me a lot. I caught a glimpse of some of the transcripts from your interrogation, and if that place is where you're from, I'd like to give something back - if I can."

Steale considered her words in thoughtful silence. "What can we do?"

"Tell them anything they want to know," the nurse suggested. "And look for any possible way to escape."

Steale's stomach tightened with apprehension. "They have no intention of letting us go, do they?"

"No. And I'm sorry."

"What about Fegan?" Steale asked.

"He's in the infirmary," she revealed. "He was unconscious when he was brought in, but I heard that he regained consciousness about an hour ago. They thought he wasn't going to make it, so there's a big uproar over his miraculous recovery."

Steale glanced to Kirin, who was beyond hearing them, then back at the nurse. "He's a healer of sorts," he explained, or tried to anyway. "He can manipulate his body energy where it's needed to heal his own injuries. Is he well enough to travel?"

"I don't know," the nurse whispered. "But they won't risk two separate flights. When they do move you, they'll move all of you on the same plane. That may be your best chance."

Steale started to say something, but stopped abruptly when the door opened to admit Schaeffer and Madison.

The young woman stood and walked out the door without looking back. Two weeks later, the plane which had been transporting her to the Philippines crashed in the Pacific Ocean. Her body was never recovered.

~

The plane was a pot-bellied camouflage transport left over from World War II. Shortly after the nurse left, three MP's came into the waiting room with a stretcher, lifted Kirin onto it despite Steale's protests, and the two of them were ushered at gunpoint through the back door of the offices toward the aircraft. Madison and Schaeffer were waiting next to the plane in a Jeep and met the entourage as the gurney holding Kirin was wheeled up into the cargo section.

Steale measured his steps carefully, ignoring the blast of desert heat as it drained the last of his strength. Walking slowly, he kept his hands raised to shoulder-height, following the MP's as they pushed the stretcher toward the back of the aircraft and secured it with cargo straps to the bulkhead.

A quick glance revealed that Fegan was already on board - semi-conscious and covered with cuts and bruises, but nonetheless alive. Strapped to a gurney identical to the one that held Kirin, he turned his face to the wall. Steale's heart wrenched for the man. Lissi was gone. The telepathic bleed emanating from Fegan was a blast of grief that caused the breath to catch in Steale's throat.

A few seconds later, Schaeffer and Madison followed the group into the plane, attempting to project an air of nonchalance which couldn't pass scrutiny. Both men appeared nervous, anxious, terrified.

"We want you to understand, Mr. Steale, that we aren't monsters," Schaeffer said. "But until we learn more about one another, there are bound to be misunderstandings."

Steale glanced pointedly at the MP's, at their guns which were still aimed at his chest. "Is all of this really necessary?" he asked of Schaeffer. "My wife and friend are injured and unarmed. Do you have to hold us at gunpoint?"

Schaeffer motioned for the soldiers to lower their weapons, though he didn't dismiss them. "You'll be flown to San Diego, California - Miramar Naval Air Station, to be specific. Some of the best scientific minds in the country can be found there, and with any luck, they should figure out a way to get you back to wherever you come from ."

Liars were the easiest of all to read. Once the guns were lowered and holstered, he allowed his arms to drop back to his sides. "It was my impression that the probe has already been dismantled," he commented. "Without it, you know as well as I do that we *can't* get back." It was part truth, part lie.

Schaeffer smiled dubiously. "We'll do the best we can," he said patronizingly. "Now if you'd be so kind as to lie down on the empty gurney, we'll secure you for the long ride to San Diego."

Steale's brows rose as he glanced toward the empty stretcher already secured to the bulkhead opposite Kirin. His lips curled to a snarl. "I don't think so."

Then, in a blistering haze of movement, he snaked his hand inside the Project Gateway jacket and pulled the gun which no one had thought to take away. Dropping into a low crouch, he sprayed the cargo hold with tranq bullets, taking out the MP's before they saw him move. Madison and Schaeffer fell a half-second later, with the cock-pit crew going down last.

"Kirin!" he shouted, moving toward her as he holstered the gun. He unfastened the straps, then lifted her into his arms and carried her down the ramp.

There were no guards surrounding the plane. In fact, as he hurried toward the Jeep and placed his semi-conscious wife in the passenger's seat, he saw no movement at all, just the eerie dancing of heat monkeys on the runway, angry spirits in a mad world.

"Steale?" Kirin murmured softly, her eyes heavily lidded as the effects of the drug kept her immobilized and confused.

He squeezed her hand gently. "I'm going back for Fegan!" he shouted over the idle of the props.

Not waiting for her answer, he climbed back up the ramp and stepped over the unconscious bodies to get to Fegan.

The horror began when the semi-conscious book-worm refused to cooperate. He wanted to die, Steale knew. Without Lissi, he was lost. The nightmare worsened when he heard a distant vehicle, siren blaring, heading toward the plane.

"Fegan!" he shouted, trying to lift the heavy, unresponsive body. "Put your arm around my neck and hold on, goddammit!"

Fegan remained limp, resigned. He deliberately fought with what little strength he had left. "Go away, Gemini man," he muttered, his voice sarcastic and cold. "Run away if you can. Play the game as if you think it matters in the end." He laughed - an out of place sound, his voice slurred with drug and despair. "You have to pretend it does, but it really doesn't, you know. One more breath ain't worth the pain. One more hour ain't worth the wait. You come to the end of the road either way. It's just a matter of when. Funny, ain't it?"

Part of him died with Lissi, Steale understood. Perhaps it was his sanity.

The siren was coming closer and despite repeated efforts, he couldn't get his old friend off the gurney in time. He had no choice but to leave him behind. Now Fegan was one of the ghosts who lived behind Steale's eyes.

~

The end of the runway seemed a million light-years distant, but Steale pointed the Jeep toward it nonetheless and pressed the accelerator to the floor. At the end of the runway, he could see a road outside the perimeter of the base. The fence which separated the two worlds ended up plastered across the grill and over the hood.

Kirin barely moved, could hardly lift her head as Steale continued across the dirt median and eventually onto the road. He watched her out the corner of one eye, reaching out to steady her as the vehicle bumped and skidded onto the pavement, the MP's less than three hundred yards behind them.

What he hadn't counted on was that they had already radioed for outside help.

With a sinking feeling in the pit of his stomach, he saw the road block less than a quarter of a mile in front of the Jeep as he rounded a bend in the road. Behind them, the sirens grew louder. The sides of the pavement were lined with huge boulders - too large and close together for the vehicle to cross. At the very best, he knew he'd roll it. At the worst, he and Kirin would both be killed, either in the wreckage or by the soldiers. It wouldn't make much difference, as Fegan had said.

He weighed his options in a fraction of a second, glancing up to take stock of the situation. The road block consisted of at least twenty men, guns drawn and ready. He'd never get even half of them with the tranq bullets before he'd be dead. And even if he was willing to sacrifice his own life, he couldn't bring himself to sacrifice Kirin's, too.

"Steale?" Kirin murmured, turning her head to look at him with wide, fearful eyes.

He jammed his foot onto the brake pedal, spinning the Jeep back in the direction they had come. Common sense told him he'd find another road block not far away even if he did somehow manage to get past the MP's.

His jaw clenched as he saw the second Jeep coming toward them. The mangled fence had slowed them down just a little, leaving them half a mile back.

He jerked his head toward Kirin as the vehicle slid to a stop up against a pile of rocks. Jumping out instantly, he ran toward the passenger door. "We've got one chance, Kirin," he told her, drawing his weapon and sliding his arm behind her. "There's a rock formation about a hundred yards to the west. If we can get to it, it'll give me enough cover to even out the odds."

Fear in her eyes, Kirin slid her arms around his neck, trying to stand when he lowered her to the ground. With Steale practically dragging her, they made it past the edge of the road and a few yards into the desert before she stumbled and fell.

Knowing they were running out of time, Steale tried to lift her, but his own strength was going, his breath coming in tortured gasps as the relentless desert heat drained him.

Kirin only smiled up at him, a sense of resignation settling in her eyes. Her voice was soft when she spoke. "I can't make it, Steale," she said. "And you'll never make it if you try to carry me."

Steale wasn't listening. "Then we'll both die," he decided numbly, lifting her nonetheless.

At that, Kirin stiffened. "We're *not* going to die, Steale," she managed, her tone suddenly sharp. "If you can get to the coordinates where the probe was supposed to land, the corridor will be waiting. Callahan will be looking for us. Get back home!."

The MP's were barely three hundred yards away. "I'm not leaving you!" Steale shouted, though he collapsed when he tried to carry her over the rough terrain in the blistering desert heat.

"Don't let your love kill both of us, Steale!" she snapped. "They won't kill me as long as they think they might learn something. You're the only one who can get back, the *only* one who can tell Callahan where to find us."

"I'm not leaving you!" he repeated, blinded by dust and tears and Kirin's psychic assault through the Way. "Don't ask me to do that!"

Her eyes hardened as she lay on the ground beneath him. "If you don't, I *swear* I will hate you forever."

She slammed the telepathic door with an abruptness which caused him to gasp. He understood then that it was no idle threat. The fact that she was right didn't help, nor did the fact that he had no time to think.

He lingered for only a moment longer, his gazed fixed on the only woman he had ever loved, the only woman who had ever existed or ever would. But she looked away and would not meet his eyes.

Insane with grief, he stumbled to his feet and started to run. Kirin's love gave him no alternative.

He never saw her again.

~

The flow of images stopped as abruptly as they had begun, and I found myself lying next to Steale in bed, my eyes open and staring blankly at the wall. His body trembled as he released my mind back to me, his expression hollow.

For a very long time, neither of us spoke. Instead, with a sudden protectiveness, I crawled on top of him, my arms tightening around his shoulders as I lay between his legs. He held me tight against him, crushing the breath from my lungs. I heard someone crying and knew it was me, my tears dropping onto his chest, my body convulsing with the sobs that tore free from my innermost Self.

No living being should be forced to live with memories like Steale's. No living soul should have been subjected to the horrors he had known. No sentient thing should be haunted as Steale was haunted.

The storm within me lasted an eternity, subsiding only when my eyes ran dry and my emotions turned numb.

"You okay?" he asked sometime later.

"No," I answered truthfully, my voice unreliable. "You?"

His arms released their crushing grip, holding me gently. "It's been a long time. I've learned to live with it."

The resignation in his voice was frightening. "I'm sorry."

Placing one hand under my chin, he encouraged me to look at him. "Don't be," he murmured. "Please?"

He didn't want pity.

He started running his hand up and down my arm in an absent-minded fashion. "They thought we were from another planet - Mars, or something," he offered with a bitter laugh. "If it had been up to me, I would have told them any goddamn thing they wanted to know. Hell, I think even Kirin would have by that time."

"But you didn't?"

Staring at the wall behind me, he shook his head. "I tried. But I didn't know enough about the scientific end of it to satisfy their curiosity. Kirin was still in shock from her injuries, and there was the added disadvantage of her being a woman."

I frowned. "What do you mean?"

"The military mind in your world - especially during that time period - couldn't believe that a woman could have piloted that ship," he explained. "And like I said, they were so damn sure we came from another *planet*, they probably thought we were lying about everything we said."

I found my hand tracing circles on his chest; it seemed to soothe him.

"Kirin was very beautiful - and very trusting," I murmured, surprised I could still speak at all.

"She had no reason not to be. Like I said, things are a lot different in my world. In all the years I was with the Argus Elite, I think I drew my gun a grand total of four times, and only had to pull the trigger once." He chuckled to himself. "Some kid in the back seat of a car with his girlfriend got belligerent and pulled a hunting knife on me - trying to impress his lady. When he wouldn't back down, I popped him with a tranq bullet and left him to sleep it off in the park while I took his date out for a drink."

But my mind was stuck in Roswell.

"I remember reading something about all of this awhile back," I said a few seconds later. "There was a lot of hoop-lah in the 50's, and then again in the 80's over the crash." It was mind-bending to realize that I was in bed with one of the occupants of that crash.

174

"I've read all the books ever written about it. One day it'll pay off," he added, almost to himself.

Tilting my head back, I looked up at him as a chill passed through my body. "Kirin's still alive, isn't she?"

His eyes closed. "I don't know."

As gently as possible, I tried to bring him out of the shell he'd abruptly crawled into. I told him what I knew, what I'd overheard nearly six years in the past. Once I'd finished with the background, I added, "Madison said there are eighteen Tourists, as he calls your people, in stasis. I almost got the honor of being the first human from *this* world, but I convinced him that would be a really bad idea. That's how I came to be here - in the desert, I mean."

Steale nodded thoughtfully. Then his eyes widened. "*You* killed Madison?"

I frowned. "I thought you knew. We talked about it last night."

His mouth opened and he drew a sharp breath. "You said that you'd killed somebody, but I didn't make the connection. *You* killed him?' he repeated.

I wasn't proud of it, but I'd stopped being sorry long ago. "Yes, Steale. I killed Madison."

The laughter that erupted from his throat caused chills to raise up on the back of my neck. He was elated and, given his reasons, I couldn't blame him. He had cause to hate Avery Madison.

When he finally looked at me once again, his eyes soft and filled with wonder. "Seems we've walked the same road a few times."

I allowed a smile to come to my lips. "Sometimes paths cross, intersect, overlap. I don't believe in coincidences, do you?" It also explained my almost irrational hatred of Madison from the beginning. Maybe - even then - I'd somehow known he had hurt Steale, a man I wouldn't meet until years later. 'All in balance', Ch'en Po had said. The circle of yin and yang.

He pulled me up against him again, sliding one arm around my back as I put my head back down on his shoulder. He seemed to like it that way; I did, too.

"You want to talk about it?" he asked.

"No."

But he was persuasive. And the secrets he had carried for so many years made my own seem pale by comparison. Within moments, lying on his chest, half-mesmerized by his spell, half in shock from what I'd learned, I told him of my own dark past - the drowning, the hospital, the coma.

And the death of Avery Madison.

CHAPTER THIRTEEN
Redefining Reality

I slept. In silent coma-crimson-vampire-darkness.

A shower of glass rained through nightmares. A man with a pink carnation pinned to his lapel tied my hands while a nurse wearing orange blossom perfume sang to me off-key.

I was flying. I was floating. I was dying.

"Clear!"

I touched the stars, my body burning.

"Again! Clear!"

Reality turned to flame. My bones melted.

And then I was lost for a very long time.

~

I opened my eyes to find a dwarf standing at my bedside - at least that's what I first believed. In reality, the man was probably of average height, yet the fact that he was sitting down reduced his stature considerably - as did the ridiculous red and white polka-dot bow tie that clashed with his cheap blue suit.

His gray hair and eyebrows gave the impression of considerable age, yet his aura bespoke the fact that he had not gained the wisdom to accompany his years.

"You're awake, Ms. Willows," he said at last, confirming my latter suspicion. My eyes were open and the heart monitor above my head had increased by several beats per minute. Obviously I was awake. Shifting weight in the chair, he offered a smile - well-practiced and not at all sincere. "I'm Dr. Madison, but please call me Avery. And may I call you River?"

Distracted by the fact that I was alive, I looked around, noting that he was the only person in the room. "Did everybody else get tired of waiting?"

"It's five a.m.," he replied quietly. "Your mother and the others are staying in the motel next door to the hospital. They've been very concerned about you."

"Ummm," I grunted noncommittally. The man had shrink written all over him, and in my half-asleep stupor I wasn't about to give him any fodder. I also had the distinct impression that he was lying - about what, I didn't know.

"May I see Dara?" It was a convenient way to change the subject.

"Maybe a little later. I'm afraid you've had a rough few days," he said, the concern in his voice too deep to be genuine. Put simply, he was patronizing me.

"Oh?" I asked. *Days?*

He leaned closer. "Do you remember what happened after the first time you woke up?"

I pushed myself further up in the bed. Only then did I notice a set of restraints which had been attached to my wrists and ankles. I tensed at the implications.

"The last thing I remember is getting hit on the back of the head with a horseshoe. I think I drowned."

He studied me closely, making an obvious attempt to discern whether or not I was lying. "Well, River," he sighed at last, "some very peculiar things have happened to you since last Thursday. For one, you stopped breathing three times - *after* you came out of the coma. Your heart stopped."

I stared at him, trying to make sense of what he was saying. I felt weak, drugged. "And?"

"You were under water for ten minutes, and even after the paramedics found you, you were on full life-support for another two days." He gestured his own words aside. "Medically, there's nothing odd about the fact that your mind entered a comatose state following the ordeal. What I'm more concerned with is what happened after that."

"I'm not following." I got the strong impression that was his intention – confuse the issue in some shrinkly attempt to force the patient to become dependent on the shrink. I wasn't falling for it.

He leaned forward again, gray brows narrowing. "To be perfectly blunt, River, you shouldn't be alive. When your heart stopped for the third time, you were technically dead for more than eighteen minutes."

"You mean I should be a rutabaga," I commented, trying to read him. He was hiding something in his sickly pale aura, in the deliberately unspoken truth.

His frown broke and he smiled just a little. "Something like that," he agreed. "But the neurologists and neurosurgeons have checked everything out and, as far as anyone can determine, you're perfectly normal. No damage at all."

"You seem disappointed." *Or scared*, I amended silently.

"No, just surprised."

"So why a shrink?" I asked, then thought better of it.

"I haven't mentioned my medical specialty to you, River. What makes you think I'm a... 'shrink'?"

"Are you saying you're not?" I'd learned to recognize one from a great distance, considering my own past experiences.

"No... just curious as to how you knew."

I tried not to let his demeanor intimidate me. "Just a lucky guess."

He sat there for a long time, watching me. "Who's Synjin?" he asked as if inquiring about the weather in Poughkeepsie.

An out-of-sync memory kicked me in the stomach and I looked away. *'Tell no one about me. Tell no one about Synjin. Silence is strength'*. That much I did remember. That and the little old man on the bottom of the lake.

"An old boyfriend," I lied, finding the words on my tongue almost before I thought them.

"You kept saying his name when you were in and out of consciousness."

"So? He was a good friend."

He smiled, but I didn't buy it. "A very *powerful* friend?"

"Why would you say that?" My stomach knotted.

Madison's jaw tightened. "Because each time you called his name, River, something happened in this room," he replied abruptly, his voice showing strain for the first time. Whatever had occurred must have scared him more than Freud's mother.

"Such as?" I asked, taken off-guard by his revelation.

He stood and walked over to the window. Outside, the sky had turned from black to slate-silver; an off-key bird sang to the morning; a siren sounded nearby. For several moments, Madison was nothing more than a very old man silhouetted against the dawn. Then he turned toward me once more and my soul chilled at the look he gave me.

"The first time it happened, there was a power failure."

"Talk to the electric company," I suggested, recognizing his attempt to force a confrontation.

He stared at me as if I were an amoeba under glass. "There was a power failure, River, but *only* in this room."

A deep chill passed through me. He came a step closer.

"At first, we all thought it was just a coincidence . But then it happened again."

I said nothing. The shrinks my mother dragged me to when I was younger had called me a liar or had patronizingly told me, *'We believe you believe it.'* Now, this man had obviously witnessed some eerie interaction between our world and the world of The People.

He returned to my bedside and stared down at me. "The second time it happened - the second time you became delirious - you called the name again. And that time, the glass in that window over there just shattered."

Trapped and cornered, my hands were - quite literally - tied. "Certainly you're a man of science, Dr. Madison. Would you stand there and tell me fairies broke windows and shut down the power all on *my* behalf?"

He looked momentarily perplexed and his face darkened. "No, of course not." He tried to smile again and failed. "I apologize for upsetting you."

I detested a liar and recognized his abrupt mood changes as an annoying attempt to gain the upper hand.

"What do you want from me, Dr. Madison? What are you so afraid of, and why do you think I'm responsible for it?" He was a charlatan, prancing about with Jungian beads and Freudian talismans like some frightened voodoo doctor; and like most dime-store shrinks, he would fight to destroy what couldn't be assigned a traditional label.

That was enough of a reason for me to dislike the man - and to fear him.

His head jerked in my direction and for a moment our eyes met, sparked, quarreled. "I don't think you understand your position at the moment, River. Whether or not you leave this hospital in the near future is entirely up to me. I've already seen things I can't explain - all of which happened coincidentally when you called the name 'Synjin'. Now I don't know about you, but I don't like seeing things I can't explain."

"Maybe *you* should see a shrink," I suggested.

He leaned over me, cold gray eyes boring into mine. "Whether or not you like me isn't the issue here. I would prefer that you and I get along together, since we're going to be spending a lot of time together over the next few weeks."

"In case you missed the Revolution, Dr. Madison, this is America," I reminded him, understanding the implied threat. "You don't have the authority to lock me up in this hospital or any other."

He didn't back down, ignoring my comment altogether. "In addition to the power failure and the window, there was another incident. An orderly who came into this room to restrain you during what appeared to be a seizure was killed - by you. And *that* gives me all the authority I need."

I felt the color drain from my face. The man with the pink carnation pinned to his lapel. "*Killed*?" I repeated, wishing I could remember *something*.

"He just vanished, Ms. Willows. There was a sound in this room the likes of which I have never heard before, and Mr. Richert disappeared," Madison whispered, stressing the last word as if I should be able to explain it. "Care to tell me why?"

"I don't know." It was the truth.

"Well maybe I do," he said. "You see, I was called in on your case by Dr. Perkins - your neurosurgeon." He paused as if that should mean something to me. It didn't. "Dr. Perkins was curious as to whether some anomaly in the brain could account for the first two incidents, and since my specialty centers around phenomena of that type, he thought perhaps I could shed some light on the subject."

"What type of phenomena?" I asked, frustrated, frightened. "You're acting like the prosecuting attorney at the Salem witch trials! I haven't done anything! How *could* I have done anything in a coma?"

His lips tightened, almost colorless. "Before I retired, I was stationed at MacDill Air Force Base as a staff psychiatrist." He paused as if that should impress me. It didn't. "I've worked on several projects of a classified nature, and the only time I've seen anything vaguely resembling what went on in this room was in 1947, and again in 1968." He paused for effect in his own drama, then pointedly added, "I don't suppose that means anything to you?"

It was obvious that he was afraid - of me, of shadows, of conspiracies that existed in his mind if nowhere else. His knuckles were white from gripping the bed rail.

"I wasn't even born in '47," I reminded him. "So unless you think I'm a time traveler from the ninth dimension, you are *way* out in left field without a mitt!"

He stared at me for a protracted moment. "Are you – a time traveler?" he asked as if he were altogether serious.

Maybe I was still dreaming, still in a coma that had turned into a nightmare. I decided to play along. "Ya caught me." But I didn't wait for him to answer. "I'm a risk to national security - confined to a hospital bed and hog-tied like a ritual sacrifice. Makes perfect sense."

His eyes darkened. "I don't know *what* you are - but I intend to find out. My guess is that you're an unwitting pawn, but I can't take that risk without certain tests. There could be a contagion factor."

"Common sense isn't contagious, old man. You're living proof," I snapped.

I hated the man in that moment, for I began to understand his plans for me. He wasn't just a shrink. He was - or had been - a *government* shrink, paid to keep things quiet, to sweep mysteries and even people under some invisible rug.

Stepping back from the bed, he composed himself like a bird ruffling its feathers after a battle with the wind. Then, going to a panel on the wall nearest the door, he thumbed a switch on the intercom, never breaking eye contact with

"Nurse McKitrick? Dr. Madison in room 309. Ms. Willows has regained consciousness, but appears to be severely agitated. Would you prepare an injection of Valium and bring it down, please?"

There was a strained silence. "I'll have to verify the medication with Dr. Perkins, sir."

Madison's jaw tightened. "Then do so at once!"

The nurse didn't respond, but the intercom switched off. For a few seconds longer, Madison stood near the panel, glaring at me with the type of disdain normally reserved for some poisonous species of spider.

Finally, taking a step nearer to the bed, he leaned down close once more. "I've already made arrangements to have you transported to a military base in Tampa," he said. "In fact, I anticipate a telephone call from the Center for Disease Control any moment now."

I frowned quizzically, willing the heart monitor to maintain a steady, unflustered pace despite the fact that I knew I was cornered. "What does the Center for Disease Control have to do with it?"

His smile returned - the smile of a man who believed himself the victor in some great historical battle. "Nothing directly. In fact, they don't even know you exist. However, in the interest of efficiency, I've taken the liberty of informing Dr. Perkins that I believe you to be suffering from some type of viral infection - one which attacks certain areas of the brain and could prove to be contagious after prolonged exposure."

I understood then. Perfectly. Clearly. Horror crept up on me like a storm. "So you called up your old Air Force buddies and told them you have another guinea pig for their labs, is that it?" I didn't wait for his answer. "They in turn will call this hospital under the guise of the CDC, recommend isolation in a superior facility, and I'll be conveniently disappeared off the face of the planet. End of problem?"

He seemed surprised, but answered nonetheless. "Something like that."

"My parents are very influential in the community," I bluffed, for I knew the threat was genuine.

"Your father disappeared years ago, and your mother's only concern is making preparations for your funeral," he replied, almost taunting.

At that, I heard the monitor betray me again. "You told her I'm *dead*?" I struggled against the restraints, then fell back with exhaustion when they refused to give. But one thing was dreadfully clear. Whatever was to be done with me, it meant I wouldn't be coming back. My obituary was already in the papers.

Madison stared at me with a self-satisfied smile. He liked the power and I hated him for that, too. But whatever he meant to say was curtailed when the intercom buzzed from across the room. Stopping in mid-sentence, he moved to answer it.

"Dr. Madison, this is Nurse McKitrick," a familiar female voice stated, sounding slightly confused. "We've just received a call from Disease Control in Atlanta regarding Ms. Willows' case."

"Yes, Nurse," Madison said condescendingly. "What was their opinion?"

A pause, then: "They say they'll back up whatever decision you feel is necessary. Their recommendation is immediate isolation at Tampa General Hospital to control any possible contagion factor. Dr. Perkins concurs."

From across the room, still holding eye contact with me, Madison's lips curved upward. "I'll make the arrangements for ambulance transport. Thank you, Nurse."

"Very well, Doctor," McKitrick replied. "Will you be riding with her or should I assign one of the senior residents?"

"I think it's in the patient's best interest that I accompany her. Oh, yes - prepare the Valium injection and bring it to Ms. Willows' room."

After an audible sigh, McKitrick agreed. "Yes, Dr. Madison. I'll be there as soon as the medication is released from Pharmacy."

Again the intercom switched off and I found myself staring into Madison's eyes as he returned to my bedside. My life had just been placed in his weathered hands.

"There, you see?" he said. "In another hour, none of this will really matter."

I glared at him, damning the restraints that held me immobile. "What makes you think you won't suffer the same fate as Richert?" I asked. I felt bad about the man with the pink carnation, but that didn't stop me from using his memory as a threat. Now it was a matter of survival.

Madison shrugged elaborately. "Quite honestly, if you had the type of power necessary to make Mr. Richert vanish, you would have used it by now. It's the people you're in league with that interest me more than any threats of yours."

I looked away, listening to the sounds of footsteps in the corridor outside the room. They came nearer, retreated, disappeared. Breathing again, I turned to glance at Madison, motivated by panic and the will to survive.

"What if you're wrong?" I asked pointedly. "What if the things that happened were just some random prank of the universe?"

He tilted his head to one side. "You seem to think this is funny."

"No, not at all. I only think *you're* funny. You're very superior over there in your bad suit and silly bow tie. You think all the answers can be found in a book you get down from some dusty shelf or one that you write yourself when the answers don't suit you."

He didn't move, didn't come toward me as I'd half expected. "I was young and full of ideals once, too," he sighed. "I suppose *you* have this one single answer to all the questions that have plagued mankind since time began?"

I think I smiled; I know I chilled. "Lesson number one, old man: there are no answers. There may not even be any questions."

Whatever he might have said after that I'll never know. It was then that the door to my room opened and a middle-aged, overweight nurse came in carrying a tray covered with a sterile blue towel. She met Madison half-way across the room with it, and I couldn't help noticing the nervous grin that slowly turned the corners of his mouth upward. He was a sadist in addition to whatever else he might have been.

For a single instant, panic threatened to overtake me and I struggled against the bindings that held my wrists. Then, subsiding back onto the bed, I made a pact with myself to at least appear sane to the nurse, though the heart monitor was chirping wildly and my body trembled.

"Nurse McKitrick?" I said.

The woman turned toward me with the kind of smile that only a nurse can get away with. "Yes, River? How are you feeling?"

I watched out the corner of my eye as Madison checked the injection, squeezing air bubbles from the syringe. Horror motivated me more than anything else ever had. I was being disposed of, taken out with the trash and thrown away.

"I feel fine, Nurse McKitrick," I said, forcing my voice to remain calm. "Could you tell me where I'm being taken?"

She came over to the bed and squeezed my hand gently. "You'll be moved to Tampa General, dear," she explained. "They'll be able to help you better than we can here. It's about thirty five miles away."

"I see," I said quietly. Then, knowing my time was running out, I made the only play open to me. Returning the pressure on her hand, I gave her the kind of look women reserve for their very best friends. "I know you won't believe me, Rachel," I began, reading her name tag, "but I honestly am not sick. I want you to promise me you'll check with my mother—."

"That's enough, Ms. Willows," Madison interrupted right on schedule. He looked to the nurse as he came closer. "She's been in and out of consciousness all morning; delirium is common in cases like this. No cause for alarm, though. The disease is undoubtedly transmitted through the blood. You haven't been exposed."

I squeezed McKitrick's hand again, ignoring Madison as he leaned down, bringing the needle against my inner elbow after a quick brush of cold, wet cotton.

"Please," I implored her, trying unsuccessfully to move away from the needle. "Check with my mother. You'll find out that she thinks I'm dead! I'm not being taken to Tampa General, but to MacDill Air Force Base! Check with TG tomorrow! You'll find that I never arrived there - that they've never heard of me! That call from CDC *never happened*, Rachel!"

"There, there," McKitrick soothed, gently petting my hand as a sharp sting announced Madison's victory. "You'll feel better soon, River..." But I saw the doubt I'd hoped to build in her eyes, the suspicion. If she'd make one phone call, if she'd call my mother or check with the CDC, she'd know Madison was lying.

"Don't patronize me, goddammit!" I snapped as the cold liquid move up my arm. "Just ask my mother! He's told her I'm dead! Ask her! Call CDC right away..."

Then it was over.

"She's been like this since she first awakened." Madison's voice. Indistinct. "Paranoid delusions... undoubtedly one of the symptoms of the disease. Her brain is trying to compensate... redefine reality... I'll speak with her mother myself, Nurse. The poor woman's meeting us at Tampa General..."

After that there was only darkness, and then The People found me again.

They welcomed me home with a ceremonial dance. I saw Synjin among them for the first time - aloof, beautiful, contemplative.

He wasn't dancing. Instead, he was sharpening a sword.

186

"Little ram? Little ram!"

The persistent old man was back again, this time a side-effect of my Valium-induced hallucination.

"River Willows! Must awaken! Bird cannot fly in river! Tree cannot grow in tea cup!"

I opened my eyes to find myself sitting with Ch'en Po on top of the ambulance as it sped down 1-75 toward Tampa. For an instant, vertigo overtook me and the world shivered, a leaf in a tempest.

"What are you talking about?" I mumbled, disoriented. "And while we're at it, where are we?" Still, I was glad to see him. He'd saved my life on the bottom of a lake. Maybe he could help me now.

"Half-way between your world and mine," he said, his accent thick and almost blown away in the wind which failed to rustle my clothes or cause my hair to move. Weird physics again. Like breathing water instead of air.

"What are you doing here?" I asked.

"Must wake up!" he insisted, squeezing my hands. "Must use budding skills to get away before find self locked up in silver box forever!"

I frowned. "What? Those things Madison said back at the hospital," I began, trying to remember. "Is Richert dead? _Did_ I cause those things to happen?"

Ch'en Po shook his head, his long gray beard seeming to hang suspended in mid-air. "Madison lied to you. Young ram did not cause. Just opened door to my world - almost let Synjin get out!"

"What?" I repeated, glancing up sharply.

"Synjin felt your danger, and came to protect you. Synjin can travel when and wherever he pleases, on road or between molecules of space. I stop him with common sense and big stick, but may not be so lucky next time. Not yet time for you to be with him."

I thought about that. I'd heard it before - on the bottom of the lake. "Why?"

Ch'en Po's very wise eyes studied me as the ambulance sped along the road, turning trees and grass into a rush of psychedelic green syrup.

"Training takes many years," Ch'en Po replied at last.

"Training?" I repeated. I knew instinctively that Synjin was already a Master many times over.

Ch'en Po nodded, then seemed to understand my puzzlement. "Ta!" he said again. "Not *his* training, little ram – *yours*! Cannot be with Synjin until you both learn what the universe plans for you," he added. "If you two come together before that, you forget the path, ignore the universe, get lazy and fat in front of TV set watching Bruce Lee movie ten times!"

I started to protest, yet I somehow knew that what he was saying was true. I tried to find some of his strength in myself.

"Don't go," I said, holding his hands more tightly. Time seemed to be moving too quickly, round in circles and back again to where it all began and ended in the same instant. "Why-? Why *now*?" I said at last. "I mean, why did these things seem to start happening all of a sudden?"

The little old man laughed. "Would you feel better if it happened last Tuesday? Nine o'clock on last Friday of third month? Things happen when things happen. Not too soon, never too late."

"All right," I conceded, though reluctantly. "Then why *me*? Why not somebody in Italy or Nepal or Outer Mongolia?"

He shook his head with a soft sigh. "Little ram butt head against innocent wall," he commented. "Not yet learn Lesson Number One."

"There are no answers," I said, before he could.

"But I tell you this: you're not alone. Many have the gift to travel between your world and mine. All children have it. But when they become teenagers, turn away from childhood, have awkward sex in back of sedan. When they become adult, forget the thrill of youth and drive sedan to pick up kids from school." He squeezed my hands in a very meaningful fashion. "Some *-few* - don't forget their dreams, don't send childhood into the past, then lament to psychologist about unhappy history. You keep child in heart, not in pretty frame on mantle. That's why government wants to dissect brain, lock up your soul in a silver box."

"I don't understand, Ch'en Po," I said. He spoke so fast I could barely understood the words, let alone what they meant.

"No time to explain now," he replied. "Understanding will come when time is right - not before, not later. Only when time is right."

I knew enough to realize that any argument would prove futile. Perhaps he *was* the temple, or some integral manifestation of it.

"You really aren't from around here, are you?" I asked, not expecting an answer. "Where *is* your world?"

He inclined his head to his left, then up, then released my hands and made the ancient martial arts system for All. "Right here," he said, his voice taking on a soft and gentle tone. "Slightly to left of tomorrow, half inch to right of quantum mechanics."

"You mean it exists in the same space as my world?"

The old man nodded. "Same space, different day. Same world, different rules. Same dirt, different worms."

I shook my head, utterly lost. "Then it's a matter of perception?"

He sighed softly. "Young ram get pain in head from butting wall," he said again. "Make old man tired."

I started to protest, needing to understand. "Then it *is* a parallel dimension," I said, mainly to myself.

"Label unimportant. What matters is that you're a traveler."

"Can I go there now?"

He looked around, ignoring my questions. The ambulance was slowing, turning onto an off ramp which would lead down into the city and eventually to MacDill Air Force Base.

"Now you must go back to *your* world," he stressed, reminding me of my all-too-real situation. "Use chi to control body and wake up from bad man's sleep. Call on skills and knowledge for strength. Wake up quick before sleep forever in cold silver box!"

That was the third reference he'd made to this mysterious silver box. I started ask him about it, but when I opened my mouth to speak, I gasped instead.

"Ch'en Po! Wait!" I called.

But I was already melting through the roof of the ambulance, slipping back into a drugged body that was too heavy and cumbersome.

From a great distance, I heard Ch'en Po whistling as he walked through traffic, over the roofs of moving cars, and into the ether. But as I struggled up through consciousness, his song became instead the siren's wail.

~

"...did the right thing, Colonel Madison... no doubt she's mixed up in this somehow... good to have you back on staff... a lot of new developments since you retired... clearance has been reinstated..."

"...I don't know, Geoffrey... thought we'd seen the last of them... eighteen Tourists already in cold sleep... might think they'd stop coming... still, she doesn't fit the profile entirely... could be just a pawn... maybe a prelude to invasion... who knows..."

"...doesn't make much difference... even if... knows something, she'll never talk... and if she doesn't know... still can't release her back into society... knows too much about the project..."

I listened to the voices for what seemed an eternity of motion, cradled in the hostile but indifferent womb of the universe. It felt safe where I was - warm, secure, unreal. Valium was good. Valium was God.

"...once we take her through those gates, she'll never leave... sure that's what you want to do, Avery? ...could be wrong about her, you know..."

"...doesn't matter, Geoff... tough little bitch... if we don't take care of her now, she's sure to come after *us* sooner or later... I'm sure she knows something... use her as bait... something was trying to protect her at the hospital... records say...to a psychiatrist a few years ago... delusions, probably, but... can't take that chance... what if... does know something about the Tourists? ...was interacting with something, that's for sure... not of this world, Geoff... experimental value if nothing else..."

"...give her to the goddamn Navy... let them worry about it... facility in San Diego's better equipped to handle Tourists... *if* that's what she is... like you said, eighteen of them already in suspension... might as well add one more... plane can be ready in fifteen minutes if need be... just don't think we should hold her here, Avery... too much chance of somebody looking for her..."

"...won't come looking... standard containment procedure... family thinks she's dead... background questionable... drowning was convenient... weren't a close-knit family unit to begin with..."

"...you're sounding like a psychiatrist again, Avery... let's just... get her in a freezer... forget about it... if she is... Tourist... only way to make sure she stays put... just like the others... throw away the key..."

Strains of the conversation playing back and forth between Madison and the other man told me more than I wanted to know. They had no intention of letting me go. Not now. Not ever. Something tingled along the edges of consciousness. Cold sleep. *'Eighteen Tourists already in cold sleep'*. There was something I should remember, but it stayed out of reach.

With a renewed sense of desperation, I cracked one eyelid just enough to take stock of my surroundings. In a split second - which was all I dared take -I saw that I was relatively unattended for the moment. The driver of the ambulance was out of my range of vision, as was anyone who might have been in the passenger's seat. Madison and his cohort were sitting near my head, one on either side, in the seats normally reserved for the paramedics. They were deeply enough embroiled in their conversation that they didn't notice when I chanced a second glance around.

This "Geoffrey" was a formidable son of a bitch - tall and stocky, dressed in a blue uniform and wearing the customary accouterments of his rank. His name tag read 'Colonel Geoffrey R. Segar'.

They continued talking about me and the "Tourists" for only a few moments longer. Then, laughing, their conversation turned to family, catching up on the past. I was as irrelevant to them as a barnacle on the back of a blue whale, and as expendable.

Taking a controlled breath, I listened to each movement, the pitch of their voices, the speed of the tires over the pavement. When their conversation turned to speculation about some new bit of construction we were passing, I surmised their attention was at least temporarily diverted.

I covertly tested the restraints that held me and was relieved to discover only two straps. One was placed across my chest, just below my breasts; the other was loosely fastened above my knees. A thick red blanket had been laid over the entire stretcher apparatus, and it provided the cover I needed. Moving with caution, I gradually inched my right arm upward, trying not to think about what I was doing.

Knowing I had little to lose, I quickened my endeavor at freedom when the ambulance sped up again, wriggling my right hand around under the blanket until my fingertips touched the cold metal fastener. Sliding the belt-like contraption back, I prayed that no clink of steel or creak of naugahyde would betray me. Luckily, whatever sound might have resulted when the strap separated was absorbed by the whine of steel-belted radials.

With the first obstacle removed, I slid my hand lower, carefully repeating the procedure until the second strap loosened its hold on my legs.

Forcing an unnatural calmness onto myself, I remembered something Master Barrows had said: *'If you have to fight, fight cold. Emotion is no companion to take into battle with you. You'll find it a more dangerous enemy than any physical adversary you'll ever face'*.

Drawing a deep breath, I found myself hoping that my body would still function according to the commands of my mind. If I understood time at all, I'd been either unconscious, delirious or comatose for a period of several days. My arms and legs felt strong enough to stand, but were they strong enough to fight, to run?

If emotion was the most dangerous enemy, then fear was worst of all. It crippled; it could kill.

For a few seconds longer, I had a pep talk with my Self. I'm not at all sure what was said, who said it, or if any of it really mattered. I was also employing Ch'en Po's advice - using my chi to control my body, to consciously dispel the effects of the Valium.

Finally, I hurled the blanket back and began to move. It was as if I were standing to one side of reality, watching it all unfold like an off-beat scene in some obscure movie.

The blanket itself made an effective weapon, and I threw it over Segar's head, stifling his startled curse. Holding it by the corners, I pulled it tight, yanking his back up against my chest as I boosted myself off the stretcher and scrambled toward the rear of the ambulance.

Not giving him the chance to fight me, I brought my left hand down hard against his solar plexus, snapping my wrist at the instant of contact to take his breath away. His arms continued to flail, however, his breath coming in tortured gasps. Too confined to adequately control him, I jerked his right arm up hard behind his back, dislocating his shoulder in the process of rendering him harmless.

Madison was shouting for the driver to stop and I was peripherally aware of a lurch as the vehicle slid to a halt. With Segar out of commission, I planted my feet against the floor of the

192

ambulance and slid backward, grabbing the inside handle and flinging the door open before Madison could get to me.

Rolling into the street, I scrambled to my feet just as the driver was rushing back to meet me. He was an MP, probably not much older than I was. Our eyes met for a fraction of an instant and I saw him hesitate, warring with his own conflicting emotions. He'd brought them into battle with him and they were to be his undoing. Startled and scared, he reached automatically for the hand gun strapped to his side.

Reacting on instinct alone, I kicked for his gun arm, knocking the weapon out of his grasp and into the street. He made a move toward it, changed his mind, then rushing toward me, he attempted a tackle which I side-stepped without effort. It all seemed so terribly easy - by the book, with Master Barrows' voice speaking softly inside my mind.

'Pivot on the right foot, turning with your attacker's momentum as your left hand catches the back of his neck. As your left foot comes back to the ground, your right hand circles, impacting with a palm-heel strike to the prominent vertebrae at the base of the neck. As your attacker falls face-down to the ground, you step through away from him, then front-thrust kick to his ribs. This will immobilize the attacker with pain so that escape is now possible. Our goal as martial artists is not to kill an attacker, but to survive the attack..'

And that's how it went. The only thing I wasn't prepared for was the young soldier's high-pitched yelp of pain and the sickening crack when his ribs broke under the force of the kick. Under any other circumstances, it might have made me give up fighting forever, but by that time, Madison had succeeded in crawling over Segar and was moving toward the soldier's gun. I was on him before I fully realized what I was doing, reacting on the instincts I'd developed over years of training.

The main thing I remember is thinking that *he* would certainly kill *me* if our positions were reversed. I saw myself go after him in slow motion, my right foot impacting with his skull as he bent forward to grab the fallen pistol. The force of the blow sent him sprawling sideways, rolling into the street. What surprised me was that he somehow managed to grab the gun at the same moment my kick landed.

I followed him down as he fell, planting my left elbow against his throat and my left knee in his stomach while my right hand caught the barrel of the weapon and forced his wrist backward. Regardless of his age, he was physically strong - perhaps because he believed he was about to die. Refusing to let go of the gun even after two fingers broke under the stress, he tried to forcibly shove his body upward in an attempt to throw me off balance.

Unfortunately, it was the last mistake Dr. Madison ever made. He might as well have taken the gun, put the barrel in his mouth, and scattered his own blood into oncoming traffic. In his frantic effort to free himself, he did succeeded in unbalancing me - which resulted in my full weight coming down on his throat when I pitched forward. Already weak from the hospital, I didn't have the strength to roll aside and spare him his life.

His larynx was crushed instantly, his stomach ruptured under the stress of my knee, and he drowned in his own blood while I looked down, horrified, into his disbelieving gray eyes.

Time stood still, pitched forward again, then back. Something touched me - something cold and misty. I had the hysterical image that it was his soul scrambling down to Hell.

Avery Madison was dead.

~

Steale stared at me for a very long time, not moving. Maybe he hadn't believed me when I first told him I'd killed Madison. Maybe he didn't want to believe it now.

Whatever he was thinking, he never revealed to me, and we never spoke of it after that day. I did not tell Steale of Ch'en Po or Synjin - at least not in direct terms. Rather, I related those segments of the story to him as if they had happened in a dream, fully and eternally aware of Ch'en Po's warning not to reveal his or Synjin's existence to another living being. Put simply, the names were changed to protect the innocent.

For a few minutes which stretched into half an hour, he simply held me in his arms, one hand tracing circles over my back.

"I'm glad he's dead," he whispered at last. "Does that make me a monster?"

I held my breath, coming to terms with my own feelings after more than six and a half years. "If it does, then I'm one, too. I didn't set out to kill him, but I don't think I'd go back and change it even if I could."

He breathed softly against my cheek, and said nothing for what felt like an eternity.

CHAPTER FOURTEEN
Little Green Men

"So *is* Kirin still alive?" I asked some time later.

"I really don't know," he said. "Kirin wasn't a fighter. She'd never had to fear for herself a day in her life. She was a gentle, trusting person, and I honestly believe that the hardest part was realizing that her brave new world was really screwed up. Me? I've never given trust easily. I knew we were being taken off somewhere to be disposed of. So as soon as we were on the plane, I pulled out my gun and started shooting."

"Why didn't they take it away from you in the beginning?"

"When they first showed up at the site of the crash, nobody seemed to know what anybody else was doing. Each guy probably assumed that someone else had already searched us, and no one ever did. I had the gun in my shoulder holster the whole time."

I stroked his chest in soothing circles, running my fingers over the acupressure points that relieved emotional tension. I began a slow and steady massage of those areas, trying to make it easier for both of us. His breathing evened out just a little.

"Once we knew we were trapped, Kirin kept saying that, if I could get back home, I could tell Callahan what happened and then send the corridor for her. And at that time, we thought we had a lot more control over the corridor than we really did. That's probably what went wrong and caused the crash in the first place - we sent the damn thing where it was never meant to go."

I could hear the sorrow and the agony in his voice, yet I could well understand what Kirin had done. She loved him enough to make him leave her. I hoped I would have had the same courage.

"There wasn't any other way, Steale," I said, holding him close. "Kirin knew that."

For several minutes, we lay in silence. I didn't remember changing positions, but found that I was lying on my back, his head on my shoulder in a mirror reversal of how we'd been previously.

"I finally made it to Arizona," he said, startling me when he spoke again. "It took nearly two weeks on foot, but I eventually got to the spot where the probe had been *supposed* to come out before the crash."

"That's how you got back home?"

He nodded against my chest. "There hadn't been any plans for something like what had happened. Neither Callahan nor anyone else had thought anything could go wrong. But they sent the corridor anyway. Every night for about an hour. Callahan told me later that he'd had to fight with the government for all he was worth just to do that much. He ended up losing his position at the university as a result, but I owe the bastard my life."

I hugged him tight against me, letting him heal as much as he could. "But you couldn't find Kirin?"

"At first, even with me in one world and her in another, the Way was clear. I knew it the minute she was taken into custody; I knew it when she was moved to San Diego; and I felt her fear when she realized what was happening to her."

My blood turned pale. "What happened to her?" Though I already suspected, I needed to hear it from him.

Steale held his breath for a moment. "It took Schaeffer's associates about a month to figure it out, but they found out how to work the stasis chambers. They must have realized that somebody would come back for Kirin and Fegan, and the easiest way to hold them was to keep them in indefinite life suspension. They didn't know they were holding a couple of scientists who couldn't have escaped from a Petri dish."

I tried to piece it together. It was starting to make a horrible kind of sense. "Why would they *want* to hold them?"

"Power," he said without hesitation. "They held them because they could. And one day, the Way went dark," he said then. "I just lost her. It was a long time ago." His words seemed out of place.

"How long?" I asked, trembling.

"Forty five years... a little more, I think."

I glanced up sharply. "You're not that old."

"No?" he said, his voice embittered and cold.

I chilled again, all the way through to my soul. I'd wondered about the time difference from the beginning, but there had been no clear opportunity to ask him about it. "You *can't* be that old."

Lifting his head, he looked up at me. "In your way of looking at time, I'm seventy five years old," he said. "Trust me; I was there every minute of it, though I often wished I wasn't."

Realities were colliding. "It doesn't make sense. In your dream, McFee said something about how time was different here - how our world was fifty years in the past."

Surprising me, Steale smiled. "As a comparison, that's right. But we're not time travelers, if that's what you're getting at. Your world is *still* fifty years behind ours - as far as technology goes, culture, social values."

I didn't understand, wasn't sure I could understand. "But...?"

"People in my world just age slower, that's all," he tried to explain, seemingly grateful to talk about something else

He was terribly casual about it, so much so that I found myself staring at him with open incredulity. "Why?" It was the only thing I could think of to say.

"Maybe because we're slightly more advanced than your world," he ventured, stroking one hand down my side. "Or maybe it's because we took care of some of the problems that plague your world before they ever got started. Like I said, I'm not a scientist. All I know is that we don't have the pollution problems you have here; we haven't knocked a hole in the ozone - although I understand from Callahan that your ozone hole will eventually screw up our world, too." He took my hand and held it pressed against his chest. "I don't know, River. Not everything."

I relaxed. "Sorry."

He smiled and I felt some of the tension leave both of us. "If it'll make you feel any better," he said a hint of humor coming back to his voice, "I should reach my so-called prime in about another fifteen years."

For that moment, we needed time to adjust to one another again. Regardless of the intimacy we had shared, the things he had told me went beyond any physical joining. He had shown me his soul, his inner Self. And I had revealed my darkest secrets to him.

We both had to be comfortable with that, with the power each of us now held over the other, before we could go any further.

~

"You don't look like a little green man," I told him over breakfast.

"The little green man story was the brilliant idea of some one-star-general at the crash site. Misinformation," he added, biting into an apple. "One of your government's favorite pastimes."

He got up and cleared away his plate, rustling around in the kitchen for a few moments before continuing. When he spoke again, he was leaning over the counter, looking at me intently. "Did you ever see *Close Encounters of the Third Kind?*"

I nodded, remembering the rainy afternoon at the tri-plex back in Tampa before my life turned upside down.

"There's a scene where the government doesn't want the contactees at Devil's Tower, so they put out a story about a freight train derailing and spilling poisonous gas, or something like that. Where Roswell is concerned, the tales of bug-eyed aliens from Mars were actually a cover story created by the military to scare people away.

"Misinformation depends on a lot of different stories, and none of it can ever be traced back to a reliable source. It's always Smith said that Jones told him that Colonel Davis said to ask Johnson. And if you're ever lucky enough to find Johnson, he's either retired, moved out of the area, or dead."

When I realized how little I knew about the UFO phenomena and the government in general, it did make sense. "So there were probably half a dozen different stories deliberately leaked. The people who first came on that crash site set the whole thing in motion?"

Steale nodded. "Apparently, some rancher had seen the probe when it went down in the storm. He called in the feds, but by the time the Army got around to coming out, there were already three different branches of the military involved. The Navy had an air station nearby, so they wanted in on it, and the Air Force claimed jurisdiction because the probe was considered an aerial phenomena. So, there were about six trucks, three Jeeps and a bunch of staff cars in the first convoy that arrived at the crash site."

There were at least a dozen questions I wanted to ask, but Steale hurried on, and I wasn't about to stop him.

"At first, in all the uproar, I had the impression that the people in charge thought it was some sort of air crash - a plane, I mean." He pushed himself up off the counter and came back to the table, sitting down next to me. "If they'd known from the beginning that it was the real thing, security would have been a lot tighter. But as it was, at least three dozen people actually saw the probe, and the majority of them weren't high-ranking officers who could be depended on to keep their mouths shut. The kids driving the trucks were just grunts, not career men with high security clearances. And once it became obvious what had happened, the military needed some way to discredit the rumors that were sure to start flying."

He reached across the table and rested his hand on top of mine, smiling softly. "How you holding up?" he asked then, surprising me with the abrupt change of subject.

I blinked. "Fine. Why?"

He inclined his head toward the clock on the kitchen wall. "Don't you have to open the studio at nine?"

I hadn't forgotten, though I realized I was procrastinating. I didn't want to let him out of my sight.

As if reading that thought, he stood up and came around behind me, bending down to place an unexpected kiss on my neck. It sent chills through my entire body, my entire being. The heat of his breath against my skin, the rough brush of his chin against my shoulder.

"Don't worry. I'll still be here when you get back," he murmured, and kissed me again.

I wanted to devour him. Or I wanted him to devour me. Either way, one thing was certain.

"I'm not going to the studio," I told him, making my decision at that moment. "You have a phone or do you just beam yourself here and there?"

He laughed softly, then went into the kitchen while I watched over my shoulder. Opening a drawer, he came back carrying a portable receiver.

"I was selfishly hoping you'd say that," he confessed. "Go ahead and make whatever calls you need to. I'll be in the living room with the papers."

I couldn't suppress the smile that came to my face as that image washed over me. "Looking for articles about people who need a one way ticket over the rainbow?"

He shrugged. "Does that bother you?"

Presented with the direct question, I was surprised to discover it didn't. "No – but it scares me. For you, I mean."

200

His brows lifted with devilment. "Still think you can save my soul?"

I met his eyes and held his intense gaze. "Maybe," was all I said. *Or you can save mine.*

That thought haunted me the rest of the day.

CHAPTER FIFTEEN
Pulling the Plug

I respected Jerry Davin because he didn't ask a lot of questions. When I told him I needed some time off - maybe a lot of it - he just said, "Okay," in that easy voice of his and let it go at that. He promised to send two of his black belt students to take over my class schedule and told me to stop by sometime for pizza and saki. I think he knew I was with Steale, but he didn't ask and I didn't volunteer.

But the time spent talking to him on the phone brought me to the conclusion that I needed to tighten the strings on my own life. I had left pieces of myself scattered from the studio to my camp site to Steale's house. And though I'd never been much for physical possessions, I understood that it was time to start pulling things together, packing the loose ends in boxes, and taking a step back to see the road where I'd been.

I found Steale in the living with his feet propped up on the coffee table and looking very normal. Not one soul in my world would ever have suspected that he was a little green man - an *old* little green man - who'd survived a flying saucer crash in 1947 and was now in the business of shuttling passengers between one universe and another. With the *L.A. Times* in his hand, he looked more like a renegade stock broker or even a travel agent.

That's what he'd called himself. He remained an enigma despite what I knew of him.

We talked for a few minutes and he agreed to drive me out to my car. The thing that surprised me was when *he* expressed the concern that *I* might not come back. I assured him that I would and told him simply that I needed some time to myself.

I realized then how true it was, and my answer seemed to set him at ease. While we drove through the desert, he relaxed considerably, reaching across the console occasionally to touch me on the arm or rest his hand on top of mine. No telepathy. Just the solidity of human contact.

We reached the Camaro a few minutes later, and he surprised me by handing me a silver house key just before I climbed out of the Lamborghini.

"I may be out for awhile this afternoon," he explained with a mischievous grin. "Business."

I felt a tug of anxiety, for I knew full well what he was talking about, but I took the key and stuffed it into the pocket of my jeans, then moved around to the driver's side and touched him affectionately on the shoulder. "Just watch your back, Steale."

"Yes, Master," he said with a wink.

The trickster was wearing that look again.

~

For the first few minutes, standing in the middle of a camp site I'd used off and on for nearly seven years, I felt good about the affinity I shared with Steale, and I knew now that our paths were inescapably connected. But as I began tearing down the tent and folding it, as I rolled the sleeping bag into a tight ball and wondered if I'd ever use it again, an unexpected tightness caught my throat until, for a moment, I couldn't breathe.

The silence of the desert pressed close, a living entity. Past, present and future collided, dancing like the heat gremlins on the hood of my car. A dark clarity overcame me, and I understood that every moment was a crossroad moment. What I did or didn't do right now would open an endless number of quantum windows into the realm of infinite possibility.

Put simply, my life was changing again – *had* changed the moment Steale walked into my studio. I'd known it then, and I certainly felt the consequences of it now.

Drawing a ragged breath, I walked into the open desert for several minutes, troubling thoughts suddenly exploding in my mind. Emotional overload. Stress anxiety. Post-trauma depression. I knew most of the clinical terms and could guess at the rest.

Whatever it was called, I found myself terrified and very much alone. When I was *with* Steale, some of that confusion was naturally diminished by the closeness of another living being. But now, alone in the desert again, it assaulted my fragile stability with a vengeance.

It wasn't *just* that Steale was a little green man. That wasn't even the half of it. Instead, it was the old human conundrum that always seemed to rear its ugly head when sex entered into an otherwise platonic relationship. Foolishly, I'd thought myself immune to its perils because of the circumstances life had dealt me.

Now – at a time when it was *most* inconvenient – I found myself face to face with the Self I *thought* I was, and the Self I had become.

I'd given myself to a man who wasn't Synjin, a man I'd hoped to help, a man I knew *needed* my help. Now, our relationship was bound to be different. I could rationalize it all I wanted, but in the end, I couldn't lie to my Self. He made it easy to want him, and I knew I wanted him still. My mind still felt the lingering tendrils of his telepathic touch. My body still ached with an unbearably pleasant pain left over from the intensity of our physical joining.

And yet...

I *belonged* to Synjin.

When Chalyn Thorne had matched us, she reminded me that it was a life-long commitment and beyond. The vows of The People didn't say, 'Until death do us part'. Instead, the words were, 'Beyond this life, until a time when the stars go dark'.

I sat down in the blistering summer heat and dropped my head into my hands, rubbing my eyes with my palms until a kaleidoscope of psychedelic colors blistered my mind.

Steale's face flashed before me, followed by the image of Synjin stolen from the astral plane. They were very much alike - perhaps *too* much alike, I thought. But one was virtue and honor, the other bitterness and despair. Yin and yang incarnate.

I thought again of the man Synjin had killed, the words Jaden had spoken, the anguish my mate had suffered as a result. And I couldn't help wondering if Steale would have even blinked an eye under the same circumstances. I wondered if I believed him when he said he'd only pulled the trigger of his gun once, and that with a tranq bullet. In *his* world, perhaps, but what had he done in mine?

The whole thing seemed beyond me. When I was a child, I had believed in another world, a better world. Many children did and, according to Ch'en Po, with good reason. But I began to realize it wasn't the perfect place I'd envisioned it to be in my childhood travels.

Rather, it was a place which had sent four travelers into my hostile and alien environment, and had never made any serious effort to get them back. There was still much Steale hadn't revealed, but from the comment he'd made about Callahan McFee losing his job at the university because of the government, it was clear that the serpent in the bureaucratic garden existed there as well as in my own world.

I didn't like that realization. My daydreams had always told me I would meet Synjin on the morning of my thirtieth birthday. We would walk together into his world along a path strewn with flower petals and twining vines. He would speak to me in his cat's-purr voice, and we would spend the day holding hands as he showed me the Temple of Kalpa. Then, at night, when the moon was full, he would take me to a secluded garden, lay me down on a bed of soft feather pillows, and shyly make love to me with the sound of bells pealing in the distance.

Hell, the moon wasn't even going to be full on my thirtieth birthday. I'd already looked at the calendar.

It was a young girl's fantasy. *Synjin* was a fantasy. Five minutes in a dark broom closet six and a half years in the past wasn't enough to sustain the process of living. I'd told myself one kiss would be enough to keep my dreams alive, even if on artificial life support. Now, while I watched in horror, the illusion drew its last breath and died in the desert, a continent away from where it was born.

The plug had been pulled.

"Is that what you think?"

I didn't even look up. Instead, I drew my knees to my chest, leaned against a boulder and rested my forehead on my arms – the classic portrait of a ball of misery.

"I've lost myself" I said without inflection. The words surprised even me.

Ch'en Po didn't answer, and I wondered if he'd simply shuffled away on the wind. Then, a few seconds later, I felt a soft thump and saw his ancient face peering up through the space between my arms and knees. He was lying halfway on the ground, head tilted to one side, looking at me with the most quizzical expression I'd ever seen.

"Might have picked a cooler spot for self-pity party," he commented, ignoring my previous statement.

"I needed to be *alone*," I said, hoping he'd take the hint.

"Can be alone in crowded street of Beijing if truly a Master," he reminded.

That caused me to look up, a moment of anger flashing through my chi. "I'm *not* a Master, Ch'en Po," I stressed, trying to make him see that.

"Ta ta ta!" he scolded. Then his voice softened. "Say the first thing that comes to mind."

"I slept with Steale last night." *And I want to do it again.* I couldn't seem to think of anything else. My years of being a virtuous virgin had obviously ended. I'd had the thrill of ecstasy and I wanted more.

Ch'en Po waited. "And?"

"And?" I repeated, incredulous. "I mean, I *slept* with Steale."

"And?" Ch'en Po said again.

Maybe he was being deliberately obtuse. "We made love." There, I said it.

"And?"

Frowning in frustration, I looked at the old man. "I've betrayed Synjin... I've dishonored myself."

He looked at me the way one might study a bug. "How dishonor?"

"Do you even know what I mean when I say I made love with Steale?" Maybe he didn't.

Ch'en Po only laughed. "Being old not the same as being dead. Made love to my pretty wife many times when younger."

I stared at him again. "You're *married*?"

"Was," he said. "Long time ago. Wife ran away with young snipperwhapper, so I went to the temple. Wanted to learn how to chop-chop snipperwhapper into dust, impress wife, make story have happy ending. Finally learned stories not always end the way we want. Long time ago," he repeated.

"You were *married*?" I said with a smile, temporarily forgetting my own problems.

"Don't look so surprised. You grow old, too, one day - if you live long enough."

I chuckled anyway. "I thought you were a priest – or a monk... or whatever."

His brows lifted with amusement. "I thought you were young ram. Instead you act like young billy goat – still butting head against wall of self-created jail."

As usual, he found a way to bring the conversation back to me. "I slept with someone else," I stressed, forcing myself to hold his gaze. "I *belong* to Synjin."

"Belong to your *Self*," Ch'en Po countered. He shrugged his small shoulders. "How old do you think Synjin is?"

I hadn't really thought about it. "Thirty." It was worth a shot.

But Ch'en Po was howling with laughter again. "Synjin sixty-eight years old!"

My stomach turned over. "Wh-what?" I stammered.

He giggled with apparent glee. "Had birthday party last October. Old man burn finger lighting last candle on sheet-pie. Number sixty-eight. Synjin have long life before you ever *born*!"

I was too stunned to say anything as the last shred of my fantasy gasped and died. Nearby Joshua trees wept, but it was only the wind scratching along their jagged fronds. A dust devil danced, carrying what remained of my sanity over some invisible rainbow.

"But we were matched by Chalyn Thorne when I was seventeen," I protested, almost to myself. The image I'd had of Synjin wasn't a day over twenty five at the time; and regardless of what I'd learned from Steale, I couldn't make sense of it.

"So?" Ch'en Po said, drawing me back to reality.

He was starting to piss me off. "What do you mean 'so'?"

He seemed to understand then, for a look of stunned comprehension came over his very wise features. "Young ram thought was Synjin chaste?" he asked with almost as much incredulity as I was feeling.

My face deepened to crimson which I couldn't blame on the effects of the sun. "I don't know what I thought," I muttered.

Reaching out, Ch'en Po took my hand, squeezing it until I looked up at him. "Would be nice thought, maybe," he said, his voice soft and gentle, "but Synjin had many lovers when young. He came to the temple to learn control over passions and domain over temper. Body not so much problem now, but he still has temper."

But I was still stuck in the groove of my own programming – what I had believed colliding with the truth.

"Then fidelity means nothing in your world?" My voice was bitter.

Sighing heavily, Ch'en Po shook his head. "Yin and yang work together, not apart. If you live with soul in balance, water in body seek its own level, seek other tree for company. Soon, forest grow."

I didn't answer, had no idea what to say or even if he expected me to say anything at all.

The old man was frustrated with me and I didn't blame him. "Time to learn lesson number three."

I wasn't sure I wanted to know. "What?"

"Life not always go according to plan."

No shit.

"It's just that a lot of things aren't like I thought they'd be," I said, trying to explain my own irrational feelings, though I probably sounded like I was whining.

He smiled very softly and squeezed my hand once more. "Humans are meant to feel, to love. Meant to enjoy touch of another's body, or the touching wouldn't be pleasant."

Synjin still weighed heavily on my soul, burdening my judgment.

"The voices of your agreements having argument in your head," Ch'en Po said, almost as if to himself.

I was hallucinating. It was the only explanation.

Ch'en Po sighed softly. "There comes a day in the life of every warrior when you must ask not just *what* you believe, but *why* you believe it." His accent had disappeared completely, his words measured and succinct.

"I don't always *know* what I believe – what I *should* believe!" I said at last.

"Do you *feel* in your chi that you've betrayed Synjin, or do you only *believe* it because your world has programmed you to believe you *should* believe it? Are you the real River Willows or just an actor in a soap opera script?"

The question caught me off guard, and something stirred in the deepest recesses of my being. *Was* I only acting out a drama because I believed I *should*? Were all humans programmed by their society and culture to adhere to belief systems which were really only transient morals assigned to man *by* man?

It was as if Ch'en Po had injected some disturbing antidote deep into the program itself, and suddenly the program was collapsing as surely as if Captain Kirk had just talked another malevolent computer into cyber-suicide.

The problem was – the computer was *me*, and the destruct sequence was anything but pleasant.

First my fantasies had died. And now my beliefs were rapidly crumbling in the wake. Nothing was real and yet nothing unreal could exist. The universe was a contradiction written in the blood of all that was sacred... and yet *nothing* was sacred.

Every event – every *thought* which was the precursor of every *action* – was a unique universe unto itself. There were no shoulds or shouldn'ts. Right and wrong had to be determined from the plateau of perception at any given moment. Even good and evil were not carved in granite as I had once believed. The yin and yang wasn't really black and white, but an infinite combination of shades of gray.

There were no absolutes.

And though this new perception I had discovered between one heartbeat and the next was appealing and undeniably real, I couldn't help thinking that it wasn't supposed to *be* like this! I needed more time – to adjust, to adapt, to evolve.

Maybe I even needed those absolutes – or thought I did.

Ch'en Po sat in silence for a very long while, watching me as I wrestled with a paradigm shift that was both life-altering and world-shattering. It was as if he had plucked me out of one reality and deposited me into another.

"Must listen to chi always," the old man reminded. "Teach students according to what you feel, to what chi tells you. Life not always go according to plan," he repeated.

"You mean shit happens," I commented without humor.

Ch'en Po shrugged. "Step in life, too, sometimes."

I laughed despite my misery; it helped a little. But I took the opportunity to talk about something else that was important, forcing my thoughts to something other than myself. "Do you know what happened to Steale and the others? About the probe, I mean."

As he often did, my Master ignored my direct question. "Young ram intend to sit here in hot sun all day while brain bake like Christmas turkey?"

"You said that Steale's a part of my path," I began again, turning Ch'en Po's own tactics back on him by ignoring his comment. "I just want to know that what I'm doing is right. Is that so much to ask?"

The old man looked at me. "Ask chi."

My mind was still too unsettled to find out anything from my chi. I was back to lesson number one. I took a deep breath, closing my eyes as I struggled to find my center.

When I opened them again, Ch'en Po was already gone. I thought I saw his shadow walking without him, but when I blinked, it was only a whirlwind.

~

It took nearly an hour to walk back to the half-demolished camp site, and during that time, I tried to make sense out of what Ch'en Po had said. What it all boiled down to was chi.

All information, all Knowledge was accessible through the gnosis of chi – which existed as a living, quantifiable force permeating the entire extent of the All. Not just my world, but Synjin's world. Not just Synjin's world, but *all* the worlds flung like diamonds and emeralds and fiery rubies into the vast void of space. And not just space, but *time* itself.

Everything that had ever happened or ever would happen was already recorded in that energetic web of the chi – which was, when all was said and done, the living animus, the breath of the multiverse, and perhaps even the essence which some thought of as Spirit.

Though I had been instructed in the importance of chi since first walking through the doors of Master Barrows' dojo, I had never really considered what chi actually *was* other than the words used to describe it. Now, I felt it moving the way the wind moves through trees – influencing their movement without controlling it, guiding the growth of the branches and the flight of the dove who makes her nest among them.

With a genuine connection to chi, one could scry the mind of all the gods – and yet, the secret seemed to lie in not only knowing what questions to ask, but in how to listen to the answer. The secret of personal power came not from brute strength, but through subtle surrender. Through vulnerability, one may become invulnerable. Unconditional love was the ultimate manifestation of chi, and as such it was a universal force that could not be contained nor even anticipated.

These things were whispered to me in the silence of the desert, the heat of an insignificant day in a long line of days and years.

Attempting to sort all of it out would have been a fool's errand. I accepted with no small measure of irony that I was no longer the same person I had been when Synjin and I had first been matched, not even the same person I had been when we had stolen five minutes in a broom closet on the other side of the continent.

We were both resplendent mysteries - servants of life, vessels of spirit, channels of the inexplicable force known to humans simply as love.

I began packing up the few things I always left lying around the camp site. One by one, I placed the items in the back of the car until, when I stood and looked over the camp site, there was nothing to say I'd ever been there at all.

I wondered fleetingly if I would have the same thought when I came to the end of the path Ch'en Po was always talking about, if I'd look back and scratch my ghostly head and try to imagine what I *should* have done. And yet... *should* was an illusion and regret nothing more than the heavy gravity of the things we had been taught to believe which had very little to do with reality itself.

One thing was certain: my life had been anything but normal. And yet, normal was just a word to describe the lowest common denominator of mediocrity. Normal was nothing more than the default landing within the drone of the syllabus – the lazy man's plateau where average and ordinary came together to create absolutely nothing of consequence.

Who in their right mind would *want* to be *normal*?

I drew a deep breath of hot summer air, perspiration pouring unnoticed down my back until my shirt was wet and clung to my body. My chi had decided to talk to me, and it was telling me the same things Ch'en Po had tried to tell me, but in words and images personal unto my Self.

I found myself breathing easier. I thought again of what I had learned from Steale. Kirin, Fegan, Lissi, all of it. *Eighteen Tourists in cold sleep.* One of them Steale's wife, another his friend. The rest had no names or faces, but their lives were unique, too. And those lives had been interrupted by men who did not understand the path of the warrior or the heart of the tree.

I knew then what I had to do.

CHAPTER SIXTEEN
Forward Momentum

"I'm glad you're here. For awhile there, I was afraid you weren't coming back."

It was Steale's voice, and I lifted my head off the couch to find him standing over me. The clock over the television read 8:45 and the room was dark save for a dim light shining through from the kitchen. I'd fallen asleep nearly two hours before, exhausted and sunburned from the desert.

I smiled up at him and accepted his hand when he offered it. He pulled me into a sitting position, then curled up next to me. The physical contact felt remarkably natural, comfortable.

I patted his arm reassuringly. "There's something I want to talk to you about," I said.

"You've fallen hopelessly in love with me and you're planning on moving in," he said with a grin. It wasn't a question.

In close physical contact, his telepathy was formidable. "Yes." Then I thought about what he'd said. "I mean – yes, I'm planning on moving in."

His brows lifted; mischief was in his eyes – an encouraging contrast to the despair normally found there. "But you haven't fallen hopelessly in love with me?"

I was learning to enjoy his teasing, though I had no idea what to do with it other than play along. "Maybe." But my smile faded and I became serious, reaching across the table to take his hand. "But I've also come to the conclusion that I can't teach you everything you're going to need to know at the studio. So if you'll overlook the fact that I'm being more forward than I've ever been in my life, I think we should start your training right away. We don't have a lot of time."

He blinked. "You're serious, aren't you?"

"There's still a lot you haven't told me, which is what I wanted to talk to you about over dinner. After that's out of the way, I'll tell you what I have in mind."

He was smiling again. "I show you mine, you show me yours?"

He had an uncanny way of putting me at ease, while at the same time making me more nervous than I'd ever felt around another living being. "Something like that. Okay?"

He didn't argue. Instead, looking at me intensely, he inclined his head toward the back of the house. "There's something I'd like to show you right now," he said suggestively.

The butterflies in my stomach gave me a swift kick in the ribs. He was terrible. He was impossible. "Steale, I'm being serious."

The sparkle didn't leave his eyes. "So am I."

He stood, pulling me up after him and gesturing down the hall. I started to argue, then gave him the benefit of the doubt as I followed to a closed door opposite the master bedroom.

With one hand resting lightly on my elbow, he opened the door, waving his hand in front of a sensor until the room was bathed in soft white light. Gesturing me inside, he stood there for a minute while I looked around.

The room was twice the size of the master bedroom and had obviously been recently remodeled. There was a scent of fresh pine and paint from where a dividing wall had been removed to enlarge the floor space. Thick mats completely covered three-fourths of the room, with a carpeted area roughly fifteen feet square left open to the north. There was even a meditation area in one corner - an intricately painted Chinese screen which blocked the area off from the rest of the room.

I didn't speak, didn't know what to say.

He broke the silence for both of us. "I'll tell you whatever you want to know, River." He put one arm around my shoulder and encouraged me to rest against him.

I blinked, gazing into the studio he'd built, once again confronted with the realization that he seemed to know what I was thinking before I knew it myself.

Maybe he did.

~

"I'd hoped I might have some pull from being an Argus," Steale was saying as we sat in the living room after dinner was finished. "But when I went to my boss after talking to Callahan, he told me to drop it."

We hadn't spoken much while we ate and were only now involved in the conversation I'd been waiting for. The two dragonfly lamps were glowing softly and the sounds of Nakai drifted through the room at low volume.

Steale was sitting on the sofa, leaning forward with his elbows resting on his knees. I'd taken the love seat a few feet away, my legs curled underneath me.

"You mean they didn't even look for Kirin and the others?"

Steale shook his head. "It wasn't that simple, really. My boss - Taler - wasn't much higher up in the Elite than I was. Project Gateway had been originally funded by the university where Kirin worked, but it was taken over by the government just before the first launch." He shrugged with seeming indifference to hide his deeper emotions. "The government had always supported independent research, and it wasn't uncommon for the feds to step in and fund projects that showed extreme promise."

"You mean take them over," I said to myself.

He turned his head to look at me. "I honestly do think Gateway was just another experiment as far as the government was concerned. But when the probe didn't come back on schedule, they got scared."

I frowned quizzically. "Scared? Of what?"

"Everything," Steale said quietly. "After Taler told me the name of the fed who was actually in administrative charge of Project Gateway, I flew out to his office. Actually, I was *summoned* to his office."

"That sounds ominous."

He didn't deny it. "The fellow's name was Vale," he began. "I didn't like him from the start, He'd stepped into the administrative offices immediately after the probe accident. He sat me down and started talking about all the same bullshit Callahan used to talk about - cultural contamination, social interference, biological contamination; but he was using them as excuses that didn't wash."

I tried to see both sides. "Aren't those reasonable fears? Maybe they just thought our world wasn't ready."

He lifted his head, his expression dark. "Vale wasn't worried about *your* world. He was talking about *mine*. He gave me a song and dance about how we'd known the risks when we accepted the assignment. I had the feeling that me getting back made it worse than if *none* of us had made it home - because I knew Kirin and

Fegan were still alive, and that made it harder for them to refuse a rescue attempt."

A cool breeze drifted in through the open window, stirring his hair. When he continued, it was with a detachment that was anything but detached. "I spent two days in his office for what he called a de-briefing session. It consisted of him asking me a lot of questions about what I'd seen here, especially about the operations of the military, and so on.

"I was still in shock from everything that had happened," he added, the pain in his voice barely concealed beneath an outward attempt at calm. "It had been seventeen days since the crash, only about seventy-two hours since I'd found the corridor in Arizona and made it back home."

I frowned thoughtfully. "Was there another ship? *Could* they have launched a search?"

"They didn't really need another ship. The corridor could be sent to any location in your world which already had a predisposition toward dimensional overlap."

"Then why the first probe?" I wondered.

He shrugged. "Ever try to carry soil samples and stasis chambers filled with live animals through an electromagnetically enhanced tunnel on your back?"

I smiled. "Can't say that I have."

He chuckled softly, breaking some of the tension. "The ship was just a glorified truck in a lot of ways. We needed something that was capable of skirting over the land and also capable of carrying back Callahan's precious specimens." He paused as if not wanting to remember, then continued more slowly. "Anyway, it became obvious that the crash had scared the hell out of our government. Vale was afraid that people from your world would take the ship apart and figure out what made it work. And he was right. To Vale's way of thinking, it was only a matter of time before your scientists figured out how to create the corridor for themselves."

"Wouldn't our scientists have figured it out anyway? Yours did. In another fifty years, wouldn't it have happened naturally in my world?"

"In another fifty years?" he repeated. "You mean right about *now*?"

I glanced up sharply. It had been forty-five years since the probe crashed. "*Do* we have the corridor?"

"Not that I know of, but that's not the problem. One of the main things Callahan was always paranoid about was technological contamination . His feeling was that, when technology develops at a faster rate than social understanding, inevitable cataclysm results."

I was starting to see what he was getting at. "Our scientists took apart that probe, eventually found out how to use Fegan's computer, and now we're in the process of destroying ourselves with what we've learned."

He nodded. "Did you ever wonder why computer science just started advancing so rapidly in the late 60's, and especially in the 70's?"

"I guess I just assumed some mad scientist discovered the microchip like his predecessor discovered the amoeba."

Steale shook his head. "They discovered a lot of 'amoebas' in the probe. Neutron radiation, for one." He looked grim. "Fegan was always working on a variety of projects, and neutron radiation was one of his pets. He developed it as a method of sterilizing soil samples, but it was later perfected by Lissi as a means to safely kill harmful bacteria in the atmosphere. I'm no scientist, but as I understand it, the formula *we* brewed up had a selective kill factor. When there were flu epidemics, or outbreaks of some new disease, the formula could be adapted and released into the atmosphere in controlled amounts. It was meant to kill germs, not people."

"But my government turned it into a weapon," I realized.

Steale didn't reply. Instead, getting up, he went into the kitchen. I heard him rattling around and when he returned, he was carrying two glasses of red wine. Handing me one, he sat back down on the couch.

"There's more," he said darkly. "Certain viruses had been artificially created in the labs in our world. One of them had to do with transplant surgery. By injecting a patient with a particular drug containing the live virus prior to surgery, the immune system could be temporarily suppressed. Rejection of a new organ didn't happen as frequently. Then, once the organ was in place, the immuno-suppressant virus could be neutralized. I don't understand all the medical jargon, but that's how Kirin explained it to me once."

"And someone in our world warped that formula the same way we warped neutron radiation," I assumed.

"The evidence is pretty damning. Your world had technology by the mid 70's that it shouldn't have until after the turn of the 21st century. Your government has taken every scrap of information out of that computer and, in most cases, perverted it into Lethe knows what."

I considered his words in silence, trying to digest it all. The things he was saying were not what I wanted to hear, not what I wanted to believe about my world or any other.

"Then why haven't we perfected the corridor?" I asked.

"It's not far away," he said. "Who knows, it may already have happened. If it hasn't, it's probably because your scientists don't know where to look for the natural doorways. As Callahan's associates found out after the crash of the first probe, we can create the corridor, but there's a danger if we try to send it somewhere it's not meant to go."

"I don't understand."

He leaned forward once again. "You said you've been into my world a few times. How did you get there?"

"Usually, I go there astrally... if I understand what that means." It sounded ridiculous; it always had. "My energy body travels."

"But you've never been there physically?" he pressed.

"Once. A few days ago. That's how I found your little operation out by Barker Dam."

"You wandered into a natural doorway," he explained with a soft smile. "There's a legend that says there were a lot of doorways between your world and mine. But when civilization grew, a lot of things changed. The doorways started to close and after awhile, only a few remained. If you listen to old stories, only the Masters can travel the natural passageways."

It certainly explained why I'd run into Ch'en Po out by Barker Dam that morning.

He leaned back on the couch again with his hands behind his head, the muscles in his arms stretching his dark skin. I still noticed. My chi said it was all right now.

"It doesn't make sense that your government would abandon two of its top scientists," I persisted, unable to get past that.

Steale took a sip of his wine. "Vale's argument was that the corridor was unreliable, unpredictable. He felt that we could end up losing *more* people. Hell, he might have been right. Like I said, we didn't know a lot about how the corridor worked. We sent the first probe into an area where there was no natural doorway and it spit us out like poison."

"So what happened?"

"For a long time, nothing," Steale said after a long silence. "It was shortly after my last meeting with Vale that I lost the Way with Kirin. I thought for a long time she was dead."

His words were spoken coldly, yet I could feel the dangerous fire burning in his blood. It reflected in his eyes.

"How long can the stasis field be maintained?"

"It doesn't matter, does it? Kirin's lost."

His voice said, *'Drop it'*, but I had learned to read him better than that.

"You said you had a falling out with your brother after you and Kirin were separated," I reminded him, trying to redirect the focus for a moment. "Was he in the government?"

Steale laughed aloud. "Hell no. He was an Argus, too. We'd been on the same unit since he joined the Elite."

"And?" I prompted.

He shrugged indifferently. "Like I said, I badgered Vale all I could and then I lost the Way with Kirin. After that, nothing really mattered. I was eventually dismissed from the Elite."

Getting up from the love seat, I went and sat next to him, slipping one arm behind his neck. I needed the solidity of human contact, and I believe he did, too.

"Tell me about your brother," I said awhile later.

He drew a deep breath which blew warm against my shoulder. There was sadness in him, but also a strength and determination I'd hoped to release.

"He always told me Kirin was still alive, that the government would change its mind eventually, and a search party would be sent. He even went to Vale on his own once without my knowing about it – which is where the trouble really started."

"You were close?"

He nodded. "He was a few years younger than me, and we'd always had this mock rivalry. Kirin thought he was the best thing the gods ever made, and he was always over at our place. I think they probably even slept together a few times."

He said it so casually that it took me off guard, especially when I remembered my own dilemma of earlier in the day. "Is that what caused the problems between you?"

Lifting his head, he looked at me oddly. "No. Why should it?"

"He was your brother, and Kirin was your wife," I tried to explain.

He laughed softly, resting his head on my shoulder again. "That's another way your world's really screwed up. I loved my brother and I loved my wife. Shouldn't they love one another, too?"

My jaw slackened. "Well, yes, but there's an old saying around here that has to do with coveting your brother's wife."

He laughed again. "You're talking about religion. River. You have to realize that things are a little different where I'm from. We're not an immoral society, but we got rid of the Victorian baggage a long time ago. Man is an animal first. Trying to change that with religious morals and social limitations only corners the animal and makes it dangerous – not to mention conflicted." He waved his own words aside.

His world, though it did sound a lot less complex, a lot less screwed up, as he'd said. "So it's a sort of free-love 1960's kind of thing?"

He gave me a wicked look. "It's not really like that, but if it'll make you feel any better, I'll buy some love beads and grow my hair long."

"Your hair's already long." I ran my fingers through it. Liquid silk.

He breathed deeply, relaxing a little. "Love is what you make it. My brother and Kirin loved one another a great deal. That wasn't the problem."

I was getting curious about something. "You keep referring to your brother in the pronoun form. Doesn't he have a name?"

Steale stiffened against me, then subsided a moment later. "When you cut someone out of your life, you don't speak their name after that. There's power in a name. I can't ignore the fact that he was my brother, but that's where it ends."

I felt an overwhelming sadness at that. "Want to tell me?"

"Not really."

"Tell me anyway," I insisted.

He took another moment to compose himself, relaxing onto my shoulder and sliding lower until his head was in my lap.

"To make a long story short," he said with a sigh, "I knew something really weird was going on. So I contacted Callahan. After a couple bottles of Scotch, he gave me the access codes to the university. Computer codes. Like the good mad scientist he was, Callahan always left a back door in his programs. I couldn't access the information from outside the university, though, since the computers were programmed to only accept input from the mains."

"So you broke in," I translated.

He nodded. "All I could really tell from the data was that two additional probes had already been launched into your world. The nature of their mission was classified - which meant that whatever information existed wouldn't be in the university's computers."

"Which led you back to Vale," I surmised.

"I was tired of screwing around, trying to be nice. I grabbed the little weasel and put him up against the wall – scared him enough that he told me everything."

I felt his aura go cold.

"The second probe had crashed, just like the first. The third came back intact, but the information they brought with them caused our government to realize that any further contact with your world was suicidal - for *both* cultures," he stressed. "Even so, according to Vale, a fourth probe had been scheduled. It was to be the last one, and its mission was to seek out and destroy the natural doorways in your universe. They were going to seal the tunnel, so to speak, so that travel in *either* direction would be impossible."

"Were they *that* scared?" I wondered, my heart beating faster. If they ever did close those doorways, I would never see Synjin again, and Steale would be trapped in my world forever.

"They had good reason to be scared," he said. "Things were already getting screwed up here because of the technology we'd inadvertently left on the first probe. Our scientists started to wonder what would happen if - *when* - your people started their next war. My government felt that the only way to save *our* home was to try to seal off the corridors once and for all."

"But what about the crew of that fourth probe?" I wondered. "Wouldn't they have been trapped on our side if they destroyed the corridor?"

"It was a suicide mission, but the crew hadn't been told about that - just like we weren't told about all the risks. Vale's people had convinced the staff at the university that the crew of the fourth probe would be able to set off a series of disruptions in the upper atmosphere which would create a chain reaction in the natural electromagnetic fields around the Earth. In theory, once the electromagnetic fields here were disrupted, the natural corridors would just short out."

I got a clear enough picture. "So how does your brother fit into all of this?"

He tensed again. "Turned out when I cornered him that he'd *volunteered* to go on that fourth mission."

"So?"

He was staring at the ceiling again. "I told him what I'd found out from Vale, but he didn't believe me. He said that the third probe - the only one that ever made it back home - had found out where Kirin and Fegan were being held. But when I asked him to tell me everything, he just kept repeating that it was classified."

I considered that. "Maybe he was trying to protect you."

Sighing, Steale closed his eyes once more. "All I know is that he betrayed my trust – *and* Kirin's. The fourth probe was scheduled to launch in six weeks, and I still had the access codes I'd gotten from Callahan, so it was easy enough to get back into the university late at night."

"To do what?"

"To fuck up the computers - and the probe couldn't launch without them. I erased everything, including all the back-up files. One thing I'd learned from Fegan was that a computer virus was more lethal to a book-worm than the plague. So I fed one into the main-frame and sat back to wait while it garbled every shred of information vaguely related to Project Gateway."

"There weren't other copies of the information?"

"I'm sure there were, but they'd fired Callahan McFee. He was the only person alive who fully understood how the corridor worked. I had to rely on his integrity not to help them out of a bind, and he was just bitter enough about the whole thing that he didn't."

His answer only awakened another question. "Then what about Barker Dam? If you destroyed the data that controls the corridor, how do you...?"

"The technology needed to make it work is actually pretty simple. Callahan had the prototype hidden in his liquor cabinet," he added with a chuckle. "When I told him what I wanted to do, he gave it to me without so much as a question."

"Then there's a device?"

He nodded. "Pandora's box," he said, as if it were a private joke between Steale and himself. "It can detect the energy field surrounding the natural doorways and amplify the affect for a period of six minutes."

I made a mental note to ask him more about the technology at a later time. For that moment, I was more interested in other areas of Steale's past. "So what happened when your brother found out about the sabotage? Did he know you did it?"

Steale snorted. "Of course he knew. After the probe was cancelled, he blamed me for the fact that he wasn't going to get his opportunity to be the big hero and rescue Kirin. He just refused to accept that it wouldn't have worked, that he'd end up dead or locked up in a stasis box, too."

"So what happened? If you're as old as you say you are, there's still a lot of time unaccounted for."

Steale sighed softly, gazing out the open window. "I disappeared for awhile and waited for things to cool off. Most of the time, I spent at my grandfather's house up in the mountains." He shrugged with that embittered indifference again. "There's a lot I don't remember. Like I said, I lost track of everything after I lost Kirin. My brother and I parted ways about five years after the crash, and I didn't see him until eighteen years ago." He had that distant look in his eye, the one that made him sad, the one that made him dangerous.

"What did you do for so many years in the mountains?" I asked, coming to the conclusion that changing the subject might be the only way to reach him.

"Read a lot of books, watched a lot of television," he explained, looking up at me for the first time in awhile. "What did *you* do in the desert for so long before you ran into Jerry?"

He had a point. "Not much. I wrote a little."

"That's about it," he said then. "Now you know where I came from, who I am, what I do."

"You said you knew Kirin and Fegan were being held," I recalled, choosing my words with utmost care.

"I know where it is," was all he said.

"And?"

His eyes closed; he withdrew again.

"Steale?" I said after long minutes of silence.

"There's no way in. And there's no way out."

That was the answer I needed. I placed one hand in the middle of his chest, trying to impart my confidence through the closeness of touch. I was no telepath, but I think I reached a small part of him.

"You've traveled from one world to another, Steale," I said, filled with awe of him. "You've done things that no one else in either place has ever done before. Why can't you understand that, if other dimensions can be breached, walls and fences are only barriers in the mind?"

He turned his face away from me, toward the window again. "You haven't seen the walls and the fences."

My destiny was stalking me. I would have run if I could, but there was nowhere to go. And in so many ways, I knew I had been running *to* this moment since the day Avery Madison died.

"I haven't seen your world either, except in the astral plane and for five minutes in the middle of nowhere, Steale, but I know within myself that it exists." I paused, letting that sink in. "And you know within yourself that Kirin's still alive, don't you?" The words came intuitively, before I could call them back.

He went rigid. "I *don't* know that."

I held on with all the love and hope I felt for him. "Yes you do. That's why you came to me to learn the Art. That's why you asked me about honor. You plan on getting her back."

He didn't answer, didn't even look at me.

"I'm willing to teach you everything I can, Steale," I promised, using my chi in an effort to reach him. "But you're not going in there by yourself."

For an eternity, he said nothing. Then, turning his head toward me, I saw the moisture in his eyes. "And what if I'm wrong?" he said, his voice frozen and bitter. "What if I go in there and find out she died a long time ago in stasis? What if *we* both die, too? What does that solve?"

I studied him, tracing the line of his cheekbone with my fingertips. "Are you afraid of dying, Steale, or are you more afraid you just *might* succeed?"

He tried to struggle up out of my arms, but I held him down by both shoulders. "If you let fear stop you, sooner or later the regret will eat you alive."

He struggled again, trying to escape my words. "Stop it, River!" he warned. "You don't know what you're talking about."

"It's all become easy for you, hasn't it? It's easier to just keep going the way you are than to take a chance," I told him, desperate to reach him even if it meant blasting a hole in the sheltering veil of his comfort zones. "Maybe you keep thinking some miracle's going to come along - a rescue party from your world? Well it's not going to happen. The crash was a long time ago, and the horrible fact remains that now you're the *only* one left who still cares enough to do anything about it. So do you want to do something, or do you want to keep searching for Oz? It doesn't exist, Steale. Believe me, I know. I buried its ashes out in the desert this morning."

He lay there in my arms for a long time. Finally, rolling onto his side, he slid one desperate arm around my waist, his weight pushing me down into the couch. I lay back, pulling him over me and holding him against my chest until the first storm subsided. An hour had passed in utter silence.

"I *am* afraid," he murmured, his voice distant. "I'm afraid she isn't alive, or maybe I'm afraid she is. I don't know which is worse."

I held him close, tightening my arms around him. "What does your chi tell you?"

He sighed softly against me, his chest rising and falling in a more natural rhythm. "I don't know how to listen."

A wistful smile came to my lips. It was the first honest response he'd given all night.

CHAPTER SEVENTEEN
Relocation

We went into his studio immediately after breakfast the next morning, and there I began teaching him everything I had learned over the years. He was a quick study, picking up complex techniques that had taken me a much longer time to master. The Art was in his blood, and now I understood the reason.

I would not have taught him had I believed he would use his skills for vengeance, or that he would use them selfishly, for personal gain. That had been my hesitation before, that unsettled inkling in the back of my thoughts that made me wonder about the past that had shaped him. But now that he had revealed himself to me, I almost envied him his quest, just as Master Barrows had once said he envied mine.

I had every intention of being with him on that journey, yet I knew I could not fully share in the joy he would feel when he found Kirin again, when he took her to him, when he took her back home. I would not allow myself to think it could happen any other way. She would be alive. She would be whole. They would be together again.

We quickly fell into a routine together, training in the morning, stopping for lunch, practicing the kata in the afternoon, dinner, then meditation. After that, exhausted and weary, we would fall into bed, sometimes together, other times not. Occasionally, we made love.

In all the chaos, I was surprised to realize that I was still traveling - in my dreams, in my sleep. I still read Synjin's silver-bound book, and Jaden often told me that my mate loved me, and that our time to be together was rapidly approaching. That made it all just a little easier. Though I loved Steale, I had come to accept that I needed Synjin more and more as my thirtieth birthday approached. Less than a year and a half away, it still seemed far in the future.

After the first six weeks of living with Steale, I spoke with Jerry Davin. He'd left several messages at the studio which I'd never received. I'd never gone back. And though I was saddened by that, I realized that part of my life had ended without my consent and even without my awareness until that moment.

When I went to see Jerry for what turned out to be the last time, my emotions were warring between wanting to tell him the truth and knowing I couldn't. Not all of it anyway. Regardless of his openness, Jerry was very normal in a lot of ways, hardly the type to understand inter-dimensional travelers and crashed saucers in the desert of New Mexico in 1947.

We had a quiet dinner at one of the local pubs, and when he asked me about Steale, I didn't try to lie. Instead, I told him about my path, how I knew Steale was a part of it. I know Jerry was hurt, but I also think he was happy for me. He seemed to believe that what I shared with Steale was only a simple romance, and I didn't try to alter his perceptions.

He brought up the studio and I had no choice but to tell him I wouldn't be going back. He smiled softly, not surprised. There were several black belt students who were qualified to teach by then, and he said only that it wouldn't be a problem. He also insisted that I take the money in the studio's account, telling me I might need it some day, telling me to come back if things didn't work out. I promised I would - take the money, come back, see him again if I could - but I never did.

When we parted, he kissed me once on the cheek, told me to take care, then left me at my car.

Just before he drove away, I grabbed something off the front seat and went to the open window of his pick-up. I wanted him to have my black belt as a personal memento, and though he protested briefly, I finally convinced him to take it. It's still hanging on his studio wall to this day, without explanation. Whenever anyone asks, he tells them that it was a gift from an old friend.

Just an old friend who disappeared one day never to return. That's what I'd like to think, anyway, though I really don't know whatever became of Jerry Davin.

~

I knew something was wrong the minute I rounded the curve which was just before the long driveway leading up to the house. The scent in the air was wrong; the burrowing owls were too quiet; there were two dark sedans parked in the driveway, their lights out.

Instinct warned me and I drove past the house, looking up the hill. The lights in the living room were on, and I could see three figures standing in the middle of the floor. Steale made a habit of telling me whenever he was expecting company, and he had mentioned nothing.

My stomach knotting, I continued past the driveway for about half a mile. Then, pulling into a place I knew to be a winter rental, I shut down the engine, leaving the car where it would look inconspicuous. From there, I jogged along the side of the road.

As I got closer, I took care to stay out of sight, paralleling the road in a canyon which ran between the house and the street. It took only about five minutes, and I skirted along the outside of the house until I came up under the living room window. From there, I could hear every word that was spoken. Most of them were about me.

"...was reported as being seen with you at the House of Happiness restaurant in July. Now do you want to tell us what you know about River Willows, or would you rather come down to the station? I'm tired of dicking around with you."

Steale's voice then. Cold. "Am I under arrest?"

"No - not *yet*." The fed again. Hostile. Belligerent. "You have no reason to protect her, Mr. Brooks. She's been wanted for murder for seven years. Now we can probably get you off the hook, but only if you start cooperating."

"I've told you everything I know," Steale replied. Ice. "And I know a little bit about the law. Having dinner with a young lady is hardly a felony."

"No, but harboring a felon is."

"You've searched the house twice already. Isn't that enough?" Steale said rhetorically.

"And I can search it ten more times if it suits me! Now you were seen with River Willows at least once. You have no means of financial support that anyone can figure out; and the mail man was nice enough to tell us that there's been another car here for the last two months. It doesn't take a rocket scientist to figure out she's been here."

The fed wasn't making a lot of sense. They seldom did.

228

"She *who*?" Steale asked. "I didn't realize it was against the law to have house guests. My sister's been visiting from out of town. She left to go back to Wyoming this morning. You're paranoid."

"Yeah? Well I get paid to be paranoid, Mr. Brooks!" the man returned.

His voice became less distinct for a moment; he must have gone around the corner toward the kitchen. "Marcus, let's get the hell out of here. Mr. Brooks, if you'll be so kind as to come with us, there are a few questions we'd like to ask you downtown."

"Ask all you like," Steale replied, a dangerous edge to his voice. "Whether we talk here or downtown makes no difference to me. I could use the money from suing your ass for false arrest."

A different voice then. "Hey, Donahue, you want me and Williams to stay behind, set up a surveillance out back in case Willows comes back?"

"Forget it, Marcus," Donahue returned, breathing heavily. "If she's managed to stay out of sight this long, she's not going to walk into any trap you two chuckleheads set up."

There was a lower mumble of conversation for nearly a minute, then the front door opened. My heart pounded wildly, though I was in no danger of being seen. I warred between whether or not to attack, for I knew that Steale and I together could easily take the three feds. But common sense told me to hold back as I watched him being escorted out the front door, down the long driveway. Regardless of Donahue's threats, they had no reason to hold Steale. I just hoped that whatever identity he'd set up for himself would pass the test, though there was no reason to think it wouldn't. He was clever. Richard Brooks. Marlon Andrews. Parker Byrd. John T. Rickster.

It was awhile after I heard the two sedans pull away before I started breathing again. I knew we could no longer remain in the desert. Somehow, after seven years, the feds had finally gotten the lucky break they'd been waiting for. Some good citizen had Big Brothered. Sooner or later, regardless of what they found out from Steale, they'd be back.

Once my heartbeat slowed to some vague imitation of normal, I slipped around the back side of the house and let myself in through the sliding glass door.

The moment I was inside, I began packing the things we might need. The teacher/student bond between us had grown to the point that I no longer needed to wonder whether or not he would run with me. He didn't have much choice.

And once cornered, a coyote never returned to the same spot to sleep.

Taking care to stay away from the windows, I switched on the police band radio Steale kept on the living room shelf. If the cops decided to come back sooner than Donahue had indicated, I wanted to be long gone.

I packed one duffel bag with enough clothes and toiletries for both of us, tossed it into the garage, and went into the third bedroom toward the back of the house. Steale kept a small computer that he seldom used and never talked about. I hadn't pressed him about it, though I suspected everything he knew about the facility in San Diego would be stored somewhere in the thing's electronic innards. For all I knew, *everything* could be stored in that computer - the corridor, the past, the future. Everything.

I quickly unhooked it from the printer and monitor, wound the cables tight and tossed them in a bag, then carried it all out to the garage. Luckily, Steale had started parking the Lamborghini inside at night, so I was able to pack everything in without having to go out into the driveway. When I had the duffel bag and computer safely stashed in the car's storage area, I went back into the house. Steale kept a large amount of cash crammed in the access crawl-way to the tub's plumbing fixture, and though I didn't count it when I stuffed it into an attaché case, I estimated there was at least five hundred thousand dollars.

I wasn't sure what he would have in mind when the feds decided to release him, but I wanted a plan of action ready and waiting. If he had a better one, I'd be happy to listen.

Once I'd scavenged everything I could from the main part of the house, I went into the studio and looked around. We'd only been working there for a little over six weeks, but it wasn't going to be easy to say goodbye to another part of my life after finding a reasonably comfortable routine. But when I recalled that the ancient masters had traveled with only the clothes on their back and sometimes a walking stick, I felt a little better about being on the move again. I grabbed a *bo* and a *jo* from the studio, then shut the door behind me as I closed off all feeling.

When I was finished tearing the house apart, the worst part came. Waiting.

I went into the master bedroom for one last time and lay down on the bed we had shared, the bed where I had given myself to him for the first time, the bed where many secrets had been exchanged. But when I felt myself growing maudlin, I got up and stood in the middle of the room for a few seconds.

After that, restless and admittedly shaken, I went outside. Crawling down into the canyon over which the master bedroom was built, I sat down behind one of the cement support beams and waited.

It was nearly three in the morning when the cab finally pulled up at the end of the driveway and I saw Steale's silhouette walking confidently toward the house. He glanced only once over his shoulder as the cab drove away, then reached into his pocket for the house keys.

The acoustics of the desert made it possible to hear tires on the two-lane road several miles away. Except for the cab in the distance, we were alone.

I climbed up the side of the canyon and met him at the driveway just as he reached the garage.

"You okay?" I asked.

He nodded, barely glancing at me. "I have a place in San Diego that I own under a different name. I just need to pack a few things and we can get out of here. Where're you parked?"

"At the old Whaley rental about half a mile up the road. Your car's already packed."

We were inside the house by then and there was very little emotion between us. It was time to go. There would be time to think about it later.

"The computer?" he asked.

"Already in the car. There's also some clothes and whatever else I could grab. The money's in the attaché in the passenger's seat. So's your gun."

He offered me a wistful smile. "I'm never eating Chinese food again."

I laughed despite myself, but quickly sobered. "How much do they know?"

"Not enough to be dangerous *yet*," he replied.

I studied him carefully. "Are you sure?"

"I can read a liar a mile away," he assured me. "The only thing they've got is a report from somebody who was in Wu's restaurant that night. They would have been here sooner, but maybe some of that good fortune you're always talking about operated in our favor. The report got lost for almost three months on some underling's desk."

I'd followed him through the house as we spoke in hurried tones. He was in the back bedroom now, looking at the spot where the computer had been.

"Did you get the disks?" he asked.

"There were about ten of them in the desk drawer. Those the ones?"

He nodded, but opened the drawer anyway. Whatever was on those disks was important.

His lips pressed together in thoughtful silence. "That's it then," he said without inflection. "Donahue's probably finishing up the paper-work right about now; they'll be back to set up the surveillance soon. Can you make it back to your car all right?"

I nodded, already headed toward the door.

"There's a place in Salton City called the Tiki Restaurant," he advised. "If we get separated on the highway, pull off behind the restaurant and wait for me."

I didn't like the idea of being apart, but there wasn't enough time to come up with a better plan. I tried to smile as I started out the back door.

He grabbed me by one wrist, pulled me tight to his chest, and kissed me hard and deep. And in all the chaos, it was exactly what I needed, exactly what I wanted, even if I hadn't known it myself. It was a stabilizing moment, a defining moment – some out of place reminder that he cared for me and I cared for him more than either of us had ever dared to confess. I took sustenance from that kiss, drinking him in, savoring him as one might savor a rare autumn wine.

And then I was out the door and running. I made it to my car in less than four minutes, scrambling through the canyon half of the way there just to stay off the pavement.

As I pulled out onto the main road, I looked one last time toward Steale's house, saying a silent affirmation for nothing to go wrong. We weren't two steps ahead anymore. We were going to need all the affirmations and all the good fortune we could summon.

~

"They had nothing to hold me," Steale was saying as we sat in the living room of his San Diego house. "I keep a lawyer on retainer for things like that; when they found out that my attorney was the one who got the governor acquitted, they backed off." He paused, leaning back on the over-stuffed couch. "I told them I'd met you at the pub in 29 Palms, that I had no idea who you really were, and that I hoped to Lethe they caught such a common criminal as yourself.."

I was barely listening, just glad to be alive and still free. "And you're sure that this house isn't traceable to you?"

"Not a chance. I have more identities than Sybil."

I didn't doubt it. I took a deep breath and looked around the room again. The house itself was located in a sort of no-man's-land between Poway and Ramona – less than two miles from the complex.

I wasn't surprised to discover that his taste in decorating this house wasn't that different from the other one. The furniture was dark and rich, covered in a deep green fabric. The kitchen was slightly smaller, but there were three bedrooms in addition to a den and family room. He liked space, room to move around.

There were no windows on rollers here, nor any mechanical blinds, but there was a king-size bed. The house had a lived-in feel to it despite the fact that it was seldom used, and the two-acre lot on which it sat was lushly landscaped with huge eucalyptus and willows. The greenery was almost shocking after the years I'd spent in the desert.

We spent the first two days recovering from the near-miss back at Joshua Tree, sorting through what had happened and figuring out what to do next. By the end of the first week, we'd converted the family room into a studio of sorts. It wasn't as large as the one in Joshua Tree had been, but it was more than adequate.

Steale had come a long way in the time we'd worked together. He might not have won any awards for style, since I had to take a few short cuts in the interest of time, but he was quick and concise in his moves, performing anything I taught him with confidence and lethal efficiency.

In another month, we started sparring. He was good. He was *better* than just good, taking the basics and turning them into a powerful system that combined intellect with ability. He was a thinking fighter and that would save his life quicker than anything else.

By the time Christmas came, I had to move harder and faster to stay one step ahead of him in the sparring arena. Occasionally, late in the evening, we would run together through the hills, and it was on one of those excursions that he showed me the complex for the first time.

I chilled the moment we came over a rise and saw it. It sat in the middle of a high valley like a blight on the landscape, its amber lights burning through the fog with an eerie glow. Its location had been chosen with obvious care, for it wasn't visible from any roads or highways, and only the seriously determined jogger would have bothered to climb the steep hills for a vantage point. Sitting on government land, it was in an area near a military base, yet far enough away to be officially denied should anyone bother to ask.

We stood there for a long time, our damp skin turning cold in the winter air. While the temperature didn't drop as low as it had on those cold nights at Joshua Tree, the higher humidity often made it seem far colder.

I shivered and wasn't surprised to find Steale next to me.

"So that's it," I said, mostly to myself, trying to wrap my mind around the implications of it.

"Hell's gate," he said, a ghostly softness to his voice.

The lights were almost hypnotic and I couldn't stop staring at them. "Looks like something out of Close Encounters. The dark side of the moon."

He held me closer, though whether for my sake or his, I didn't know. "In the daytime, it doesn't look like much, just a few buildings scattered here and there. The real circus is underground."

"Do you have a lay-out of the place?"

He nodded. "In the computer. It's a few years old, though. Things could have changed since then. But bribery works wonders; I can buy a more recent blueprint for the right price."

"Don't bother. If this place is as hush-hush as you claim it is, not everything is going to be on the plans," I explained.

He sighed softly. "Then we're boned."

I smiled despite myself, my eyes affixed to the complex as if in a trance. "Not yet."

He tensed again. "I don't think they give guided tours, River," he said. "So unless you know some way of making yourself invisible, we're back to square one: we're boned."

He had a point. The place was intimidating to say the very least. "It ain't over until the fat lady sings, Steale."

He gave me a peculiar look. "What fat lady?"

I smiled up at him. "Never mind."

He shook his head, then stood looking at the place for a very long time, his breathing gradually slowing to normal.

"What are you thinking?" I asked.

He released a weary breath. "Not much. Everything. I was thinking that I'm standing less than a mile away from Kirin - *if* she's still alive," he quickly amended.

It was an uncanny thought and I followed his gaze instinctively. "She is."

"What makes you so sure?" he asked cautiously.

"Chi," I told him truthfully. "Some things you just know." I touched his chest, trying to impart that to him. "In here." I touched his forehead. "In here."

He didn't argue, didn't say anything at all for a long time. Instead, he breathed very softly, almost reverently. "I want to believe you, River."

I held him close. "You will when you're ready."

I sensed some of the strain leaving his body. "You're one weird cookie."

I patted his arm and nudged him back down the hill. "Thanks," was all I said.

It was all right not to be normal.

~

I continued training Steale to control both body and spirit for the next several months, and by the time spring came, he'd managed to fight me to three stalemates in the sparring arena.We walked or jogged to the vantage point in the hills several times a week, often at dusk or sunrise. He had been right about one thing: in the daytime, under the harsh light of the sun, the facility seemed downright uninteresting.

There were four long buildings constructed almost flat against the landscape, a few parked cars here and there, and nothing at all to point to the fact that eighteen visitors from Steale's world lay in cold sleep beneath the ground. The place looked far more like a row of chicken coops than a top secret para-military installation.

The complex was surrounded by three consecutive tall fences, and a camera with a long lens revealed that the razor wire strands along the tops of those fences slanted in as well as out. Whoever was in charge wanted to make sure that whatever was out *stayed* out, and whatever was in *stayed* in.

It took awhile after I first saw the complex before Steale agreed to look at the lay-out on the computer, and I could imagine what he felt whenever he forced himself to do it. His beloved Kirin was somewhere in that maze of architectural drawings, plot plans and blueprints.

But with a little encouragement and a lot of late-night talks that bared both our souls, I finally started to see his determination, his strength, coming back to him. He had always been the silent, brooding type. Now, other than on rare occasion when it rained, there was a different kind of fire in his eyes. He was starting to believe that we could get inside the place and *maybe* even get out again.

When I asked him about his reaction to the rain one March evening, he told me only that it was raining the night he and Kirin were married. He'd liked the rain after that. But it had rained again the night the probe had crashed. Then he began to hate the rain, the storms that came to San Diego in the winter and made the world wet and cold.

On those darker nights, I either took him to bed early and made love to him, or sat with him in the living room in front of the fireplace. Occasionally, he turned on the television, in his words, to 'see if the world's blown itself up yet'.

One Tuesday night in early May, he was sitting in front of the TV when an old re-run of *Unsolved Mysteries* was aired. It was a special report done in '89, the kind of thing the networks dug out of mothballs for special occasions. When it first started, the announcer came on to say that the recent flap of UFO sightings in the midwest had reawakened the public interest in the age-old phenomena. He chattered on for a few minutes, then dramatically said he was proud to present a journey back through time, to Roswell, New Mexico.

Chills raised up on my arms as the report began. The production crew had done a good job recreating the rumors. As Robert Stack's voice explained the scene near Roswell that night, he spoke of the storm in the desert, the brilliant blue flash that was taken to be lightning by Mac Brazel, the owner of the ranch where the vessel had crashed.

The picture on the tube showed a silver craft not unlike the one I'd witnessed in Steale's dream. But that's where any similarity ended. From that point forward, the audience was shown four alien bodies, over which was dubbed the voices of witnesses. As Steale had predicted, those witnesses were usually the friend of a friend of a friend. There was a retired Air Force man, who claimed to have loaded the bodies onto a truck for transport to the base in his younger years; but other than that, it was back to stories of four-feet tall grayish-green men with insectoid eyes, slits for mouths, and hairless heads.

Steale turned off the set with the remote control during the second commercial break, studying me from across the room. The jacket of his gi hung open to the waist, his chest rising and falling.

"Misinformation," he stated. "They almost had *me* believing it, and I was *there*."

"I've had a little experience with it myself. After I first escaped from Madison, the news had me killing three guys and stealing an ambulance, as I recall. I almost turned *myself* in after hearing it for the tenth time."

He smiled softly, wistfully, and I felt the force of his chi in the room. "How much longer do we wait?"

The question startled me, causing my stomach to tighten. I asked my own chi for the answer and accepted it when it came. "Until October."

His brows narrowed quizzically. "Why October?"

"You mean why not now?" I asked. I was edgy from what I'd seen on the tube; my voice was sharper than I'd intended.

"No, that's not what I meant. I'm just curious. Why October?"

I listened to my inner voice again as it told me what to do. It didn't always speak in English, however. "Because something else has to happen before then. There's something not yet settled."

"What kind of something else?"

"We'll know when it happens," my chi told me then.

After a long silence, he nodded as if to himself. "All right." He got up off the couch and came to stand next to me. Reaching down, he messed up my hair with unexpected mischievousness.

He didn't say a word. Instead, he padded softly down the hall and into the family room which had become our studio. I saw him practicing the kata, and my instincts told me to let him be.

We both slept alone that night.

~

My birthday came the following week. One more year. Less than a year. One more winter, one more summer, one more fall.

I lit a candle at midnight in the meditation area of the studio and placed it in the window.

It was Synjin's candle.

And I was terrified.

~

In July I began to wonder if I'd been mistaken when I told Steale something else had to happen before October. The summer had turned lazy, and there was a virulent storm off-shore, making the air still and humid. After so many years of living in the desert, my body had grown accustomed to the heat, but not to the thickness which clung to my flesh, leaving my body wet and alien.

Nothing at all had happened. Steale had progressed in his learning; we often stayed up late at night sipping tea or wine; we

238

studied the lay-out of the massive underground complex both on the computer and from our vantage point in the hills; he'd beaten me in the sparring arena twice.

But there was no revelation.

By mid-August, I began to doubt myself.

When the last week of the month came around, I was staring at September with a knot in the pit of my stomach. My chi hadn't gone silent, but it was speaking that alien language again.

Occasionally, I took long walks through the hills alone at night. Steale had said there was a natural doorway about a mile and a half to the southeast of the house, explaining when asked that he never liked to be far away. But even when I located it just off a horse trail in a secluded canyon, Ch'en Po didn't come wandering through the mist with words of wisdom or to hand me the road-map to my life.

I was back to lesson number one.

CHAPTER EIGHTEEN
The Twenty Seventh Day of October

When summer finally retreated, there was still no insight into the statement I'd made in May. Now, with only four days left before November, I stood in the middle of the sparring arena with Steale. We'd just fought to another stalemate, our bodies damp with perspiration, our breath coming harder than usual. The gi which had been shiny-black unwashed cotton when I'd given it to him over a year and a half ago was now faded with age, ripped in several places, well-worn. My own had long- since been retired; I wore a pair of loose-fitting sweat pants and a tank top.

Our eyes met and held for a long moment.

"Well?" he said with a half-smile.

"Well what?" Over the time we'd lived together, we had developed almost a short-hand form of language. Usually I knew what he was thinking when he spoke only one word. But now wasn't one of those times.

"It's October," he reminded me, going to the far wall of the training area and sitting down on one of the mats.

My stomach knotted as I went to his side. "I know."

Looking over at me, he shrugged. "Well?"

I couldn't hold his gaze. It had grown too intense. We hadn't become distant from one another, though we hadn't shared a bed in over two months. I missed that part of our relationship, though I understood why. We had work to do. He was thinking of Kirin, and I of Synjin. We both spent a lot of time in silence.

After a few moments, I forced myself to look up at him. "I've taught you everything I know, Steale. Do you feel ready?"

"Ready?"

"Ready to go into that complex," I explained, my stomach fluttering again. "Do you think it's time?"

He smiled softly. "You're asking *me*?"

I shrugged, nervous. "Yes. I'm asking you."

He closed his eyes, leaned against the wall. When he opened them again, he looked at me without expression. "I don't know."

I couldn't fault him for that. He had learned to listen to his chi, but like my own, it was undoubtedly speaking in tongues.

Surprising me slightly, he reached across the space that separated us, running the back of his hand over my face. "You okay?"

I started to give him the pat answer that's usually given to the grocery clerk, the mail man or the Avon lady. But I *wasn't* fine. "Not really."

"Want to talk about it?"

In the training arena, where we spent the vast majority of our time, I was the one in charge; I'd gotten used to it. It might be nice to start trusting him with some of the responsibility, trusting him with my feelings again.

I looked up at him, forced myself not to glance away. "Sometimes I just wonder if it wouldn't be better to go down to the local arms dealer, buy a couple of shotguns, a few Stinger missiles, and get this thing over with."

He laughed softly, pulling me over to lean against him. "I've still got my gun if that makes you feel any better."

His humor had gotten us through a lot of tense situations. "Do you ever feel like everything we're doing here is a waste of time?" I had to ask. I needed to know.

"This is why we've spent the last year learning to even out the odds," he reminded me. "So in answer to your question, no, I don't feel that everything we've done is a waste of time. Most of the time, you have me believing I could walk through walls."

My lips curved upward. "You can."

He turned me until my head rested in his lap, then began stroking my hair, soothing me into a lazy exhaustion that made talking to him easier than it had been in weeks. I realized then that he was using that power of his again. Telepathic suggestion. Subliminal seduction of the tension in my body.

"You do that very well," I told him, looking up into his eyes with a smile.

He winked, one hand warm and comforting on my shoulder, the other in my hair. "We make a good team."

He was right. We did. "Do you ever think about how weird it is that you and I ever met, Steale?"

He looked down at me. "No."

"Oh?"

"You're the one always talking about paths," he said with a grin. "After everything that's happened in your life, isn't it obvious that we were meant to meet?"

I considered that. "Just for the sake of argument, I've met a lot of people in my lifetime. Not everybody I meet is significant. I had no idea where I was going when I left Florida. I could just as easily have ended up in Boise, Sioux City or New Orleans - and we certainly wouldn't have met then."

"But you *didn't* end up in any of those places," he stressed, holding me close.

Releasing a sigh, he slipped out from under me, letting my head come down softly against the mat. Then, gesturing for me to turn onto my stomach, he got up on his knees, straddling my hips and beginning a deep massage into my back and shoulders.

"Looks like you need the full treatment," he commented lightly, his hands working magic on me again.

I could feel him inside my mind, a gentle presence that encouraged my body and spirit to relax. Within a few minutes, he lulled me into an easy laziness.

"You're just scared," he said after a long silence – not an accusation, just an accurate observation.

His words gave me pause. The truth again. "I hate it when you do that."

"Do what?"

"When you can see through me." My mind was getting lethargic. "When you make me feel like limp asparagus."

"Want me to stop?"

"Do and I'll kick your butt," I threatened with a smile.

"Think you could?"

I was no longer sure. That was good. That was what I'd worked for. "I don't know, but it might be fun to try."

He stretched out next to me, the length of his body pressed against my side. Propped up on one elbow, he continued stroking my back, keeping the telepathic contact open between us.

"If it'll make you feel any better, I'm scared, too," he said, more serious. "Regardless of all we've learned about that place, there's no way we can know everything. The computer can tell us most of the nooks and crannies, the corridors and the underground mazes, but whether that'll be enough, there's no way to know."

His words awakened a question, perhaps even an answer. "Do you think we'll be killed in the attempt?" My question surprised him, but not nearly as much as it surprised me.

I felt him tense, then relax. "No. I *don't* think that."

I lifted my head to look at him.

He glanced away.

"What?" I asked quietly, afraid of the answer as the hairs lifted at the base of my neck.

He shook his head. "No, nothing."

"You don't lie any better than you ever did," I told him.

He met my eyes a moment later, his gaze intense, almost grim. "My chi tells me you'll be all right, River."

I stopped breathing, listening to my own intuition. It scared me with its silence. "And what's it saying about *you*?"

His hands slowed their massage for an almost imperceptible moment, then continued again. "I don't know."

"Steale, if anything happens to you—"

"Nothing's going to happen," he interrupted. "I shouldn't have said anything."

I twisted my head around until I could look at him. His face was unreadable. "Did you have a premonition?"

He shook his head, smiling down at me. "Nope. Tired?"

"Steale," I warned.

Finally, releasing a heavy breath, he told me what was on his mind. "I've just never been able to picture myself together with Kirin again. It's not something I can see inside my mind."

"Even chi has a hard time seeing through fear, Steale," I reminded him. "Besides, do you really think I'm going to let anything happen to you after all of this?"

He leaned over me, kissing me on the cheek. "You'd better not. My ghost would probably be a lousy lover, all that ethereal mist, not much substance."

His words took me off guard. We *were* lovers. It didn't matter that we hadn't slept together in awhile. That realization made me fiercely protective of him. I rolled over onto my back and took his hands, holding tight.

"Are you telling me the truth, Steale? No premonitions?"His smile was soft and understanding. "I didn't mean to scare you,

River. No premonitions, okay? We're both just a little nuts right now - which is probably normal, all things considered."

He was right. Again. He started running his fingers over my shoulders, down my arms. There was still a sense of uneasiness within me, but it slowly dissipated as he soothed away our mutual anxiety with touch.

"I've missed this," I said, meaning it.

The mischief was back in his eyes. Then, before I realized what he was doing, he slid his arms under me, lifted me up against his chest, and carried me down the hall. I couldn't help laughing as I held on to him, my hands laced together behind his neck.

"One of these days, Steale, I'm going to carry *you* off to *my* lair," I threatened, relaxing under him as his weight came down over me on the bed.

The tension that had built up in both of us over the past months erased any awkwardness. I clung to him with a renewed sense of desperation, sliding my hands under the jacket of his gi to pull him against me.

His arms had grown thicker over the time I'd spent with him, his shoulders broader. There was power in his body, in his heart, in his chi. He'd once told me in a rare moment of shyness that there was nothing to compare with making love to another martial artist except making love with a mate; and when he drew me into his unrelenting embrace, I understood fully what he meant.

There was no gentleness in him this time. Instead, there was a passion that expressed itself in hard angles and sharp breaths. He held me tight by the wrists with a ferocity so intense it might have been alarming had I not craved to be taken so completely. The need was mutual, and when we kissed, it was with a gravely dark obsession that brought with it a brief flicker of blood. He tasted of alien waters and wildfire, molten gold and the broken heart of a fallen seraphim.

Clothes were torn away, thrown aside without reverence. His weight against me became both sanctuary and prison, and though I had never experienced such feelings, I longed to be dominated by him utterly – to give up control for one night, to allow him to lead us both into the most hidden corners of our most forbidden desires.

He didn't need his telepathy to tell him what I was feeling, and so he took command without hesitation and without apology, bringing us together as one with a driving force that caused me to cry out with the sheer intensity that came from being filled so completely by the living essence of this splendid creature.

Making love with Steale had always left me overwhelmed, but now the roller coaster had fallen off its track and was plummeting upward, out of control, past the safety zone of the atmosphere and into some realm of rapture that lies well beyond the ability of words to describe.

I was obliterated.

I was reborn.

I stopped breathing. Started again.

Tears fell from my eyes. Joy. Pain. Love.

His body slowly settled onto me, into me. We held to one another for a long time, and when he finally lifted his head to look down at me, the confident power had returned to his eyes.

"Now I'm ready," he said. He lay down against me, his heart beating boldly on my chest. He wasn't even winded. I liked that. A lot.

"Tomorrow," he murmured sleepily.

My eyes closed with apprehension. The time had come.

~

I awoke less than an hour later with an uneasy feeling. Steale lay at my side, one long leg thrown protectively over both of mine, his dark head resting against my arm. He wasn't dreaming, yet the feeling of uneasiness continued - the same feeling I often got when jolted awake by one of his nightmares.

Without realizing it, I was holding my breath, reaching out with my intuition until I pinpointed the source of my apprehension. The room was in total darkness. When Steale had carried me to his bed, the light was on in the studio; its glow had filtered down the hall when we made love, shining on his face, his body.

I wondered briefly if he had gotten up and turned it off, but I never slept that soundly. It was an old habit from the desert. The slightest sound or movement was sufficient to awaken me instantly.

Not moving, I listened to the house. A light rain was falling outside, dripping off the roof to patter softly in forming puddles. Still, the rain wouldn't have wakened me.

Taking a moment to center myself, I drew a deep, silent breath. Once I was more balanced, I looked around the room again, though the darkness was so intense that I could see nothing out of the ordinary. I wondered momentarily if the autumn storm had caused a power failure, yet I could hear the refrigerator running in the kitchen.

My apprehension grew, my heart beating faster as adrenalin rushed through my body. Something was wrong. Something was *very* wrong.

Moving as quietly as the Art had taught me, I leaned over Steale and placed one hand on his shoulder, my lips less than an inch from his ear. He stirred and I tightened my grip on him, whispering so softly that someone a foot away couldn't have heard.

"Something's wrong."

He felt it, too. His telepathy surged against me, his body preparing for battle. He nodded soundlessly, then reached toward the night stand, groping for the gun. I felt him tense, then he pulled me against him.

"Someone's in the house; the gun's not where I left it," he whispered against my ear.

I didn't need to ask if he were sure. He always was.

My heart slammed against my chest and I reminded myself to fight cold. Master Barrows was still with me, and his Masters before him. They were all there, in that room.

I felt Steale move though I never heard it. He pulled on his gi pants, tying them without making a sound. I mirrored his actions with my sweats and t-shirt, grateful that I hadn't thrown my clothes all the way across the room the way I sometimes did in my midnight encounters with him. Once dressed, we lay side-by-side in the bed, breathing in eerie unison, our bodies tensed for action.

He pulled me against him again, his lips to my ear. "Get to the garage. The keys are in the car."

In the back of my mind, an odd thought told me that whoever was in the house definitely was not the feds. They wouldn't have been polite enough to wait for us to put our clothes on. We would have had bright lights in our eyes and guns in our faces long before then.

Steale rolled soundlessly off the bed as I followed behind him. It was ten feet to the bedroom door and another fifteen feet down the hall to the garage. But it seemed like miles.

I could vaguely see his body as a shadow of darker darkness in the room, silhouetted against the void as he moved cautiously toward the bedroom door. But then I saw something else - another figure against the backdrop of the open door, blackness outlined against the lighter paneling of the hall.

"Steale!" I shouted. "In front of you!"

Abruptly the world was bathed in light which caused my eyes to water, stinging. I blinked frantically as life turned into a slow-motion nightmare. The man in the doorway was only a silhouette, dressed in black, holding a gun.

Steale moved toward him, looked up, faltered, gasped, started to move. I was a half-step behind him, my only instinct to get to the intruder's gun arm before it was too late. Someone said something. I'm not sure who or what. I heard Steale's name spoken in a dark voice, like something I'd heard in another world.

A flash of metal and the intruder aimed the weapon at Steale's chest. He was still too far away, for the shadow had taken two steps back into the hall, his face masked in shadows that weren't really there – shadows created in my mind because I did *not* want to accept what I already knew, what I had failed to *see* all along.

The surge of my chi was like a rush of fire breaking through a wall, my own instincts and my protectiveness for Steale awakening with a vengeance.

The conversation we'd had the night before flashed through my mind. *'No premonitions'*, he had said. I wondered if he'd lied.

"Don't do it, Steale. You're too far away."

It sounded like something I wanted to say, but the words didn't come from my lips. The intruder spoke them. Cold. He knew how to fight cold.

I tried to get past Steale, knowing that my smaller size would allow me to move quicker. My mind was imploding, turning inward, shutting down all outside distraction. There was one thought in my head: disarm the intruder. He was further back in the hall. Another two steps.

Steale was to the bedroom door by then, and I couldn't get past him. His body blocked me, perhaps deliberately, his back pressed against my chest as I tried to shoulder in underneath him.

That's when the horror struck me. I felt him flinch, gasp with disbelief, curse. He staggered backward, the weight of his body almost knocking me down. I hadn't heard a gunshot, yet I knew he'd been hit.

My eyes misted over with terror and I tried to steady him, but my balance was already off. He slipped through my arms and slid down the door frame, his dark head resting on his chest as his long legs curled underneath him.

From that instant forward, my sanity was gone. I launched my body through the open door and into the hall, coming upon the intruder before he could back away. I kicked for his gun arm and missed, though I did connect with the weapon itself. It flew out of the shadow's hand and landed somewhere out of reach.

Then I was on him, using every skill I had ever learned. I kicked again, aiming for the solar plexus. But I was aghast when the intruder caught my foot in a well-practiced move and used my own momentum against me.

I went flying past him to land in a heap half-way into the living room, ten feet from where I'd started. Not only was the man a cold fighter, he was also trained. The guy in the alley was usually a street thug. The kid who robbed the 7/11 with a knife couldn't defend against a trained fighter. But another martial artist evened out the odds.

Another light came on then as if from a separate world, and the intruder walked slowly, almost casually around the corner of the hall before I could pick myself up off the floor. I started to scramble to my feet, knowing I would get no second chances, then stopped instantaneously as I saw his face for the first time.

Since my feet had touched the floor when I'd gotten out of bed, no more than a minute had passed. I couldn't think. I couldn't see. The color drained from my face; my body went limp. I think I screamed for the first time in my life.

He looked a little surprised, too.

"Are you all right?" he asked in a voice I remembered from the past.

He moved toward me, offering a hand to help me up. But I couldn't move to take it. He stood over me for several long seconds, then knelt down beside me, a distant smile in his eyes.

He was approximately six foot four, with hair that reached almost to his waist, and obsidian eyes. His features were finely-chiseled, as if cut from marble, his skin as smooth as autumn rain when he took my limp hand and pressed it between his own. He was dark, not unlike Steale, and looked to be about thirty years old. But he was much older than that, and I recognized him whether I wanted to or not. He was a black book with blank pages - the book I had written for Chalyn Thorne so many years in the past.

"Synjin?" I finally managed, my voice coming out as little more than a whisper.

He nodded, smiling very softly. "Are you all right?" he asked again.

I could think of no answer. The one which came from my lips shocked me when it burst free. "What the hell are you doing here? I could have killed you!"

His dark brows lifted in surprise for a moment, his hair brushing around him as he laughed. "I'll try to explain a little later," he promised, helping me to my feet. "But for now, maybe we should see to Steale." His voice was utterly controlled, his aura steady.

My heart wrenched as I thought of Steale crumbled on the floor. "You didn't...?" I stood facing my mate now and saw genuine alarm in his eyes at my unfinished question.

"Kill him?" he finished. "Hardly. He might be obnoxious, rude and half crazy, but he *is* my brother."

I stared at him. My knees shook violently. I couldn't breathe. Someone had turned off the lights again.

"Your... *brother*?"

I think Synjin caught me when I fell.

~

The lights had been dimmed and I was lying on the bed. Steale was next to me, still unconscious, and Synjin was sitting in a chair beside the bed. He smiled when I looked at him, though I glanced away before either of us spoke. Instinct told me I'd passed out cold; my time sense said I'd been out about two minutes.

"I thought you would have known," Synjin said, taking my hand once more. "I'm sorry, River. Please believe me."

I had no choice. Like his brother, Synjin used his telepathy naturally. I felt him inside my mind as he'd been nearly eight years before.

I hadn't seen his face then. I had only felt him. But it was the same presence. Comforting. Natural. Perfect. It scared me that it was so perfect, for I understood then what Steale had shared with Kirin.

With a little effort, I managed to sit up, leaning against the headboard and fighting back the dizziness.

"What the hell just happened?" I asked.

Synjin smiled, applying a soft pressure to my hand. "It was time," was all he said.

"Time?"

"For us to be together."

I tried to understand that. "But... I thought all of this wasn't going to happen until I turned thirty." My image of reality was getting thrashed again.

He stroked my hand with long fingers. "As I recall, Chalyn only said that we'd be together *before* your thirtieth birthday. Isn't this before your thirtieth birthday?"

It was seven *months* before.

"There *is* a door, you know," I muttered, still irritated enough to challenge him. "There's a thing called a doorbell? You might have used it."

His lips curved upward. "I saw the lights and thought you were still awake. When I saw you sleeping, I turned them off. I'd planned to wait in the living room until morning, but apparently I didn't move quietly enough."

I stared at him for a long time before I spoke. "Steale's your *brother*?"

He nodded. "We haven't seen one another in a long time. It's time for that to change, too."

His words were soft-spoken, gentle. He *was* a Master, for there was no animosity within him. There was only love. For me. For Steale. But I knew it wasn't going to be easy for them.

"I take it you shot him with his own gun?" I said.

250

"I was an Argus before I went to the temple," Synjin explained. "Putting Steale to sleep seemed more humane than fighting with him, maybe injuring him."

My brows lifted. "Oh? What makes you so sure *he* wouldn't have injured *you*?"

Synjin laughed – that warm rumble from deep in his chest. "It might have been an interesting contest, but fighting a brother *and* a mate isn't usually a good way to rekindle relationships."

He had a point. I looked up into his face. He was flawless. My match. Still, I felt awkward with him.

"You... uh... you know about me and Steale?" It was important to me to be up front with him.

"Ch'en Po told me some months ago," Synjin murmured. "I'm glad you've had one another to lean on, to learn from."

I released the breath I'd been holding. "He's a very extraordinary person, you know - a bit crazy sometimes, not that I blame him."

Synjin nodded, his hair moving over his shoulders again, an entity unto itself. "I know. I've always regretted what happened between us. You've brought us together again."

I hadn't thought about it quite like that. "Maybe. Just don't forget that he's lived in my world for a long time. He's not likely to be as understanding as you are when he wakes up."

Synjin's demeanor was one of absolute serenity. "In time."

Unexpectedly, my stomach knotted. "How much time do we have?"

He frowned. "How much time?"

"We're going into that complex to get Kirin and the others," I said. Nothing even *he* could say would change my mind about that. "We can't very well do that if you and Steale are at one another's' throats."

His lips curved upward. "A lone man can only shadow-box. I have no intention of fighting with Steale. A lot's happened since the last time we were together. I've changed; I hope he has, too."

I wasn't so sure. "He won't even say your name. If he had, I might not have passed out in the hall." I felt a bit lame for that one and probably always would.

"He'll come around," Synjin assured with far more confidence that I felt. "In time."

I wasn't going to ask again. How much time we had was secondary to what was going to happen when Steale regained consciousness. Turning my head, I glanced at him. His eyes were closed, his hands at his side. He looked more peaceful than I'd ever seen him.

"He should be waking up in another few minutes," Synjin said, reading my thoughts with apparent ease. Getting up, he went to the other side of the bed, motioning for me to stay where I was.

Then, sitting on the edge of the mattress, he looked over at me with tender affection and reached down to take one of his brother's hands, undoubtedly using the physical contact to open a telepathic channel between them.

Steale moved slightly, his body tensing as a low moan passed through his lips. His head started to thrash, but I held him still with one hand in the center of his chest..

"Steale?" Synjin asked tentatively.

His voice had a commanding quality which couldn't be ignored. I felt Steale tense again, his eyes fluttering open, then snapping closed again. Squinting against the light, he moaned softly, trying to pull his hand away.

Synjin held him effortlessly, leaning over to brush the shaggy hair back from his brother's face. "Come on, Sleeping Beauty," he murmured, surprising me more than a little. "You never did like to get up, did you?"

They were brothers all right. Whether Steale liked it or not, whether Synjin would be able to deal with him or not, that one sentence told me they'd shared a past together. Two dark-haired little devils playing pranks before school. I didn't envy their mother.

Steale's body went taut for a moment. I held him as still as I could, stroking his hair in an effort to soothe him. I remembered when I'd been shot with one of his tranq bullets that the world had seemed a bizarre and unnatural place for a few minutes.

His eyes fluttered open a moment later and he threw one arm around my neck, pulling me down next to him.

"Sorry," he muttered. "Bad dreams again. What time is it?"

I glanced up at Synjin, my heart hammering again. Steale was only half-way back. "It wasn't a dream, Steale," I told him as gently as I could. "Synjin's here."

At that, he tensed, his head jerking in the opposite direction as he pulled abruptly free of our awkward embrace. I made a grab for his shoulders, unable to predict what he might do next. As it was, he scrambled up in the bed until his back was pressed to the headboard, his eyes widening as he confronted the man sitting next to him.

He tried to swing his legs over the side, but Synjin was in the way. Then he simply subsided against the bed, staring at his brother until I was certain a fire would start in the room.

Synjin made the first move, though it wasn't what I expected. "Have a nice nap?"

I felt Steale's chi surge violently. Moving on instinct, I placed a restraining hand on his arm. He turned his head toward me, looked pointedly at my hand, then up to my face.

Finally he looked at Synjin, then at me again. I think that's when he first made the connection, undoubtedly through the telepathic rush of panic that overwhelmed me.

"*Him*?" he said to me, incredulous. "You have *got* to be kidding!"

I didn't know what his reaction was likely to be, but I owed him the truth. "Yes. I didn't know either. I mean, I didn't know he was your brother. I didn't know my mate was your brother." I was babbling; I shut up.

Steale looked at me for a long few seconds, then turned his attention back to Synjin. "You prick," was all he said. He glanced at the night stand, but the gun wasn't there.

Synjin's brows lifted. So did the corners of his lips. "Good to see you, too, Steale."

I wasn't sure why Steale didn't attack. But he just sat there, leaning against the headboard, his arms folded stubbornly over his chest.

"A lot's changed since you've been away," Synjin said at last. "I was wrong."

Steale glared at him. "I know."

Synjin didn't react. "We were both a lot younger then. I didn't - *couldn't* - fully understand what you shared with Kirin. Now I do," he stressed, looking at me again and giving me chills with his words. "I want to help."

Steale continued staring at him. "Still looking for glory, little brother?" he asked, his sarcasm like a knife in the room. "I don't need your help." He jerked his head in my direction, bitterness in his dark eyes. "And I don't need yours, either, River. You've taught me what I need to know. I was just about finished with you anyway."

Something inside me broke. It hurt to be shut out so abruptly after all we'd shared. His telepathy struck me like a physical blow regardless of the fact that we weren't in physical contact. I reacted badly before I knew what I was doing.

"Good!" I snapped, rolling off the bed on the opposite side as I unconsciously mirrored his psychic anger back at him. "Close yourself up in that ball of misery and feel sorry for yourself again, Steale. It's what you're best at, isn't it?" I paused just long enough to let that sink in, then added, "You haven't learned a thing! *Not. One. Thing!*"

I was on my feet and around the end of the bed, heading toward the door, when Synjin caught me by one arm. I twisted away until he let me go. Everything I had ever dared to imagine was crumbling like so much quicksand. It wasn't a moonlit night at the temple; it wasn't how I'd imagined it; it wasn't right.

"I need your help," Synjin said, his voice unruffled, cool.

I blinked, my face darkening. I looked over to where Steale was sitting on the bed, his head turned away from both of us, his arms tightly closed over his chest, his aura seething. The coyote was cornered and he was lashing out. I made myself understand that, though there was a tightness in my throat that made it impossible to speak. His anger had taken me off guard. It was a tangible thing in the room, a separate entity sitting on his chest like some invisible demon. It was a side of him I'd never seen.

"I see you still have your temper, Steale," Synjin said to him. "That'll help - once you learn to direct it in the right places."

Steale turned toward him, eyes narrowed, jaw tight. "I'll start with you," he threatened. "Get the hell out of my house. And take her with you. That *is* all you came for, isn't it?"

I flinched, started to say something, then stopped when Synjin spoke for me.

"That's one thing," he admitted, never raising his voice. "But I also came to help. As I said, a lot's changed while you've been away. Once Vale was eliminated - which you can tell me about sometime - attitudes softened. Even though I haven't been given any additional manpower, I'm authorized to take whatever means are necessary to insure the return of our people."

Steale sat there for a long time. "You're lying," he said at last.

"Our government has authorized a rescue attempt," Synjin explained. "It's not official, of course; that's why I'm here instead of half the Elite. We've got one chance, Steale."

Steale stared at him awhile longer, and though he tried to maintain the aura of hardness, the lines of his mouth eased very slightly. "Why?"

Synjin relaxed a little. "I think the three of us should sit down in the living room and talk. You can even get us something to drink if you haven't lost all your manners."

Steale's long brows lifted, his expression hardening. "I don't have any beer."

"I haven't touched alcohol in over forty years, Steale," Synjin said without animosity. "I've been at the temple since I left you."

Steale remained taut and unbending for a few seconds longer. Then, surprising me, he rolled off the opposite side of the bed. But before he made a move toward the door, he glared at Synjin once again.

"I'll listen to what you have to say, little brother. Beyond that, no promises," he warned.

Synjin inclined his head in acknowledgement. "I have a name, you know."

"Not in my reality," Steale assured him, moving past me as if not even seeing me, and into the hall.

I wanted to reach out to him, but our eyes never met as he left me standing in the middle of his bedroom. I looked at Synjin, only then starting to breathe again. He moved to my side and placed one reassuring hand in the middle of my back, then pulled me against his chest. It was a familiar embrace, a distant memory awakened as if by some half-forgotten scent. I realized only then that I was trembling. A very important part of me had just been assaulted, a part I didn't realize I even had until it was injured.

"He's going to say a lot of things he doesn't mean over the next few hours," Synjin murmured, his voice penetrating deep within me. "Don't let him drive you away. That's what he'll try to do because it's easier for him right now than dealing with me."

I didn't look forward to next few hours.

"I'm all right," I muttered miserably.

Synjin's brows rose as he looked down at me. We both knew I was lying.

~

I took the safest spot I could find in the living room - one of the overstuffed chairs in the corner next to the fireplace. Steale sat on the sofa, still wearing his gi pants, barefoot. Synjin had taken the love seat and I really looked at him for the first time since his unorthodox arrival.

He was dressed in soft cotton pants, a deep green shirt which had appeared black earlier, and canvas shoes of the type occasionally wore for outdoor practice. The sleeves of his shirt were rolled up to the elbows and as he leaned forward with his arms resting on his knees, I could see the lean musculature he'd developed from years of studying the Art.

He and Steale even looked alike. Not so much that anyone could have mistaken them for twins, but enough so to tell they came from the same genetic pool. Both had the same sharp features, angular, cat-like. And though Steale's eyes were considerably lighter than his brother's, they both had the same almond shape, the same brow-line, the same dark skin. I remembered Steale saying that his brother was a few years younger, and if what Ch'en Po had told me were correct, they were seven years apart, though for all practical purposes, neither of them looked any older than thirty.

Steale sat stiffly, deliberately not looking at either one of us. Instead, he stared out the window, his eyes riveted to some distant point. His embittered indifference shredded my soul, but it was up to them now.

"Let's hear it," Steale said finally, toying with the cord on the mini-blinds. "I don't have all day."

Synjin looked at me, set his tea cup on the table, then leaned back on the love seat. "Several years ago, shortly after Vale disappeared," he began slowly, "our government came to the conclusion that there's a much greater danger leaving our people here than attempting to get them back. A lot of public pressure occurred once Callahan McFee told his story to the press. I believe you knew him?"

Steale shrugged coldly. "I knew him. So what?"

"Living at the temple, I hadn't heard of the unrest," Synjin continued, his voice cool and controlled. "I only learned of it three weeks ago, at which time I was approached by someone in authority to plan the rescue and oversee it."

Steale turned his head toward his brother. "Why you?"

Synjin smiled softly. "The majority of the information concerning Project Gateway was destroyed several years ago. I'm sure you haven't forgotten."

Steale said nothing.

"At any rate, it quickly became obvious that the government may indeed have had the technology to use the corridor, but they either wouldn't, or couldn't. The reasons and the history no longer matter."

Steale took another sip of his tea, then set the cup in the window sill behind him. "It matters to me. *Why?*"

"I don't know," Synjin replied. "It's possible that they didn't want to risk turning the public opinion against them in the event of another crash. That's why they came to the temple - a man named Justan; Vale's successor. Apparently, the legends led them there."

Steale frowned. "Speak English."

Synjin wasn't dissuaded by his brother's coldness. "It's been said that only the Masters can pass through the doorways without the enhancement of Gateway. Justan came to the temple to speak to Ch'en Po."

"Ch'en Po?" Steale repeated.

Synjin glanced at me. "You haven't told him?"

I shook my head, speaking for the first time since we'd moved into the living room. "Ch'en Po told me a long time ago to tell no one about you or him. I never did, other than in vague generalities."

Synjin nodded thoughtfully. "It seems that my Master has set many things into motion which are only now becoming clear." He looked at Steale again, then back to me.

Frowning, Steale turned toward me, his gaze hard, demanding. "Did you know from the start?"

I drew a deep breath, centering myself. His words were a cold silver blade. "I'm not sure what you mean."

He jerked a finger toward Synjin. "Did you know that *he* was my brother? Did you set this whole thing up from the beginning?"

That was the problem. We'd *all* been very much in the dark - even Synjin, it seemed. Each of us had a small piece of the map to the maze, though none of us had the key. Ch'en Po probably kept it in his pocket.

"I didn't know, Steale," I said truthfully, holding his icy gaze as I spoke. "I knew I had a mate among your people and I knew you had a brother. I didn't know they were the same person any more than you did."

Steale stared at me for a long time as if trying to decide whether or not to believe me.

"Steale," I said fervently. There was power in a name; he'd said so himself. "You've been inside my *mind*. Now maybe you can't read direct thoughts any better than I can, but you would have known. Think about it."

He seemed doubtful. "I told you a long time ago that my brother got me interested in the Art. You didn't make the connection? Certainly, you knew what the prick over there did. You knew about the temple. You never said anything to me about it."

"A lot of people have brothers who take a few karate lessons," I pointed out. "And yes, I knew Synjin was a Master at the Temple of Kalpa. And sure – maybe I was dense for not making the connection and maybe you were, too. But it's a big planet - with two different worlds sharing it."

I paused, trying to say the right thing without anger or hurtfulness. "As for why I never told you about Synjin, you never *asked* about my mate, other than in general terms. As I said, Ch'en Po warned me years ago to keep my silence. If you ever meet him, you'll understand that he doesn't make requests lightly."

That seemed to reach him. His eyes weren't as dark when he spoke to me again. "I didn't mean to hurt you, River. There's just a lot of water under the bridge between me and Syn— between me and *him*," he corrected.

"If that's an apology, Steale, I accept," I said, hoping that was how he meant it. "Just don't let your problems with Synjin overshadow everything you've learned. We've come too far."

He continued staring at me, still unconvinced. "Are you telling me you still want to help?"

That surprised me. "Of course that's what I'm telling you! You pissed me off and you hurt me - you're still hurting me when you shut me out like this - but even if that's the way it has to be, I'm not willing to let that change anything."

I wasn't sure what Steale's response would be. He glanced at his brother, who was still leaning back on the love seat. He looked at me again. Then he turned to Synjin, his eyes narrowing once more as he spoke.

"I won't compete with you, little brother," he said.

I frowned, not understanding what in all the worlds he was talking about.

"Compete?" Apparently, Synjin didn't know either.

Steale glanced away, staring out the window again, playing with the cord to the blinds, winding it around his finger. "You were a competitive little bastard when we were younger. Not even you can deny that."

"There is no competition, Steale. There never was," Synjin replied, his voice softening considerably.

Steale didn't look at him. His gaze was fixed on some point outside the window. The first rays of morning sunlight were filtering through the red and gold liquid amber trees. A car's tires crunched on the gravel street outside. Somewhere in the world, people still went to work in the morning.

"So if you're here to play the big hero, what do you need with me?" Steale finally asked. "Why now and not years ago?"

Synjin released a heavy breath. "We weren't the same people then. Perhaps we both foolishly believed in miracles at the time."

"It'll take nothing *short* of a miracle to get into that place and back out again," Steale countered. "If you don't believe in such things, you're in the wrong ball park."

Synjin only smiled. "I don't believe in miracles. I do believe in what I know, what I've learned. You obviously haven't spent so much time perfecting your skills only to ignore them now. Listen to your chi, Steale. It'll tell you that I'm not lying."

"Fuck chi," Steale muttered under his breath. He was winding the cord of the blinds tighter around his finger, undoubtedly imagining it was Synjin's neck. Or mine.

"Steale," I said softly, my voice trembling, "you have to listen to him. We've both known all along that two people against two hundred doesn't make for very good odds. If Synjin can help us, why not let him? This isn't about him and it isn't about you. It's about Kirin."

He turned his dark head toward me, his eyes suspicious, his aura guarded. "You don't even know him, do you?"

"The way you're acting, I don't know you either."

I'd trapped the coyote again and he didn't like it. "Some things go beyond honor, River," he muttered to himself.

"Why?"

"Some things go beyond honor," he repeated enigmatically.

Synjin glanced at me again, his eyes filled with warmth despite the blizzard his brother was bleeding into the room. "Your pride will be your epitaph, Steale," he said softly. "There's no shame in admitting we were both wrong. We had neither the skills nor the knowledge we have now. The time wasn't right. Now it is, but there can be no animosity between us if we're going to work together."

Steale laughed, a chilling sound from deep in his chest. "Maybe you've gone deaf in your old age, but I meant it when I said I'm not working with you." He glanced at me as if trying to decide. "You've taught me everything I know, River, but if your path lies with him, then go now."

Something within me was breaking again. I tried to build a wall around it, tried to fight cold. But then I understood that it wasn't a fight; it wasn't a war; it wasn't a contest. As Synjin had said, one man alone could fight only with himself.

"You can't cut me out like ripping pages out of a book, Steale. It doesn't work that way - with me *or* with Synjin," I said, meaning it. "We're both part of your life, whether you want it that way or not. You're just being an ass out of pride."

His head jerked toward me but he stopped himself before his mouth opened. Turning back to the window, he began playing with the blinds again.

"You can't even look at me," I told him.

"I don't want to."

"Bullshit."

Synjin's brows lifted; I think he wondered if it were about to turn physical. "She's right, Steale," he said, leaning forward to rest his elbows on his knees again. "If you take my hand, if you look inside me and inside yourself, you'll know that I loved Kirin as I love you - as a part of who I am."

Steale's lip curled to a snarl. "I *have* been sleeping with your mate, you know."

He could be a dick when it suited him.

"You've been away from our world too long," Synjin said with obvious disappointment. "Have you started thinking like that, or are you trying to initiate a brawl?" When there was no response, added, "On the other hand, if you're just trying to start a fight, we could go into the studio and spar. But then you'd have to sully your hands on me, wouldn't you?"

Now *that* wasn't what I expected to come from the mouth of a Master. I shot a dangerous glance at him, but he motioned me to silence with a gesture that went unseen by Steale.

After a moment of lethal stillness, Steale turned toward him, fury in his eyes. "Fuck the studio, little brother. How about right here?" He started to get up.

My heart dropped. "Stop it, Steale!" I snapped, getting on my feet and starting toward him. I intended to push him back down onto the couch and sit on him if need be. Despite all I had taught him, Synjin could tear him asunder without breaking a sweat.

But Synjin moved before I could close the distance. "Why harm fragile artifacts, Steale?" he said, gesturing toward the decorative lamps and the pottery on the shelves. "If this is to be a battle of honor, shouldn't it be done in an honorable place?"

Steale was standing by then, only the coffee table separating them. His lips curved upward into a threatening smile. "It makes no difference to me where we do it. But if you need the comfort of a studio, let's go!" With that, he gestured elaborately toward the archway which would lead into the sparring arena.

Synjin started to move, but I reached out, grabbing him by one arm and turning him to face me, my eyes hot and wet with disbelieving anger. "Is this what it means to be a Master? Some arrogant display of male pride?"

He looked down at me, trying to tell me something with his eyes. Steale was right; I didn't know him, couldn't read him.

"This is your *mate*, River," Steale told me with a scowl of derision, coming around the coffee table and heading toward the studio. "Sure you want to spend the rest of your life with the little bastard?"

My soul was shattering again. I blinked back tears that had collected in my eyes. "Don't. *Please*," I said, looking up at Synjin. "If you fight him now, you'll only validate everything he's been saying. Can't you *see* that?"

Synjin's lips pressed together as Steale disappeared around the corner and into the studio. Then, surprising me more than I'd thought possible, he leaned down, whispering close to my ear.

"Trust me, River," was all he said.

That old line used by men since the dawn of time. *Trust me.* My jaw tightened in utter disbelief and I battled the heartfelt urge to slap him stupid.

But he didn't wait for my answer. Instead, he followed Steale into the studio, leaving me alone in the living room for a fraction of a second.

I went after them, furious.

~

It was over before it ever really got started. Steale had withdrawn to the far side of the room and, as Synjin entered, my over-anxious, angry student lunged, attempting to hit him in the mid-section with what might have been a nice spinning roundhouse kick under other circumstances.

As it was, Synjin caught his leg, pulled him through the kick as he'd done with me a few hours earlier, and dumped him in the middle of the floor. But this time, he didn't casually saunter up and offer a hand down to help.

Instead, he slipped around behind Steale, pinning him easily with one forearm against the back of his neck, his other hand catching the attempted elbow strike and sliding down to seize his brother's wrist. From there, twisting the arm up behind Steale's back, he subdued him without effort.

I looked down at the floor, away from them, overwhelmed with a sense of loss and regret. I loved them both, yet they seemed filled with bitterness, even hatred for one another. Steale was the one with the problem, but Synjin was feeding the fire, and I began to wonder if he were no more disciplined than his brother.

I started forward, violently angry with both of them, then stopped cold when I really looked at them together, as I *saw* what was happening between them.

Steale had been cursing steadily since he was pinned, but now his body had subsided for no reason I could detect. He lay face-down on the mat, his cheek pressed to the floor, the tension abruptly gone from his body. I wondered in a flash of terror if Synjin had changed his mind and had killed him in cold blood. But as I took an instinctive step closer, I saw the lightning-fast movement of Synjin's hand on the back of Steale's neck. I knew what it was then. Eagle Claw *chin na* – a technique that could render a victim unconscious or in a paralyzed daze, depending on the skill of the practitioner.

As Steale subsided into semi-consciousness against the mat, Synjin's eyes filled with compassion. He released the effective hold, sliding his arm lower until one hand was laced through Steale's fingers, the other pressing into the middle of his back.

I blinked, not fully understanding what I was seeing; and then I understood what Synjin had meant when he'd asked me to trust him.

The telepathic contact was undoubtedly wide open between them. Synjin was doing with his mind what he'd been unable to do with his words – reaching into the dark places where Steale kept his secrets and his wild dog spirit, removing the cobwebs of distrust and rage that had formed over the years, giving him the truth with some degree of force.

In my world, some shrink with a hard-on might have said it was no less than mental rape, yet Synjin was incapable of vengeful violence. Steale's words - no matter how bitter, how angry, how cruel - were not sufficient provocation to a Master. I watched with a sense of awe as they seemed to melt, one into the other. Physically, they were very much alike, emotionally very different. But in the mind, separate identity was temporarily lost. At that moment, Steale and Synjin no longer existed. They were one in the same, their identities blending together until the memories and experiences of one instantly became the memories and experiences of the other.

For several minutes, neither of them moved, and when I realized where I was, I found myself sitting on the floor a few feet away. My eyes closed. There was a stillness in the room, as if the world had stopped for those dangerous moments. Whatever happened between them now, whatever acceptance or rejection would come of the communion, the sharing itself was a precious thing, almost sacred as I understood it.

I could not say how much time passed.

Just when I was considering sliding out the door and disappearing into some other part of the house to give them some privacy, I saw Synjin's hand slacken. Steale's eyes had opened. Synjin straightened his back. Steale breathed again.

I'd been holding my breath, too, and as I looked up, Synjin gave an almost imperceptible smile.

Steale's breath was coming in a regular rhythm, his body lax. He looked at me, too, giving me chills with his intensity. I couldn't help remembering the night before, when we had made love with such a ruthless passion I had been propelled out of my body.

"River?" he said.

His voice went through me. I jolted back to a reality somewhere between two worlds. "You all right?" I asked cautiously.

Steale nodded. "Come here."

My stomach tightened; I froze. He looked a little dazed to me, and definitely unpredictable. When I glanced at Synjin, he held one hand out to me, the other pressed against Steale's back, keeping the mental communion open between them.

"What Steale's trying to say is that we want you to join us," Synjin explained with a soft smile.

I glanced at Steale. He winked, taking me completely off guard. "My brother can be a prick at times, but he's okay once you get to know him." His voice sounded lazy, drugged. I recognized the feeling well; I'd had it every time he'd slipped inside my mind.

I looked to Synjin again. "What'd you do, give him a happy pill?"

Synjin's expression was soft, serene. "I gave him knowledge."

My brows rose. "Knowledge?"

"An understanding of the way things are." He held out his hand to me again. "Come join us, River."

The color drained from my face.

"She's shy," Steale mumbled, his face still pressed to the mat like some lazy sunbather on the beach. He was basking in his brother's light, in the Master's warmth.

I wanted to choke him. I *was* shy.

Synjin chuckled, then reached across the space separating us to grab me by one wrist. "That can change," his deep voice murmured as he pulled me up next to him and drew me into their gestalt.

After that, I understood how things were.

CHAPTER NINETEEN
Triunion

Sharing a gestalt with two telepathic brothers was both exhilarating and draining. I don't know whether I fell into a natural sleep or if my mind simply disappeared into unconsciousness for self-preservation. All I'm sure of is that I came back to the living nearly four hours later.

The storm that had come in the night was gone; the studio was hot; it was Indian summer. The only thing that surprised me when I woke up was that Synjin and Steale were gone. I was lying on my back in the middle of the studio floor, staring up at the ceiling as if it were the most fascinating thing I'd ever seen, a vacant smile on my lips.

I could hear their voices further away and, when I was able to move, I crawled on my hands and knees to the wall and pulled myself up using the exercise bar. My body was exhausted, my mind more at peace than it had ever been before. It was an interesting contradiction.

When I was able to stand, I moved toward the studio door and started up the hall. But when I heard my name mentioned - Steale's voice – I stopped just around the corner. I was eavesdropping, I admit.

"...River was teaching at a studio in Joshua Tree. I felt something click the minute I met her. I guess I just knew. Weird..."

A pause, then Synjin's voice: "I'm glad the two of you had one another, Steale. It was disturbing to think of my brother and my mate both alone. Ch'en Po often told me to rest my spirit, yet I know how this world can be at times."

"To call it a madhouse would be a kindness, Synjin."

Steale's voice. He'd spoken his brother's name. I closed my eyes and whispered a silent thank-you to whatever restless spirits or wayward deities happened to be eavesdropping with me.

"So," Synjin said then, sounding very much like a normal human being. "You've been sleeping with my wife, big brother?"

Whoever said that men don't gossip was deaf.

"Want to drag me into the studio and kick my ass again?" Steale replied. A question for a question. Typical.

"Hardly. I'm sure you were good for one another," Synjin said, his voice calm, sincere.

Steale chuckled. "If I hadn't met her, I probably would have given up. I'd become bitter - worse than the last time I saw you before you first went to the temple."

"You knew where I was?" Synjin asked.

"I knew," Steale said. "Your old partner told me where you'd gone."

"You could have visited, you know. The Masters wouldn't have turned you over to the Elite regardless of what you'd done," Synjin said quietly.

There was a long silence, then Steale spoke once more. "They never told you?"

Another silence. "Told me?"

Steale: "Four years after you left, I went to the temple. I spoke to an old man by the name of Freelin. I wanted to study there, maybe try to work things out with you..."

"And Freelin turned you away?" Synjin asked, surprised.

"All I was told was that the Masters had decided it wasn't in my best interests to study there. I thought you would've known, since you're one of the Masters."

"I was never told," Synjin replied, his tone sincere, compassionate. "I didn't achieve Mastery until I'd been at the temple for seventeen years - and then only a student-initiate status. I didn't know, Steale. I'm sorry."

It started to make a lot more sense than it had before. I'd always felt that Steale's motives for hating Synjin went deeper than what I'd been told. He'd never intimated to me that he'd been turned away from the temple; obviously, the emotional injury he'd suffered as a result had deepened the rift between them.

"...just revenge at first, I guess," Steale was saying, confirming my suspicions. "I wanted to hurt people. Hell, the Masters probably knew that in the first place; that's why they wouldn't take me."

"If there were any doubts as to your motives, if the Masters believed you would use your skills for harm or vengeance, you would have been denied," Synjin explained.

"Whatever their reasons, that was the last straw," Steale commented. "I blamed you for the fact that I was turned away, and I wasn't capable of understanding at the time why you did what you did."

"You mean why I went to the temple?" Synjin asked.

"That. And why everything went to hell between you and me after Kirin was gone," Steale said. "So I figured out Fegan's computer and learned how to send the corridor into this world myself. He'd shortened the process considerably; the amplifier that used to fill a room now fits in a shoe-box. Fegan might have been a chronic pain in the ass, but he was one hell of a bookworm."

"And so you began using that technology to send people from this world into ours," Synjin surmised.

"At first, I made a point of sending the most ruthless criminals I could find," Steale confessed, his voice filled with regret. "Our world - our government - had hurt me, and I wanted to repay the favor. I turned materialistic and cold. Did you know your big brother's worth upwards of twenty million dollars?"

I almost choked. I'd known Steale was well off. I just hadn't known *how* well off.

"Could you spend so much money in a lifetime?" Synjin asked, incredulous.

Steale chuckled. "Probably not, but I had a good time trying for awhile. Before I met River, I made most of my money from the kind of slime you usually only see in the movies. For a fee, I'd send them to a brave new world."

"Losing a mate is like losing oneself," Synjin said, gently reassuring.

Steale was silent for a long moment. "River's taught me a lot, though I'm surprised she stuck with me. I feel like an ass for what I said to her."

"She forgives you, Steale. You saw that - felt it - in our triunion," Synjin murmured.

"You really think we can get in that place and back out again?" Steale asked.

"Yes." Typical of Synjin. Seldom said more than was needed.

"You have a plan?" Steale asked.

"Not yet. Show me everything you have."

That's when I heard them get up and start down the hall. I tried to duck back inside the studio, but Synjin was around the corner before I made it. Feeling like an utter idiot, I shrugged, looking up at both of them with a sheepish grin.

"You should have joined the conversation, River," Synjin murmured, his eyes filled with the same devilment I'd often seen in his brother. "Were you more comfortable in the hall?"

My mouth opened, then closed again. I looked at Steale, then at Synjin. "You bastards," I muttered.

It was going to be all right.

~

For two days, we didn't sleep. I didn't realize it at the time, but a link had been created between the three of us when we'd joined minds in the studio. It made the Whole greater than the sum of its individual integers - something I was finally starting to understand. As long as we were in close physical proximity, our energy levels remained higher than any of us alone could have maintained.

During those forty eight hours, Steale explained the layout of the complex to Synjin, and I gave whatever assistance I could in the form of shooting holes through their plans. When they discussed going under this fence or over that wall, I tried to think as the paranoid feds who'd built the place would think. Every fence was electrified; every wall was laced with closed-circuit cameras.

I'm not sure what Steale and I had been thinking, but now I fully understood what I'd meant by my off-the-wall statement back in May. Without Synjin, the picture was only half-finished. Steale and I were the rough sketch; Synjin was the paint on the canvas. On our own, Steale and I would have been caught or killed despite our best efforts and all our skills. It took the presence of a Master to let us see that.

By the time sunset of the second day came around, however, I could find no serious holes in the plan we'd formulated.

If - *when*, I amended - we found the chambers, Steale had said it would take no more than fifteen minutes to awaken their occupants. Even assuming the effects of such a prolonged stasis would reduce the capacity of the prisoners, he assured me that no more than an hour would be needed. He'd grimly added something along the lines of, 'If it takes longer than that, there's nothing worth reviving.'

Steale made it clear that he was taking his gun with him, and though I preferred a more direct confrontation, I couldn't fault him for his reasoning. What surprised me was when Synjin agreed with him. Not only did he agree, but he'd brought two additional guns with him - one for himself, one for me.

I didn't argue when he handed it to me and showed me how to load it.

Getting out of the underground would probably turn out to be the easy part. Getting to the natural doorway, located nearly a mile away, was likely to be harder. If we were fortunate, we would have not only ourselves to worry about, but eighteen others as well, assuming all of them were still alive.

It was the only chance we had. Terror was a good motivator, and Steale informed us that even the book-worms had been required to pass a physical fitness test. They wouldn't set any speed records, but they could run as well as the average American. That wasn't very reassuring.

Once we reached the natural doorway, we could activate the corridor immediately. We planned to conceal the shoe-box-sized mechanism near the doorway the day before; it would be ready for us when we arrived. After that, it would be a matter of holding off the wolves for the six minutes it would take to get through to the other side.

When I questioned Steale about the length of the corridor, he looked at me with those intense eyes and said he didn't know what I was talking about. The corridor was six minutes long, he told me. Physical length was unimportant. It existed as an anomaly of time more than one of physical dimensions. Its length was how long it took the hands of a clock to travel six minutes.

I gave up trying to understand it long before he gave up trying to explain it. Neither of us were scientists, and we were on the brink of frustrating one another to the point of a confrontation. Luckily, Synjin stepped between us, placed one hand on each of our shoulders, and we all managed to laugh it off. In the end, I was left only with the explanation that the corridor was long enough to reach from here to there. Precisely six minutes long, to be exact.

On paper, the plan looked as good as any we were likely to come up with. Personally, I wanted to move as soon as possible.

But then Synjin said something which, at first, almost insulted me. In a very calm and level voice, he said simply that Steale and I had completed the basics. Now, he told us, our skills would become more refined. He, of course, would be in charge of that fine-tuning.

I didn't know it at the time, but it would be another six weeks before we were ready to make the attempt. Most of that time would be spent, day and night, with Synjin teaching us to smell the color of blood, taste the sound of wind, and hear the sensation of fear.

"Listen with the heart. See with the third eye. Hear with the chi. Only then will you truly Know." Words often repeated until they became more than just the words themselves. He called it a crash course in awareness.

But I didn't learn of that crash course until the third morning Synjin spent with us. We finished formulating the plan late in the evening of the second day and, after that, we all slept together on the mats of the studio floor.

When I awoke the next morning, Steale was gone. There was a note attached to the refrigerator.

> *Gone for a walk. Be back tonight sometime. Don't do*
> *anything I wouldn't do, little brother.*
> *River, my gun's in the dresser if he gets out of hand.*
> *Love to both of you...*
> *Y. Lee Coyote*

I understood that Steale was giving us time alone together. What took me off guard was when I realized I didn't quite know what to *do* with that time.

I had been in love with Synjin – or an *idea* of Synjin – for longer than I could remember. And yet, even with the telepathic communion that was a natural extension of our triunion, I realized I didn't really know him at all.

~

We had oatmeal for breakfast, then sat at the kitchen table, the light filtering through the paned windows as we stole glances at one another over a glass of orange juice. The breeze wafting in through an open window was cool, the sky a late autumn slate, predicting rain. In the distance, a dog barked erratically, a sad and lonely sound.

Conflicting emotions overwhelmed me, unbidden.

I had little experience with men. With Steale, it had been a natural progression from one part of our lives to the next. With Synjin, I wasn't even entirely sure what I wanted. Nervous, I looked away.

Synjin smiled softly, reaching across the table to rest his hand on top of mine. "When I was younger, I had a fantasy about how we'd meet," he began, surprising me with how closely his words paralleled something I'd thought not too long ago. "I imagined it would be at a wonderful celebration given by the Masters to welcome you to the temple. We would walk together in the gardens; it would be a warm summer night; you'd tell me about your world, how you came to be who you are..."

I understood then how alike we were even though we had always been worlds apart. "And you would show me the temple, all its meditation gardens and secret passageways," I finished for him. "Later, we'd make love in some special place you'd prepared for us, sleeping in each others' arms until morning."

It *was* a little silly, the flesh of fantasy, not reality.

His lips pressed together with an ironic little smile. "Instead, it's Halloween."

I hadn't realized it. "Well, I could dress up as a witch and brew a love potion."

He laughed again. "Not necessary. I have always loved you, River." His expression grew seductive, devilish, as his brother's often did. "But it might be entertaining if you're in the mood for that kind of thing. I haven't been trick-or-treating since I was a boy."

Relaxing, I tried to imagine him dressed up like an elf or a ghost, grateful for the light-hearted banter. "Do the children do that kind of thing in your world? Trick-or-treat, I mean?"

"Though traditional calendars are discouraged at the temple, even the children there know intuitively when Halloween comes. The Masters quit trying to fight it years ago. In that way, our worlds aren't so different."

I smiled, tightening my grip on his hand. My heart quickened at the closeness; my body surged. My next words shocked me more than anything I'd ever said, for they weren't a request, and they defined in an instant *precisely* what I wanted. "Take me to bed."

His long brows lifted. Obsidian eyes darkened.

Outside, the winds quickened as if in response to the intense need that seized me. Raindrop fingertips tapped at the window.

Without speaking, he came around the table to meet me when I stood. I was in his arms then, our bodies tangled. My hands slid under his shirt, my cheek pressed to his shoulder. For several minutes, we remained that way, affirming one another's reality, drinking in the solidity of flesh and bone.

His essence was sandalwood and wild mint, scents of the temple which I knew without knowing how I knew it. The beating of his heart against my chest was slow and measured, quickening when I lifted my face to him in an unspoken demand to be kissed.

It is impossible to describe the erotic and exotic texture of that kiss – no longer the shy and tender dalliance from so many years in the past when we had first met and first kissed in a janitor's broom closet somewhere on the outskirts of a nightmare.

No, this was a kiss of a different color. Darker. Deeper. A kiss to seal the past and open the door to the future.

He held me to him reverently at first, but that was quickly replaced with a fierceness that left me breathless.

Lifting me as Steale occasionally did, he carried me down the hall with a strength that was effortless. I'd learned to like it – to be vulnerable and yet still in control. But instead of taking me to the bed - the only bed in the house - he turned into the studio, knelt, and placed me on the mats.

Looking up into his face, I tangled my fingers in his long hair as he leaned over me. "You don't consider it sacrilege to make love in the studio, Master Synjin?" I asked, teasing him.

When he spoke, his voice was thick with wanting. "These mats have tasted your tears, the sweat from your body, even your blood. How can love be wrong in such a sacred place?"

After that, he could have done anything he wanted with me. He was my match, all right. Romantic bastard.

I don't remember him undressing me, nor do I recall how he came to be suddenly naked before me. All I remember is looking at him, his body, his spirit. His flesh was smooth and without flaw, its only mark being a small scar about two inches long just below his left collarbone. I unconsciously traced the length of it with my fingertip, wondering.

His eyes smiled down at me, his hair forming a canopy which shielded my face from the morning light streaming in through the large window. "Nothing as dramatic as you're imagining," he said, reading my thoughts.

"Not the scar from a dragon's tooth or the wound from a battle with some evil warlord?" I persisted, enjoying the easy rapport between us.

He laughed again, shaking his head in mock dismay. "A sai," he explained, his breath warm against my face. "A gift from Ch'en Po. It was attached to the wall of my room at the temple. One night, an earthquake jarred it loose while I slept. Now my bed's on the opposite wall."

I couldn't stop laughing at the image. "Wouldn't it have been easier to move the sai to the other wall?"

He shrugged, leaning over me, the long strands of his hair tickling my breasts. "Ch'en Po feared I'd hurt myself trying to drill another hole into the stone. It was his suggestion to move the bed instead."

Tears ran down my face from my laughter – a laughter that was cleansing and healing and altogether necessary. Perhaps not surprisingly, it was also contagious, and Synjin's weight collapsed on top of me when he joined in my amusement.

"Actually, he said that a Master should have felt the earthquake and caught the sai by the handle as it fell... and that it never should have been attached by such a puny nail in the first place."

I lay together with him for several minutes more, our laughter gradually subsiding as my hands ran up and down his back, tracing the line of muscle and bone.

"You make me crazy," I told him, meaning it. He made me laugh; he made me happy; he made me crazy.

And then, in a manner that is impossible to describe, time simply stopped. The mirrors on the walls of the studio caught our reflection, repeating it to infinity. When I looked up into his eyes, I saw myself reflected there and had the thought that I had always been there and always would be – since before I was born until long beyond the day of my death.

I love you, my thoughts affirmed. My lips wouldn't speak the words, not when they were so important, so frighteningly and infinitely real.

"I love you," Synjin whispered, his warm lips pressed to my ear, his voice so soft that I knew the words were meant only for me, so soft not even the ascended ancestors could have heard them.

Even the confession of our love became an echo, a reflection, synapsing back and forth through the telepathic union that lay open between us. The mirrors seemed to shimmer, and though it made no rational sense, our infinite images vanished from them altogether, causing me to entertain the uncanny notion that we had disappeared from the world of matter and men altogether, living wholly within the newborn entity that was the union of two-into-One.

"This is the Way," Synjin explained, pressing his lips to the center of my forehead, the third eye, the eye of the chi. I felt the world dissolving – for there is no other way to express what was happening between us. We were not two separate beings poised on the edge of passion. Instead, we were a single being that had been split apart for an eternity, now becoming whole again.

Matter and time did not exist. There was only the penetrating luminosity of infinite energy which had gathered us into a single cocoon and sewn it together with filaments of light which were comprised of the starstuff of life and love itself.

This was the Way.

When I breathed, it was through Synjin's lips.

When I opened my eyes, I was looking down into my own face, seeing myself as my beloved saw me. My body appeared to glow as if illumined from within.

And simultaneously, I was looking up into Synjin's face, which had become my own. He was the dark light of moonbeam on the surface of water – the mystical muse I had been chasing all my life. More than human. Greater than the totality of his experience. More, even, than a Master of the art. He was Spirit made flesh and Life incarnate.

There were no more secrets between us, yet we became more of an enduring mystery to one another than ever before – for the consummate unknowable was the core ingredient in the elixir of love.

When he entered me, I dissolved into nothing, then just as quickly solidified into a woman who was dangerously vibrant and viscerally alive – a feral cat filled with a hunger that transcended all else and made me wild with needing this creature who was no less fierce than myself.

This was not the tender introduction to my beloved that I had envisioned in fantasies. Instead, it was dark and mutually brutal and driven by a starvation that had been years in the making. I didn't want him to be gentle with me. I wanted him to take me with all the power that was in him; I wanted to give myself to him as a willing sacrifice – and at the same time I longed to devour him utterly with my body, drawing him into me deeper than the limits of flesh, into the very core of me.

We rolled and tumbled like wolves in a battle to the death, propelled by an ecstasy that crested time and again. At one point, he pinned my wrists with a grip so powerful it bruised, looking down into my eyes with such an uncontainable turbulence that I knew he was not human and never had been. He was Other. Alien.

He was *mine.*

And I took what was mine with the same intense aggression that he had unleashed on me, rolling him onto his back and filling myself with the totality of him, swallowing him into me until I cried out with the pain of him, the perfection of him, the life essence of him that wept into me until I was filled and finally sated, collapsing onto his chest with a cry that left tears streaming down my face.

With his masculine strength, he rose up to meet me, wrapping his arms around my trembling shoulders, bringing us into a sitting position. My legs wrapped possessively around his hips, clinging to him, holding him deep inside me as he kissed at my tears, tracing their path with his lips, taking the earthen salts of me inside of himself on the tip of his tongue.

Somewhere in the uncontrolled ferocity of our joining, I must have scratched him. A single drop of blood had welled just above his right nipple, and without hesitation I placed my mouth over the little wound and drew the alien essence of his world into my mouth. It was an intimacy that left me dizzy, taking me higher and further into the dark realms of passion that I had ever dared to tread.

276

The self I had always known was dissolving, disintegrating, disappearing, yet at the same time I was being recreated and rebirthed into some hybrid being that could only now begin to conceive of how alone she had been before.

This was the Way.

In awe and wonder, I clung to him long after the storm had passed. We did not speak, for there was no need for idle small talk or epic soliloquies.

We lay together in silence for an hour or more, sharing the mystery of the rain on the roof, the dappled intervals of sun throwing shadows across the floor, over our faces, our bodies. Our reflections had returned to the mirrors, but they were altered forever – brighter perhaps, not as well defined at the edges where one stopped and the other began.

Twice more that afternoon, we coupled with a fervor that would have shocked most humans, rolling and tangling together until the heavy gravity of exhaustion dragged us down into sleep, our bodies still conjoined with the Way pulsing between us like a shared heartbeat.

~

The fight was a bitter one.

Steale sat tucked into a corner of a tiny room, a pale amber light shining across his face from the glow of a computer monitor. His arms were folded across his chest and he glared up at Synjin with open hatred. He looked as if he'd gone without sleep for a very long time. His body was thin, drawn, pale.

Synjin stood with his hands on his hips, anger bleeding off his aura in red spikes. Their minds were touching, tangling.

"Go, then," Steale said, his voice colder than the mountain air outside. "But if you go, don't you *ever* come back, little brother. Go see the world if you think it'll do you any good. Look at it long and hard, look for beauty and serenity and all those pretty fantasies that don't exist."

"Better than staying here and watching you kill yourself slowly," Synjin countered, his voice tinted with bitterness. "What's happened to you?"

"What's happened to *me*?" Steale repeated, incredulous. "Kirin's gone! Fegan's gone! Lissi's dead! And you can ask what happened to *me*?"

"It's been five years, Steale. If you don't let yourself heal, you never will!" Synjin snapped. "You can't spend the rest of your life trying to get back something you lost a long time ago."

"Well it's my life, isn't it? You were pretty gung-ho there for awhile, too, or did you think I wouldn't find out about your glory hunting, volunteering for the probe?"

Synjin took a step away, turning his back on his brother as he bit his lower lip. "You're killing both of us, Steale. You've lost Kirin and now you're killing both of *us*, too."

"You know where the door is. Don't let it hit you in the ass on your way out. Unlike you, little brother, I'm not afraid to die."

Turning on him, Synjin glared down at his brother. "There's a sharp knife in the kitchen, Steale. You want me to bring it to you?"

Steale stood up, jerking his fingers to the door. "Get out, Synjin." Cold again. Permafrost.

Synjin glared at him for a very long time, his body trembling violently. His head ached; the world was insane and he was the world. Then he walked out the door.

But he didn't listen. He came back twice more after that. The last time, Steale half killed him with his bare hands.

~

The woman underneath him was pretty but unintelligent, her wide blue eyes blinking up at Synjin without emotion as he slammed into her.

When it was over, she rolled off the bed and lit a cigarette, taking a sip of warm beer from an open bottle.

Her name was Jozet. Synjin remembered that much.

He pulled on his clothes and walked out her door, leaving the money on the dresser.

~

Liquor. It dulled the senses, but not enough. He drank one night until consciousness left him. And still he dreamed. His dreams. And Steale's dreams. Dreams of the past.

Nightmares. The telepathic link still existed between them, pulling their thoughts together like whirling atoms around a common nucleus of madness.

Like his brother, he was going mad. Unlike Steale, however, he had no outlet. He didn't have Fegan's computer. With the information about Project Gateway destroyed and the probe cancelled, he no longer had the sanctuary of another universe to disappear in to, no purpose for living.

Alcohol made it go away. But not far enough, never far enough.

~

Silence.
It lasted for a very long time.
Just the silence.
Time passed.
And the silence grew deafening.
Just the silence.

~

He came to the temple in rags. The silence drove him there when there was no place else to go. The women were gone. So was the liquor. And the money. The apartment had been repossessed by the co-op. He was alone.

The night before, Steale had almost killed him in the silence. Steale heard it, too. Deafening. Snow storm silence.

The last of the money brought him to the city. He'd walked the rest of the way, sixteen miles south of the last house, into the middle of nowhere. The temple was there in the desert, as it had always been. But it was silent, too. Like the world. Like the birds who sang without making a sound. Like the children who laughed and played, and yet were utterly silent.

Now he sat at the gate, his clothes torn, stained with blood which was partly Steale's, but mostly his own. His body was numb, without even the company of pain.

An old gentleman by the name of Ch'en Po found him there the next morning and led him inside without speaking. If he did speak, there was no sound.

It took three accomplished Masters half a season to nurse the foundling back to health. After that, they started to train him.

Gradually, the silence lessened. But it was a long time before Synjin smiled, and then only on rare occasion. After that, he began to heal inside just as his body had healed externally.

But it took years.

~

I was sitting in the middle of the mats, wearing Synjin's long-sleeved shirt and my own sweat pants. He'd swiped Steale's gi jacket and a pair of loose-fitting white jeans from the closet and now we sat facing one another in the center of the floor. We'd showered together, and finally gotten dressed.

I hadn't spoken to him of what I'd witnessed in his dreams. He knew I'd been there inside him as he slept. I knew he knew it. We didn't talk about it, though I understood then who and what he was, what had shaped him, what had molded him. He'd shared Steale's madness for a very long time, and only when *he* healed, only when *his* mind was clear could his brother begin to mend.

Drawing myself out of my reverie, I looked around the room, taking a deep breath to steady my nerves. The sun was low on the autumn horizon and soon the witches and warlocks, the devils and the angels would come to our door. All Hallow's Eve. Steale must have bought a bag of candy, for I found it sitting in a bowl next to the door.

Still, we had some time before the spirits arrived.

"What really happened to Steale before he came here?" I wondered.

Facing me, Synjin took both my hands, holding them as he spoke. "How much has he told you?"

"Almost everything, I guess. He told me about the probe, the argument the two of you had, how you went away," I recalled. "He never specifically said that you'd gone to the temple, though."

Synjin smiled softly, warmth radiating from his aura. "Steale and I were very close as children and into our early adult years," he

280

continued, tilting his head back and closing his eyes for a moment. "Our parents died when he was twenty-two and I was only fifteen. He became my guardian."

"Weren't your parents rather young?" I asked, surprised by his revelation.

"They were returning from a party at a friend's house one evening. Their car was struck by a train; they were killed instantly," he said, his sorrow a tangible force through the Way.

"So you and Steale became closer still," I surmised.

Synjin nodded. "By the time he met Kirin, I was already a legal adult. He'd been with the Elite since he was eighteen, and I joined when I was eighteen, too. The commander put us on the same unit."

"You were partners?" I wondered.

Synjin chuckled softly. "Not partners, exactly, but we worked together quite often. We still spent a lot of time together after work, too. That's how I met Kirin. Steale had been introduced to her after they both just turned twenty-five; I think they fell in love the first time they were alone together. He married her when he was twenty-eight."

"And the probe accident happened when he was almost thirty," I recalled.

Synjin nodded.

"And after that?" I asked, curious.

He released a heavy breath, squeezing my hands. "I almost lost my mind when the accident happened. Being on the Argus gave me access to a lot of information that the public normally didn't get to see. I knew about it long before it was all over the media. Our government had tried to cover it up, too."

I frowned. "Why?"

"A lot of people in my world felt we had no business playing around with something like inter-dimensional warps," he explained.

"*Did* you blame him for what happened to Kirin?" I wasn't being unfeeling, I simply needed to know.

Synjin's lips pressed together in thoughtful silence. "For a long time, I suppose I did. I had this image of him, you know. He was still my big brother regardless of the fact that we were adults. I thought he should have been able to make it right somehow. I was also impatient, moody, selfish. I said a lot of things I didn't mean; so did he."

It made things come clearer. "So that's why you went to the temple."

He nodded. "I felt as if my mind were going to shatter. Nothing helped. I tried drinking for awhile, anything to numb my brain," he explained. "I'd always had an interest in the Art, and I knew after that last night with Steale that I had to get some distance, get some perspective on everything. That's when I went to the temple."

"And you've been there for the last forty years?" I asked, still finding it hard to believe at times. He looked no more than thirty, yet he'd been at the temple much longer than that.

"During the time you were apart, did you ever feel him? In your mind, I mean?" I asked, saddened by the years they'd missed, the time they had spent apart.

Synjin shook his head with a soft sigh. "The night we fought - physically - the telepathic link between us was destroyed. That almost killed me, more than the bruises and the broken bones. I'd gotten so used to him being there that the silence was like death."

That's what I'd seen in his dreams. A jumbled, abbreviated version of his life. I let the subject drop after that, knowing - *hoping* - we'd have a lifetime together to sort it all out.

He asked me about my past then, the paths I'd taken, the roads I'd traveled, and by the time we heard the front door open, it was late in the evening. It occurred to me that no trick-or-treaters had come. The world was afraid. Afraid of the dark, afraid of poison apples.

I looked up a few minutes later to find Steale standing in the door of the studio, leaning against the archway and looking down at us with a questioning, mischievous smile.

"Did we have a nice day, kids?" he asked with a grin.

I felt myself blush, a silly reaction, all things considered. "Yes, we did, Steale." I patted the mat next to me, encouraging him to sit with us.

He came over and joined us and whatever awkwardness I'd feared never happened. I slept between them that night in the bed, feeling more safe and secure than I'd ever been before. Their telepathic link had almost destroyed both of them before; now it made them stronger, made them whole again.

We woke up the following morning in a tangled heap, sore and stiff; but we did it again - every night for the next six weeks.

In the daytime, we worked together on the kata, the fighting techniques, the mental disciplines. At night, we slept beneath the warm comforter, occasionally waking in the early morning hours to watch the stars through the open window.

And finally, it was time to go.

CHAPTER TWENTY
Winter Solstice

Church bells rang on the morning of the winter solstice.
Christmas services were in progress somewhere. People dressed in
fine clothes were attending the morning mass and talking about the
chicken waiting at home in the oven, the presents under the tree.
Four days before Christmas, and normalcy still existed somewhere
in my world.

I awoke to find myself pressed like a slab of tuna between two
dark pieces of bread. Synjin was already awake and staring at the
ceiling; Steale was just beginning to stir. One of them, I'm not sure
which, lifted a stray arm off my chest. I felt impossibly blessed in
the stillness of that morning, and had the thought that if my life
ended in whatever battle lay ahead, I would have no regrets.

Outside, the world was gray and cold, a light rain falling and
clutching the window-pane. Leafless winter trees glistened with
tears, and a strong wind howled around the house like a disturbing
aria of restless spirits.

In many ways, I was grateful for the rain, though I understood
it was disturbing to Steale. It had stormed the night he'd lost Kirin;
it seemed fitting to rain on the day he got her back. I wouldn't let
myself see it any other way. At the very least, on a more practical
note, the rain had a tendency to make security personnel lazy. It
was easier to sit in a Jeep with the motor running and drink coffee
than to patrol the perimeters of a complex that no one had ever been
crazy enough to attempt to break into.

Without speaking, each of us alone in our thoughts, we rose
from the bed that morning and went to the kitchen. Someone
shoved a glass of juice into my hand. A few minutes later, eggs and
fruit came. I ate without hunger.

As soon as we'd finished eating, Steale came around behind my
chair, his hands soft and warm on my shoulders, working their way
under the robe I'd thrown on and massaging sore muscles. We'd
trained with Synjin almost constantly for the past six weeks. The
only day off we'd taken had been the day before - to recover, to
meditate, to try to talk ourselves into changing our minds. I'd used
the early part of the afternoon to take the steel box into the canyon
near the complex. I located the natural doorway, placed the

amplifier nearby, and left it shielded in the crevice between two large boulders. The pre-set controls would activate on voice command from any of the three of us.

We never did change our minds.

Synjin was in the kitchen, clearing away the dishes and stacking them in the dishwasher. It occurred to me that it was all rather strange. We'd probably even turn off the lights when we left the house that night. Not that it would really matter; whether we were successful or not, we weren't coming back. We would either be in another world, or we'd be dead. Yet Synjin was rinsing the dishes as if nothing at all were out of the ordinary.

When the kitchen was clean, he raised his head to find both of us looking at him with amusement in our eyes.

His dark brows lifted and he chuckled softly. "Habit."

I returned his smile, relaxing a little as Steale's hands worked their magic. Over the past few weeks, I'd grown accustomed to their peculiar ways. It no longer seemed odd to have Steale give me a massage while Synjin washed the dishes, or for me to play with Synjin's long hair with Steale looking on in amusement. *Triunion.* That's what Synjin had called it.

We spent the rest of the day doing nothing in particular. Late in the afternoon, while Synjin was outside meditating in the rain, Steale lured me into the bedroom and made love to me again - wildly, without gentleness, without explanation. I think we both wanted it that way. It wouldn't have mattered if Synjin had come in. He would have smiled and said he was happy for us. Or for that matter, he might have climbed in with us.

What I felt for Steale and what I felt for Synjin wasn't dissimilar. I'd tried to convince myself that I wasn't *in* love with Steale, though I came to understand that I was only human. And it wasn't that I loved Synjin more because he was my mate. I loved them both – differently but equally.

Once, when I'd expressed some dismay to Synjin over my confusion, he'd told me with a fair amount of amusement that love wasn't like a peaceful lake which might go dry if too many people drank from it. Actually, I think Synjin *wanted* us to be together sometimes, for he would often disappear into the hills for long walks at sunset. Once or twice, he came back to find us sitting at the kitchen table with mischievous smiles. He lifted his brows on those occasions, shook his head, and talked about such things as how beautiful the mountains appeared when the sun was at a particular angle in the sky.

On that afternoon of the winter solstice, however, I don't think Synjin noticed anything at all. He told us simply that he needed to meditate, to be alone for a few hours, and that we should find strength in whatever manner suited us.

We found it in one another. In that way, Steale and I were very much alike - very much grounded in the physical world. Our passion was a fire we built to summon our chi. We were reckless with it that afternoon, for I think we both knew it might be the last time.

Without ever saying it, we all knew we might not see another morning. We might all die in a blaze of glory that wouldn't be so glorious after all. No one would ever know. It would be covered up before it ever hit CNN.

By the time the sun was lower on the horizon, Steale had gone into the studio and was working out alone. I went through the back door of the house and found Synjin sitting under the willow tree which hung her branches over Rattlesnake Creek. Most of the year, the creek held no water. Now, with the rain still falling, a muddy stream wound its way through the valley and toward the distant ocean.

I stood at his side for several minutes, marveling at his beauty. His long hair was slick and clung to his white shirt like a wet shadow when I sat down at his side. The water from the ground penetrated my clothes, cold against my skin. I didn't notice.

His eyes remained closed. The late afternoon rain made the world silent; the air was cold and still; the winds had stopped. Overhead, the sky was dark with storm clouds, overcast and gray. Night was approaching. And destiny.

For several minutes, I sat in silence next to Synjin, barely noticing when my own hair went flat against my head, drenched with rain that fell so softly I barely felt it on my skin.

Synjin opened his eyes then and looked at me, his lips forming a wistful smile. "I thought you were Steale."

"Oh?"

He nodded. "I smelled his cologne."

I held his gaze, feeling a desperation I hadn't felt in a long time. "I wanted to take him with me tonight."

Synjin smiled very softly, reaching out to caress my cheek with a hand that did not tremble. "Will you take me into battle with you as well?"

His words awakened a fire within me. "Yes. If you'll let me."

The sun was down. The sky had turned dark. In the cold and wet grass, Synjin took me to him, leaving his scent overlaid with Steale's, his essence inside me, too, now.

I never felt the cold, never acknowledged the fact that my body was wet and shivering. After that, I was no longer afraid. I had them both with me and it would be enough.

We went inside to dress to find Steale already waiting. He was lounging lazily on the couch in the living room, dressed in black, watching some old rerun on the tube. Some mechanical contraption was shouting, "Danger! Danger!"

I hoped it wasn't an omen.

~

By midnight, we were ready to go. The third shift had just come on duty, and it would be no later than 1:15 when one of the vans would come out through the southern-most gate, drive into town, and order three dozen donuts to go.

I felt slightly bulky in the clothes I was wearing, even more so whenever I noticed the weight of the gun against my left breast, suspended in the shoulder holster.

We stood by the front door for several minutes, and I saw Steale glance just once over his shoulder, down the hall, toward the studio. He drew a deep breath, but said nothing.

When we left the house, Steale reached automatically for the light-switch. I caught his hand, then smiled up into his eyes. But I locked the door behind me, never realizing the significance of it at the time.

CHAPTER TWENTY-ONE
Yin and Yang

None of us spoke throughout the entire time we were in the car. There was nothing left to say. As for what Steale was feeling at the time, I was never certain. He was scrunched down in the seat, his long legs pressing into my back as I drove. He looked lazy, relaxed.

The rain was still coming when we parked the car out of sight near the donut shop frequented by the guards every night at precisely the same predictable time. Once I turned off the engine and the lights, raindrops glistened on the windshield, forming intricate patterns that reminded me of fairy dust glitter in some long ago childhood I barely remembered.

Perhaps because of the storm, only a couple of cars pulled into the lot for the half hour we waited. Sane people were tucked in their beds, sleeping. The world was safe. At least that's what they thought, what they had to believe if they wanted to go on the next morning.

A plethora of thoughts like that one strayed through my mind. I wondered if the coyotes singing in the hills had warm burrows to shield them from the cold. I thought about Christmas and all the colored lights. Why *did* we have colored lights during the holiday season? I counted forward to three hundred, then back down again. I thought about the rain forests and the ozone. I thought about dying.

And then the van came. The driver took his time getting out, then quickly skittered into the brightly lit donut emporium without so much as a glance at his surroundings. At least two other patrons were in line ahead of him, but we would still have to move quickly.

Drawing a deep breath, I got out, held the seat up for Steale to untangle himself from the back, then moved under the covered walkway which ran in front of the entire shopping plaza.. Aside from one old man pushing a grocery cart, the world was devoid of life. We skirted along the edge of the building until we came even with the van.

During the thirty seconds it took Steale to pick the lock, only one patron exited the donut shop – a man with a newspaper over his head who never looked up as he pattered through the rain to his car.

Once Steale had the door open, he motioned us forward. Taking a deep breath and muttering a prayer to no particular god, I moved silently across the parking lot and climbed inside, relieved to see that the partition behind the driver allowed only a partial view into the back. From the bed of the van to the top of the headrest, the divider was solid metal.

Synjin and Steale were inside an instant later, and the door closed. We settled ourselves quickly, lying flat on the floor, or as close to it as their long legs could manage. There were various boxes and crates stacked close to the front of the vehicle, a tool box that was jabbing me in the thigh, and two dark tarps folded atop the cargo.

After what seemed like hours but could have been no more than five minutes, the squish-squeeze of tennis shoes on rain-slick asphalt announced the return of the driver. My heart pounded eerily inside my chest, but I reminded myself that we'd been through it all a thousand times. The guys who drove the vans were little more than glorified gophers. The chances of him looking over his shoulder and into the back of a van he knew he'd left locked were about the same as the chances of being attacked by a rabid beaver on the streets of L.A.

A few seconds later, keys fiddled with the driver's door, a rush of cool air caressed my face, and the engine started. I smelled gasoline and donuts and fought the urge to throw up.

The door closed then and the van started to move. I shut my eyes and concentrated on breathing silently. Had it not been for their warmth, I would never have known that Steale and Synjin were with me. Other than the engine and the tires on wet streets, there was no sound at all.

I tried to see Synjin's face, or Steale's, but there wasn't enough light. I had to settle for their scent which still clung to my skin.

And the van drove on into the storm.

~

All in all, from the time the van left the parking lot until it pulled up in front of one of the long buildings near the rear of the complex, it had taken approximately twenty minutes. Now, as I listened to the driver padding away from the vehicle, I started breathing again.

Even though there were no windows in the back of the van, I could tell he'd parked it under a bright light just outside the building. I could see Synjin and Steale now and was somewhat relieved to note that neither of them looked much better than I felt. Aside from trying to lead eighteen book-worms over rough terrain at night, the most potentially dangerous part of the journey was over. We'd been more exposed in the van than we planned on being from that point until we reached the stasis chambers.

After a few minutes had passed in silence, Steale moved toward the rear door, opening it without making a sound. Once it swung back, Synjin and I slid out onto the ground, hit the dirt, and made it into the shadows. Steale was a half-second behind us and, a few moments later, we were pressed against the side of the building, listening for movement.

Getting inside proved to be easier than we'd thought. When we came around to the side of the structure that couldn't be seen or photographed from any vantage point, we discovered massive hangar-type doors standing open as if they'd been waiting for us to arrive.

Maybe they had...

I clamped down hard on my paranoid thoughts, staying close to the ground as we slipped through the doors and found ourselves inside an almost-completely-dark building. Apparently, the structure was a left-over from World War II. It not only looked like a hangar, it *was* a hangar. And the fact that it was almost completely empty made it even more eerie than it might have been under other circumstances. Other than a few older vans that had obviously been retired and what looked to be a rusty engine from an old plane, the place was a hollow, a broken egg with dirt floors and windows completely obscured with decades of dust.

We found the elevator easily enough, and Steale and Synjin worked together to force the outer doors apart. After that, one of them attached the grappling hook to a ledge higher up in the shaft itself, then dropped the rope down into the darkness.

Without hesitation, Synjin wrapped the rope around his hand, swung out away from the door, and started the long descent to the sixth level. I followed after him a short time later.

I was almost grateful for the darkness, because I couldn't tell whether the drop was five feet or five hundred feet. I tried not to think about it, walking the shaft of the elevator wall and coming down the rope hand-over-hand. It took me longer than it had taken Synjin, but I eventually found myself looking down toward a patch of light where he had opened the door onto the sixth level.

In another minute, I swung through the opening, breathing a whisper of relief to have my feet on solid ground again. I tugged twice on the rope to let Steale know I was in, then slipped around a corner where I found Synjin waiting.

The sixth level was eerie. The elevator shaft had opened onto a long corridor which went about sixty feet, terminating in a staircase to the left, a service conduit to the right. Along the corridor were several doors, opening into what the blueprints had labeled as offices, storage areas and supply rooms. The staircase was our next destination, for it would lead a half-flight down, open onto a landing, then back into another corridor leading in the direction we'd just traveled - the beginning of the maze.

I mapped it out in my mind for the thousandth time, my back pressed against Synjin's chest as we waited for Steale to make the long climb down. He came through from the darkness a minute later, caught his brother's eye, and nodded curtly. He pressed the button on the wall which would summon the elevator car up from the seventh and deepest level, where it normally waited. It arrived, pinging loudly and echoing off the corridor walls, causing me to jump with unexpected anxiety.

But when the doors slid open, the car was empty.

Synjin moved out from behind me then, slipped into the waiting car and began unscrewing the panel while Steale and I stood sentry. It took no more than a minute to disconnect the alarm. With that done, he put the panel back in place and locked the car off at the sixth level.

We moved quietly down the long corridor and came to the stairs a few seconds later. Still there had been no movement, no sound. The first thing I'd done when I came out of the shaft was to look for surveillance cameras. Fortunately, there weren't any.

Anyone who had made it to the sixth level was supposed to be there – at least that must have been the attitude of the arrogant builders.

We continued down the half-flight of stairs and into the corridor between the sixth and seventh levels, then slipped inside one of the service tunnels which would take us the rest of the way. There were three labs which had been marked on the blueprints as classified, but there was no way to determine which one would house the stasis chambers.

It took another ten minutes to stealth through the dark tunnel. The only lighting came from bare bulbs which had been attached to the ceiling with cheap fixtures. Located approximately twenty-five feet apart, they gave off an eerie, dim glow. The part of the complex we were in now was used only as a conduit for servicing the facility. Electrical wiring and air ducts criss-crossed haphazardly; boxes filled with food, water and medical supplies lined the walls. The entire place was obviously meant to withstand a major catastrophe, perhaps even a nuclear attack.

At one point, we came to a bend in the tunnel where a cold wind blew against my face. Instinctively looking up as I passed underneath it, I saw one of the many air shafts leading to the surface, venting onto the various levels and providing breathable air for the entire complex. We'd discussed the possibility of dropping down one of those instead of the elevator shaft, but now I understood why Synjin had vetoed the idea from the beginning. The walls of the shaft were smooth metal with unfinished seams in several places. One wrong move and a rope could be slashed instantaneously.

The complex was designed to be a maze. After we'd dropped down the half-flight of stairs and emerged into the corridor, a bizarre series of twists and turns were necessary to get to the classified areas of the underground. In all, the area beneath the surface was no less than a square mile; and the deeper down it went, the more complex the maze became. The seventh level was primarily the power source, where massive generators, heating units and air processing equipment were stored.

After confirming that the hall was empty, Synjin motioned for us to follow. The blueprints had shown a T-intersection to the north, with the three classified labs in that area.

It seemed reasonable to assume at least one guard would be posted in the corridor. Steale already had his gun drawn and was providing back-up for Synjin. I was in the rear, covering our backs as we proceeded toward the intersection.

We were approximately ten feet from the corner when I heard a door open behind us. Knowing I was too far away for any direct physical confrontation, I drew my own gun, pressing my back to the wall and taking aim in the direction of the sound.

A second later, a man in a common business suit stepped out into the corridor and started in the opposite direction without looking up. Then, almost as if sensing something, he turned toward us, his eyes meeting mine and widening with surprised disbelief. He started to say something, his mouth opening.

I didn't hesitate. Instead, I squeezed the trigger, aiming for his mid-section as Steale had taught me to do. I saw him flinch, heard his gasp of astonishment just before he crumbled in a heap in the middle of the floor.

In my mind, I felt an abrupt rush which I recognized as my link with Synjin. The Way. Looking up, I nodded, telling him without words that I was all right.

When I reached the fallen man, I glanced quickly around. Steale had followed after me a few steps and was covering my back. I found what I was looking for in the form of a door labeled 'Major Kittering'. A quick check confirmed my guess; no light shone through underneath. The room was empty.

Opening it, I returned to the sleeping man and slipped both hands under his arms, dragging him into the dark room while Steale stepped in front of the open door to cover me.

"Shoot him again," he whispered. "Twice!"

I looked up, surprised. "What?"

"One load's only enough to keep him down for twenty minutes. We might need longer than that," Steale insisted.

I didn't argue. Instead, after propping my victim up against the wall inside the office, I drew the gun and pulled the trigger two times at point blank range. He'd have one hell of a sore shoulder in the morning, but he'd be alive.

Closing the door behind me, I came into the hall at Steale's back. Synjin had remained a few feet further down the corridor and we caught up quickly, inching our way along the wall until my mate came to the corner.

With a movement I barely saw, he jerked his head around the wall, taking in every nuance of what lay behind the T-intersection in a fraction of a second. Turning to glance at his brother, then at me, he held up two fingers, then pointed to the left and the right.

Two guards, one at each end of the hall.

That rattled me a little. They were awfully quiet.

As Steale and Synjin stepped around the corner, I covered their backs at the intersection. I didn't hear anything at first, other than the pound-slam-thump of my own heart. Then, half a second later, there were two soft thuds. The guards were out without ever knowing what happened.

My wrist watch read 2:18.

When I came around the corner at the intersection, I saw why the guards hadn't been talking. The hall was much longer than the plans had shown. Undoubtedly, the classified projects had been expanded. Instead of being fifty feet long, the corridor was ninety feet long, altogether - forty-five feet on either side of the intersection.

Synjin took the passage to the right, Steale the middle; I went left. The only inscriptions on any of the doors were useless. All three had stenciled letters with black ink reading: 'Security Clearance Required; Restricted Area'. The one I found myself in front of also bore the additional placard which said: 'CBU 947'. It meant nothing.

I was slightly unnerved by the guard who was slumped, snoring, in a straight- backed wooden chair next to the door, a copy of *Playboy* on the floor where he'd dropped it.

Reaching out with my instincts, summoning my chi, I ignored the unconscious guard and placed my hand flat on the door. I'd never been particularly psychic, but I'd been gifted with something I'd come to think of as deep logic. Subtle temperature changes or inaudible sounds had occasionally told me whether or not a room was empty. I felt nothing, heard nothing, sensed nothing.

Synjin had already opened the door at the far end of the hall. I saw when he cracked it just a fraction that no light came through. Looking up, he shook his head, then started back to his brother.

Whatever he'd seen in the room was enough to tell him it wasn't the right place.

Looking at me for a brief instant, Synjin nodded sharply, telling me without words to open the door. Like Major Kittering's office, it wasn't locked. With guards and top security precautions, they'd overlooked the most obvious thing.

They usually did.

Putting my hand on the cold knob of the door, I started to turn it, then stopped abruptly when I heard Steale take a sharp breath. My blood turned to ice and I snapped my head in his direction. He had already closed the door after a brief look inside, and when his eyes met mine, I knew we'd found what we were looking for.

I stopped what I'd been doing and started down the corridor toward where the two brothers were only a few feet apart. When I reached them, I could see Steale trembling. Worse, I could feel his turmoil in my own body through the link of our triunion.

I glanced at Synjin; if Steale crumbled, we were finished. Reaching out, I placed one hand on Steale's shoulder just as Synjin steadied him from the other side. We didn't dare speak. Light was shining underneath the door; at least one person was inside the room, probably more.

I squeezed his shoulder hard, trying to impart my own strength through touch. A moment later, he nodded that he was all right. What I felt inside *myself* said otherwise, but I had to trust him even if we all knew he was lying.

Synjin took the lead then. He guided Steale behind him, me in front. I was to be the first one through. I was the shortest. They could shoot over my head once I swung the door open; I couldn't even see over theirs.

Taking a deep breath to steady myself, I placed my hand on the knob and turned it very slowly. An instant later, I pushed it open hard and took four steps inside the room, giving Synjin and Steale enough room to maneuver behind me.

My eyes turned cold and hard, looking for movement rather than detail. I saw it soon enough - two white-coated lab technicians with pale, pasty faces. The woman screamed when we burst through the door; the man dropped a sheaf of papers he was holding. Leveling the gun at their chests, I pulled the trigger three times on each of them, ignoring them as they fell.

Out the corner of my eye, I saw that Synjin had taken out two more; Steale was occupied with three who had been behind a glass divider wall when we came into the room. He picked off the older of the three men with relative ease, but the other two ducked behind a bank of equipment.

I felt myself moving before the signal ever reached my brain. Synjin was a half-step behind me, Steale a half-step ahead. I ducked around behind the electronics bank while they went to the far end to cut off any possibility of escape.

When I first came around the blind corner, I was surprised to see one of the two men crouched down behind a turned-over chair, pointing a gun in my direction. But before he could pull the trigger and alert anyone else within ear-shot, I fell to the floor and slid toward him, feet first, in a move it had taken years to perfect. My tabi boots impacted with the chair an instant later, throwing the gunman off balance and toppling him over backward.

I seized his gun arm in a numbing grip, bending his wrist backward until I heard the bone snap. He yowled with pain, then let the gun drop to the floor, clattering as it fell. With an outward hand-sword strike, I caught him across the carotid artery and the sensitive nerve center in the neck. He collapsed, unconscious. I pulled my gun then and shot him three times, vaguely aware of the uproar taking place a few feet away.

I looked up to see Steale break his adversary's ankle with a thrusting sweep kick. An instant later, Synjin fired his gun and a dangerous silence fell into the room.

We were alone.

Yet we were not alone.

~

The three of us stood utterly still, waiting for the barrage of gunfire which never came. There hadn't been time for any of the stunned victims to get on the intercom and yell for help.

I went back to the door and soundlessly closed it. Then, pulling a chair and a heavy metal desk over to it, I wedged the back of the chair under the knob and used the desk to block it.

Finally, turning around once more, I looked at the room for the first time, a sick feeling creeping into my stomach as I did.

The pale green glow that filled the room came from an area near the back, thirty feet away. And when I forced myself to really look, I saw something I recognized from Steale's dream more than a year in the past now.

Stasis chambers. Or, in Ch'en Po's words, silver boxes which kept souls locked up forever.

Five of them were identical to the ones I'd seen in Steale's nightmare, probably because they *were* the ones I'd witnessed there. The rest were what appeared to be a military representation of the same thing. I understood then at least part of what had happened. The technology we'd stolen from the Roswell crash had been sufficient for our scientists to duplicate the results even if not the complete design. The five chambers from the crash were sleeker in appearance, almost completely made of glass except for the bottom. The others – I didn't take the time to count at that moment - looked more like silver coffins with glass-bubble lids. The same green glow came from each of them and, as I took a halting step forward, I realized for the first time the horror of what I was seeing.

Each of the chambers was filled with a human occupant, lying as if asleep under the life-suspending green light. I didn't need to fully understand the technology to know that at least some of these people had been asleep for more than forty-five years.

I felt my legs tremble, then looked up to see Synjin and Steale standing across the room, a few feet in front of the chambers. Regardless of how well we'd prepared ourselves, it could never be enough to fully soften the shock of what we saw, what we knew, what we were feeling in our chi.

I stood there in a reverent silence for several seconds longer, then forced my legs to move. When I came up next to Synjin and Steale, I placed one hand in the middle of Steale's back.

"Kirin?" I asked.

He inclined his head toward one of the five original chambers and, when I made myself look, I recognized his beloved wife from his dreams. She appeared to be no more than thirty years old, dressed in what I recognized as a standard-issue military hospital gown. Her eyes were closed, her sandy-brown hair resting on the leather-like pillow beneath her head.

She looked to be asleep.

I wouldn't let myself think anything else despite the fact that none of the chambers' occupants were breathing. But perhaps the most chilling thing of all was that Kirin's arm was in a cast, as it surely had been forty-five years ago. She hadn't changed; the arm had never healed; she had no idea that so much time had passed without her.

I realized peripherally that Steale was shaky, and when I looked at him, I saw the moisture in his eyes. That was enough to force me into action. We'd have time to digest the horror and the injustice of it later.

"Come on," I said gently, guiding him away from her chamber. "Let's get started."

He drew in a sharp breath which startled me, then collected himself as much as possible.

I knew nothing of the technology other than what Steale and Synjin had explained to me, so it was my job to serve as sentry while they worked the controls that would bring the dead back to life. I was grateful to watch the door, not knowing what to expect, not daring to believe anything could go wrong now.

Unconsciously holding my breath, I kept my gun drawn, pacing back and forth while they worked together in silence. Occasionally, I glanced over my shoulder, and for nearly ten minutes, nothing at all seemed to change.

Then, abruptly, I heard a rush of air like steam being released. At first, I thought we were being gassed, but as I turned instinctively toward the sound, I watched with nervous fascination as the top of one of the original units slowly slid back. It wasn't Kirin's chamber.

It was Fegan.

He was alive. He was breathing. He was sitting up.

Steale was saying something to him that I couldn't quite understand at first, something about the corridor, something about how much time had passed.

I saw that Synjin had moved to another of the chambers, and another rush of air soon burst into the room.

Keeping my attention divided between the door and what was happening, expecting the guards to come at any moment, I listened intently to what was being said.

"...told you to go without me, Steale." Fegan's voice.

It caused me to chill. It had been almost half a century, yet to Fegan, it must have seemed like only a few hours.

"We don't have time to discuss it, Fegan," Steale was telling him. "Can you stand?"

"I can stand, Steale. I'm not an invalid, you know," Fegan protested in his typically whiny voice. In that moment, it was pure music.

I glanced over my shoulder again to see Steale helping him to his feet, practically lifting him out of the chamber.

"It's been forty-five years, Fegan," Steale was explaining. "Don't ask questions, just help me wake the others."

"I know what time it is, Gemini man," Fegan muttered.

There was a silence. "What?" Steale's voice again.

"You dream," Fegan said as if Steale should have known that. "You sleep and you dream. Why are you looking at me like that?"

Their conversation wasn't making a lot of sense, but I understood that very well. Fegan knew about the passage of time, what had happened. Somehow in a nightmare that had lasted longer than I'd been alive, he understood. Maybe the others would, too. It would save a hell of a lot of time. It might save our asses.

I looked at them again and saw that two more were awake. I didn't recognize them; I didn't need to. In some out of place reality, I heard a man crying. One of the book-worms. Maybe they had nightmares. Maybe he was just scared.

I know I was.

Hissing again. More chambers opening. At least Steale had been right about one thing. The occupants of the stasis chambers awakened as if from a natural sleep. It wasn't like the horror of cryonics that the media often liked to exploit in the 80's. There was no liquid nitrogen, no frozen bodies. Whatever the stasis chambers really were, they acted like long-term anesthesia. The only major difference was that, instead of just terminating consciousness, the chambers stopped *all* bodily functions.

Except, according to Fegan, dreaming.

I counted seventeen hisses before I turned around again. There was still no sound of footsteps rushing down the hall to discover us; other than the man crying and a low rumble of unintelligible book-worm conversation, there was silence.

Finally, turning slightly toward the chambers, I watched with awe and hope as Steale and Fegan moved to the chamber where Kirin slept.

A few seconds later, when some of those who were well enough came closer, the top of the device slid back, hissing like a serpent as the green glow dissipated. I held my breath for a moment longer, then blinked back the tears that came when I saw a slender arm slide around Steale's back.

Kirin was alive. *Somehow.* Kirin was still alive.

I was vaguely aware of their conversation, though they weren't saying so much in words. Instead, Kirin was crying softly, her face buried in Steale's neck, her arms holding him as if she might never let go again.

Synjin was trying to get some sort of order among the chaos, trying to explain to the newborns that we still had a long way to go. I had the feeling that most of them weren't listening. Instead, they seemed to be dealing with the shock of coming back to life. Several of them were couples. In fact, as I watched the scene out the corner of one eye, I saw that only Fegan and Synjin were standing alone.

My heart wrenched again. Fegan kept his head lowered, kicking shyly at the floor with one foot. I took a few steps closer, careful to keep my eye on the door at the same time.

"Fegan?" I said, glancing over at him, motioning him toward me with a gesture of my head.

He looked perplexed, but seemed to decide I was one of the good guys, for he came over to me without question.

"Fegan, we have to get these people out of here," I said. "There'll be time for all of this later, but for right now, we have *got* to get moving."

He nodded thoughtfully, always soft-spoken, I would soon discover. "How'd you get in?"

I gave him the Reader's Digest version, finishing with, "The elevator's locked off on the sixth level. We should be able to get to it without a lot of interference, but once we reach the surface, things are going to get crazy. Think you can get these people to understand that?"

He looked at me as if I'd gone completely out of my mind. "Why'd you come in that way?"

I blinked, staring at him. "It was a hell of a lot safer than an air shaft."

He shook his head. "It's a wonder any of us are still alive."

"What are you talking about?"

He shrugged just as Synjin came up to stand next to me. "They just finished a new escape tunnel about seven months ago."

I frowned. "How do you know that?"

A wistful smile came to Fegan's lips. "I overheard them talking."

My blood chilled again. "You *what*?"

He shrugged. "I overheard them talking. You want to take the tunnel? By the way, what's your name?"

He seemed downright oblivious to the danger we were in. I answered him anyway. "River Willows. What tunnel?"

"Nice name," Fegan commented. "The tunnel that's down on the seventh level. They built it after a fire broke out in CBU 947."

At least he hadn't been delirious when he'd said he knew what he was talking about. CBU 947 had been the inscription on the door at the end of the hall, the door I'd never had to open.

"Do you know where it is?" I asked, my voice rushed. Synjin was covering the door now; I could concentrate my attention on Fegan.

"I've never been there, but I can find it," he said. "Old Doc Kittering always bitches about it every time they have a fire drill. 'I don't get paid enough for going down those goddammit rickety stairs into the bowels of the Earth and crawling through some hole in the side of a mountain'," he mocked.

I glanced up at Synjin. "It might be easier than trying to get this bunch back out the way we came in," I suggested.

Synjin nodded, then glanced at Fegan. "Do you know where the tunnel emerges?"

The book-worm shook his head. "Probably still inside the perimeter, but a lot further out than the way you got in here."

He had a point.

"We have to go, River," Synjin warned.

I couldn't have agreed more. I looked around in the swarm of bodies for Steale. When I finally spotted him, he was standing toward the back of the throng, Kirin still in his arms, her head resting on his shoulder.

I made my way through the crowd until I came up next to them. I didn't want to intrude on their reunion, but we were rapidly running out of time. The longer we waited, the greater the chance of some peon discovering the guards in the hall or the man I'd stuffed in Kittering's office.

As gently as I could, I tapped Steale on the arm, waiting until he opened his eyes and acknowledged me before I spoke.

"River," he breathed softly. "This is Kirin. We..."

I knew what he was feeling. At least I think I did. As Kirin turned toward me, her eyes swollen from crying, I smiled very softly, touching her on the shoulder to impart my feelings for both of them. I hoped it would be enough, for there wasn't time for long-winded introductions.

"Steale, we have to move right now if we're going to make it," I said softly. "Fegan says there's a tunnel down on level seven - something that wasn't in the plans."

Kirin nodded with an enthusiasm. "I heard them talking about it, too," she said, her voice deeper than I remembered from Steale's memories. "They said it takes five minutes to get to the surface. At first, I thought it was just another dream. But if Fegan heard it, too..."

I'd go into shock later, I promised myself that. But for now, the adrenalin would have to keep me going.

I smiled a thank-you to Kirin, then looked up at Steale again. "You ready to travel?"

He nodded, then held his wife at arms length, looking down into her bright lavender eyes. "Can you make it?"

Kirin smiled, first to him, then to me. "I'll make it if I have to crawl," she promised.

I liked her. I also hoped the other book-worms shared her conviction. I touched each of their hands in an attempt to convey what words could not, then went back to Synjin.

Fegan was chattering incessantly while Synjin stood watching the door, and I put a hand on the book-worm's arm to shut him up for just a moment. The others were instinctively crowded around him, and when I came up on them, I overheard him telling them what we planned. Luckily, there wasn't one dissenting vote, though I heard someone crying again.

Emotional trauma. I'd felt a little of it myself and was going to feel a lot more if I lived long enough.

I glanced again at my wrist-watch. 3:11. Almost time for coffee break. We had less than four minutes to get the hell out of there before someone thought to check on the good folks in the stasis lab. As I drew up alongside Synjin, he looked down at me with a questioning gaze.

"Damned if I know how to talk to them," I muttered, "but Fegan seems to have them under control."

"Steale?" he asked tentatively.

"Overwhelmed but functional." I considered what I'd said. "Make that two of us."

It broke a small amount of the tension, and Synjin smiled. "I'll lead; you follow behind the group. Put Steale and Kirin somewhere in the middle."

When I found Steale again, he had already started toward us. I met him half-way across the room.

"Synjin wants me in the back of the bus and you in the middle," I told him. "You okay with that?"

He nodded, looking down at me with those intense eyes. I felt Kirin's gaze on me, too, and glanced over at her. She looked stronger, more ready to travel than I'd thought she would be. I felt a little better.

"Yeah, sure," he said. Then, unexpectedly, he reached out to mess up my hair. "Don't worry about me, River. We're going to make it."

I tapped him on the chest with my gun, trying to impart a confidence I was far from feeling. "Just make sure you do."

Synjin had already started to move. By the time I ushered the last straggling newborns toward the door, he had already slid the desk aside and was peering cautiously into the hall. My heart was hammering in my chest again, especially when the entire group of book-worms fell into utter silence. They weren't half-bad at stealthing, and only one person tripped after we made it to the stairs. I promised to kick myself for it later.

As Fegan had promised, the tunnel was there on the seventh level. It was even politely marked with a glowing red 'Exit' sign pointing south. If we were in luck, if the tunnel continued south, we'd have some kind of head start toward the natural doorway where the corridor could be summoned.

I felt somewhat better once we were actually in the tunnel, though I noticed the claustrophobic feeling immediately. The passageway was no more than three feet wide in most places, less than six feet tall, and had been carved from solid rock. All the men and a couple of the women had to crouch just to clear the top.

The most disturbing thing was that the tunnel itself had no light, and not one of us had brought a flash-light. We hadn't planned on needing one. But I trusted Synjin's lead implicitly, and resigned myself to the darkness as we continued along for what seemed to be about two hundred yards. That's when I felt the rush of cool air against my face and heard the book-worms mumbling to one another in hushed tones. In the closeness of the tunnel, the sound was almost deafening to ears that had grown accustomed to the silence.

It was obvious by that time that no guards were going to come after us through the tunnel, so I began making my way forward through the throng until I found Synjin in the lead. Steale was already at his side, with Kirin a half-step behind.

The entrance to the tunnel was no more than fifty feet away; I could see the lighter gray of the clouds through an opening that led out through the side of the mountain. I smelled the rain again. I began to taste freedom, victory.

Keeping my gun drawn, I walked at Synjin's side, my elbow brushing his arm in the closeness of the tunnel. I could feel Steale at my back, his presence a formidable shadow.

When we reached the mouth of the tunnel, I took the lead again, for the same reasons. Steale and Synjin were taller; they could shoot over my head if needed.

I hoped it would never happen.

I was wrong.

~

The horror came an instant later. The moment I stepped from the tunnel and into the misting rain, my breath caught in my throat. A bright search light shone on me from about a hundred feet away, and four voices were shouting simultaneously.

I knew then where the tunnel had emerged: near the southern perimeter. We weren't surrounded. Yet. Undoubtedly, the four lazy guards had been on their coffee break just like almost everyone else in the complex. Bored, the boys from the western perimeter had shown up to share donuts and coffee with the fellows from the southern perimeter. As my eyes adjusted, I could see two Jeeps with their headlights turned off silhouetted against the silver-gray night sky. Two Jeeps. Two men per Jeep.

I forced myself to remember everything we had learned. No more than twenty-four guards at any one time, *if* they all showed up. It was possible that some of the higher-ups might also be armed, but the chance of any of them being able to shoot straight through the rain and their own fear was slim.

I forced myself to believe that anyway, my body hitting the ground instinctively as some fool who'd seen too many movies shouted, "Halt or I'll shoot!" at the top of his squeaky lungs.

I felt Synjin go down next to me, but I lost track of Steale for a moment. I thought at first that he'd gone back into the tunnel to cover the book-worms' backs, but then I saw his silhouette a few feet away, crouched low among the rocks, out of range of the search light. Kirin had pressed herself back inside the tunnel, and the rest of the book-worms were utterly silent. They knew what was at stake. They'd been the victims of it for half a century.

What surprised me was when Synjin suddenly stood up, just to the left of the search light, half in shadow, half out.

"Hold your fire. It's Kittering," he shouted. "The fire alarm down on level six went off. And get that search light out of my eyes! You're blinding my staff!"

"Dr. Kittering?" someone yelled from one of the Jeeps.Synjin *was* a Master. I just hoped he could lie like one.

"Turn off that light and get over here! My staff's getting drenched as well as blinded. How about giving us all a ride back to the parking lot so we can go home?"

I almost passed out cold when, abruptly, the light was turned off and someone shouted again.

"We'll be right there, Major." And then the Jeeps started their engines and came ambling toward us over the rough terrain.

"Shit!" I half-whispered, clamoring to my feet at Synjin's side. I pressed my arm against him for a moment to steady my nerves. "I don't remember *that* being in the plan!"

The headlights were bouncing eerily over the land and shining up into the sky whenever they hit a bump in the off-road terrain. A few seconds later, the first one reached our group and two guards in raincoats hopped out. By the time they looked up, they were already falling, taken out by tranq bullets. I got the one on the left, Synjin took the one on the right.

By then, the second Jeep had pulled up, and I hoped it would go as smoothly. But that's when I heard the shouting.

"That's not Kittering, you fool! *Shoot!*"

I saw the driver of the Jeep slump over the wheel when Steale took him out with a tranq. The vehicle rolled to a stop with its front tire in a rut. But that's when I heard the gunshot, deafening as it echoed off the low cloud cover. I thought at first that I'd been hit, but realized later that the pain I felt in my arm was Synjin jerking me down to the ground, out of the line of fire. I heard one of the book-worms scream; then another.

And then I saw Steale. He stood up from his cover, leveling the gun on the only guard left standing. I think he pulled the trigger, but his vision was undoubtedly hampered by the headlights shining directly on him.

Another gunshot. And then he fell.

After that, I went undeniably insane. Without thinking of the danger, not daring to look back, I broke free of Synjin's grip and lunged for the guard's gun arm. He didn't see me coming around the Jeep until it was already too late, and when my flying thrust kick caught him hard across the throat, he fell to the ground. The force of my chi when I hit him would have stopped a truck.

But it might not be able to save Steale. I thought of yin and yang. Dark and light. Good and evil. It seemed in that moment of utter horror that the balance was struggling to maintain itself - to take a life in exchange for the lives we had brought back.

That thought hit me hard and, struggling to breathe, I turned toward where Steale lay, face-down, on the ground.

Synjin was already there, his hands covered with blood as he tried to stop the flow of red emanating from his brother's chest. I couldn't tell exactly where the bullet had hit him, but it seemed to be somewhere between the shoulder and the sternum.

That's when everything stopped. All sound. All rationality. All reason. I looked at Synjin, horror in my throat. I saw Kirin, too. She was leaning over her husband, her eyes haunted, her lips pale and drawn. She didn't seem to be breathing, yet she called his name over and over, screaming, whispering, crying.

"How... bad?" I asked, my throat constricting.

Synjin's eyes were terrified, empty. "He's loosing a lot of blood. I don't know."

My heart stopped beating. I gasped, disbelieving. Steale seemed so still, so silent. He was barely alive, slipping quickly away.

Then Fegan was there. I don't know where he came from, but he was leaning over Steale next to me, taking Synjin's hands and gently forcing them away until he could see the wound.

"Not good," he said softly, shattering my reality again. "He won't make it if we don't get him some help soon." He looked to me, then to Synjin. "Where's the corridor? If we can get him to a warm place somewhere, I might be able to do something."

It was a mile away. Steale was dying. A mile away from a home I'd never seen, I was losing him. But somewhere deep inside me, a stray thought that disguised itself as logic made me look up.

"Get him into the Jeep," I said, my voice barely a whisper. "Just get him in the Jeep, Synjin. We'll drive through the corridor if we have to!"

Synjin was staring at me as if I were speaking some alien language.

"Get him into the Jeep!" I shouted then, trying to break through the telepathic shock. "*Get him into the fucking Jeep!*"

Finally he moved, sliding his hands under his brother and lifting him into trembling arms. I heard Steale moan with the pain, coughing, finally slipping into merciful unconsciousness.

What happened after that is largely a blur. I remember Synjin's reasoning coming back to him when his brother lost consciousness. He said something about the newborns, something else about the other Jeep, and then he was gone, not giving me time to argue. Somehow, I'd ended up in the driver's seat of one of the vehicles; Fegan was next to me on the passenger's side, cradling Steale's unconscious body in his arms. Kirin was jammed behind them, and several of the other book-worms had managed to grab onto the roll-bar, standing or slouching or trembling in the back. Not one of them spoke.

Then we were moving again. I must have driven, though I don't remember doing it. I also don't recall seeing the other Jeep at all, but it was there when we came up to where the natural doorway opened into my world. I wouldn't understand until later that Synjin had led us to the spot; I'd followed behind the other Jeep without ever seeing it, my eyes blinded by tears and rain and grief and horror. Only the Way between us had allowed me to react at all.

In a haze of rain and shadows, I saw Synjin moving through the night, going to where I'd hidden the box. Whatever he did must have worked, because the next thing I remember is seeing the blue light. There was no rumbling, no high-pitched screaming, no sound at all. There was just the light, like a beacon guiding me toward some distant sanctuary.

Synjin came up next to me then, his face a whisper of light at my window. "Get him through, River," he told me, his voice choked with pain. "I'll stay here until the corridor closes, then follow you through the natural doorway."

"No!" I heard myself shout. "I can't do this without you, Synjin!" If he didn't make it back, I would lose him, too.

But he was already gone.

Fegan was rattling on again, telling me how to drive. I guess I didn't understand that I was the first to put a Jeep through a hole never designed for that purpose. He kept telling me to stay away from the sides of the corridor, move, move, move, stay away from the sides, don't be afraid, move, move, move, and for Lethe's sake, stay away from the fucking sides!

In some part of my mind, he must have been getting through to me. I didn't have the time to be afraid of where we were, what I was seeing. To say it was like nothing I'd ever seen before would be a detrimental understatement.

To say I actually remember it would be a lie.

The only thing I recall with any degree of accuracy is when the vehicle abruptly stopped; the blue light had gone out, or so I believed at the time; the air was cold and stinging in my lungs.

I knew intuitively that we were on the other side, somewhere in the equivalent of the High Sierras at the cabin where Steale had lived for so many years.

Fegan later told me that I carried Steale inside the house and put him down on a dusty bed after kicking down a locked door. I don't remember doing it, though my shirt was covered with blood, sticking to my chest with the scent of death.

Kirin was clinging to me and I to her while Fegan worked to stop the bleeding.

That's when Synjin came through the door, bringing the Masters with him.

CHAPTER TWENTY-TWO
Circle of Knowledge

Synjin came to my side, kneeling by the small bed and looking up at me. I was peripherally aware of other people in the room - the Masters, Fegan, some of the book-worms - but I saw Ch'en Po above them all.

I realized I was in shock, my body trembling violently as I sat on the edge of a wicker chair next to Steale's bed. My eyes filled with terror, I looked to Synjin for some answer, some hope, some explanation.

"The Masters will help him, River," he promised, though his voice was shaky, his body shivering as if from the cold.

I drew a ragged breath, forcing myself to believe that, knowing I had no other choice. Putting one hand on his shoulder, I tried to find the Way. It was clouded with pain and grief, but it was still there.

I noticed then that someone had chased the book-worms from the room; only Kirin, Fegan, Synjin and I were left.

And the Masters. Ch'en Po. Five others that I didn't recognize. They were dressed rather normally, I observed. One woman wore a black gi, but the rest looked like anyone I might have met walking down a crowded street. They were gathered around the bed, four of them working in silence, doing things that I couldn't see, couldn't understand.

They weren't speaking.

A fifth came to me and placed a hand on my shoulder, gesturing toward the door. He had a kindly face, elderly, gentle. But I had no intention of leaving the room.

"I'm staying with him," I said, meaning it.

That's when Ch'en Po looked up. He'd been gazing down at Steale's unconscious body from the other side of the bed, and when he heard my voice, he came to stand next to me.

"She's his Master, Silke," he said in perfect English. "She will stay with him until this has passed."

I looked up at him with surprised disbelief. But I didn't ask about his perfect English. Instead, my eyes filling with tears, I began to cry, getting up and putting my arms around his back, holding on with a desperation I had never before experienced.

"Don't let him die, Ch'en Po," I begged. "Please... just don't let him die!"

He embraced me with gentle strength, then took me to another chair on the other side of the room. I let myself be led, knowing I could do nothing for Steale, knowing I couldn't leave him either.

Sitting me down, Ch'en Po knelt in front of me, taking my hands and reaching up to brush the wetness from my cheeks. "Is it wise to grieve for someone who isn't dead, River?" he asked gently. "Be silent in your spirit lest your student hear your sorrow in his chi."

I blinked, drawing a deep breath that hurt my lungs.

Ch'en Po smiled very softly - an out of place, tender smile. "If you want to save him, you must give him your strength, not your grief."

I bit my lower lip until it bled, trying to hold back the tears.

He glanced again toward the bed. The Masters were working quietly, Synjin among them. I wondered how he could have such control at such a time. I'd felt his anguish as a force no less than my own.

"Synjin knows this," Ch'en Po said, interrupting my thoughts with reason. "You must know it, too. Belief is not enough, River. Only knowledge can save him."

I frowned, starting to breathe again. "I'm not Synjin. I don't have his skills, his strength."

Ch'en Po only stared at me, admonishing me with a frown. "You don't have his years of experience, but you do have his strength, little ram. Look inside yourself for it. Go to Steale and lead him back."

I blinked, started to get up, not knowing what I was going to do, but knowing I had to do something.

But Ch'en Po placed a restraining hand on my shoulder as I started to rise. "Ta ta ta!" he scolded softly. "Not like that."

I looked at him, not having the ability to reason at that moment. "Then how?"

He tapped one fingertip to his forehead. "You're a traveler, aren't you?"

I knew then what he meant, though I was terrified when I understood it. I trembled again. "I – I can't."

Ch'en Po sighed softly. "You can do nothing for him in this plane," he said. "The Masters can heal his body, but only if he wants it so. His fear - and yours - can just as easily kill him. Silke is a talented surgeon, Freelin a gifted herbalist. Your own Synjin can stop his brother's body from bleeding, but not one of them can find Steale's soul where it hides in the darkness, River. That is *your* gift. That is what *you* must do if you want him to live."

"But Kirin-."

"Kirin loves him, yes," Ch'en Po stressed. "But she doesn't have the knowledge to travel."

"But the Way-."

"Ta ta ta!" Ch'en Po said again. "The Way between them has long been silent. Even love cannot be enough sometimes, young ram. You know Steale as he is *now*. You know where his spirit will go. You must go to him, you must go alone, and you must go *now*."

The shock and the fear were too much. I looked toward the bed and saw only the blood, tasted the color of death in my soul. My eyes closed. "I can't," I whispered again, terrified and ashamed.

I heard Ch'en Po sigh. "Where would young ram be if old man had said 'can't' on bottom of lake?"

His accent was back again, but his words made me look up, reaching some part of me that could still reason. I'd be dead. That shocked me enough so that I stopped crying and looked up at him, desperation motivating me.

The old man nodded as if reading my thoughts. "Knowledge must travel circle. *You* must travel full circle, too."

I hadn't realized it, but Kirin had been gradually urged away from the bed and was standing a few feet away, looking down at us with an expression I couldn't read. She took a step closer, her eyes swollen and red, her breath trembling.

"*Can* you help him?" she asked, her voice barely a whisper.

I held her gaze, biting my lip again. "I don't know."

Tears started down her cheeks again. "I don't understand a lot of this, but I know Steale needs you," she managed painfully. "I know you've been there for him. If you care for him at all, won't you try? He's *dying*, River. I can feel it... and there's nothing I can do for him."

My eyes bled tears again. I had to glance away. But I found some whisper of a strength deep inside myself. I looked up at Kirin, hearing the horrible truth in her words.

Steale was dying.

No words came.

I'd seldom traveled when I was awake, certainly not without a lengthy meditation to prepare myself. But I'd never had the motivation I had now. With Ch'en Po still kneeling in front of me and Kirin at my side, I closed my eyes and summoned whatever remained of my chi.

The door to the Dream was smeared with blood.

~

Despite popular myth, the astral plane usually isn't a place of mist and shadows. In my own experience, it was no different from the physical world; it was simply reached by different means and existed in a different corner of non-time and no-space.

I found myself in Joshua Tree again, at the house on the hill, the house where we had lived, the house where we'd first made love.

I was standing in the bedroom, looking down to where Steale lay on the bed, his arms stretched behind his head, the covers pulled up to his waist. I knew intuitively that he was naked. He'd come into the world with nothing; he would leave with nothing.

He looked grim.

I went to him with the full knowledge of everything that was transpiring at the cabin, and sat on the edge of the bed, reaching out to place one hand in the middle of his chest.

"I thought this might be a more comfortable place to wait," he said, his voice as I'd always remembered it. Deep. Penetrating.

"Wait?" I repeated.

He nodded, then made a slicing motion across his throat. "I'm not going to make it, am I?"

I swallowed hard, my eyes closing for a moment. But then I remembered Ch'en Po's words. I couldn't let him feel my sorrow; I couldn't grieve for a man who wasn't dead. And I also understood something else. I *had* come full circle. Just as Ch'en Po had found me on the bottom of the lake, I had found Steale at the bottom of a great abyss, at the crossroads between life and death.

"That's up to you," I said, running my fingertips over his smooth skin, distracting my heartache with sensation. I looked at his face, his eyes, remembering *his* old tactics. "If you die, I swear I'll kill you, Steale."

He laughed despite himself. "If I die, you won't have to kill me, Master River." But the amusement faded from his eyes. "Did we make it?"

I nodded, smiling for him. I had to. "Every last one of us - including *you*," I stressed. "Kirin's waiting for you - back at the cabin."

He looked away from me, his eyes darkening. "I know."

I frowned. "What?"

He shrugged, his dark skin stretching over the muscles in his arms. "I don't love her anymore."

"Bullshit," I said. "Don't use a lie as an excuse to give up. You've spent more than forty-five years grieving over losing her. Don't lose her again. Don't put her through what you've been through because you're afraid."

He didn't argue at least.

I smiled softly. "The Masters are with you."

He studied me with a peculiar expression, one I hadn't seen before. "Why?"

"Synjin brought them," I explained. "I didn't get a chance to ask him how he did it, but he told me once that the temple is sitting on a natural doorway. Maybe they just walked through. It doesn't matter. They're there - with you - in the cabin, I mean. You're going to make it."

He turned away again. "You don't know that."

Reaching out, I took his chin and turned his head toward me, forcing him to meet my eyes. "I know it, Steale. *You* just don't know it yet."

He sighed wearily, closing his eyes. Stubborn ass.

"Remember what you said about paths being connected, destined?" he asked.

"Yes."

He looked at me again, his intense gaze going through me. "Well what if I've come to the end of my own? What if I've done what I'm supposed to do in the world?" He paused, his expression turning dark. "I mean, what if this really is the end of my road,

River? Even you can't see into the future. Maybe this is where the bus stops. Maybe this is *it* for me. Did you ever stop to think about that?"

I hadn't. I didn't. I couldn't. "It isn't."

He was slipping away. I could feel it in my chi, an empty coldness where the tangible essence of him had been.

He seemed unconvinced, resting his head on the pillow and staring up at the ceiling. "We had some good times, didn't we?"

My heart ached. "Stop it, Steale," I warned.

"I'm going to miss that," he said, ignoring me. "I'm going to miss the way your hair always got in your face when we sparred, the way you used to be edgy when we hadn't made love in awhile. Hell, I'm even going to miss Synjin."

Before I realized what I was doing, I slapped him hard across the face, astral tears stinging my eyes. "Damn you, Steale! Words and thoughts have power! Stop giving it energy!"

He was rubbing his cheek with the back of his hand, looking surprised. "That hurt!"

"It was meant to," I told him. But my voice softened. "I love you, goddammit."

"You've never said that before."

He was right. I hadn't. "I'm saying it now."

He glanced away. Then, reaching out, he ran his fingertips down my cheek. "You're crying. You've never done that before either."

"You just never caught me," I replied, thinking of the day I'd spent in the desert after my first night with him. There had been other times, too, times when I'd slept alone. Times when I'd *felt* alone. Times when I was afraid to admit what I was feeling for him.

"It's going to be complicated if I let you take me back," he pointed out.

I frowned; he had a habit of thinking a few steps to the left of me. But at least he'd acknowledged the possibility of going back. "Complicated?"

He nodded. "I don't want to give up what we have."

"Neither do I." I had to be completely truthful with him now, no matter how much it scared either of us.

He smiled, devilment in his eyes. "I *won't* give it up, River."

"What's Kirin going to say about that?"

He shrugged. "She likes you. Why?"

That easy, peculiar attitude again. "I like her, too, and I'm not going to do anything that's going to hurt her. You two need some time alone together - maybe a *long* time, Steale. Hell, by the time we figure any of this out, I'll be old."

He looked at me as if I'd gone mad. "What are you talking about?"

I found myself glancing away from him. "Life spans," I said, my voice undependable. "It's a fact that I won't live as long as you or Synjin." It was something I'd tried not to think about, but now I used it as a weapon - the only one I had left to try to reach him. "But I don't intend to let that screw up what time I *do* have. Every moment contains infinite possibility, an infinity of choices leading in all directions."

He was still looking at me, incredulity in his gaze. "You still don't get it, do you?"

I blinked. "Get what?"

He moved further up in the bed until his back was pressed against the headboard. "You're not *from* here, any more than I am or Synjin is," Steale said, holding my hand tightly, trying to make me see.

"Bullshit," I said again. "I was born-."

"Under weird circumstances, if I'm right – and you know I am. You're also a Taurus, but I don't hold that against you, either."

I blinked, not breathing. "What the hell are you talking about?"

"Look, River," he said, "I don't know all the background, but Synjin told me you 're one of *us*. Your father was one of us - what you'd call one of The People. Apparently, he was also a traveler."

I was afraid to believe that. I stared at him. "Bullshit," I said again.

He shrugged. "Taurus."

I gave up crossing swords with him, becoming serious again. "Okay, so it'll be a little complicated when you come back with me. We've worked out worse problems."

"*If* I go back," he corrected, causing me to chill.

I didn't let his negativity dissuade me. "Tell me one reason why you shouldn't."

"Pain, for starters," he ventured.

I looked at him. "The Masters can help with the pain, Steale. You're lying again."

He wouldn't meet my eyes.

I tried to find another angle. "Are you afraid of starting over?"

He didn't answer, but I saw his lips tighten. That was part of it. Finally, surprising me, he turned his head toward me again, his eyes more intense than I'd ever seen them.

"We've done it all, River," he said then, his voice deep and filled with what I could only define as awe. "We've already *done* it - everything that mattered."

I understood then. I'd felt a twinge of that myself down on the sixth level, a moment of wondering what I was going to do with the *rest* of my life. I hadn't known then that it was going to be such a long life, and I still wasn't sure I believed him. But I took his words inside me, analyzing them with care, comparing them to my own feelings.

Then, running the back of my hand down his face, I smiled softly. "If it's excitement you want, I'm sure we can think of something. Getting the others back was just a start, Steale. There's a lot more injustice in the world - *both* worlds, probably."

He looked up at me as if trying to decide whether or not I was lying, leading him on. Finally, shaking his head, he sighed softly. "Like what?"

"Everything from ozone to whales to rain forests to children not going trick-or-treating on Halloween. If you're worried about being bored, about not being able to live up to your own illustrious past, I'm sure we can think of plenty to do."

He seemed dubious. "Kirin's not going to like it," he said with that mischievous grin back in his eyes.

I laughed gently. "Kirin's a book-worm. She'll love it - all that new information to analyze and catalog. It'll be your gift to her, mine to you. Okay?"

Steale released a heavy breath, the amusement fading from his eyes as he held my hand tightly. "Synjin might not like it either."

The Way sang to me, tender and wild at the same time. "He was never meant to stay behind temple walls forever, Steale. He *is* your brother, you know."

Steale laughed, a warm, sincere release of emotion. "You make it hard to say no."

"I don't intend to let you say no," I told him, meaning it. "Now, do I have to carry you back to your body, or do you plan on coming peacefully?"

He held my hand, squeezing it so tight I thought the bones would break... if astral bones could break.

"Will you be there?" he asked, a melancholy resignation in his aura.

"Yes."

"And Kirin?"

"Yes. And Synjin."

He smiled again. "Can't get rid of him, can I?"

My lips curved upward. "You don't want to."

Then, releasing a heavy breath, he looked up at me, no longer trying to hide his fear. "I don't know the way back," he said, his voice quiet, too quiet.

I pulled him to me, taking his hand as I stood and drawing him into a lover's embrace. I gave him my own confidence, the force of my chi. "I do."

He let me lead him back, along a road I'd never traveled before. At one end of it was a white light that shone with an incredible brilliance. I saw Lissi there. And my own mother. I hadn't known she was gone, but she assured me it was all right now, that she understood, that she approved of her little girl. She even said she was sorry we'd never been close.

Steale started toward the light once, drawn by its serenity; but I kept my fingers tightly laced through his, guiding him away from it when he strayed, strengthening him when he weakened. It was a long and treacherous journey, the path strewn with pale white bones, the staircase leading back to life rickety and unstable.

CHAPTER TWENTY-THREE
The Healing

When I came back to my senses, I was lying on a bed in what I took to be another room of the cabin. I had no sense of time having passed, yet I knew it was several hours later, perhaps days. My body felt drained and tired, exhaustion taking its toll.

For a few seconds while my mind existed half-way between sleep and wakefulness, I stared at the dark wooden ceiling of the room, watching a graceful spider spin her web in a corner. It was as if I'd just been born, my memories still sleeping in some shadowed part of my Self.

But when I remembered Steale, the long walk back through the darkness, the light calling us, I snapped up in the bed, gasping myself awake.

The moment I made a sound and started to rise from the bed, Synjin came around the corner, motioning for me to stay still. I blinked, gazing up at him with a question in my eyes. He didn't have to ask what question.

Coming to the bed, he sat on the edge, placing his hands on my shoulders and pushing me down against the soft mattress. His eyes were tired; I could tell he hadn't slept; his hands trembled.

"Steale's resting," he said, causing the tension to ease from my body as I released a heavy breath. "He's weak and fatigued, but he'll live. The Masters want him moved to the temple, though; it's going to take time for him to heal."

Impulsively, I pulled Synjin down next to me, shielding myself in his body, his strength, his warmth. "I thought I'd lost him."

Stroking my hair, he relaxed against me, his weight coming to rest on the bed at my side. "Ch'en Po told me you went to find him - his Self. You've slept ever since."

I drew a deep breath, my arms tightening around Synjin's back. "How long?"

"Nearly two days," he murmured against the top of my head. "Were you traveling?"

"No. I was dreaming, I think."

I felt Synjin's contentment through the Way. "Of what?"

"All of it - you, Steale. Everything. I haven't dreamed in a long time." I only then realized it.

He stroked my head, the sensation reverberating all the way through me, his love a tangible force in the room. "I sense questions in your thoughts," he murmured. "Tell me."

Closing my eyes, I thought about what he'd said. I did have questions. Lots of them. But one was more important than the rest.

"He's really going to make it?"

Synjin nodded, his lips brushing my ear as he spoke. "Silke was able to repair the damage; Freelin is treating him with healing herbs. The wound was severe, but he'll heal. In time..."

I remembered what Steale had said. On the astral plane. In his bed. Where he'd gone to die. "He wants us to be there, Synjin. I promised him we would."

Synjin smiled; I felt it. "There are quarters at the temple for guests, Masters who occasionally visit from other places," he explained. "Until Steale is well again, the Masters can tend him and we'll have time to talk, to learn of one another."

"We haven't had much time for that, have we?"

He pulled me close against his chest. "So much energy was spent preparing for the rescue that we haven't done much else. Now we can."

The questions were coming back again. I supposed they always would. "Have you talked to Kirin?"

He nodded again. "She's anxious to go to the temple. She told me she'd never had much time to be with Steale before the accident." He smiled inside my mind, warming me. "Her memory's a bit faulty, I think. They were inseparable from the day they met."

I had a feeling I was going to be the same way with Synjin. But I remembered something else Steale had said. "I don't want to give up what I have with him."

Leaning back to look at me, Synjin's brows lifted with amusement. "Why would you?"

I shrugged. "Living in my world did a trip on my head, as Steale's so fond of telling me. It's going to take some time to get used to it; that's all."

He studied me curiously. "You'll have to tell me more about this other world, River. It sounds terribly bizarre."

"For almost thirty years, it was the only world I knew," I explained.

He frowned thoughtfully. He didn't understand me yet and I didn't really expect him to. We were still new to one another, with a lot to learn, a lot of healing still to be done.

"Where love is concerned, River," he said, holding me close, "I draw no boundaries. Neither does Steale or Kirin."

I wasn't ready to talk long-term plans just yet. I changed the subject, realizing the house was silent. "What happened to the book-worms?"

Synjin smiled softly. "They left last night, all but Fegan. He's out in the living room trying to determine what damage Steale's done to his computer over the years."

I relaxed, or tried to. "Is he all right? I mean, he lost Lissi."

Synjin stroked my face with genuine affection. "Time has helped him heal. He says her spirit visits him in his dreams."

I didn't doubt it.

I made myself trust Synjin. But as I looked at him, images of everything we'd done together kept flashing through my mind.

"Did we really do it, Synjin?" I asked, barely able to believe it myself.

He laughed gently, a purr of contentment against my side. "So it would seem. Once you took the Jeep into the tunnel, the others followed. I stayed behind until the corridor had closed - to make certain no one from your world followed."

"And after that?" I wondered.

Synjin smiled. "In time, little ram."

I smacked him on the arm. "Don't be superior."

He laughed again, the tension leaving him. "I didn't mean to be. Sorry."

"Yes you did. So tell me," I persisted.

"I was at the temple for only a few minutes," he said. "Once the Masters agreed to help, it took us only six minutes to get from there to here."

I elbowed him. "You're every bit as evasive as your brother, Synjin."

"Am I?"

Clenching my fists in a combination of frustration and amused disbelief, I rolled onto my side, climbed on top of him, and pounded his chest. "Yes!"

He pulled me down over him in a smooth movement, taking my wrists and throwing me off balance. I ended up on his chest, feeling his heart beating next to mine. He was inside me again, in my mind, in my Self. His telepathy told me to be patient. It also told me that he loved me - which was enough.

We stayed that way for a long time, and I think Synjin had finally drifted off to sleep when I saw another shadow come around the corner, into the room.

"Ch'en Po," I said, smiling softly.

He shuffled into the room and sat down in a wooden chair, looking at the two of us with open affection. "I see fire in young ram's eyes," he observed. He was probably right. I felt alive again. "Does this mean you're going to take my best pupil and leave temple?"

I remembered then what Steale had said, the promises I'd made. "After awhile, probably." I felt Synjin beneath me, his breath coming in the steady rhythms of sleep. I took care to speak softly.

Ch'en Po was playing with the long strands of his beard. "Where will you go??"

I shrugged. "I'm not sure. Steale's afraid of getting bored, I think. That's part of why he hesitated to come back."

The old man smiled softly. "But come back anyway. Young ram good teacher."

It was a meaningful compliment. "I had a wise and relentless Master."

I think I actually saw him blush. "Make old man proud."

"I'm just sorry that Steale was hurt."

"Sometimes pain make good tutor," Ch'en Po pointed out. "Student be more careful next time before trying heroic bang-bang in middle of night."

I laughed very quietly, careful not to awaken Synjin. "I'll tell him you said so." I thought about what he'd said. "Will there be a next time?"

Ch'en Po's lips curved upward into a wistful smile, but he gave no direct response.

"I just feel that my skills are meant to be used. I think they do, too - Synjin and Steale, I mean."

"Umm," the old man commented dubiously. "Didn't use skills enough getting eighteen people back home?"

I considered that. "It's enough for awhile. But wouldn't it dishonor you and me both if we just stopped there?"

He smiled again, very softly. "Must do what must do, young ram. Right now, should be quiet and let Synjin sleep."

I chuckled despite myself. "Questions getting too hard for you, Master?"

His long brows lifted. "Questions easy. Answers hard."

"I thought there *were* no answers," I reminded him with a teasing grin.

He opened his mouth to speak, but closed it again. Finally, getting up and shaking his head, he bowed elegantly to me for the first time ever, bringing his right fist together with his left palm - the ancient gesture of respect from one martial artist to another.

Then Ch'en Po shuffled out of the room with a pensive little smile, leaving no footprints in the dust at his feet.

EPILOGUE
Coyote

I awoke in the middle of the night with the feeling of something left undone and, rising on instinct, I followed my intuition into the bedroom where the Masters were caring for Steale.

The lights had been dimmed, and I noticed upon entering the room that only one of the elders was there. Freelin sat in a chair next to the bed, and I smelled the familiar scent of smoldering herbs. A closer look showed several acupuncture needles glistening from Steale's body.

But as I came closer, the old Master smiled at me, bowed his head in acknowledgement, and left me alone with my student, my lover, my friend.

I sat next to Steale for a very long time, looking at him, honoring my word to be there for him when he awakened. His color was almost back to normal, and I could tell by the gentle rise and fall of his chest that he was out of danger. Still, it would take time to heal, as Synjin had said. It would take longer to get his strength back, to mend his chi.

But we had time now.

Reaching out, I took his hand, holding tight until I felt his pulse. Steady. Strong.

I looked up when I sensed another presence in the room, and found Kirin standing in the doorway, looking over at us with a soft smile. She still seemed weak and exhausted - a feeling I could share with her. The cast was gone, though her arm was bandaged with gauze.

She came into the room and took the chair on the other side of the bed, glancing to where I held her husband's hand pressed between my own. I didn't let go, knowing I didn't need to.

"You saved his life. " Her voice was delicate and melodic.

"I just showed him the way home," I said. "His strength and his love for you are what really brought him back."

She looked at me as if really seeing me for the first time. I was having a similar reaction. "But you gave him that strength, River. He's never followed anyone in his life – but he followed *you*. You probably know him better than I do at this point," she murmured, almost to herself.

She looked at him again and reached out to run one fingertip down his cheek. Then, glancing up, she smiled at me once more. It seemed only a little odd for both of us to be touching him at the same time, though I suspected I could get used to it. She was obviously at ease with it, and I let myself be comfortable, too.

"I'm not sure either one of us really knows everything about him, Kirin," I said, only then realizing it. "Synjin probably knows him best."

She touched his face again, looking down at him with love and awe for a long time. Then she met my gaze again, a quizzical smile in her eyes. "Will you tell me what you know?"

I frowned thoughtfully, the warmth of Steale's hand easing some of the tension of the past few days. I could feel his chi in my mind – his telepathic gift reaching through the darkness toward both of us, encouraging us to talk.

She took his other hand then, enfolding it between both of her own as I had done. One of us on either side of him, we looked at each other for a long moment, sharing Steale, sharing understanding, sharing the commitment to help him heal.

"Tell me how you met him," she encouraged. "I want to know everything about him – and about you, River. Please? Tell me?"

I did the best I could. At times, lesson number one weighed heavily on my mind, yet as I spoke with Kirin throughout that long night, I began to realize for the first time the importance of lesson number two.

There are no answers – but there are also no accidents.

I called the story Coyote.

THE END

About the Author...

Della Van Hise is a native of Florida, transplanted to California at the age of 21, who has subsequently sunk her roots into the high desert near Joshua Tree National Park. She has not personally seen any aliens since around 1992, but there is rumored to be a secret UFO base underneath her house.

Della's writing started around age 11, when she would bang out some of the very earliest "fan fiction" on an old Smith Corona typewriter. No, not an electric one. A real antique, made of metal and heavier than a wet coffin. Her first professional novel was *Killing Time* - the controversial *Star Trek* book which was recalled and re-edited in 1984.

Della has written extensively in the non-fiction genre, with titles such *as Quantum Shaman: Diary of a Nagual Woman* and *Scrawls On the Walls of the Soul. Quantum Shaman* focuses heavily on the author's metaphysical explorations and experiences, while *Scrawls* is a continuation of those journeys many years later. If you enjoyed the works of Carlos Castaneda or Don Miguel Ruiz, you'll enjoy the non-fiction works of Della Van Hise.

In addition, Della has written professionally for *Tomorrow Magazine* and other prominent science fiction publications. Her fiction works include *Ragged Angels* (an award-winning vampire novel); *Year of the Ram* (a space-faring gay romance); and *Coyote*.

All of the titles mentioned here are available through Amazon, or through Eye Scry Publications.

http://www.eyescrypublications.com

SONS OF NEVERLAND
an erotic vampyre novel by
Della Van Hise

"The virtuosity shown here is only the beginning of a pyrotechnic talent unfolding into the hidden dimensions of the human and nonhuman spirit."
-Jacqueline Lichtenberg

"Sensual! Sexy! Surreal!"
-North County Times

"A literary triumph where the undead have more heart & soul than the living."
-The Readers

One Amazon Reviewer said...
"What Sons of Neverland resembled to me was the creative hagiographies of Nikos Kazantzakis, where a few stylized characters deliver a message that goes way beyond the parameter of the characters themselves. And much like Kazantzakis, this book zones on the question of immortality. However, this is not just the decadent historical immortality of the long-lived vampire, it is immortality as a change in one's perception. This is the story behind the story, delivered by characters that are hyper-real – each one loaded with symbolism. Sons of Neverland will have you filled, even brimming over with the sense of Mysterium Tremendum et Fascinans. Go there for a full helping of the numinous."

Set against a backdrop of contemporary culture, SONS OF NEVERLAND explores the universal questions of life & death, sex & love – the most crucial challenges every human being faces – through the eyes of the immortal vampire.

Readers have compared SONS OF NEVERLAND to the works of Anne Rice, Carlos Castaneda, and Anais Nin. One reader summed it up as follows: "SONS OF NEVERLAND is one of the most erotic books I've ever read. I found it totally uplifting regardless of the gritty story In the end, it made me realize that light can't exist without darkness. Thank you for a truly exceptional read!" (Charlene J.)

A shorter version of this book was published in TOMORROW MAGAZINE, under the title "Kiss of the Black Angel." The novel in its entirety was published as a limited first edition under the title "Ragged Angels."

http://www.amazon.com/Sons-Neverland-Della-Van-Hise-ebook/dp/B00O4GUH2W

YEAR OF THE RAM
Della Van Hise

Year of the Ram was described by one reviewer as... "A space-faring gay romance full of love, angst, and longing."

Only after Star Commander Morgan Diego becomes an exile as a result of a Galaxy Corps political blunder does he begin to realize how much he valued the companionship of his second in command - the mysterious Lucien, an Alfarian who is more elven than human, with peculiar powers & abilities which begin to unfold as he, too, realizes what he has lost.

Separated by circumstance from his former life, Morgan is thrust into a world where he must survive by his wits. When he meets a peculiar little old man calling himself Kim Le, Morgan finds himself in a situation where he is required to master The Art - not only a form of human & extraterrestrial martial arts, but a way of living and being that will alter his life forever.

At the temple, he is introduced to his new teacher, another Alfarian who begins to steal his heart - a heart which is already promised to Lucien. Torn and conflicted, Morgan struggles with the world he left behind and the world he now inhabits.

Beginning to believe he may never again return to his ship and to the friends and loved ones he left behind, he is all the more frustrated and heartbroken when a new Master arrives at the temple: a man to whom Morgan is immediately drawn both mentally and physically, a man who is strikingly familiar... yet utterly alien.

Year of the Ram is a fully-fleshed novel, approximately 97000 words, with a focus on the love story and romance angle. Set against a science fiction milieu, it explores the infinite possibilities of the human and alien heart. Sexual content is explicit, though is not the primary focus of the novel.

For those who like a romance that forces its characters to contemplate the ecstasies AND the agonies of love... you will enjoy *Year of the Ram* immensely.

http://www.eyescrypublications.com

Quantum Shaman: Diary of a Nagual Woman

Della Van Hise

"Diary of a Nagual Woman brings a quantum understanding to what has traditionally been believed to be a mystical path alone. This book picks up where Carlos Castaneda left off to take us on a roller coaster ride of our own forgotten power..."
- Michael Grove, Independent Reviewer

Scrawls on the Walls of the Soul

Della Van Hise

"If you've ever felt like a stranger in a strange land, this book is your road map to survival in the spiritual wilderness!" (Michael Grove)

The long-awaited follow-up to Quantum Shaman: Diary of a Nagual Woman. Stands alone, or order together!

"It's not your neatly typed essays that interest me, but the scrawls on the walls of your soul."

Both titles available through
www.eyescrypublications.com

329

The Foundling
by Wendy Rathbone

Diego is a powerful man with a tragic past. Out on the expansive ocean in his private yacht, he discovers a beautiful and mysterious man adrift on a raft, near death. The bond that forms between them in the aftermath of Alec's rescue is one of fierce passion, though lacking in trust. Can they make it work, or will Alec's amnesia bring forth secrets so disturbing as to tear them apart? A passionately erotic love story of desire and darkness, exquisite and explicit.

I can see his struggle between gratitude and uneasiness. He is buffeted by all things new and strange. He does not know where he is from, who he is or what happened to him. He does not know me. There has not been enough time to transition between strangers and friendship.

This isolation of his is something I can identify with, but it is also a feeling no one can help him with until or unless he gets his own life back. And his memory.

If that doesn't happen, then it will take time for him to build a new life. He is polite to me, even friendly, but even a night together during a storm with his arms wrapped tight around my waist doesn't calm the surge I see inside him, the emptiness, the loss, possibly even panic. That night may have reinforced some trust in me, but so far not enough for him to completely relax.

He seeks me out, though. That's something. He sits by me at dinner when he can have any seat of his choosing. I watch him closely when he does not realize it. At dinner the following night after we had only 'slept' together, and before we go to bed again in separate rooms, I notice everything about him, how he moves, the way the air warms when he is closer to me, the dry sheen of his lips as they part for more air when he is reacting to something, or speaking, or eating.

His hands still shake. Anyone else might not notice because he keeps them clasped into fists at his sides or, while sitting, pressed tight to his lap.

I spend another fretful night alone. I dream restlessly, wild, loud and colorful visions I cannot recall at all as soon as my eyes open. All I know is the dreams leave me unfulfilled, impatient.

www.eyescrypublications.com

None Can Hold the Dark
Wendy Rathbone

In the eagerly-awaited sequel to Wendy Rathbone's homoerotic romance "**The Foundling**," Diego and Alec meet new challenges in private and from the outside world. Diego is being investigated by the local police for murder. Meanwhile, Alec's amnesia and the trauma of his kidnapping by white slavers continue to plague him. And the danger to Alec is not yet over.

Distracted by their new love, both men fail to see certain threats until it is almost too late.

"Why do you keep doing this illegal business?" Now Alec's gaze turned toward him, open as the day and lit with a sad frenzy, a challenge. "You could go anywhere, do anything, be anyone."

Diego had asked himself that question on rare occasions. In truth, he got used to what he was, what he did. Even a dangerous known was perhaps preferable to the unknown. "People depend on me."

Alec shook his head, but smiled a little as he said, "That's so weak." He leaned forward, over the arm of the chair, and put his shaking hand on the back of Diego's head. The kiss was cool, lingering, moist with salt. When Alec pulled back, he said almost matter of factly, "It's like there's sharks and there's goldfish and one can't decide to become the other."

Diego was still stunned by the kiss. But the words hit him hard. In them was the unfair conjecture of a locked fate. He believed in making his own fate...or luck. Did Alec think only one kind of man lived inside him and that was all there was to it? To life? It hurt. Badly.

Diego sat back on his heels, catching himself with his hands on the smooth, plank floor. "So, Alec, which am I?"

Alec frowned.

Diego said, "I made choices in my life. I made them. No one made them for me. If I need to be strong I'm strong. If I need to be vicious I can be that too. So what? I'm stuck there? In a pattern, a role...with no free will? Huh?"

Alec watched him inquisitively now.

"Because," Diego went on, "I'm solely responsible for my actions. Me. Could you say the same of the shark?"

They both waited, the silence covering them in muggy discomfort.

"You think you understand me?" Diego finally asked.

UNEARTHLY
by Wendy Rathbone

A Collection of
Award-Winning Poetry

Intro by the Author: This book contains all my out of print chapbooks (mini-collections of an author's work usually published by smaller presses.)

The chapbooks published within include:
Moon Canoes, published by Dark Regions Press, 1994
(Im)mortal, published by Shadowfire Press, 1996
Scrying The River Styx, published by Anamnesis Press, 1999
Autumn Phantoms, published by Flesh and Blood Press, 2000
Dreams of Decadence Presents: Wendy Rathbone, published by DNA Publications 2002
Dancing in the Haunted Woodlands, published by Yellow Bat Review, 2003
Vampyria, published by Eye Scry Publications, 2005

She Sleeps With Vampires

She sleeps with vampires
courting velvet breaths
poem-dreams
chill-stopped hearts

Wrapped in her arms
like teddy bear thoughts
purple lips trembling
at her quiet throat
they love her more than
somber rain
more than autumn
more than ash-soft hearths of night.

Teachings
of the
Immortals

So... You Want To Live Forever?

The teachings are presented as brief vignettes in no particular order of importance. This is not a book you read from start to finish in a single night. It is a grimoire of self-creation, intended to be contemplated slowly so as to be assimilated wholly. Pick it up and turn to a page at random. Where your eyes come to rest on the page is your lesson for the day. Go no further until you have assimilated the lesson totally.

The teachings are seduction as much as instruction. This is the way of The Dark Evolution.

Two Brief Excerpts...
The Ruby Slippers

The danger of the consensual continuum is that its natural gravity exists at the lowest common denominator of human experience, and because of this it will automatically make you forget those elusive truths you've fought to learn, and before you know it you're lost in petty dramas again, sinking into the mire of old familiar scripts.

The only way to overcome this is to be continually cavorting with worlds and events beyond human experience, journeying into the unknown so that it can become known, expanding knowledge and awareness to become more than you were, bringing back from the Dreaming those secrets which will teach you how to use the ruby slippers to transport yourself over the rainbow to the vampyre wizard's secret lair.

Perception

This is the nature of reality: to be precisely what perception dictates, as solid and whole as your interpretation of it, or as changeable and eternal as you permit it to be.

It wasn't knowledge god tried to keep from Man, you see. It was perception, for perception alone has the power to destroy god and obliterate comfortable consensual realities to create unending immortality.

Take the apple, my embryonic children. Nibble its red red flesh. Open your vampyre eyes so you may finally begin to See.

Eye Scry Publications
A Visionary Publishing Company

www.eyescrypublications.com